THE LAY OF LADY PERCIVAL

Jennifer R. Povey

1

The ancient hill fort loomed, torn by the wind that came off the sea. From its ramparts one could almost see Gaul, the narrowest part of the sea splashing, beneath it, against cliffs as white as snow. Tucked below, not far from the port, the villa seemed cozy in comparison, hints of flickering light coming from the windows.

The young woman had walked some distance from the villa. The ships she watched were all leaving the harbor. Galleys, and even from where she was, she heard the drums. Beat, stroke. Beat, stroke. She imagined the slaves, large men, bare torsos sweating in the summer heat as they bent to the oars.

On the decks, the soldiers milled a little, finding places offering a modicum of comfort. Was her soldier amongst them, the last of the Legionnaires to depart Britain's shores? Rome could simply no longer afford to garrison these far reaches.

The Empire had not fallen with a resounding thud, but slowly, withering away like an unpicked grape. Persy watched. Was he with them?

He had been an officer, a leader of men, but would he stay for her? She felt her heart lift towards her throat. If he stayed, they would wed. Even in these uncertain times, with the Saxons on every shore and the Norsemen a-viking in the north, marriage meant something.

The fact that her soldier was of those northern bloodlines meant nothing. If he stayed, then she would know he had chosen...

"Are you Briton, Norseman, or Roman?" Her own words from the last time they had spoken echoed in her head.

"Did I not agree to a handfasting in the old style?" Even the recollection of his voice was enough to cause a stirring within her.

It had been properly done, quietly, by a woman who still remembered such things, who had not fallen entirely into the Roman style of worship. Dangerous, these days, with the Christ-cult now the only religion it was legal to practice.

Persephone lowered her hands to her belly. It was still flat. She had not told him, wanting him to stay for her, not out of obligation to a child. True, by the old ways, he should wed her, fertility having been proven.

She simply did not want to hold him, to trap him.

So young, he was, for the position he had held. Too young to retire, but under normal circumstances, he would have wed her and stayed. Many did, legionnaires and auxiliaries sent to serve in other parts of the Empire, where it was felt they would be less likely to desert.

Persephone had a childhood friend who's skin was as dark as wood, her father having come from some place far to the south. From Nubia, south of Egypt.

With what seemed like the strokes of a thousand oars, the ships streamed south. A tear rolled down her cheek. He must have gone with them. He knew where she waited. He would have come by now.

Slowly, she turned, and walked away, but not to the villa. There had been a grove, once, past the fort. That was where her steps led her. The Christers had not yet claimed the site, as they had so many others, for their temples.

They were almost like a plague, she thought. Some were good men and women, but some...

Some did nothing but try to convert everyone in sight. They had, no doubt, rejoiced in Constantine's conversion. And it seemed that they were always miserable.

Persy would not follow their path, which would condemn her child as a bastard.

"Gwydion, Gwydion, slow down!"

The toddler stopped, but punctuated it with, "No."

She had chosen a British name for her son. Perhaps it was because they had to be British now, not Roman. Perhaps because she did not want to remember the other half of his heritage.

There was much of Arthur about his features, although he had his mother's dark hair, sure to be black before he matured. She quickened her pace, caught him up in her arms. "Do you want to see the warlord or not?"

He squirmed, but briefly. The warlord. The man the tribes had chosen to lead their united warband. Dux Bellum, the Romans would have said.

His name flowed through her mind and almost reached her lips. Arthur. It could not be her Arthur, yet...the name was the same. How rare a name was it? Rare in Britain, yes, but not in the lands of the Norse and the Dane and the Saxon. Thor was one of their gods.

He had been named after a god, just as she was. Yet, had he stayed, he would have come to her on that clifftop. Had he stayed, she would be at his side now, and Gwydion riding on his shoulders.

For a moment that vision was clearer than the reality. The one servant she had brought helped her clear a way through the crowds.

He would be acknowledged outside the Cathedral, a nod to the Christians. That was not how it should be. They should be in the great royal circle of Avesbury, not that teeming city, diminished yet still vibrant.

Gods. Persy hated Londinium.

Yes, there they were on the steps, the most important of the royals of Britain, gathered. She should be with them, her blood was as good. Something about her urgency was picked up by the crowd, who parted, leaving a clear route to the center of it all.

Gorlois of Lyonesse, his wife Ygraine and daughter Morgan. Lot of Orkney, with his wife, Gorlois' sister Morgawse...once considered the most beautiful woman in the land. Their two sons...Gawain and Galahad, the latter barely fourteen. And Leodegranz of Wales with his daughter, the fair Guinevere.

She knew she should not, but nonetheless she let her track drift to the edge of the group.

A white horse came through the crowds. It bore a figure in armor akin to that a Roman general might have worn, but a longsword rested at his side.

The warlord dismounted and removed his helm, and her heart skipped a beat. "Arthur."

His eyes turned to her, lingered, and then glided away. It was almost as if he did not recognize her.

No, his eye had gone elsewhere once it had rested not on Persephone, but on Gwydion. It was the child he denied, and the mother with him.

Then he turned to face the Kings. The Bishop of London stepped out onto the steps, where the highest of the druids, Merlin, should have stood.

"Arthur," he greeted. "Do you truly take the charge of leading our defense?"

"I do." His eyes were entirely on the bishop now.

Persy's were entirely on him. As were Gwydion's, the boy too young to understand but fascinated by the ceremony.

"Then..."

It was Morgawse who interrupted. "The Christian kings will accept him. But for those of us who follow the old ways, we want more."

Arthur turned towards her.

"If this man is to lead above even the Kings, he must be bound to the land."

"Meaning?" That word came from the bishop, and in it sounded a volume of disaste, every aspect of his tone and the shift in his stance revealing that he wished nothing of such pagan rites.

"He must wed a woman of our royal line." Morgawse's eyes fell first on Morgan, then on Guinevere, then, after a long moment, on Persephone.

She bit back 'He already has'. Why was he betraying her? For his eyes did not move towards her.

Instead, he regarded the two other women, one dark, one fair who faced him. And she knew the truth of his choice. Morgan was as pagan as they came, rumored to be both a powerful witch and priestess of the terrible Morrigan. Leodegranz was Christian, as, one could presume, was his daughter.

"Then, I will wed Guinevere of Wales."

Hatred and confusion boiled up within Persephone's heart. She would see him brought down. She would...

...she could not. Without one unified leader, they would fall. So, instead, she stood there, watching.

Watching as he vanished into the church. Then, she understood. Arthur had converted to Christianity. A wife named after a Greek god could be nothing but an embarrassment to him and a bastard child could only be worse.

Yet, he owed her. Could he not see that?

She vowed to speak with him, before he could wed fair Guinevere. She had one thing that delicate, blonde woman with the slender hips did not.   ·

She had his son.

The next day, Persy considered leaving Gwydion with the servants. Yet, he was her one weapon.

Did she really want a man who so deserted her? Not exactly, not any more. But if she simply dismissed her own claim, then she could gain nothing. Besides, it was not for her, now, but for her son. A man needed to know his father.

The morning was typical for Londinium, fog having settled over the valley in which the city rested. She kept Gwydion on her hip despite his weight, the mist swirling around both of them. The air weighed her down and the faint smell of too many humans too close together reached her nostrils.

The streets were already beginning to fill up. The city had shrunk, but not significantly. It would take a sack akin to what had happened to Rome to drop the number of people to reasonable levels. As the fog faded to thin tendrils, the colors of their garb assaulted her. She even saw a group of Scotti in their brilliant wool togas...kilts, they called them. The rest mixed Roman and British, as they always had. Sometimes on the same person.

She was herself no exception, a simple wool dress covering her form under a faded Roman palla.

Arthur was staying in a rented town villa, one that had once belonged to some Roman functionary. His choice had been made clear, the new ways, over the old. She feared that the old days altogether numbered. She had paid them lip service while the Romans had required it, but once they had gone, returned to giving honor to her namesake.

What would Gwydion do? What gods would he serve? If he did have a place with his father, then could he balance the two?

But she would rather lose him to the new religion than have him grow up not knowing his bloodlines. Not knowing an important part of who he was. What could she say or do if Arthur did not wish him to know him?

By the old ways, Gwydion was legitimate. To the Christians, he was a bastard. Perhaps that would be the final test.

The villa was neither modest nor grand. A manservant stood in the doorway. "Can I help you?" he asked, in tones that indicated he intended nothing of the sort.

"I'm looking for Arthur."

"And who are you?"

"Persy." She gave the short form of her name. Did he still have the right to use it? Could she truly deny him? She remembered the feel of his body and ached for him for a moment.

Did she still love him? Perhaps.

"I will find out if he wishes to see you." The servant vanished, and then Persy saw who was behind him.

Guinevere wore white, and so fair was she that no color seemed to adorn her. A silver torc encircled her throat. She had her pale gold hair loose, as befitted a virgin. Her eyes heaped scorn on the woman who was so obviously not one. An ironic thing, for she should not be here, spending time in her betrothed's temporary residence before they were wed.

"Princess," Persy greeted. She was unsurprised by the woman's visible scorn towards her, even though they were of equal rank and blood.

"I'm afraid I don't know you." It sounded like she did not care to.

"Persephone Caracti," she introduced herself.

A golden eyebrow lifted momentarily. "And where is your husband?"

Persy answered with a smile, feeling the woman's distaste. "That is what I am trying to establish."

"What are you implying?" Guinevere's voice carried with it the accent of Wales, the heavy breath instead of the l.

"I need to talk to her. Jenny, enough. I'll explain later." His voice came unexpected, a moment before the man himself stepped around a doorway and came into view.

Jenny, he called her, as if he had known her all of his life. Under his gaze, though, she left, leaving the two of them standing in the atrium.

"Arthur."

"What, exactly, do you want?"

"You left me."

"You were not exactly a suitable bride. Even less so now, I see."

Suitable... "I am a princess of Britain."

"A pagan princess." Then, a softness came into his words. "I'm sorry, Persy. I feared even then that I would have to...placate...the Christians. Guinevere is the only woman who can allow me to do that, and I most certainly cannot marry a woman who has a bastard child."

She exploded. Her anger almost carried her into him, almost caused her to resort to fist or knife. "He's yours, you idiot."

She had set Gwydion down. Fortunately, he paid no attention, distracted by a display of flowers set within the hallway.

"I wish that could make a difference. I'm..."

"Don't you dare apologize. What if I tell your perfect princess..."

"What of it? You know that they always consider these things the woman's fault."

Her look became a glare. "To think I once loved you."

He softened once more. "I did love you. Past tense. I thought a clean break was better. I thought..."

"You didn't think. Fine. I'll vanish and you'll never have to look at me again." With two steps she scooped up Gwydion. "Or him."

It was the only sanction she had, but if he did not acknowledge the boy then she would find a father worthy of the name. Or she would win Arthur back. There was, at that point, no possible compromise. No middle road.

Even after the way he had treated her, she still wanted him.

2

She left Gwydion behind in the capable care of his nurse. At least she was no longer in the city, no longer trapped by the crowds and the walls. She felt a weight upon her, almost as if they all, past, present and future reached out towards her, wanting something from her.

Her pony made its way at an easy trot along the old road. The roads were becoming overgrown, but it seemed as if their cobbled surfaces would last forever. Perhaps they would. Perhaps they would outlast mankind itself. She felt the weight of past and future on her again.

One hand reached forward to scratch the base of the dun gelding's mane. Three days would take her to Avesbury. To the place where kingmakings happened. Or did they any more?

It seemed that Arthur wanted more than to be Dux Bellum. He wanted to be High King and he was willing to discard anything that got in the way. Placate the Christians, indeed.

Place the Christians first, more like. But she knew who would be at Avesbury. She hoped. She could not be away from her child long...or could she? He was too young to foster, she decided, reluctantly.

She wanted to push the pony into a canter, but she knew she could not afford to. The countryside she passed through had not yet really been hit by raiders, as that to the east and the north had been.

Too young to foster. Yet...she knew of only one way to gain Gwydion his place. To make it so that Arthur could not ignore his mother. Even if he only acknowledged him as a bastard, he at least would have his father.

Would cold Guinevere allow such a thing? Given how meekly she had bowed to Arthur, possibly. She did not strike Persephone as a real princess.

Thus, Avesbury. She saw a path, but to follow it, she needed advice. She had, herself, only a trace of magical ability. Her gift was with sword and spear, not the talents of a witch; but every so often, the sight came to her. Too rare to be of use. There had, though, always been a grove at Avesbury, even when the Romans suppressed the Druids. They had not dared to touch the Great Circle. It had not been built by the Druids, of course.

It was far, far older.

Night descended upon her and she knew she must find some hostel. There was a village, one villa and a group of old-fashioned roundhouses. She was traveling as a common woman. Incognito seemed best. It seemed even more appropriate when she saw that even this village was building a church. A small one, and of wood and wattle, but a church nonetheless, betrayed by the rough temporary cross somebody had set outside it.

She scowled in its direction, then decided she was being unfair. They were not all bad people, and they had not made Arthur abandon her. No, he had done that all on his own. He had set her aside for his ambition.

Yet, he might still be the best person to lead Britain against the Saxons...in no small part because of his Norse blood, his kinship with them, albeit distant.

Those were the thoughts she took to bed, and they had gone nowhere by the time she rose. Nothing had changed. Nothing would change as she returned to the road, her horse's hooves muffled by the heavy fog as mist rose from the Thames.

She had a sword at her side as she rode, but as yet had no cause to use it. Its very presence was enough to keep highwaymen at bay. They would wait for some unarmed merchant. She hoped.

On the third day, the weather changed, and not to her favor. She wrapped her cloak around her as she rode through the dripping rain. The gelding bowed his head and tried to hide inside his own shaggy mane. She let him, for such was weather unfit for man or beast.

Thus it was that when she reached the Great Circle of Avesbury, the rain dripping down on her from grey skies, she did not immediately recognize what she saw.

The circle was large enough to hold a good-sized village, but none would dream of placing a permanent structure within it. Until now.

She reined in the gelding at its edge. A simple wooden building, set in the circle's very center. It should not be there. Slowly, the rain cleared a little.

Slowly, she saw the truth of what it was.

Somebody had built a Christian church in the Great Circle of Avesbury.

Frozen, she wondered how long it had stood there. It was finished, but not yet aged, the wooden boards that made it up still clean and pristine.

How would she find what she sought now? The grove trees were still there, most of them, but the church had pierced and desecrated that inner circle.

For a moment, the rain closed in on her, and through it she saw a prosperous village, set within the circle itself, even spilling out past it. As if the banks were no more than some forgotten fortification, to be abandoned once the enemy had gone.

Her tears mingled with the rain. It was wrong. It was all wrong.

She saw a man emerge from the church. She wanted to whirl her pony around, gallop back the way she had come. To her home, to her son. There, at least, she was safe from those who denied the existence of all Gods save one and condemned everything they didn't understand.

Instead, she forced herself to nudge him forward. The man was a Christian monk, wrapped in the brown robes they favored.

"Brother," she greeted, being as polite as she could.

"Perhaps you would care to come in out of the rain."

She shook her head. "I'm looking for Vivian." It was in vain, though. How had Arthur known which way to jump?

He had known who would win in any conflict between the old ways and the new.

The Brother's eyes took her in. "Vivian." He spoke the name as if he knew who it was, and, surprisingly, with no distaste.

"Vivian," she insisted. She would not enter the Church, but where was she?

"She left earlier today, for Avalon. She was in a wagon. You may be able to catch up with her."

Left. "Then there is nothing here for me." She spun the gelding away, digging her boots into his ribs and pushing the already tired beast westwards.

Avalon. If they could not meet at the Great Circle, then Avalon was the next best choice. The mound that resembled the Earth Mother's swollen belly, the altar on its top. Or had that, too, been altered, transformed, taken over?

She thought she heard the sound of church bells. If she rode fast enough, and the Brother told the truth, she could catch up with Vivian. And at that moment, she did not care if she foundered her horse in so doing.

Only after she had ridden away did it occur to her that maybe, just maybe, she had been rude to a man who had not treated her ill and had, in fact, helped her.

The road was not Roman, and the mud slowed her. It sunk beneath the level of the surrounding land, as unpaved roads in heavy use were wont to do.

Despite that, she caught up with Vivian just as the light died. A wagon, covered with cloth and two figures on the buckboard. One was Vivian, the other a child, a girl of no more than six or seven.

Granddaughter or fosterling?

"Hail, lady!" Persephone called.

The wagon stopped and the woman's head turned. It was, indeed, Vivian. A woman no longer young, just as she had been two years before when she had blessed Gwydion's birth.

"Persephone. You are a long way from home."

"So are you." There was just enough room to squeeze the gelding between the wagon and the bank. A shaggy piebald drew the wagon, long mane and forelock all but hiding his head.

"I do not know if I have a home any more."

"Arthur is going to marry Guinevere." Persy fought back the expression that wanted to mark her face. "He does not care about me or his son."

"He also?" Vivian breathed in, then out. "Merlin is at Avalon. Perhaps he has answers."

If anyone did, it would be him. Merlin, who supposedly had so much fairy blood he did not grow old. Persy shook her head. She had never been, quite, sure she believed that particular story. "Maybe Arthur will listen to him."

"Do you ask this for yourself?"

"For Gwydion," she said, finally.

Persy had never been so far west. Avalon was, to her, a legend. A gateway to the Otherworld, she knew. A path through which the Faerie could come.

The fog settled again, and Vivian reined in her horse. "We must leave the horses here."

Persy nodded, remembering that Avalon was supposedly surrounded by treacherous marshland. A roadhouse of sorts loomed out of the mists.

From it, a large man emerged. He nodded, but did not greet them out loud. Instead, he took charge of the horses while a second, as like as another pea from the same pod guided the three to a boat.

Persy realized the irony. Maiden, Mother, Crone. Not that Vivian was that old, but she was too old to bear more children, and that was sufficient.

She should have brought Gwydion. But no, he was safer at the villa, well protected. If they were attacked, the servants had orders to flee to Arthur's side. He might not be willing to acknowledge his son, but he would, surely, protect him.

The boat was flat, propelled by a pole that the man thrust into the mud. He did appear to have a tongue, albeit seldom used. "Lady Vivian...you may not find all to your liking."

"They are here also, then?" Her voice was always soft, but it carried a tremor when she spoke, a weakness.

"I could not deny them passage. That is the law."

Persy felt her heart drop into her stomach. Yes, they were a plague indeed. Decent people, taken one at a time, but their determination to rule the souls of the people? That frightened her.

Softly, "Then perhaps we will flee further. They can drive us into hiding, but they cannot harm the gods. Their time will be fleeting." That was Vivian's promise, but as she gave it, she looked at the little girl.

Nimue, her name was. One day she would be a woman. And Persy knew that she was intended to be Vivian's apprentice, perhaps even her successor. A priestess and a witch, fostered young for such training.

The even rhythm of the pole and the motion of the boat lulled her. Persy did not realize she had dozed off until she woke with a start as the tip of its prow touched solid ground. Some marsh bird lifted off from the bank nearby. Grey wings guided it upwards into a grey sky.

For some reason, that was enough to make her shudder again.

The island had always had permanent occupation, but it seemed to have been split into two camps. The Christians were not just there, they were there in force. Men and women worked on constructing a church.

It was not right, and she felt a rising panic within her. The image that came into her mind was a tower and cross on the Tor itself. "No," she whispered. "They mustn't."

Vivian shook her head. "They can do as they wish. If we fight them, then we destroy Britain. Come."

At least there, the groves still stood. Rowan and oak and hawthorn. Other plants too. Persy knew the uses of some and not others. For a moment, breathing in the scent, she could forget, then a dropped tool and a curse reminded her.

"Don't give in to hatred, Persy. It's an ill-fitting garment...it makes the wearer ugly."

Knowing Vivian was right, she took several deep breaths. The scent, again, rich and deep, flowers and trees and with it something else, something she could not place. A bell-like sound that was remembered, rather than heard, and then there was a man standing in the grove.

Either the rumors were true, or Merlin was more than one man, passing the title on as Vivian would some day pass the mantle of High Priestess. He did not look much older than Arthur, dark hair unstreaked with grey, skin darker than most Britons.

Persy swallowed, then curtseyed.

He stepped forward, extending his hands to grip Vivian's arms firmly. "Lady," he greeted her. "You came."

"And saw," she said, almost grimly.

"It must be," he said, softly. He smiled at the little girl, who grinned back, making dimples. "And...Persephone."

Persy took a deep breath. "Lord Merlin."

"No, no, no. No Lord," he said, simply. "Just Merlin."

"I...I was hoping for some advice."

He glanced at Vivian, something unspoken passing between them, then, "Walk with me."

Persy did so, and they stepped between the trees of the grove. "The man I thought I loved is marrying somebody else and refuses to acknowledge our son."

"He will," Merlin said, simply.

"Acknowledge Gwydion?"

"He will have no choice." Merlin glanced sidelong at her. "I see no issue from Guinevere."

"Then he's making a poor decision...but I suppose there's..."

The lips quirked. "On some things, he will listen to me. When it comes to the weather, the best time for a battle, he listens. When I told him not to wed her, he would not."

"There is Morgan, too." She too had been scorned, although there was no deep past or attraction to intensify her feelings.

His face changed. "Do not cross that one. If she is not stopped, she will bring nothing but destruction."

"Is she stopped?"

"I don't know. She hates Rome and all it stands for, and thus, everything connected to it. Including Arthur."

"Good job he didn't pick her, I suppose." Then, angry, "He should have chosen me."

"He insists he must have a Christian bride."

"I fear he has already converted." Persy's eyes drifted towards the sound of tools. "He will accept Gwydion, but not me."

"Yes."

Did she let her son go with... "So, what, now I'm supposed to give my son up to him?"

"It's the only way, Persy." He turned towards her, and only then did she notice just clear the blue-grey of his eyes was.

"It's not fair." She regretted the words the second they were out of her mouth, but in truth it was not. How could it be? What was she supposed to do? "What can I do? Forget him and love another?"

That, she almost regretted too. She knew in that moment she would live apart.

Merlin sighed gently. "As I said. He will not listen to me. But in a few years, he will send for Gwydion. Ask to foster him, as is so commonly done. Eventually, he will make the boy his heir. That is crucial."

"Why?"

"Because otherwise it will be his son by Morgan who inherits."

Persy flinched, reaching up for her hair. "He's going to bed her as well?"

"She has always been that way, ever since she changed from girl to maiden."

"You know her, then."

He closed his eyes. "Morgan of Cornwall is not Gorlois' daughter. She is mine."

3

Gwydion could run. His mother, who remembered the time when he could not walk, was constantly startled by that.

The villa on the coast was gone. Raiders had destroyed it, and they had barely escaped. The survivors fled inland. That had been two years ago, but she remembered it. Her aged father, others of her kin, dead holding off the Saxons so the women could escape.

She would have fought with them, but she had to get Gwydion out of there. He had been five then, he was seven now, a sturdy lad.

Arthur had been war duke for three years before they had finally named him King. That too had been two years ago. Five years, and no whisper of an heir from Guinevere. The pale queen, it appeared, was as barren as Merlin prophesied.

She waited for the other part of the prophesy to come true. When would Arthur come for Gwydion?

She watched her son run across the heather, and then stop and look up.

They were here. Arthur, and next to him his closest comrade, the huge Kay, so large that the only horse that could carry him was bigger than the biggest ox. She remembered him, for he too had fought with the Legions and, she had believed, departed with them. There were others, too, but it was at Arthur and Kay that Gwydion looked.

And then, the king slid down from his saddle, handing the reins to Kay. "Hello, young warrior. What is your name?"

"Gwydion."

"Where is your mother? I want to talk to her."

She strode across the ground towards them. "I am here." She saw his body language shift, from gentle toward the boy to hostile to her. No,

15

not hostile. It was more as if he did not quite know what to do or say.

When he spoke, it was soft, "I wish to foster Gwydion."

"Had you chosen me, you would have four children by now," Persy said, equally softly.

"I did what I needed to do." Then there was a pause, a hesitation. "I'm sorry."

She did not want to believe him. "And now you will take my son." She paused. "Take me as well."

"You are no court lady."

"I can ride with your warband."

"No," Arthur said softly. "I do not let women fight for me."

"Is that the Roman influence, or Guinevere's?" Those were words worth regretting.

The way in which he turned away gave her all the answer she needed. Despite that, she pressed her words. "Will she treat my son poorly?"

"No. She has promised to treat him as her own...and if she does..." He tailed off.

"If she conceives, then her son will have..." She glanced at Kay.

His eyes closed. "I would that conceiving were the problem."

Pity flowed through Persy. She could not help it. Some women could not conceive, and that was bad enough. But others could conceive but not carry, and that was by far the worst of it.

"I cannot ask her to try many more times. I have said she should have the healers give her something...something to stop conception."

Such potions did exist, although they were hardly reliable. "Have you talked to Vivian?"

"I have, but Jenny will not. She calls Vivian and Merlin witches, she tolerates Merlin at court only because I won't budge." A pause, then, "Perhaps I should have chosen you, but in truth I could not."

"Barrenness is enough reason for a man to take a second wife."

"The Church does not allow it. Or even divorce."

Persy shook her head. "Do you not see their folly now?"

"It is one matter amongst many, Persy. The Son of God said that a man should not divorce his wife, so I will not."

Given how far away the man, avatar or not, had lived, Persy wondered if that had been accurately translated, but she held her peace. "Take him. He will be safer at Camelot than here in any case."

The plan that formed within her mind was as half grown as an unborn child, and might need almost as long to come to birth.

"Thank you."

Gwydion had not heard the conversation. He was too busy feeding his lunch to Arthur's horse.

Persy looked at him, and vowed in that moment that it would not be for the last time. "We must eat before you depart...and as late as it is...I welcome you to spend the night."

Would he come to her bed anyway? If he did, would she allow him? No, she thought. She could not risk conceiving again, not now. She had done so so easily with Gwydion.

He should have picked her. Instead of saying more, he nodded, walking over to speak with Kay.

Persy called the stablehands, two of them, to help with the horses. Kay's giant would dwarf the ponies, she thought with amusement.

"Can Gwydion take his pony?" she inquired

Arthur's brow furrowed as they stepped inside. "We brought one, but of course, if he's attached to the animal."

"He is," she smiled, making as if...for all who watched, she was at least resigned to the situation, if not happy with it. Would Arthur buy it? He would probably not even rent it. But that did not matter. A bit of time would convince him that there would be no more 'trouble' from her.

"Then I will have to give him something else." Arthur smiled. "Perhaps a puppy. I have a litter sired by my favorite that will be weaned soon."

"Hunting dogs or war dogs?"

"Hunting," Arthur said. "Good, fast staghounds. I'm very fond of that line. And as for gifts, I have one for you."

He signaled one of his men, who brought a small box from his saddlebags.

Inside it was a silver bracelet with an amber charm. It had to be very expensive. Persephone slipped it onto her wrist, feeling its weight. "This came from Rome."

"Yes." And then he lowered his voice, as in a confidence. "Jenny hates amber."

So, she got the queen's rejected castoff jewels. But then... "Blondes as fair as her shouldn't wear it anyway. Garnet would be far better."

"Exactly."

She led them to table, and before long food was served. "I would offer a real feast, had you given more warning."

"Who killed the boar?" Kay asked, reaching for a rib.

"I did," Persy said with a slight smile.

One of the other men made some comment about women and hunting under his breath, but Kay looked at her with some approval.

Maybe that would be another way to get to court....court one of Arthur's warriors. Kay, perhaps.

No. She had a plan, and she would stick to it. To be a lady of the court was not her desire. To prove the Christians wrong in every way she could...now that was worth it. To see Guinevere's face...

But the face that floated into her mind was Merlin's.

Merlin. She could not, yet, ask him for his advice. "So, tell me, are you recruiting warriors?"

"We will be come spring." It was autumn. "There will be trials held at Camelot."

Then she had the winter to prepare. To consider. And while she could not ask Merlin...she might, perhaps, be able to contact Vivian.

Or, perhaps, she could ask the gods themselves. She was no skilled witch, but there was a circle not far from here, a small one. She doubted she would be struck down for asking what she intended to ask.

No, the worst case would be that her question would receive a 'no', and then, at least, she would know it was a stupid idea. "I know a couple of young men who would greatly appreciate attending."

Arthur smiled, magnanimous now. "They would be most welcome." Then his visage changed. "Persy, I..."

"Don't." Soft, but firm. "Arthur, just don't."

He shook his head. Long after he and those with him had retired, Persy sat staring into a candle flame, trying to see the future in its flickering light.

As usual, she failed.

When they rode out the next day, Gwydion was with them. He was young to be fostered, but not too young. The break had to happen sooner or later. A man could not be too close to his mother, or he would not grow into a man, but something neither one thing nor the other. Or so they believed.

Of course, some were that way from birth, but that was different. That was the will of the gods. Such made powerful witches.

Persy had little ability in that regard. She was sure and certain that the weight of history she sometimes felt on her was her imagination. Or her fear.

She watched until the last of their horses' tails vanished over the horizon and the sound of hooves faded into nothing.

She went back inside. "I am leaving," she told the servants. "I wish to travel, to see the old shrines before the Christians claim all of them. I don't know when I will return."

They accepted that. With Gwydion gone, what was to hold her here? Some women, no doubt, would have sat with their spinning, but then most women would have found another man to share their bed and fill their bellies with more children. She knew the servants thought her fay, or, at the very least, obsessed.

Perhaps they were right. They would certainly believe more of it if they knew her true intent.

She took two horses; the dun, Blazer, and a dark grey. She took sword and spear and her armor. In armor, it was all but impossible to distinguish a man from a woman. The curve of the breastplate would hide her breasts, but she would need to flatten them when unarmored.

She went north, then turned off the road once out of sight. There was a copse...not a grove, but perhaps the closest she would find. Further away, the great forest closed in, but the small copse was safer. She saw no chance of anyone seeing her. She picketed the horses, and then pulled out her belt knife.

Ruefully, she regarded it, then tested the edge. It would do. With three quick movements, she hacked off her hair. A proper barber could finish the job, but no woman would wear it that short. Almost, she wept for it, but it could be grown again in time.

Once she convinced him.

She bound her breasts then donned her armor, tucking the shorn hair beneath her helm.

As long as she avoided the bath house, going there only at times nobody else would be present, she knew she could continue the masquerade indefinitely. With one exception. A body servant would know, would have to, to dispose of certain things. She would have to find one she trusted, or do without.

None of her existing ones would do. She was better off with some boy who wanted to be a warrior. Or, perhaps, some girl who wanted to be one, bound by the shared secret.

She hid the dress she wore, buried it and her hair under the earth. Her head felt oddly light as she rode on. She felt light, as if freed of some burden.

She did not ride for Camelot. The trials were in the spring, and she had to be ready for them. She was well trained, but aware of the several layers of rust on the top of her training. So, she rode for the plains around Avalon. Perhaps, Vivian was still there.

Each day, she rode for half of the day and then worked for a couple of hours on her swordsmanship. She was in no hurry. Rapidly, though, she found herself in need of a sparring partner.

Winter was closing in and the campaign season over. Some of the warriors would be returning home. The raiders would not cross the seas now, while winter storms roiled the waters.

She reached Avalon, but Vivian was no longer there. Somebody had placed a cross on top of the Tor and she wept openly to see it. It was not right. They were determined not to co-exist, but rather to take over. To rule.

Even Merlin, she remembered, had been resigned to that.

She brushed back the tears from her eyes, succeeding in getting rid of them before the monks came.

Two of them, wearing brown robes.

"Brothers," she greeted them, dropping her voice. So far, her masquerade had fooled everyone.

"Do you come to the shrine?"

Not yours, she wanted to say. Instead, she shook her head. "I'm going home." A lie, of course, but one that explained her presence on the road so late in the year.

"Pray with us."

She hesitated. It would be impolite to refuse and wrong to accept. She had never felt so trapped as she did in that moment. Forgive me, she thought, and felt a warmth. It was alright. The gods understood...or did they? Did she want them to? Did she want to accommodate?

Arthur would raise Gwydion as a Christian. She herself was part of a vanished past.

Then she knew what was really wrong. She could no longer sense the gate to Faerie that lay under the Tor. It was still there, but sealed, barred. Britain's strength came from the Otherworld. Without it, what could they be but a pale shadow?

A mere remnant, putting its trust in a foreign god. Despite that, she slid down, wincing as cold feet touched the ground. She picketed the horses and followed the monks.

They did not cross the swamp, but had a small road shrine of sorts. She was relieved...she had never entered a church and did not plan on starting now.

He prayed in Latin, which she did understand, although the words of the prayer were unfamiliar. She listened, feeling the wind around her, and feeling...yes, a strong sense that his god was real. At least there was that, but did that god really want every human to worship him? His followers certainly did, and the prayer that came to her mind was highly irreverent, 'Jesus, save me from your followers'.

They weren't so much dangerous as annoying, though, she mused. If they could find room to acknowledge those of other ways, she would have no problem with them.

At least he hadn't asked her if she was baptized...initiated into their religion. No, she realized, worse, he had assumed. She shivered inside at that. Would there be a time when everyone was? When the old ways were completely forgotten?

"What is your name?" he asked her, finally. "I am Brother Malcolm."

"Percival," she said, still keeping her voice deep. He seemed fooled enough. Or, perhaps, he was one of those who did not care about women fighting anyway.

"Do you ride with the King?"

"I hope to." Ride with... Arthur was very much into fast raiding from horseback. He always had been.

"Ah. Good luck with that. At least we don't have to worry about raiders here."

"No, but I'd imagine you have some problems with bandits."

"It's hard for them to get to the island, but yes, they're active in the area."

She nodded. "I was afraid of that. I'll have to keep my eyes open."

"They're unlikely to attack an armed man, at least." He paused. "Do you have work for the winter?"

She shook her head. "No, but..."

"We could use some extra blades here. Just until the campaign season starts again."

What did she do? She could use the money, the training...but at the same time, wasn't it hypocritical of her to take the monks' pay? "I don't know."

"You can't tell me you don't need the money, and you're clearly a good man."

The fact that he didn't interject 'Christian' in there both relaxed and disturbed her. He was assuming again. She wondered if her great-grandchildren would even be allowed to know their ancestors had followed different beliefs.

She wondered where Vivian was. "Do I have to commit to the entire season?"

He hesitated, then shook his head, "No. You can sleep with the lay brethren."

"My horses?"

"There's a stable nearby for the use of pilgrims. Their board, of course, would be included in your pay."

She would not be the only one with animals to care for. Finally, she nodded.

She did not realize she was soon to get one of the biggest surprises of her life.

She was not the only soldier there for the winter, nor even the first. And when she saw one of the faces, it was all she could do to hide the recognition that flowed through her.

It was Galahad of Orkney.

What did she do? Brazen it out as a good test of her disguise? Then again, they had seen each other but once, and he a child then. She was not even sure why she felt such a shock of familiarity.

For the first moment, he showed no sign of recognizing her, but then it seemed to flow across his youthful face. "Persephone?"

She shook her head. "I'm sorry...you're mistaken, although...it's a mistake people do make. I'm Percival. Persephone's half-brother." The lie came easily, it had been the explanation she had come up with if people noticed the resemblance.

"Oh." He wasn't exactly disappointed. "You look a lot alike."

"I know," she said. "We've been confused before. Have you been riding with Arthur?"

"Not yet." He was younger than her; she remembered him as a boy at Arthur's recognition. Yet, he was a man now.

Would it be dangerous for them to travel together? "I was going to the trials in the spring..."

"We can ride together, then. Two blades are always better than one. Have you seen the shrine?"

"Not yet." Joy, he was going to drag her to see some Christian relic.

"Come on."

She could do nothing but follow...but absolute shock came over her face. In the middle of the courtyard was a young thorn tree.

"They say that Joseph of Arimathea, the first missionary to Britain, came here to speak with the priests. He demonstrated the power of his god by planting his staff in the ground, and it sprouted into this tree."

That was not magic. Some trees could be propagated that way. It was certainly no tree she had seen before. A foreign tree, transplanted as a symbol of a foreign religion. Rowans were far prettier. "Mmmhmm."

"Have you ever actually seen a druid or a Roman priest..."

"I'm not going to argue with you, Galahad. I believe that's what happened, I'm just not sure whether it was magic or a good, solid knowledge of trees and plants." But then, that was often considered part of magic. "It's more like somebody giving you a healing potion than real magic."

"I can sort of see that. But can you deny it's pretty?"

It was, in its own way. It also explained why... "Pretty, yes, but foreign. It doesn't belong here."

And she had agreed to ride with him. Now he'd be attempting to convert her every step of the way.

The scene shimmered and she felt that weight again. She saw the thorn, not just fully grown but bent with age...stone buildings surrounded it, not wood. Yet, those buildings were worn and tumbled, fallen. Paved paths, like the Romans could have built, led around it.

Then she was back in the present, blinking. A raven flew overhead. Messengers of one of the Saxon gods, she recalled. She watched it for a moment.

"Those things are big," Galahad murmured. "Not as big as sea eagles, though."

"I don't think anything that flies is as big as a sea eagle short of a dragon, and from all I can tell they're extinct."

"If they ever existed."

"Those bones people find are either dragons or giants. Or maybe some of each. But I don't think they exist now." Which was a sad thing, Persy thought. Seeing a dragon would be...special.

"Some people say that dragons are just a symbol of the evil one."

Persy tried not to frown. "I thought his symbol was a snake."

"That too. They sort of put the two together."

"I can see being afraid of snakes." If a viper bit a man, the man might die. Not always, but he might. They were very definitely beings to respect. She could see connecting them to evil, but they were also connected to rebirth and renewal. It felt all twisted around, for a moment, as gnarled as her vision of the thorn tree in the future.

Had that been the future she had glimpsed, or just her imagination running rampant?

The raven circled back overhead.

"I think it has more to do with snakes being small and looking harmless but being capable of killing. They have snakes in the Holy Land that will kill you before a healer can even try to do anything." Galahad shook his head slightly in obvious distaste.

Persy shivered a bit. She was abruptly glad most snakes were harmless grass snakes. Not that she would want to be bitten by one, it would hurt. But it would not be serious.

"Scorpions, too."

They had scorpions in Rome. "Let's talk about something other than poisonous creatures." For some reason, she thought of Morgan of Cornwall. There was something poisonous about her. And if Merlin was right, she pursued married men.

Abruptly, Persy recalled that Arthur was married to Guinevere, so what was the difference? The difference was that she wanted him to divorce 'Jenny' and marry her. She wouldn't jump into his bed while they were still married. Unless he took her as a second wife.

"Let's go to the Tor. It's a nice day and I've never actually been up it."

She hesitated, but it was no holiday when such would be an act of disrespect. Besides, the Tor, too, had been desecrated. "Neither have I. I hear it's a nice view from the top."

She was beginning to relax in Galahad's company, despite the fact that his beliefs were different from hers. He was obviously a Christian, or at least leaning that way. Did that mean she had to dislike him? Definitely not.

"So, have you been to Camelot at all?"

She shook her head. "No, not yet."

"I hear he has built baths there, in the grand Roman style."

"Now I really want to go there," she said, ruefully. She hadn't been able to get as clean as she would have liked in weeks.

Galahad started to walk towards the Tor. At least, she thought as she followed, he had believed her. That moment of recognition scared her, implying bound breasts and short hair might not be enough..

It worried her. It was a good test. Arthur would ask the same questions.

Arthur knew she had once had brothers. Hopefully, he would forget that none of them were named Percival, or assume her to be some half-brother he had never met. She had needed to come up with a name that she could shorten to Persy or Percy. Percival had been the first that had come into her head. It could have been worse, but also better. She was, in any case, committed to the name now.

The masquerade had to last, in any case, only until she had proven herself to him. She had to do well enough in the trials to make him look like an idiot if he didn't take her. "Maybe we can spar some time?"

Galahad offered a smile at that. "I could use the practice."

She reminded herself that he was competition...but then, they could easily both be chosen, especially if they helped each other. "Thanks."

The way up the Tor was a spiral...true, one could cut up the banks, but it was easier to follow the old processional route. In any case, Persy was not about to take short cuts.

"Do you follow the old gods?" he asked her.

"Yes," she admitted, bracing herself for the conversion attempt that was bound to follow.

"What the monks are doing must displease you."

Her shoulders relaxed. "Displease is a mild word for it. I..." She tailed off, glancing upwards.

"In time, you'll come to understand."

That irked her more than him telling her she had to change. He took for granted that she would convert, rather than consulting her on the matter. Why, the arrogant... "I doubt it," she snapped.

"You will."

Now his words sounded like a promise. The tones of a faith so secure that he could not imagine others following a different path. "Maybe we should be thinking about living side by side, not arguing about it."

He fell silent, and she judged by that that she had scored a point. A small one, anyway.

The trees had been cleared from the top of the Tor and replaced by the simple wooden cross. Galahad dropped to one knee, regarding it with an expression she recognized as true devotion. Perhaps even love.

In that moment she understood that he truly believed, and nothing she could do or say would change that. If she could show him her faith, show him the same thing, they could be friends.

She regarded him for a moment, but something in the light shifted. For a moment, Galahad of Orkney appeared to be covered in blood.

She shivered, and the moment passed. Her imagination...or, perhaps, not.

Perhaps it was another vision.

4

Spring returned slowly. It was no longer possible to skate, Norse fashion, across the swamp. Boats came out of storage.

Near the thorn, the sound of wood against wood could be heard. Galahad and Percival practiced, sparring with wooden blades rather than risking live metal.

Persy knew she was doing well. He had been ahead of her at the start, for the men of Orkney fought as soon as they could walk, but now she beat him as often as not. She had, in fact, learned all she could from the other warrior, although she did not voice that thought.

He had proven a good man. Had he been her first introduction to the Christian religion, she might have converted...were it not for their attitude towards women.

She stopped. "I yield."

Galahad lowered his blade from her throat. "A good match."

"My sister's as good as you are."

He shook his head. "Women should not fight."

On that point, he was as adamant as Arthur. It was not so much a Christian thing as a Roman thing, but it seemed to be spreading. "Then, what should women do? Have babies?"

They'd had the conversation, the debate before. The spreading trend seemed to be to view women as wives and mothers first, anything else last or not at all. She was not the kind of woman who could live that way.

She suspected now that Arthur would send her away if he found out. Perhaps she would have to live as a man for the rest of her life. And Galahad could be no confidante. He would betray her for her own sake, her own safety. Unless she could convince him she was truly the better fighter.

"Percy..."

She sighed. "I'm sorry. I just don't think that things are that...that set. That people need to be in such narrow roles."

"And if a woman goes into battle pregnant, without knowing it?"

"You can be more careful than that." She sighed. "We're going to have this fight until we're both old and grey." If they both survived, of course. Perhaps she would not have to keep her secret for long.

"Then let's have a different one."

She laughed. "Defend yourself."

Swords lifted again, and their sounds echoed off the rude buildings used by the monks. For a moment, Persy saw real battle, heard its sounds, smelled the sickly sweet stench of blood. Yet that was as likely to be memory as vision. Perhaps it was both. It lifted her, the memory or image, and she drove Galahad back across half the courtyard.

"Whoah, enough! Just because I disagree with you!"

She laughed and stepped back. "One each. Shall we go for a third to settle it?"

"Why not. Just give me a moment here."

As they turned to face one another again, the sound of bells distracted them. "What?" both said in unison.

The sounds of a commotion reached them. Persy dropped the useless practice weapon and, one hand on her real sword, ran towards the noise.

She heard Galahad's footsteps behind her. Hopefully, it was nothing important. Somebody dropping something on his foot, maybe...

...but the noise came from the chapel itself. As she stepped inside, warily, she felt the stirrings of sacred space...except twisted, wrong. It had been desecrated.

And she instantly saw how. Lying on the altar where the monks prepared their sacred feast was a woman. She had been killed with a single knife blow to the heart.

She was nobody Persy knew. "All the gods." Whatever she felt about them and their new religion, she would not...

It was blasphemy, in their religion, to sacrifice a human. The druids had done it, but only on the rarest occasions, the most desperate need.

This had not been that, and she saw the ropes that still bound the girl's hands. "Unwilling," she whispered.

"Jesus Christ, son of God, have mercy on me, a sinner." That was Galahad, the prayer spoken no louder than she had.

Three of the monks also stood staring at the girl. "What do we do?"

Persy closed her eyes. "Seal everything off. Let nobody leave."

Galahad stepped forward, reached for the girl's wrist. "She's been dead at least a couple of hours, Percy, they're probably long gone."

"Who would do such a thing? Druids?"

"No..." She frowned. "At least, none I know."

"They practice human sacrifice."

"Rarely, and always either of willing victims or prisoners taken in battle. This woman has never held a sword and she was..." Persy felt it tightening around her. "We have to cleanse this place. Where's the abbot?"

"Here." He pushed his way through the crowd, and made the Christian sign of the cross over his chest. "We must remove her."

Two of the monks lifted the body and carried it outside in the light. The abbot turned to the others. "Water, from the font."

Persy took the excuse to leave, before they began their cleansing rites. She would only be in the way, but she vowed to do some of her own, outside the building, later. She felt unclean even from being in that presence. Outside, she saw for a moment, an old woman watching, but when she looked again, the crone had slipped away.

"Does anyone know who she was?" Persy asked of them...half the abbey seemed to be gathered there.

"A girl from Glastonbury village. The daughter of a farmer. A nobody."

"A virgin?"

The monk blushed scarlet. "I'd hardly know."

Persy forced herself to breathe. "Somebody, go to the village, bring her parents here. Try to be easy on them."

They were probably simple farmers who had never before witnessed violent death.

The darkness still flowed around her, and Persy knew that the girl's soul was trapped between life and death. She was no witch of skill to reach it. "Are any of you..." She took a deep breath "Skilled at the art of exorcism?"

She wished with all her heart that Vivian was there.

They buried the girl in the monks' own graveyard, once her spirit had been settled. Persy had sensed - she seemed to be becoming more sensitive - her depart, free, to the Summerlands.

Yet, there remained a tension, and some of it focused on her. She felt she was no longer entirely welcome. But it was time to leave in any case.

She secured the grey's pack load and glanced at Galahad, who rode a black mare. Riding a mare was setting oneself up for trouble, but it was a nice animal, tall, some old Roman cavalry blood in it, no doubt.

"I suspect you are glad to leave."

"I had nothing to do with it." She realized how defensive she sounded, and sighed. "Sorry."

"I know you didn't. But I understand how they feel."

"If I find out who was behind it, I'll kill them," Persy said, with meaning. "They no doubt thought they would drive the monks away. Instead..."

"...instead they've made those people actively determined to stamp out the old gods. I swear, that was never..."

"You would rather people followed their hearts and came around on their own than be pushed or forced as the Emperor tried to do."

"Constantine probably wasn't even really Christian. I think it was all politics to him. Things were already falling apart." Galahad paused. "You're not so bad, for a pagan."

"I'm not sure it really matters. What's the difference between our priests and yours?"

"Some in the church say the practice of magic should be banned."

Persy laughed as she tightened Blazer's cinch. "I've seen the Christian mass. If it's not magic, what is it?"

"It doesn't purport to do anything. It's not like..." He paused. "It's not like the wine literally turns into blood."

"I heard a monk trying to argue that. That at some level it does."

"It's a token representation." Galahad considered that. "But so is a lot of pagan worship, I suppose, like the Beltane marriage."

"Actually, that serves a practical purpose. Most of the women who participate have been unable to become pregnant. It allows them to try and conceive with a different man with no shame on the husband."

"The Church doesn't even want to let Arthur set Guinevere aside. Of course, could it be his fault?"

"No." Persy frowned, then, "You know Arthur is fostering my nephew."

"Gwydion is his bastard?" Galahad's eyes widened slightly.

"Yes."

"So that is why she was so upset. She was hoping he would marry her."

"She was hoping he would have the sense to marry a woman he knew was fertile." She mounted, neatly. "I think he's regretting it now..."

"...but he'd lose the support of the Christian lords if he divorced Guinevere, without a better reason than barrenness."

Persy snorted. "Barrenness is the one good reason to divorce. Especially as sometimes a woman who is barren with one man can be fertile with another."

Galahad frowned a little. "Is that really true? I had heard it, but thought it an old woman's tale."

She nudged Blazer outwards. "It's unusual, but it happens. Besides, most of the time it is the man's fault."

He looked like he was going to say something. Opened his mouth, then shut it. "I've never heard any man admit that."

"You don't seem too shocked by the idea."

"Yeah, but I wouldn't say it like that."

"But given Arthur has a bastard, it's definitely Guinevere who's the problem." Persy sighed. "Poor woman." She did feel some sympathy for her.

She envisioned Guinevere in her mind's eye. Small breasts. Narrow hips. She even looked like a woman who would have problems carrying a child. Not that appearance meant everything, but Persy knew that a woman with hips like a man was in for lengthy and painful labor. Gwydion had not exactly hurried on his way out.

Of course, he had been quite a large baby. And had she had childbearing hips, this masquerade would have been a lot harder.

"Poor woman," Galahaed echoed.

"Then again, I've met women who would have been just as glad to prove barren. Not every woman wants a horde of kids." She didn't mention the number of women who died in childbirth. At least Guinevere was spared that risk and Arthur that grief.

Pheh. That man would not grieve. He'd wait a decent time and turn around and wed Morgan of Cornwall. She had seen the way he looked at her.

"Women are weird."

"That they are. Talking of women, do you know if Morgan's at court?"

Galahad made a face. "At court and sleeping her way through lords and warriors, from what I hear."

No, Persy thought, she's sleeping with Arthur. Anyone else is camouflage. Of course, with a reputation like that, any child she bore would be no threat to Gwydion. That reassured her. "Somebody should make her marry one of them."

"There's one who would take her. He's been, from what she said, seriously courting her, but she doesn't seem sure about it."

"Probably lousy in bed."

"Percy!"

"Well, it sounds like she has a lot of comparison." So, Morgan of Cornwall was playing the court whore. Of course, if what she had heard about the woman's parentage was true, her mother had hardly been a woman faithful and true.

"She's an embarrassment. Gorlois should just plain order her to marry this man and have done with it."

"If you're going to be a mistress," Percy agreed, "stick to one guy. What if she gets pregnant?"

"Gorlois wants her sent back to Cornwall, but he has no real say given he only visits at midsummer." Galahad shook his head a little.

He had no say either. "I doubt Morgan would let herself be 'sent' anywhere."

"Probably not. At least she's not my sister or daughter..."

Persy let him have the last word, falling silent as they rode east towards Camelot.

5

Arthur's main base of operations blended Celtic and Roman in ways that were only mostly harmonious.

Baths there were, indeed, in the building constructed at the base of the hill, outside the defended area. It would, Persy thought, be a shame if that Roman-style villa fell, but she supposed it had to be where there was water and fuel.

Camelot itself was a hill fort of the old style, bounded by banks and ditches and a wooden palisade. To her distaste, she realized that one of the buildings within carried the cross of the church.

The fort, though, was too small to hold all those who had come. Arthur was creating an elite legion, if that was the right term, and while he welcomed all who wished to fight, entry to this force was determined by merit.

That merit was tested in trials, in a grand tourney that demonstrated skill of arms. Naturally, anyone who was anyone; and not too afraid to travel, had to be there.

There would be battles, both on foot and on horseback. There would be feasting. Persy saw that a hippodrome of sorts had been set up for horseback and chariot racing. Arthur was too Roman to use chariots in battle, but there was nothing quite like a chariot race. Not in her mind, anyway. She patted Blazer thoughtfully, and eyed the grey, Winter, but no...they were not well enough matched and unlikely to be competitive against taller Roman-bred horses.

She would content herself with watching the races. There would like as not be footraces too. Didn't the Greeks compete in such contests naked? Then again, Greece was supposed to be very warm. She also saw archery targets.

There were so many people. Tents and makeshift shelters burgeoned on the lower slopes of the fort, and that was not counting those who had brought only bedrolls. Stable hands tossed hay to long lines of horses, whistling cheerfully. Their strident neighs and whickers mingled with the lowing of oxen.

Then, in the midst of it, she saw Arthur.

He was on foot. On one side of him walked Gwydion, the boy seeming slightly overwhelmed. On the other was a huge hunting dog, white with black ears. Persy was pretty sure she had seen smaller horses.

There was no sign of Guinevere.

Persy watched her son until he and his father vanished behind a tent, and tried not to sigh too obviously. She should be there with them.

Arthur did not seem to want his wife at his side either. No...that was unfair. Guinevere might simply have other things she wanted to do than wander through the camp. For that matter, from what little she had seen of the woman...

Christian women did fight, or involve themselves with fighting.

She found a place for Blazer and Winter, and made sure they were fed and watered. She rubbed them down herself, unwilling to turn them over to hands she had not yet observed in action.

Then she sought a place for her bedroll. She had, at some point, lost Galahad and realized she felt it keenly.

True, he was a little young, but Arthur had been a little old...and she chased that thought away. She was not there for that and she would not, could not, betray herself so. Galahad disliked women in battle...

Galahad wanted to protect everyone, to be the perfect warrior and the perfect Christian. Yet, he seemed so secure and certain in his faith that nothing could shake him. That, she realized, was the only way they could...

...and she almost walked into another young man. Thankfully, she caught herself in time. Even a casual brush could be dangerous.

He was bearded, in what seemed to be a desperate attempt to look older. Red hair and beard...Scotti, perhaps? There were not as many of the northerners there, but definitely a few.

Then he opened his mouth, "Excuse me. I should pay more attention."

Erin. His accent was pure southern Erin and her jaw almost dropped. The Irish had never bowed to Rome. Why was he here? "No, no, it was me," she managed, almost losing control of her voice in her agitation.

The man of Erin was wearing a cross, she noticed. So, Christianity had reached them to. Or, perhaps, him after he left. He regarded her, then made introductions. "Bedivere. Of Connemara."

"Percival Caracti," she introduced herself.

"Roman, eh? No, that is not an entirely Roman name." Then he shrugged. "What does it matter? You are British."

She had another echo in that moment. A group of people, exploring a Camelot that had returned to the woods, no longer needed. One seemed to be Saxon or Norse, two more dark-haired Celts, and the last two, two women, dark skinned Nubians. All British, eh? Perhaps.

Perhaps it meant...and she shook her head. "Sorry. Woolgathering."

He frowned, then, "Do you have the Sight?"

She had no clue how to answer that. "Maybe. It could just be my vivid imagination."

"Sometimes that can be every bit as good," Bedivere mused. "There's some good ground past that small copse that nobody's found yet, if you're looking for a place to camp."

She smiled at him. "Thank you."

A decent man, she thought, as he walked away. There seemed to be so few of them.

She had to walk through a good part of the camp. She saw few women, and those she did see seemed to be camp followers...servants, cooks and, yes, a couple that were probably the non-sacred variety of prostitute.

She ignored most of them, seeing that she would have more in common with the warriors. Besides, the whores were probably diseased. That type tended to catch anything that was going around.

She did stop when one of the women offered her a bowl of stew and refused to take payment. She was not about to turn it down, even if it was rabbit. She hung out with the bowl and spoon, tucking into the rich food and watching.

She did not see Arthur again, but she did see the hound. Somehow, it had slipped its leash, and it padded up to her. The look it gave her was utterly pathetic and it drew its sides in in an attempt to appear starving.

"Oh, come on, I know you get fed well," she told it.

It wagged its tail at her, a slow sweep of the stern in true hound fashion. Man. That was one huge dog. "You're a big fellow."

Wag, wag, wag. She didn't immediately see the boy approach. "Cafall, that's where you got to!"

Gwydion's voice, and her heart skipped a beat before she registered the pun in the dog's name. Cafall was friend in Welsh, but it was also very close to the Latin for 'horse'. Appropriate. "Tell your father he caused no trouble. He just wants rabbit stew."

Gwydion laughed lightly. "He can catch his own."

There was supposed to be some deep connection between mother and son. Grimy, short haired and in man's clothing? There was no spark of familiarity in his eyes.

She watched him take the hound's collar. "Sorry..."

"Percival." She didn't tell him she was his bastard uncle. She did not think to until he and the dog were gone.

Then she finished her stew and, fighting back tears, headed for the small copse.

Bedivere had been as good as his word. She claimed a sleeping place in the hollow of some trees, where the wind was mostly broken. She felt no qualms about leaving her bedroll, but not her valuables. Those, and her weapons, she kept close. She estimated she had an hour until dark.

Could she get inside the fort? A quick reconnoiter indicated...no, not yet. The entrance was well guarded and, on top of that, she saw the huge Kay talking to the guards. She did not want to test her masquerade to that level just yet.

She saw the point of the guards. Such a gathering would attract thieves and lowlifes, and she kept a hand on her own pouch. Like as not, they would not try to fight an armed man, but they might try to slit her purse or do her some mischief in her sleep. She was suddenly quite glad that the large Bedivere's spot was so close to hers. And, perhaps, he had an ulterior motive for pointing it out. To want another blade nearby made sense, even if the man was small.

Then again, people knew better than to judge by size. Gwydion, she had noticed, was getting at least some of his father's, although not the fair hair. Fair hair could show up in any line, but was most common with two fair haired parents. She wondered why.

Who knew. The gods worked the way they worked. She saw three stray puppies chasing through the camp. Maybe she should get a dog. No, she had no real use for one.

Then, she saw a familiar face, albeit shifted and changed. Merlin, using a glamor to appear a more reasonable age, rather than his normal self.

Something quickened within her, something completely non-sexual, but strong. She changed course towards him. Finally, somebody she could trust.

He turned, and their eyes met. His were blue, and showed only curiosity in their depths. That, she might have expected. "Per...you came."

She nodded. "Of course I did. Did you expect anything else?"

"Come. Walk with me."

She fell in next to him. "I tried to find Vivian."

"She has disappeared," Merlin said, softly. "I think she went north, perhaps into Scotland."

"Given the Christians have found their way to Ireland, I doubt anywhere is safe."

"Ah. You met Bedivere. Don't judge him by his choice of gods."

"I don't. It's not him, or Galahad, or even Arthur I worry about. It's that plague of monks." They were walking, she noticed, a bit away from the camp. Towards the hippodrome, which was empty except for a small group of horses picketed nearby.

"There is nothing wrong with their beliefs...as long as they don't listen to..." Merlin frowned. "They are not the problem. Those who use and abuse the idea of a monotheistic religion are. They always have been. Ever since anyone came up with the concept that there might only be one God."

"Which is bull," Persy said, stubbornly.

For a long moment, he fell silent. Then, "There is one." He held a hand against her protest. "There is one god, from whom the many gods come, in whom they partake. That is part of the Great Mystery."

She bowed her head. "I am not a druid."

"No, but you hold the spark in your heart. Gwydion may follow his father, but his daughter will come to her grandmother. If all else is forgotten, let that be remembered through the dark times to come."

"Why?" She turned towards him. "What does it matter?"

"Because one day humanity will have to relearn that basic truth in order to survive."

She shivered, feeling the wind flow around her, through her. "But you will be there."

If the rumors were all true, Merlin was over two hundred years old, fae-bred and immortal.

"No," he said, softly, sadly, "I will not."

She wanted to argue, but something in his tone halted her words. Merlin? Not there? That was unimaginable to her. He had not changed. "Merlin..." she managed, finally.

"Don't worry. In the end, everything will work out."

Why did she not believe him? Rather, she watched him stride away. She had forgotten he was barely taller than she was.

He seemed far larger than life.

Persy slept surprisingly well that night, albeit with one hand on her sword and her money pouch tucked under her.

Nobody attacked her or robbed her, and she was able to slip off to bathe. She regarded the bath house with longing. She did not dare. Not indulging would mark her as a barbarian, but she had no chance to do so without being caught.

Arthur might remember that Persy had never mentioned a brother named Percival, but she had an answer to that, an easy one. A bastard, but recently acknowledged. Allowed to compete in the trials, but on the fringes of noble birth.

Would he support her? Once, she would have said yes, when raven-haired Ffion fought at their side. And she was expendable. As long as Gwydion lived long enough to father a child of his own, then the line was secure.

Would Arthur give her a say in the boy's marriage? She supposed that depended on whether he made him his heir or not.

Walking through the morning camp, she kept her eyes open for Merlin or Galahad. Or, for that matter, anyone she knew.

Seeing no one, she frowned. She wanted...no. Gwydion was the last person to whom she could reveal herself. He was far too young to safely keep such a secret.

A shiver abruptly ran down her spine. She glanced around, then up. Standing on the walls of the fort, facing the rising sun, was a woman. She wore a red gown and was not recognizable from this distance, but Persy knew it was Morgan. She raised her hands and Persy wondered which god she honored.

A dark one. Could that possibly be Merlin's daughter? Echoes came into her mind, and she decided she did not want to be in the woman's field of view. She made a quick passage to find one of the cooks. Her coin would not last much longer...but then, if she failed, she might still get on the payroll as a common soldier. That, she had more than enough ability for.

What was Morgan up to? She shook her head. There was no rational reason to mistrust the woman. No, if she was honest, she was jealous of her. Jealous of her lack of fear to pursue the men she chose, even if she did not always choose well.

Merlin's words echoed in her mind. If something happened to him. He might be immortal, but if one knew how, he could probably be killed.

She could not do it...if she tried, she'd end up stabbing a glamor. Taking Morgan out would have the same problem. The Christians were making noises that magic was inherently evil. And, of course, they would see Morgan's habits as proof of that. Persy herself would not judge, except that it was *rude* to go after other women's husbands when there were plenty of single men around.

Galahad stood by the cooks' tent, eating his breakfast without bothering to sit down. She felt an attraction stir and forced it down.

But, they could be friends. "Hey."

"Percy! I was wondering where you vanished off to."

"Easy to lose somebody in this crowd." She shrugged a bit. "Not so easy to find them. This place is chaos."

"I bumped into that weird old Druid. He told me to be careful."

"Merlin?" she asked, keeping her tone neutral.

"Yeah. Him. I don't know what to make of him. Too many hazelnuts, I suppose."

Percy couldn't help but laugh. "Nah, too much time spent alone." She had, to be honest, to admit Merlin was odd. "But he's a good man."

"I can tell. Just a little bit...off."

"He's better than that Brother Cadan at Glastonbury."

Galahad laughed. "Oh, God, *him*? The guy who would only talk to God, not men and spent half his day walking around the courtyard widdershins muttering."

"That's the one. I was tempted to tell him that he was going the wrong way." Widdershins, after all, was for darker magics and banishment.

"I'd call that superstition, but the guy was so off it wouldn't surprise me if he did accidentally summon a demon." Trust Galahad to forget about the banishment part.

Despite that, Persy shuddered. "I think there are those there who could send it home if he did."

"I think that's why the abbot lets him stay, despite how annoying he is. Best to keep a nutter like that close. You're right. He's worse. Merlin just says cryptic things."

"What did he say to you?"

"To be careful about drinking blood."

Persy frowned. "Be careful who you accept Mass from." She knew that the Christian sacred feast symbolized their God's body and blood, his sacrifice.

"Oh! You think he's worried one of the priests is going to drug the wine?"

"Yeah. For now, I need to check on my horses." She tossed her bowl on the stack of dirty ones. "Want to come?"

"Sure, give me a second," Galahad said, quietly, finishing his own gruel. "It's nice to see a friendly face."

"Definitely. Oh, there's this Irish guy, Bedivere. You might like him...nice, polite, Christian." She could see the possibility of a friendship there.

"You not being so doesn't bother me."

"Yeah, but there have to be things you can best discuss with one of your own faith." If they were all like Galahad and Bedivere, Persy would have no problem with the Christians. Sure, Galahad would like it if she converted, but he didn't push the matter.

"And if he's nice...besides. I need to spar with somebody other than you."

"Watch out. He's not much smaller than Kay."

"Even better."

The mists started to lift as the day began in earnest. The breath of the horses seemed to contribute to the rising fog.

Somebody was already putting out hay for them, there not being nearly enough grass along the picket line itself. Another lad led them to the stream to water, three at a time.

She would have smiled at him but found most of her attention fixed on Galahad. Of course, if he knew the truth, he would tell her to get herself home and make babies.

Part of her thought it would...no. Her son was here, and here she would stay until he was a man. That meant surrendering any chance of further children, but so be it. Besides, he was too young, barely of marriageable age, and she old enough to have a son heading rapidly towards manhood.

Such a union could never work. Thus, she resolved to be sure he never learned her secret. Yet, she feared he suspected, such was his tension with her.

She found a brush, to groom her ponies herself.

"You care for your beasts."

"I prefer to know for sure the state of all of my equipment, living and otherwise."

"I don't blame you. A friend of mine broke his arm because he trusted a servant to tighten his saddle girth."

Persy winced. "Could have been worse."

"Could have been his fool neck. Not exactly the most careful of riders," Galahad admitted. "But even so..."

He glanced along the lines. "I'm going to find mine. I'll..."

"Same tent, lunch?"

The trials would begin the next day. Was she ready? Her stomach knotted as Galahad walked away, and she turned her attention back to the horses. The smooth, even stroke of the brush calmed her. Winter, though, had elf knots in his mane.

6

The gods did not seem happy about the timing of the trials. Rain fell in grey streaks from a steel-colored sky. Even before the first pairs stepped out onto the tourney grounds to demonstrate their skills, the soil had turned to mud.

That time, Persy did see Guinevere. Dressed in blue, she sat between Arthur and Kay...pointedly ignoring the latter.

Some quarrel, she supposed, and at length she and Arthur changed seats, reducing the tension visibly.

The variance of skill between the first two opponents was visible. Bedivere had his opponent on his knees and screaming 'Yield' before, almost, one could blink. He was good, Persy thought. He was very good. The next pair saw Galahad square off against another very young warrior.

Too young to be there, she decided, even as he dodged right into a blow of the training weapon and went down. Of course, Galahad immediately stopped to check on him.

Naive, she thought. Somebody would like as not fake it before the end of the day. A real opponent would use such tricks.

Water on the face awakened the boy and he was helped from the lists. His day was probably over...at least, he did not return to the group of fighters.

Then they called her name. She assessed her opponent quickly. He too seemed very young...of course, they would probably think her younger than she was. Most of the older men wore beards. This one only had peach fuzz on his cheeks.

The first bout was under tournament rules, sword only. She watched him for a moment, wary eyes fixed on his blade.

He struck first, but she found her rhythm quickly. Her blade lifted to block his, the faint thud of wood against wood quite audible. Quick. Take him down quick...she would have two more bouts and then the obstacle course they had set up that afternoon. She wasn't going to waste any energy on that guy.

She saw the look on his face as she quickened her pace. One, two, three, and his blade was on the ground. Four, and hers was at his throat.

"I yield," he whispered, looking a little pale and definitely out of his depth.

She actually felt sorry for him. But that was one solid point in her favor. Even if it was, in truth, the warmup.

She heard people cheering. One of them, she was sure, was Galahad. As she walked back to the group, the boy followed. "Can you teach me that disarm?"

"Sure." In the end, they were all on the same side. In the end, she should teach what she knew to anyone who wished to learn and vice versa.

"Fast work," Galahad said, moving over.

"They're boys," Persy frowned.

"They're not that much younger than we are."

"True." She did not correct him about her age. She was still worried he was the greatest threat to her disguise.

Two more bouts. The first one was against one of the few older warriors here, a man with grey in his beard. He was canny, but slow...it lasted a while before she gained victory.

He should, she thought, be detailed to train the younger people. She felt she could learn a lot from him.

In the third bout, she drew Bedivere. She expected the same thing...smart but slow...from the big Irishman.

She underestimated him. He was easily as fast as Galahad, and she found herself on the deck with his sword tip between her breasts...glad they were properly bound.

"I yield." There was a man she wanted on her side, now and forever. He took her hand.

"You have the finest hands of any man I have fought," he murmured. "And you fight well." There was something in his tone that made her wonder, for a moment, if he practiced the Greek vice. None of her business, if so.

There was still an hour before lunch. She should have expected what happened next. Two huge men stepped out into the lists.

"Who is that?" she asked Galahad.

"I believe that is Bors...and Kay." The two big warriors faced one another in the center. Kay stood six inches taller than his opponent, not far from being a true giant.

"Looks like they're planning on showing us how it's done." Persy focused her attention. A spar between those two men would certainly be interesting to watch.

Bors swung his arms and his blade, then gave Kay a come hither look. The big man had a sword to match his scale. He lifted it over his head and brought it down. The light flared from it.

They used live steel and Persy found herself leaning forward. Only two men who trusted each other absolutely, who knew each other's moves, would spar with combat-sharpened blades. She was not the only one. On the far side, she saw Guinevere.

She watched Kay. It was clear even from that distance which man she rooted for.

Arthur watched. It didn't seem that he cared who won. The fight felt as though it lasted forever. Blade against blade, sparks flew across the field.

They were perfectly matched, she realized. Trained together, working together, living together. A bond that she envied...and might never be able to fully share.

Her secret was a barrier between her and all of them. It darkened her.

And then it was over, both men stepping back. They saluted Arthur and the audience, then walked from the area together.

Persy watched them go, still wistful.

Galahad shook his head as he ladled stew into a bowl. "I'll never be that good."

"I think that was meant to encourage us, not the opposite." Persy made a wry expression. "But I feel the same way."

"Neither of us could fight like them anyway. You're half Kay's size and I'm not much bigger." He smiled at her. "I'm more interested in seeing the scrawny little weasel who did so well against Bedivere. What's his name..."

"I don't know his name. But yeah, he seems more our speed than the giant types."

Persy studied Galahad for a moment. He fell silent and she focused on her stew, tucking into it with considerable aplomb. It was actually pretty good even if she was fairly sure, from the nutty flavor, that it was squirrel. She had never objected to 'wood meat', although she would bet all the game had fled that place.

She was not overly tired. She was pretty sure she would be fresh for the next test. Or as fresh as she could manage. "This is going to wear me out," she said, finally.

"Pellinore," Galahad mused. "His name's Pellinore." Then he seemed to come back into the conversation. "Yeah. It seems they're making it multiple times harder than the real thing."

"Do you blame them?" She stretched a bit, regarding him, careful of the angle even though she was sure her armor hid her bosom well enough.

"No. But I'm starting to feel that I have no chance."

"Chin up, Gal. You're better than I am." She was pretty sure that was true. If only one of them got through, she knew who it would be. But she could try again next year. She could keep trying until..

...until she got caught. Sooner or later, she would be, and she knew it. All she could do was hold things together as long as possible and hope she made her point.

She sighed. "I am the one who isn't going to be picked, not you. I promise." She smiled at him, weakly.

"Don't be silly. Besides, we don't have to be as good as Kay and Bors."

"I'm not sure anyone is. I want to see Arthur fight."

"So do I. I hope he hasn't been focusing on tactics at the cost of his edge."

Persy hoped so too. Officers did that, far too often. She rolled her shoulders backwards. "We don't need him to get killed."

"I hear he's talking about making Gwydion his heir...after any issue of Guinevere, that is."

"That's why he fostered him. As a backup. He made the wrong choice."

"The right one politically."

"No. The wrong one all round. Of course, he wasn't to know she was barren when he picked her." He wouldn't be the first or the last.

"Poor woman. No woman should be left childless, and I don't think she cares for Gwydion much."

"He probably reminds her which of them has the problem." Persy finished her soup. "I'm going to lie down for a few minutes, see if I can get some energy back."

She slipped away from him, but the peace she sought was not to be found. When she made it back to the hollow, Bedivere was there.

With Gwydion.

"Hey there," she greeted them.

"You look like my mom."

Persy took a deep breath. "I'm your uncle."

"No you're not. I've never met you before."

"Her father was not...entirely faithful to her mother. It happens." And she knew she was not slandering her father. He had, indeed, committed adultery more than once. Most men did, with the common wisdom saying it was harder for a man to remain faithful, although Persy thought it rather that they found it easier to get away with it. She thought of Morgan.

"Oh. That kind of uncle." He shrugged, not at all concerned.

"The boy was wondering who you were," Bedivere commented.

Persy was torn between relief that Gwydion had not recognized her and pain at being a stranger to her own son. It seemed none of it showed on her face. "I meant to say a proper hi, but..."

"You don't want my father knowing who you are until after the trials."

"Yeah. I don't want any kind of..." He was as likely to be prejudiced against her as for her. It might even out. But at the same time, she seized on the excuse Gwydion offered.

Bedivere glanced at the two. Then he said, "You fight well, but you should consider doing some work left handed. Strengthen that side."

"I'll bear that in mind," she said, wryly. His comments made sense, picking up on a weakness she knew she possessed. Why did she resent them a little? Because she wanted to be perfect?

She always craved perfection. She wanted to be the son and the daughter her parents sought. She had dreamed of being a warrior queen like Boadicea.

Nobody was a warrior queen anymore. Even Morgan, who disdained rules, did not fight. Maybe in her case it was cowardice. Persy would believe anything of that woman.

"Trust me, you're getting there."

Gwydion glanced at Bedivere. "None of you are as good as father."

"I hope that Arthur will spar before the end of this."

Gwydion grinned. "He will. He'll take anyone who goes against him, especially from horseback."

Persy felt a twinge of pain and regret. It was clear where her son's loyalty now lay, and it was not with her. Well, she had given him up, in many ways, for his own good. He was better off. Still, she would have felt...

Her thoughts were interrupted by words. "He'd better. No man wants to follow a commander who can't walk his talk." Bedivere glanced towards the fort.

"You sound as if you're not sure you want to follow him."

"No. I just don't offer my loyalty on the merits of a man's reputation, but rather his deeds."

Persy glanced at Gwydion. The boy scowled.

"A man should be loyal to his father, unless said father isn't doing a good job." She hoped her words would remove the scowl.

They did not. He stalked off, tossing parting words over his shoulder. "My father's the best..."

She didn't hear the rest of the sentence. "Eh. At that age, they should hero-worship," she told Bedivere.

"As long as it's not misplaced."

"No. Arthur's a true warrior, I've seen him fight.." His faults, she felt, were not hers to mention. Besides, his flaws were not as a leader but as a man.

"When?"

"A long time ago. Assuming he's kept his edge and practiced, then I have no problems following him into battle."

"That's a big assumption." Bedivere glanced at the fort. "And I fear that his...woman troubles..."

"Woman troubles?"

"Just rumors. Guinevere going to witches for fertility potions. Morgan of Cornwall sleeping her way through the male population, but going back to him when she can."

"Fertility potions don't seem to be helping her." Sometimes they worked, sometimes they didn't. Persy was not a healer or midwife and had no clue why that was. "I can see why she would try, though."

"I don't know. I don't trust the young one."

"Young one?"

"There was a witch and her apprentice. The apprentice was, oh, maybe eight or nine, and she bothered me."

Vivian and Nimue. "Bothered you how?"

"I can't put my finger on it. Maybe it was the fact that...I wintered here, you know, and so did they, and she seemed to be spending all of her time with Morgan, not the old lady."

The hairs rose on the back of Persy's skull. "Don't trust Morgan. Don't even listen to her."

"Don't worry. She hasn't managed to seduce me yet. She tried." Bedivere shrugged. "Her charms have no effect on me."

"She's a dangerous enemy." Persy knew she needed to talk to Merlin again. "But she hates Christians. If you need to get away from her, I doubt she'd follow you into a church." She was even more sure he was of the Greek persuasion, as he seemed to be the only man capable of resisting Morgan. Rumor had it more than one woman had also found her way to the princess' bed.

Bedivere considered that. "She could, though? I mean...I hear witches can't walk on holy ground."

Persy shook her head. "She could, but she probably wouldn't. She'd be too uncomfortable. I find it hard enough."

"You're not a witch..."

"No, but I'm not a Christian either."

Bedivere frowned. "Yet. Hopefully one day you will understand."

Merlin's words echoed in her mind and trailed around her thoughts. There is only one God. What differs is... "See, I don't think what God you serve even matters."

Bedivere shook his head. "If there is only one God, then serving anyone else is lying to yourself."

"Is it? I think trying to believe something you don't is lying."

She was not sure how much sense that made, even to herself, but she said it anyway. Her voice had become very, almost dangerously, soft. "I'm sorry, Bedivere. I'm not going to change.

"No, I suppose that you are not. But there's always hope."

She did not see it that way. "It matters more, I think, that we're both loyal to Britain."

"Definitely."

She wondered, though. He was not British, that Irishman. He was probably here as a mercenary, looking for experience and money. "Or loyal, at any rate, to those we fight with."

Bedivere considered that. "Arthur has to earn my loyalty. Does he have yours?"

She considered for a moment. "Yes. At least for now."

7

The fact that she had to consider whether Arthur had her loyalty was enough to make Persy wonder if she should stay.

If she was not loyal to him...then she was loyal to Britain. Arthur was the commander they had, he was the unifying force they needed.

Therefore she would stay. And Gwydion was happy. That meant something, even if she had not been the one to cause it.

Gwydion would be king. Assuming Guinevere did not manage to carry a son to term. Sometimes, a woman could have ten, twelve, fifteen miscarriages and then finally settle. She could not be confirmed as barren yet. Except Persy knew she was.

She knew it with certainty, having heard it from one of those she trusted the most.

Speaking of Merlin, finding him to talk was proving harder than she expected. She supposed she should have known he would be in the fort or similar, not the camp. That was her guess, anyway, until she finally saw him coming out of the trees.

He had a dog, of all things, at his heels, that she suspected was of Cafall's bloodlines, although considerably smaller.

A good thing. Staghounds were not meant to be that unnaturally large. "Ho, Merlin!"

She crossed the distance between them and immediately got tackled. The dog wasn't smaller because it was smaller, it was a year old puppy. "Hey, hey! Enough of that!"

Merlin could not help but laugh. "Down, Aura. Down."

A bitch, then, although she could see nothing golden about her. Unless she was named after Aurelius. Some claimed he was Arthur's grandfather. She knew no evidence of that, but it would grant him a certain legitimacy. She pushed the dog down, then scratched her behind the ears once she started behaving. "Am I right in thinking she was sired by that great beast of Arthur's?"

Merlin nodded. "He was a gift from one of the Irish kings. I think they use them to hunt wolves, but he's been crossing him into the staghounds."

Persy could see a dog that size taking down a wolf. "I need to talk to you. Privately? Please?"

"Come, then." They ducked back into the trees, the hound bitch padding at Merlin's heels. "What troubles you?"

"Morgan has been subverting Vivian's apprentice."

Merlin frowned. "That is why Vivian left. The girl is somewhat impressionable, given her age."

"So's Gwydion."

"Morgan wants Gwydion replaced, not..."

Her hair stood up again. "Morgan is going to end up wanting Gwydion dead, if she really wants...but there's a difference."

"Everyone knows Morgan has many lovers, whilst Persephone can honestly swear to Gwydion's paternity." She spoke of herself in the third person, just in case.

"Exactly. Which means that she has to discredit Gwydion's mother. Who has, conveniently, vanished. That may be good or bad."

"Not here to trick anyone into anything, but also not here to defend herself."

"Still, children at that age are impressionable. Gwydion, too, and he was fostered young."

"Old enough to understand, I think." She thought of her son as he was now. "And you can't say Arthur has been a bad father to him."

"Definitely not. It is women Arthur cannot deal with."

She thought back. "He's afraid of women. Maybe he picked Guinevere because..."

"He picked her because it was the most politically expedient option. They don't love each other."

"You sure of that?"

"Thrown crockery," the druid said, wryly. "Other things too. Kay once had to forcibly separate them."

Persy rolled her eyes. "That's normal for some marriages."

"Not when it's the only interaction they have. They don't even share a bedchamber any more."

Persy frowned. "That's not because he doesn't love her. He as much as told me he doesn't want her going through another miscarriage."

Merlin glanced back towards the fort. "Then she'll just seduce him. She's desperate for that child, but nothing will give it to her. Actually..." He paused. "I've been sneaking potions to prevent conception into her wine. There's a very real risk that she could die if she keeps trying."

"Politically, that...no, he'd marry Morgan."

"Yes, likely he would."

"Morgan as queen is definitely a worse proposition than Guinevere, but I don't understand..."

"Morgan acts like a woman. Persephone always acted like..." He tailed off, regarding her. "You know what I mean."

"Stupid Christians." She shook her head. "What happened to..."

"Rome happened. Christianity happened. Change happened. It will not last forever."

"Long enough for me." She hesitated before she spoke again, unsure if she should voice it even to him. "Merlin, I saw the future."

"What did you see?"

"The abbey at Glastonbury in stone with an aged thorn at its heart."

"And what do you believe it meant?" Merlin regarded her.

She shook her head. "I think I was seeing Christianity in its dotage."

"Nothing lasts forever, Persy."

"Some things do," she said, looking towards him. "The love of a mother for her son." Even mares and bitches felt that, she had seen it so often. "The love of a man for a woman. Those things endure..."

"...until the stars themselves die. Which they will. Even the world must die in order to be reborn."

She shivered again. "But not today."

"Nor tomorrow, nor any time in lives upon lives."

"I would not wish to be a druid."

"We know bare fragments of what has been known, and what will be." There was an intensity to his gaze.

Persy could not face him for a moment. She looked away. All she saw was approaching rain. Through it, hints of silver seemed to shimmer, but they never formed into coherent shapes. If it was a vision, it died stillborn. After a moment, it was gone. "Will we learn more?"

"Yes, but only after centuries of darkness and fear and pain. Would you believe that..." he indicated the villa, "will be the last bath house built for many centuries?"

She shook her head. "People need to be clean. If they forget that..."

"Then their children will die, but they will still forget."

"A couple of the monks at Avalon seem to think God wants them to be dirty." She wrinkled her nose.

"Exactly." Merlin reached out, placed his hand under her chin. "Never allow your grandchildren to forget."

"I promise."

He released her, then turned and strode away, towards the fort, the hound padding beside him.

Perhaps while Merlin was there, there was hope.

The trials lasted five more days. By the end Persy was exhausted. She had run, ridden, fought on foot and on horseback and no longer cared if she passed or failed. She knew she would get over that feeling once she had had a good night's sleep, but for the moment she sat by her bedroll, leaning on her sword. At least she was clean, having managed to find a time when nobody was likely to use the bath house.

"Percy?"

Answering to that was easy, especially in familiar tones. "Galahad?"

"Gawain."

She felt disappointment. "Sorry."

"It's the Orkney accent. Nobody can ever tell our voices apart."

He stepped around in front of her. He was taller than Galahad and a scar marred his cheek. It had not been there the last time she had seen him.

It improved his appearance, gave him a warrior's dignity. He was a handsome enough man that she was glad certain reactions were not visible. "Let me guess, Galahad's been telling stories about me."

"Good stuff, I assure you." Not that he was smiling.

As she recalled, he had not smiled last time either. Perhaps it was simply not a habitual expression for him. On the other hand, he was a good man according to his younger brother. That made him likely to be a candidate for sainthood. "I was afraid he'd tell you about all of my scrapes."

"The only scrape he mentioned was the chapel murder."

Persy repressed that memory, but at the mention it sprung into stark relief. She shivered. "You had to bring that up."

"I have a horrible thought on who did it."

"Oh? I'm not...good at that kind of thing," she admitted.

"One of the monks."

Horror flowed through her. "Why?"

"To make the old ways look worse." He had stubble, maybe he was growing a beard to hide that scar. "I...wanted to run it past somebody else."

She remembered Brother Cadan. Walking the courtyard withershins, over and over again. "I don't know. Not all of them were entirely sane, but desecrating their own temple seems a bit much."

"Very religious people tend not to be sane." Gawain cracked a smile. "Seriously. Both Merlin and Father Duncan - that's Arthur's Christian priest - seem a little off at the edges."

Persy shrugged. "Yeah, but it's a different kind of insane from the insane that causes somebody to do that. One of those monks was seriously nuts...but a murderer? I don't think so. Unless he thought God told him to do it, and that seems unlikely."

"Oh, one of those?"

"Yeah. Spent half the day walking withershins around the courtyard." Persy shook her head. "But I'm pretty sure he was harmless. No, it wasn't one of the monks. But I'd buy somebody trying to make us look bad."

Gawain showed no surprise. Probably, Galahad had warned him about her tendencies. He shook his head, instead. "I really stopped caring what people believe a while ago. You do realize Arthur tries to haul all of his people into the church, right?"

He was giving her fair warning. She tried not to shiver. "Tries? Or makes it mandatory?"

"Not mandatory...yet. But he is trying to be very, well, Roman."

"So, as soon as he thinks he can get away with it." Persy frowned. Would he choose Christians over pagans? Would he...

Yes, she knew, he would. She would have to be twice as good to get 'in'. That was the future. Could she pretend to convert to be close to Gwydion?

She might have no choice. She could see it...but could she compromise who she was? "Gawain? Thank you."

He arched an eyebrow skywards. "I don't want to see Galahad hurt. He's become fond of you. Too fond."

Oh gods, she thought. He knew. But Gawain left without another word.

8

Persy did not have much time to muse on Gawain's words. The trials were over, and she had failed.

Not by much, but failed nonetheless. After what he had said, she had to wonder. Was it because she refused to bow to the cross? The painful need to see her son hit her like a blow. Yet, she realized, she would always be separated from him. The barrier of secrecy had to remain. She could not trust a boy so young to maintain security. He would forget.

She still wanted, needed, to keep an eye on him. She needed inside that fort.

Galahad had been chosen. Could she confide in him? Truthfully, she wished to avoid him, still sure and certain that he had seen through her. He might be trustworthy, he might not...

...he was still her friend. But not the man to ask about it. Instead, she sought out Merlin, and she found him under an oak tree, talking to a squirrel. Of course, to her ears, the squirrel did not talk back. To his? She was sure it had a lot to say. Probably about nuts.

"Merlin."

"Arthur is...I don't know how much longer I can stay," he said, softly. "He listens to his priests, to this new monk..."

"New monk?"

"A Brother Cadan. Duncan was...messing around with the kitchen wenches and now this monk has taken his place in Arthur's heart."

The temperature dropped. "Make him send him away," she whispered. "He has to."

"He won't. Cadan is Guinevere's new confessor."

And lover? No, that was unfair, although if any woman could get away with affairs, it was a barren queen. "He must. Talk to Gawain."

Maybe Arthur would listen to the heir to Orkney where he would not to a crazy old druid or a mediocre warrior.

"Gawain?"

"There was a murder at Avalon, a virgin killed in the chapel. He thinks one of the monks did it to discredit the surviving druids. Now one of those monks is here..." Cadan. An ordinary enough name. Yet not so ordinary that she could be sure it was not the man she remembered. "...and supplanting you."

A plague of monks. She had been joking, almost, when she said it. Now? Now she was not sure. "I said I didn't think Cadan had anything to do with it. But, all the gods, he's an obvious nutjob."

"He seemed lucid enough to me."

"Maybe it's not the same Cadan. I'd have to see him, to be sure..."

"...which means getting you close to Arthur."

"I could don skirts and play the camp follower."

"I doubt that would work. The cooks are invisible to him."

"Maybe that's what I need to be. Invisible." A plan began to formulate in her mind. She could see inside the fort and identify Brother Cadan. It was a shame. Most of the Christians were...okay. Good people, even. Had Bedivere and Galahad been the first she met, then maybe she would even have looked into the religion. Maybe, but then again, sooner or later she would have encountered his type.

"I can see an idea in your eyes. I don't think you need my help."

A compliment, she realized. "Or we could do this openly."

Merlin shook his head. "A warrior who failed at the trials and a druid who is being visibly displaced. It would look like revenge."

He was right. "So, we need some evidence against him...and it can't be obtained by magic." Had Cadan killed that girl? "Maybe there isn't any. I still find it hard to believe he had the physical and mental strength to kill. He used to walk around the gardens widdershins talking to God."

"Then maybe it was not God who talked back."

The temperature seemed to drop further. "Arawn?"

Merlin frowned. "No. Some entity that would benefit from the extension of Christianity. I wonder if their Satan, their fallen angel, is real."

"Sounds like a corruption of Set to me." And that would be enough. Set, an Egyptian deity...dark, chaotic. Unpleasant.

"It could be, and Rome long had trouble with the priests of Set. They have unsavory habits."

"Like human sacrifice."

"Exactly."

Persy glanced towards the fort. "My plan is going to take some preparations." And it would be layers upon layers, for she still needed to keep the Percival identity intact. Her biggest question, in fact, was whether she should create a completely new one or accept the risk of being caught.

For some reason, Galahad's face floated in her mind. Too fond of her? But perhaps that made him a potential ally. At some levels, he already was her ally as well as her friend.

"Then, perhaps, we will speak again soon." He stepped behind the oak tree...and vanished.

She could not help but walk all the way around it, just to check for a crack in the trunk, but the one she found was too small for a grown man to enter.

Fae born, indeed. Two hours later, she rode out of camp, leading the grey. Glancing back, she thought she saw Galahad quietly watching her depart.

Three days later, Persy was seriously regretting her plan. She failed to find work as a cook and had returned to her male guise. Just a poor boy, desperate for whatever work he could find.

They put her to work in the kitchens...as a dish washer. She had never, in her life, descended to such menial labor. It gave her a new appreciation for servants.

Yet, it was surprisingly perfect for her needs. Everyone came into the kitchen at some point. They came to sneak food, to talk the cooks out of a bottle of wine.

At the moment, the current visitor was one who made her want to vanish into the floor.

Morgan of Cornwall. She wore a simple red dress...ah yes, she would wear red. It was clearly an every day gown not one for important affairs. She wanted a 'snack', but none of the food already there was good enough.

Persy kept herself out of sight as much as she could. If anyone other than Arthur was going to see through her disguise, it would be Morgan.

The woman did not give her the vibes she expected. Oddly, what Persy felt hovered between sorrow and pity. She wanted to hate this woman for sharing Arthur's bed when she could not. Guinevere, perhaps, she could.

Why? By all accounts, Guinevere was a victim of her own ill luck and Morgan...

Their eyes met. Persy looked away quickly, not afraid of that gaze but of recognition. She seemed invisible to the woman who was, to be unfair, Camelot's whore. Persy did not feel like being fair.

But as she finally claimed an apple and left, she watched her go before turning back to her task.

In but days, they would leave on campaign. She still had not seen Cadan. He was the only man who didn't try to wheedle the cooks. That fit the man she remembered, as nothing else that had been said about him did.

Crazy, really. A waste of time she could have spent more productively. Especially with the growing...pressure. Pressure to attend the little church...

"You! Boy!"

Her thoughts were interrupted by a cook. She had not stopped working, but she might be in trouble nonetheless. Sometimes, they looked for excuses. She turned. "Yes?"

"Take this tray out into the great hall. You seem to be about the only person here without grease spots."

Relieved, Persy moved over and picked it up. The great hall was built in the Norse fashion, the roof made to distinctly resemble an overturned boat. Probably because the same people, in that culture, built both. It was full of people, and one long table had been covered with a buffet of food.

She almost tripped over two different puppies as she made her way in. The animals needed to be kept under better control. Really. Dogs should be under the benches or tables, not chasing around.

Then she saw him, as she set down the tray of sweetbreads. Cadan. Undeniably the same Cadan.

Their eyes met, and he stood, slowly. He started to walk towards her...and then she felt somebody grab her arm. "Psst."

She turned.

"Don't piss him off," came a painfully familiar voice. "Per..."

"Hush!" she insisted, before he could finish the name.

Cadan looked at her, looked at Galahad, then sat back down.

She turned to dart out of the hall, but the warrior followed her into the corridor. "What are you doing? And what did you do..."

"He must have recognized me from Avalon. Ask your brother." She kept her voice even. "Some of us think Cadan is responsible for the sacrifice."

"Christ," Galahad muttered.

Funny how everyone took the name of their gods in vain. "And he's replacing Merlin as Arthur's advisor."

"Not good if he's a murderer. But can we be sure?"

"No..."

Persy did not like how Galahad had left her with the last word and vanished. It seemed he wasn't about to betray her, at least.

But Cadan would. It was time to leave. She had no things worth mentioning in the court and hardly cared about her paltry pay. There was a way out to the open bailey.

And then she fell, something on top of her, pinning her to the ground. "Cafall!"

Oh, she remembered the hound's name all to clearly. He did not harm her, but neither did he allow her to move.

Arthur approached, reaching for the hound's collar. "So, having failed to gain admittance to spy on me by one means, you sneak in through the kitchens, Percival."

She was, in some ways, honored he remembered her name. Slowly, she rose. "Persephone asked me to come, to keep an eye on Gwydion. That was the only 'spying' I was doing, Liege."

He studied her. "You *are* her brother. I see it in your face. Come."

She followed him, having no real choice. Even if she suspected Cafall would not actually rip her throat out. His tail was wagging, as if it was all a great game.

"What is between you and Father Cadan?"

"We wintered together at Avalon. As far as I know, he has nothing against me." That was, in fact, the truth. Cadan could know nothing of those who suspected him of murder.

"Then why is he accusing you of murder?"

Persy shook her head. "Do you really think I would have anything to do with sacrilege? I might not be Christian, but I wouldn't want to anger your god."

"So, you do know about the murder he speaks of."

"Somebody either tried to scare the Avalon monks away, or to discredit the druids. I have no clue which. But my only connection to the matter is that I happened to be there." She shivered a bit.

"Cadan says you are part of a druidic conspiracy led by Merlin."

"Has Merlin ever led you false?" She could not turn him against Cadan, but could she plant some seeds of doubt?

"No, but neither has Cadan."

"The Cadan I saw at Glastonbury was a madman." She had to tell him. He needed to know, deserved to know, even if she did not trust him to use the knowledge.

"A madman or a holy man. Sometimes, they're the same thing."

"I know." Cadan had, she realized, pulled her teeth. If she or Merlin accused him of murder now...

...well, they would find another way to discredit him.

"So, what am I to do with you?"

"You're the king. It's your decision."

"I am torn between keeping you close and exiling you to Erin."

"Erin's very nice this time of year." She regretted the words the moment they were out of her mouth, but she had not been able to resist them.

Perhaps her manner was what did it. Arthur laughed, and while not the same laugh she had once known from him, it was at least a real laugh. Genuine. Almost painful, that, reminding her of happier times. That once she had envisioned the man as her own. "Stay," he said, finally. "I may have use for you."

She knew she had no choice. "My liege."

"And get yourself some better clothing."

Did he know? She could not be sure, but if he did, he gave no direct sign of it. "I won't be long."

At least she could keep an eye on Cadan.

9

As she came back out of the barracks, dressed in clean clothes, Galahad crossed the courtyard towards her. "What is all this about?" he asked. "I thought you had left."

"My sister asked me to keep an eye on Gwydion, so I stayed. Also..."

"There's something else. I can hear it. Out with it, Percy."

"Brother Cadan is not a good Christian man." With him, she felt it safe to be honest. He would not dismiss her.

"I know," he said, with a slight sigh. "I think this may be what the warning about blood is about. Taking mass from him feels like eating and drinking ashes."

"Find somebody else?" The central ritual of their faith required a priest. A good priest. A better one than Cadan.

"I'm trying."

"Shame we can't catch him and Morgan in bed together."

Galahad laughed. "Even she would have better taste. Besides, I think Brother Cadan ascribes to the idea that priests should be virgins."

Persy wrinkled her nose. "How can somebody who hasn't experienced life advise others on it?"

Galahad shook his head. "Are..." He tailed off. "For some of us, celibacy is the best idea." A pause. "Bedivere tried to..."

She laughed a bit. "Don't judge him too harshly." She frowned, and then headed for the palisade, where they were unlikely to be overheard. "Galahad. Talk to me."

"Bedivere was flirting with me." Galahad shook his head. "I have no problems with the Greek vice, but I do not share it. Meanwhile, it seems that every woman I am attracted to is one I can't have."

"Galahad." Persy shook her head. "I think I know exactly how you feel." She could not act on any feelings she had, not without betraying her secret.

"You? You're a Christian monk," he teased. "Or are you…"

"No, I'm not inclined towards the Greek vice." She wasn't, particularly. Other women had never interested her that much. To be honest, neither had any man but Arthur. Until now, and now she was interested in one she knew was a bad idea.

"I know. You aren't that way, and neither am I." A pause. "So, what do we do?"

Persy teased, "You could try Bedivere. It might stop him from watching Arthur's butt."

Galahad shook his head. "No thanks. I think even if I was inclined that way…I'd be more interested in you. But, the Church says one should not lie down with a man as with a woman."

With those words it became dangerously close to a Greek farce. Bedivere going after Arthur and Galahad, Galahad half-confessing attraction to her all unknowing.

She kept her voice low, moving so the wind would carry it away from the fort. "Galahad. You're cute, but you're too young for me even if I was…."

He blushed scarlet.

She sighed, "Look at me, Galahad."

"The Church."

"No." A deep breath. He had to know, otherwise, she was leading him on. "Galahad, you great lump. I'm a woman."

He stared. And then he laughed. "Oh, Christ. You're Persephone's…" His voice tailed off.

"I'm not her sister either, and I have no brother named Percival."

He shook his head. "Arthur didn't want you at court, so you dressed as a man and then…"

Persy laughed a bit. "Yeah."

"Star-crossed. You *are* too old for me." He paused, studying her. "But your secret is safe with me."

Persy smiled. "I know. Or I would never have told you."

He reached both hands out to her. "You are a true friend, Percy. I won't ever press for more." A pause. "Maybe the church is wrong about women fighting. Some women, anyway."

Her lip quirked. "Galahad, you are the best." She meant it. Despite the fact that she was, in reality, years older than him…she knew she could not ask for a better friend, then or ever. Except, that she knew it might not end with mere friendship, that if he was star-crossed then so was she. The years between them made little difference. But he needed a younger woman, one more likely to give him children.

"Let's go spar," he offered. "And if anyone can convince me that some women can fight...it's you."

The fact that he was still willing to do that sent a new current of relief through her. She had not been, could not be, sure. "I just need to convince Arthur."

"Do you love him?" Galahad asked.

She paused, considering her answer. Letting her feelings flow for a moment. "Not any more."

That not any more was a sad truth that dogged her heels as if she were a stag pursued by hounds. Or the Saxons, who were harrying as far inland as Eboracum and well into the fenlands.

They had to move. There could be no more time spent integrating men into units and gathering supplies.

Other armies were already riding east. And now Arthur rode, at the head of his men. Guinevere did not ride with them.

She would stay at Camelot, and manage the fort. Including, Persy suspected, its defense. Despite Arthur's attitude to such things, Persy had no doubt that Guinevere was capable. She had seen the steel which lay under the frail exterior, and the woman's father was one of the best. She stole a glance backwards and, indeed, the queen was speaking with the women and those men too old, too young, or too incompetent to ride with them. In that moment, Persy saw that she could have been a true queen, had she not been so tied down by her own beliefs and by the pain in her heart.

Morgan also stayed behind. Brother Cadan did not. He did not ride with the warriors, however, but back with the supply train on a mule that had seen better days. Persy herself rode next to Galahad. "Did you see Cadan's noble steed?"

"Arthur should give him a better animal. That thing needs to be put out to pasture."

"And it wasn't that great to start with. I don't have a problem with mules, but that one has a ewe neck." Persy made a face. "Now that mare of Arthur's...did you see her hooves?"

"Round and nicely striped. I'm betting he could take her shoes off and she'd be as sound as ever," Galahad said, thoughtfully. "Never been big on the spotted horses, though."

"Might be as hard to see in the woods as a dun, though."

"That dun's a nice animal. Maybe you need something bigger, though."

It relaxed her to discuss something as utterly mundane as horseflesh. "Yours, on the other hand..."

"Don't knock him. I know he has a goose rump, but he's as agile as a stag and he never, ever does anything bad."

"He does have a nice eye," she mused. "Unlike Cadan's mule."

"Maybe he's not a good enough rider to handle anything better," Galahad accused.

"Maybe not. He is a scholar, after all." She could not really expect the monk to be able to ride. On the other hand, she predicted that that mule would be lame within a day. She was wrong.

East, they rode, and north. They crossed the Thames and kept going, heading up into the wilder lands of the northeast. With the exception of the great city of Eboracum, Persy could think of nothing in the north that was worth protecting.

As Blazer's feet beat their four-beated rhythm, she told herself she was being unfair. There were farms here and there, even the occasional hamlet. Most were in the old style, a cluster of round buildings. These people had as much right to not fear the Saxons burning them out or worse as anyone else. Even if they probably were barbarians.

Galahad drifted through the line. He rode next to Arthur, a position she would very much have liked to claim for herself. Or did she wish to be riding next to Galahad.

Confusion, for a moment, flowed through her. Especially considering he could be blowing her cover, could be betraying her to her king. What would he do?

Send her away, was the cold answer. It would undermine his position with the Christian lords to allow a woman to ride with him, openly.

Apparently, the Christian lords were all that counted anymore. She shook her head, as the sky dulled to dusk and they slowed to make camp.

Perhaps she did not want to ride next to Arthur after all.

Cadan approached her the next morning. The priest wore brown robes, wrinkled and slightly stained from travel.

"Percival," he greeted her.

"Brother." She did not know what else to say, and the opinion she held of the man did not lend itself to politeness.

"Walk with me for a few?"

She fell in next to him, but a small voice within her said to be careful. A warning of what he might attempt? Or know, perhaps? Had he really been involved in that murder?

"You follow the old ways."

"Do you wish to change that?"

"Of course. But I have a feeling you will be slow to see the light. Which is a shame. I would not wish to see you, or anyone, die unshriven in the battle to come."

Here it comes, she thought. The hard sell. She thought of the goddess for whom she was named, and the months she was forced to spend in the Underworld with her dark husband. Maybe it was an unlucky name after all, for it seemed she had spent much time there. "I have my own beliefs. We are on the same side."

"The Saxons are pagans."

"You really think that is the point of this?" She turned towards him, hoping he would not see anything in the...no. He was a monk, what contact would he have with women?

"The point is to bring the light."

"The point is land," she said, bluntly. "The point is that the sassenach want our land and we don't want to give it to them. It has no deeper or greater meaning than that." Put that way, it was enough to make some question why they fought, what the point was. For her? She needed no other reason. The Saxons and Angles and Jutes were the aggressors, they had started the war.

The Celts and Romans would finish it. Losing did not enter into her mind or thoughts.

Cadan actually regarded her thoughtfully for a long moment. "Come to me when you understand what it really is that you risk."

She shook her head as he turned and walked back to his tent. It was a long moment before she did the same. Her immortal soul? It was safe in the hands of the gods she knew and trusted.

She did not fear the Underworld. If she feared anything it was that murder, it was the violence that was brought by Celt on Celt.

No. What she feared was that they would be divided, and thus fair game for the oppressor. The Romans had done it that way, had bought loyalty with wine and olive oil. Had traded for slaves and then brought in people from afar, causing some children to be born with darker skins.

Yet, the Romans had only ruled, they had not taken, pillaged, destroyed or raped. Given the choice, and she more than a little Roman herself, she knew which she would prefer.

She murmured in Latin, as if reminding herself that she could still speak the tongue, and went to strike her tent.

10

The hours of riding blurred into one another. Their pace was relatively slow, both because of the wagons...several of them drawn by oxen...and to spare the horses.

The horses were their big advantage. The Saxons used neither cavalry or chariot, and seemed to hold a superstitious fear of the beasts. Perhaps it was something akin to the Greek legend of the centaur, so that they saw not riders but monstrous hybrids of horse and man.

She did not care. She cared only that cavalry was the best weapon they had against the raiders, who came on foot.

They came on the third day. A less bold commander would have harried the column or, perhaps, sneaked behind them to burn farms. Whoever was in charge of the band fancied his chances.

Despite that, they came from the rear, and one of the outriders went down before he could raise alarum. The second, however, had a chance to call, and a chance to strike down two men with his sword before he fell from the saddle.

Persy wheeled Blazer, glad the pony was not one of the larger Roman-bred horses. Sweat beaded her as she drew the gladius. She would have used a bow, but there was no clear shot. The spare mounts milled in a panic as cooks and camp followers spilled from the wagons. She wanted to scream at them to stay inside, in the cover.

Somebody fired past her. A poorly aimed shot, all it did was bury itself in the side of a wagon, and then she was amongst them. The sword she had was almost too short for mounted work. She should have taken a spear. She leaned low over Blazer's neck, felt the sharp edge of the blade cut through a man's arm. Not quite severed, it hung limp at the man's side, dangling.

His scream mingled with others, with moans and the sound of blade on blade.

An axe cut through her boot, dug into her leg, she swung the blade over the pony's neck. It struck the man's helmet, bouncing off, but the axe withdrew as the Saxon stepped back a little.

A flesh wound. She knew that for sure, although her blood pooled with the rest that was being shed. The tip of her blade crossed the man's throat.

He fell without even crying out, landing in the rapidly reddening mud.

Saxon fools, she thought. Worthless and stupid. Unless they were a distraction. The king? She spared one glance over her shoulder.

Spear and shield in hand, Arthur rode his spotted mare hard towards the mass of Saxons. His blonde hair streamed from under his helmet.

She could spare no more thought for him, for one of the Saxons had thrust the butt of a spear up towards her stomach. It was intended to get her out of the saddle, and would have worked, but Blazer reared, knocking it aside with his shoulder. With no cue from her, the gelding struck out, his hooves striking the man in the head.

He crumpled, his helmet and skull dented, even as she reached forward and grabbed the flying spear, dropping the reins.

Oh, to have a horse one could trust! Blazer stayed under her, responding to knee and seat as she tucked the gladius back into her belt and swung the spear between her hands. It was not a spear designed for mounted work, but it still had reach on the short sword. She blocked an incoming blow with the fire-hardened shaft, then spun the weapon to thrust it into the Saxon's throat.

As he went down, she became aware that there was a clear space around her. There seemed to be no more adversaries. Her heartbeat slowed a little. Arthur? Galahad? She saw the former cleaning blood from his spear head. Galahad?

There he was, coming around from the far side of the wagons, grim anger on his face. She wondered what he had seen to make him so angry.

With the fight over, her leg began to hurt in earnest. Not wanting to put any weight on it, she sat there on the gelding. The horse was trembling.

No, she was.

Two of the cooks were dead, as had a woman one of the men had brought with him for other services. They had also lost one of the outriders and the other would not fight again any time soon. The insult to injury was that the Saxons slashed some half a dozen ale skins in their raid. Waste of good ale.

Persy found herself missing good wine. The cold winters were damaging the vines, and there seemed to be less every year, and of less quality. No wine came from the sunlit south.

Her leg had been cleaned, pronounced not serious, and bandaged. She could ride, but walking was a bit of a challenge. And she had acquired a spear. She was not going to be caught like that again.

The Saxon weapon she abandoned. It had been crude and ill-balanced for mounted work. Oddly enough, nobody suggested that she needed a better horse.

Blazer too had picked up a couple of cuts in the fight, but he was not lame. He picked his way along the road carefully, but easily. He had also somehow lost a good chunk of his mane.

Arthur had spoken but two words to her, but they were words she cherished as she rode. 'Well done'.

His praise, though, did not mean as much as it once had. She still envied Guinevere her place, but something had come over her feelings. A confusion that flowed through her.

Galahad.

He was, she knew, the source of those feelings. He had not betrayed her to his king and captain, even though he had every chance and reason to do so. He was Christian, but he seemed to be slowly escaping their trap. Their tendency to treat women as women were treated in Rome itself.

That was one part of civilization that had always stayed in Londinium and the rare villas outside of it.

Galahad. Yet, he was respecting and understanding her. His beliefs and his conscience were no longer quite in line on the matter. Perhaps he was just glad to have a blade he trusted at his back.

He might use his hold over her, for he undoubtedly had one, in some manner. Should she trust him?

She had no choice. If he tried to use his influence, she would go straight to Arthur and tell him who she was.

He would send her home, but there were worse alternatives. The horse moved under her easily. His hooves beat on the dirt, for there was no Roman road on the route they took.

Then there was, as they hit the Street, the road from Londinium to Eboracum. A rider, switching off horses at relay stations, could do that run in an easy day. It was rumored some had managed to do it with only one horse.

Persy would never do that to a good horse. Or would she? If she had to? If lives were at stake?

She patted Blazer absently. He had not been such a good horse when she got him. Now? His hooves echoed on the cobbles. Worn as they were, it was still better than trudging through the mud. Even the oxen began to move faster.

She still did not know where they were going. It was rumored Eboracum was the primary target of the Saxons; did they go to aid in its defense? Could that city's walls stand if the barbarian hordes really came?

She had never been there, thus had no good visualization. She knew only the walls of Londinium. Eboracum was smaller and poorer, its defenses would be less.

Then, misery descended on them in the form of clouds and of rain. She tucked her hands under Blazer's mane for warmth. They made camp early, but at least there were no more attacks.

Galahad sought her out, and he brought with him broth from the kitchen tent. Judging by its quality, the Saxons had killed the best cook.

It was still warm, and nothing else mattered at the moment. She curled her half-frozen hands around it. "Thank you."

"You looked like you needed it."

"Just remember one thing. We're on the road. The Saxons aren't. Can you imagine plowing through the mud?"

"Assuming they're not five miles behind us."

She had not wanted that thought. She glared at Galahad. "Don't you dare be a doom and gloomer. The weather's enough to turn me into one without comments like that."

"I swear, the world is getting colder. I'm sure of it. Or perhaps it's just our mood." His tone was a little wry.

"Maybe that's the real reason the Saxons are here. Maybe their land is getting even colder and they're fleeing hideous winters."

"You could be right." He stared out into the rain. "All I know is we can't get wine any more and it's not just because Rome is gone."

Once more, it seemed, they thought alike. "The light is going out of the world." Pessimistic, yet, she knew it was, at least at some levels, true. The world was changing.

"But one light is coming in." He hesitated. "I don't want to preach at you."

"If Cadan was like you..."

"Cadan's a jerk. He doesn't want to say words for Bronia because she wasn't married to her man."

"Hasn't he heard of a proper handfasting?"

"He believes in marriage in the Roman style, no handfasting and no separation."

"Stupid. And I suppose..."

"Arthur believes the same way. Or he would divorce Guinevere."

"Thus, he has taken Gwydion." The boy was too young to be with them. Persy was glad of that. He was not old enough to face war.

"But not harmed him."

"Arthur would never do that. But he's going to have to risk him." Persy brushed back her hair, which was getting long. She needed to cut it again. "He will have to be proven in battle if he is to inherit."

"Yes, but he will. With his bloodlines he is the only choice."

Persy could not argue with that. Her shoulders rolled backwards. "But not yet, thank the Gods."

Galahad glanced at the sky. "Do you think we can win?"

"What kind of question is that? You've seen the Saxons fight. They're brave, but undisciplined and they have no horses. All we need is to get the high ground on them." She glared at him.

"But we also need open ground. If they get us in the woods, then our advantage is negated."

She frowned a bit. "Or the city."

"Or the city, although I suspect the people of Ebor will defend their homes fiercely."

More and more people were shortening Eboracum to Ebor and Londinium to Londin or London these days. She supposed it was easier, but she wondered if the time would come when the true names were forgotten.

Would she be remembered? She shook her head, and a flash of an image came to her mind, of a book in a language she did not know. She saw amongst the letters the name 'Percival'. Remembered, then, but only under the false name, not the true.

"You looked fey for a moment."

She shook her head. "A passing fancy, no more." She hesitated, then admitted, "I was wondering how future generations might remember this time."

"That," Galahad said meaningfully, "depends on who wins."

That night, Persy did not sleep well. She might have called the vision a passing fancy to Galahad, but it returned once she was alone in her tent. She saw flickers of images. She saw an infant king being shown to the crowds from a platform built into the wall of a great castle. She knew he was a king, without being told. Or a future king, perhaps. A flicker, and she saw a tombstone, weathered and worn. The name on it was Artor...the rest lost. Nothing else marked it.

She saw Galahad crumpled to the ground, a cup in his hands. She knew with cold certainty that she had foreseen her friend's death.

Friend?

He was too young to be anything more than that, or was he? Arthur was lost to her, it was time to accept that, and she could not escape the feeling that drew her to that man.

She shook her head. A bad idea. Galahad was Christian, he would not...but then, he had criticized the Roman form of marriage.

She and Arthur should be married. Except then she would not ride with him. He would not have permitted it. She would wait behind safe walls for his return, behind Camelot's walls.

She saw those walls crumbled to dust, but did she see the near future or the far one? She did not know.

Finally, she gave up and slipped out into the night, sitting in front of her tent. It no longer rained, and a myriad of stars glimmered through the forest canopy. The moon was new, which probably protected them from Saxon attack more than those who watched at the camp perimeter. The night was very dark.

Toweeeet! came from her right and Towhoooo! answered from further in the woods. There was no mistaking the two cries as coming from the same bird, as some ignorant city folk thought. The owl husband calling to the owl wife in the night. Toweeet! Towhooo! Their calls came again, echoing in her mind.

She envied the birds. They could have no worries beyond finding the small creatures that were their prey. Their marriage was solid and natural. Birds did not commit adultery, birds did not get divorced. They chose their mates carefully and they kept them.

Toweet! Towhoo! She heard them again, closer together. Now she might think it was the same bird as they converged on their nesting site. Would they still have eggs, or by now, were fluffy owlets crouched in the nest? She had seen a very young owlet once. A white ball of fluff it had been. A cloud crossed over the stars, drifting by. She knew now that sleep would not come.

For a moment, in the distance, she heard the roars of battling beasts.

Then she saw a figure moving across the camp. Galahad. She identified him by his gait, and then he moved towards her.

"Let me guess, you can't sleep either?"

"Blasted owls woke me up."

She could not help but laugh, although she did so quietly, so as not to disturb those who yet slept.

It was not appropriate for a woman and a man to do this, alone in the night, with no chaperones...for they were not close to the watchers.

Why had she had that thought, when she had ridden with him, fought with him? Her eyes sought his. She saw echoed within them the mirror of her own heart.

It was by no conscious thought of either of them that they came together, that their lips touched. The kiss sent electricity through her, and she forced herself away.

"We should not."

"No. They would think us both inhabitants of Sodom."

"No," Persy said, "they would guess."

She wondered if she was already suspected of the greek vice, given she never visited the tents of the camp followers. But she wanted another kiss, she felt that electricity, that energy flow through her again. She wanted more than that. It had been too long, and there was nobody else.

Reluctantly, she pulled further away. "They would guess. We have to remain friends."

"But perhaps..." Galahad tailed off. "No. It would not work."

At least he knew it. At least he understood without having to be told. In silence, they stared into the night. There could be nothing more between them, but neither returned to their tents before dawn began to steal across the sky.

11

Ebor's walls were lower than those of Londin, but not much. Persy frowned at herself, catching herself using the shortened forms. They would be what survived, but she wanted to cling to that little part of Rome.

To the Latin, if nothing else. To the baths...which she had not visited in far too long. She did not notice her stench or that of the others.

Ebor had baths, but she doubted the good citizens would allow the warband within their walls.

Arthur and a couple of others - with a wince she noticed Brother Cadan riding with him - rode to the gates. Perhaps, she thought, Cadan wished to contact the local Church. He had, after all, been without contact with other monks and priests for some time. She could be charitable.

Yet, it should be Merlin who rode at Arthur's side, and he, she had not seen since they had left Camelot. MEven organ would have been better than that priest.

It should be her on the other side. Yet, when she thought that, she also remembered the feel of Galahad's lips.

He had not been visiting the camp followers either. The gates opened after a pause, admitting the king and his delegation.

Persy turned away a little, then walked Blazer to the picket lines. She hoped they stayed a day or two. All of their mounts could use the rest. She had been tempted to switch out Blazer for a spare, but she feared ambush and trusted none of the spare mounts.

She gave him a handful of grain, water and a brushing down. Then, she walked a bit away from camp and regarded the walls.

They should hold, she thought, but the city flickered before her eyes.

For a moment, its walls were higher, a barbican in front of the gate, and a party in rich dress rode through. A good vision, that time, a vision of an Eboracum prosperous and well-protected.

Perhaps she was seeing what would happen if they won. The horrible feeling though was that it might be what happened if they lost.

She shook her head and the vision faded away. She saw only the physical city, its walls towering over her. There was somebody standing on the top of them.

It was not a soldier. After a moment, she realized it was a little boy, waving to her. She waved back. No doubt his parents had no clue where he was. Children did such things, and he was only a little bit younger than Gwydion.

Who was in the care of Guinevere, who resented him and Morgan, who...who knew? Who could begin to guess what went through that woman's mind.

Yet, she had been sent no visions of he who should have been the closest bonded to her of any.

Footsteps behind her. She turned. Bors emerged from of the mist. He towered over her, although not as much as Kay.

"An *as* for your thoughts?"

"Not sure they're worth that much. I miss my nephew."

"At least he's safe. Imagine if he was a few years older..."

Persy shook her head. "He is a young man. Young men will face danger."

"You aren't that much older yourself," Bors pointed out.

"I feel it." An honest admission, even though the life she lived was a lie. Maybe one day she would be able to tell all of them.

All would know the truth, and she would be remembered for who she was. That thought, though, sent a cold chill through her. A feeling as if she was being caught up in a web. A web of her own deceit.

"That's the travel."

"No. It's not having bathed in days."

"Same thing. At least I can't smell you...I can't smell anything over me."

Persy laughed a bit, careful to keep its tones deep. She sometimes felt as if she could not, dared not, laugh.

She wanted Gwydion. She feared that she would never see him again. No vision came to answer her fears, to confirm them or to deny them. On the point of Gwydion's future, her sight remained blind. "But

I am worried about him. I'm worried about what Guinevere might do. In her position..."

"She has a cuckoo in her nest. That can't be easy."

Persy knew how she would feel. She knew that Guinevere would be giving Gwydion a very hard time. As long as it went no further, though, it would be good practice for being King. She had seen how people snapped at Arthur's heels, hoping to bring him down.

With all that, did she still want to be queen? It was probably a moot point. Arthur had married Guinevere in the Christian fashion. He would not divorce her.

But he would not even take Persy as a mistress. Galahad's face drifted into her mind.

"You and Galahad are unnaturally close. You should get some distance."

For a moment, it was as if he had read her mind. As if he knew all she was feeling.

"Trust me, it's not like that. He's my friend." She was able to say that evenly.

"Good, because if Cadan...he's bad enough on the camp followers, if he found out *that* was going on, he'd go into apoplexy."

"Would that be a bad thing? He's only that way because he has no fun himself."

Bors laughed. "Probably so, but Arthur respects him. Too much, if you ask me."

"Too much for sure." She frowned a bit. If only she could prove the truth about Cadan. "I don't trust him."

"You're Old Religion."

"That's not why. I don't trust Morgan either." Maybe that would convince Bors she was not speaking out of prejudice or even envy.

"Anyone who trusts that woman is blind. She's a serpent."

"Arthur isn't blind. He just trusts very easily. Especially women."

"I noticed." Bors turned towards her. "But we follow him."

She glanced towards the walls of Ebor again. "There is nobody else. And in battle, there is nobody to match him. It's a shame he can't handle his relationships as well." It was more honesty than she wanted to give.

"He dumped your sister, didn't he?"

"I don't know that he had the choice. He had to placate the Christian lords. He had to marry a Christian woman, and I don't see her converting. Not in a million years."

She remembered the church in the center of Avesbury and shuddered.

"Are you all right?"

"Just tired of it all, I think. I'll be fine." She turned away from Bors, away from the city, away from everything, and walked back towards the camp.

She was tired of it all, and she had a battle to prepare for. She knew that. Would it be there, by the walls of Ebor?

Or did they have further yet to travel? For want of a better idea or thought, she sought out the company of her horse, letting her arm fall over the shaggy neck.

He searched her for apples, giving her a dirty look when he found none.

She ran her hand through his mane. Part of her wanted to ride all the way back to Camelot. If she did so, then she proved that she was...no. She proved them all right about women if she turned back now.

She would fight. She would, quite possibly, die. Then they would know.

Her eyes began to cloud into a vision. "No. Not now." Unbelievably, a blink cleared it; she saw only the camp and the trees and the horse's mane.

She hid her face in it, aware she was not acting like a man. But then, she was not the only one. Pre-battle jitters flowed through the camp. The horses, picking up on it, stomped their hooves and shook their manes, although Blazer was still searching her for apples.

With a wry face, she went to see if she could find any.

The king did not return that night. Perhaps he was closeted with the city fathers. More likely, he had found himself a bath and a feather bed. Persy begrudged him that as she sat in the cold dawn, a hand wrapped around a mug of broth.

She was not the only one. A bit of a mutter went through the camp. Arthur, Kay, Cadan and Galahad's brother, Gawain, were in the city, and showed no sign of wishing to leave. She would not either, were she them. But she could not take a bath anyway, not unless she sneaked away.

The stress of her masquerade flowed over her for a moment. She felt isolated and alone, she wanted Galahad's arms. She wanted Arthur's. She wanted her son's.

Instead, she finished the broth and then pulled out her sword. She ran the whetstone over the already sharp edge. It needed very little honing, but the task occupied her hands.

From the city, fog drifted, rising from the river that flowed through it, the river that was why it existed. A sizable river, one that no doubt flooded every spring, spilling out across the water meadows in the valley.

A pleasant place to live. How soon would it be marred by conflict? And it was cold, that morning, she felt the chill. It was still getting colder. She could feel that.

What was it the northfolk believed? That the end of the world would be an endless winter. No. Her visions told her the world had not ended, was not going to end.

For the first time, she sought them. She set the stone down, closed her eyes.

The first thing she saw was a sword. Not a short sword, either. Not a gladius. An officer's sword, and she knew she had never seen it before.

She also knew that they needed that sword. As if by opening her mind to the visions, she had opened her mind to the gods.

The sword was in the hands of Vivian.

Vivian. Where on Earth or in the Otherworld was she? Silently, Persy opened her eyes, sheathed her blade and stood up.

She had to find that sword. No. Because as she stood, the sword was in the hands of Arthur.

Arthur had to get the sword from Vivian. And Vivian was here. Nearby. Persy could sense her presence. But where was Arthur?

The city gates opened even as she had the thought, and he rode out, Cadan the ever-present shadow at his side. Like a dog, she thought unkindly. And unfairly...that was an insult to every dog ever whelped.

Arthur's hounds, tethered at the edge of the camp, howled greeting. But how did she approach him?

Then she knew.

Percival could not approach him. The Lady could, but if Vivian came into his camp, with all of those Christians? There would be an argument between her and Cadan they would probably hear in Londinium.

Persy left the camp, softly, moving past the perimeter guards. They gave her odd looks, but did not challenge her.

She had feared Vivian dead, but if she was there? If she was trying to offer help, even to those who would not accept it?

Persy had to do what she could.

Rain started to drip down upon her, and she scowled at the sky. Maybe the Saxons had invoked their storm deity upon them.

Nah. It was just ordinary northern rain. Which came, more and more often, south of the Wall.

She wondered what was going on amongst the Picts and the Scotti. Would they too try to come south if snow fell more often?

Maybe, maybe not. Those peoples prided themselves on their stubborn toughness. It would take a lot to make them run. They would make fine allies, did they not also pride themselves on their independence. She dismissed them from her thoughts. The Cymry, at least, were helping, even though it would take much for their western fastnesses to be threatened.

Where? She closed her eyes, took a deep breath, and simply followed her instincts. Followed the thoughts and feelings that flowed through her. Had things been even a little different, would she have been the Lady's apprentice, not Nimue?

No. It was not a path she would have chosen. She was too fond of spear and sword and a good horse under her. The air was cool in her lungs and...there. That was the way.

Vivian's wagon was parked in a clearing. Her spotted horse grazed nearby, tethered loosely to a tree, but Persy did not see the woman herself.

Then she did. And she knew instantly that Vivian was dying. It showed in her thin skin, like fine parchment, in the slow hesitation of her movements. It was the last help she would give to Britain.

Then she would walk in summer and return... A thought for later. Vivian moved to hug her.

"I see you have fooled the man."

"He would not take me as myself. He has fallen too far into the Christian path."

"This entire land will, and for many, many generations. Do not fear. Some will hold the light."

"My Sight has become stronger."

"Did it guide you to me?" Vivian released the younger woman, moved slowly to sit on the wagon board.

"Yes. But it shows me other things. It shows me the future. The distant future. It also showed me the sword."

"Ah, yes. It is for Arthur, but with that monk there, I fear to approach."

"He's a murderer," Persy pronounced. "And a bigot."

"The latter seems more and more common. I fear that the old ways will be forced into the mountains of the north and west."

"Or integrated into the new."

"Stolen."

"Perhaps," Persy said, softly. "There are some things...do you really think the village folk will ever give up the may?"

Vivian smiled. "Not likely. Nor the logs of winter, nor..."

"The old ways will remain. They just might have to hide a little."

"Have you Seen that, Persy?"

She nodded, for in her mind men and women in strange clothes danced the may, laughing.

"Good. But if Arthur does not fight well, the Saxons will burn Eboracum."

Persy shuddered. "And this sword?"

"It is simply a sword. Just an exceptionally fine one. And with, perhaps, a blessing or two upon it."

"He will not accept it from me, and he dare not from you, not with Cadan watching."

"Then we will just have to make sure Cadan is not there."

There were no immediate plans to move the camp. Arthur and Kay and a couple of others pored over maps she doubted were accurate.

Her plan, and Vivian's, was a simple one. But approaching Arthur was hard. He would take nothing from her, seeing her as an embarrassing reminder of her 'sister'. If he knew the truth...

But he had shown no sign of guessing. Arthur, as she had said, was a good fighter, but his relationships. Oh, in those, he knew nothing. When it came to women, he was a naive fool, and she not the only one who thought so. He might understand men a little better. A little.

She bowed to him. "Arthur. There is a white hart in the woods."

Not just the king but all those present perked up as if they had arrows pointing at them. A white hart was the ultimate in luck, a symbol of the goddess Genovefa to the Celts, of Diana to the Romans and Artemis to the Greeks. Could it be hunted before the battle, then their victory might be assured.

Whether it would actually do that or whether they would believe it did not matter. The best part was, she was not lying. There truly was a white hart. She almost pitied the creature, that would undoubtedly be brought down by men or dogs. But it would serve two vital purposes...morale and getting Arthur away from Cadan.

Cadan, as was well known in the camp at that point, hated to hunt. Furthermore, he would not brook the superstition. He grumbled in their wake as the hunters left.

Blazer, rested, pranced under Persy. Obviously, as the one who had seen the hart, she would be included in what was otherwise a small party. Arthur's hounds, including the giant Cafall, paced at his mount's side.

The woods seemed very silent. Mercifully, the rain had stopped, although a few drops still dripped from leaves. It felt, sometimes, as if it would rain for forty days and nights, breaking the Christian god's promise to the world.

At least their religion had some good stories attached to it, as crisp as any bard's tale. But she wondered if they understood the meaning. The promise that it would not rain forever.

Kay dismounted to examine some spoor on the ground. "Deer for sure, but be it the one we seek..."

His voice was deep and rumbling. Kay was rumored to be part giant, and Persy might well have believed it...had she not seen a larger man once in the arena, in the Games at London. That man had been a Nubian, so black his skin almost hued blue, far darker than most of the Moors and Nubians that found their way to the north.

She had watched him fight, watched him win. She wondered where that man was now. He would have made a fine addition to the war band. Perhaps he had retired in the arena and become a trainer, or joined the army, or experienced some injury that forced him into a more peaceful occupation.

She shook her head a little. She did not miss the Games. She would rather watch an honest spar than a fight rigged for her entertainment, some reenactment of legend. She suspected that even those bouts which were not supposed to be predetermined were, or at least carefully choreographed. Women fought in the arena. She had considered it once, before she had decided she preferred real fighting to theater, and the law tended to look unfavorably on women of rank who fought.

A glint of white brought her back to the present. Was it the hart, or Vivian? The former, from the way it moved. There was a sudden stillness over the party. The beast had no fear of them as yet, the wind blew from it towards them. It stood, its ears twisting in every direction at once.

Nobody seemed able to get arrow to bow. Nobody breathed in that moment, and then the hart heard them. It was gone in moments, a white pattern through the trees.

The hounds gave voice and chase, and it was that which seemed to break the men from the spell.

Yet there was no way even her pony could follow them through the trees. Leaving the youngest of them, a beardless boy whose dark skin hinted at a father who might have come from the same place as that gladiator, with the horses, they followed the hounds on foot. Bracken fern surrounded their feet, and a bramble, unnoticed, tore at Persy's clothing and scratched the skin beneath. A yelp indicated another plant had caught one of her companions.

"Hush," Arthur breathed. As if it mattered, with the hounds singing their joy of the chase. They ran, Cafall at their head, leaping over a stream that the humans were forced to splash through. Water sloshed into Persy's boots. Startled, a dipper sprung from the water and, with a few wing beats, vanished into the mess of roots along the bank.

It seemed that they had been running forever. Would they catch the hart? She almost hoped not. If they did, then she might have more problems getting Arthur...and the hounds ran into Vivian's clearing.

How she had managed it, Persy would never know. The wagon and horse had gone, but the old woman herself stood in the center, a staff in her right hand and the sword in her left. She no longer looked as if she was dying, but seemed to glow with an inner luminescence.

"Lady," Arthur breathed.

Perhaps he was not lost to them after all. Persy herself felt frozen, and she saw the same reaction in others. Nobody moved except the king. He stepped forward, then hesitated.

"I have a gift for you, my king." Vivian stepped forward, and in one quick movement offered the hilt to Arthur. "May it serve you well, but when you no longer have use of it, it is to be returned."

Not passed to Gwydion? Persy felt an odd chill through her, mingled with the desire to race back to Camelot.

Yet, it was not a vision, only a mother's concern. And perhaps...no. Vivian would not live long enough to determine Gwydion's worthiness. That would be Nimue's task.

A vision did come over her at that point. A man's hand, casting the sword into the water. That was not what Vivian meant.

Yet, it seemed, it was what would come to pass. Such a weapon, sacrificed to the water gods on its warrior's passing. Persy might be in favor of the old ways, but...

Arthur bowed to Vivian. The king was not supposed to bow to any. Then he took also the sword belt she offered and girded the weapon.

They did not, however, find the white hart, not that night or any night.

12

"I tire of these superstitious mutterings!"

Persy turned at the voice. Brother Cadan strode through the camp. They were a day's ride from Ebor now, north and east. Arthur harried the Saxons, trying to lead them to the ground of his choosing. To the hill fort the locals called Bail's Dun, but often shortened to Badon.

Its approaches would be bad for any army.

"The witch did not turn into a white hart, nor vice versa, nor..."

So that was what they were saying, now? Persy laughed inwardly. Vivian might well have called the hart to her, used it to lead them, but she had most certainly not turned into one! That was an ability only one with the gods' blood in his or her veins could possess.

But she had, it seemed, tricked them almost too thoroughly.

Cadan had been trying to get Arthur to ditch the blade since they returned from the hunt. Arthur, however, was not about to give up Caliburn, as he had named it. Why would he give up a weapon so sharp it could cut a thrown hair on the fall, or slice an apple in six pieces in one move. She had even heard Arthur say, "I would keep this blade were it a gift from the devil himself!"

That was the cause of Cadan's sour mood. For once, he had been outmaneuvered, and his star was no longer on the ascendant with the king.

"I know what I saw." That was Bedivere, stubbornly loyal, but not as smart as he might have been. Even if he had once soundly defeated her in the lists, she acknowledged his strengths and his failings. For that matter, so did he. Of course, she knew that part of his loyalty to which Arthur remained oblivious.

"Brother," Persy said, turning sideways to maneuver through the small crowd.

Cadan turned his gaze on her. As their eyes met, she sensed power within him, growing and building. He was her enemy, and that would not change. Yet, she also could not allow the division.

"I suppose you saw it too?"

Persy shook her head. "Honestly? I don't know one way or another. I do know that fighting over it will weaken us. Truce?"

He regarded her. "Truce." But his eyes said something quite different as he turned to walk away.

Bedivere shook his head. "That man is so narrow minded he can look through a keyhole with both eyes at the same time."

Persy laughed. "Nice image, but no, it is not that his mind is narrow. It is that it is closed and locked and he lost the key somewhere."

"Why can't we be tolerant of each other?"

"Because if he is right, we are wrong, and vice versa. Both truths cannot exist together."

Bedivere shook his head again. "I know what I saw."

"I hate to say it, but I think we all wanted to see it. Otherwise we'd have to admit we were lousy hunters who let the deer get away."

Bedivere laughed out loud at that. "I hope you're wrong. Arthur is not a lousy hunter."

Persy smiled. "I did say 'we'."

"You're not a lousy hunter either."

"How about 'out of practice'? We've been spending so much time hunting Saxons that we've had none left for hunting game."

Bedivere chuckled as Persy turned to walk away. The look in Cadan's eyes was absolute hatred. Did he suspect? Or was he afraid of admitting any middle ground, any reality to the old gods? Perhaps he did truly believe that if they were real, his god was a liar. His god claimed to be the only one.

Or did he? Maybe he was just jealous and didn't want his followers praying to anyone other than him. Persy found that image, too, rather amusing. It spoke of insecurity, which struck her as strange for a god.

She shook her head, walking to the edge of the woods. It was better to believe in Lugh and Apollo...who might or might not be the same person...than in some deity that had walked a different, alien land.

In the shadow of the eaves, she saw a figure standing in a valley looking up at a ruined hill fort. Persy did not recognize the place, but she felt a sense of the gods. Of the old ways. That they would survive. The world might change and all of those strange things could happen, but the gods would not be forgotten.

That was, almost, enough for her. Almost. Yet, they had to win. They had to.

She sent a quick prayer to Artemis, whom the Romans called Diana. The huntress, the maiden of the woods.

In the eaves, white moved, and she held her breath for a moment, but if it was the hart, it did not come close enough.

She shook her head. "Thank you." And she turned to walk away, but her mind was disquieted.

Her mind became even less quiet when they reached Badon. It was certainly the valley from her vision. The fort rested at the high point of the ridge, wooden palisades set on earthen banks in the olden style. Not as solid as a Roman stone fort, but in this defensible position it did not need to be.

In the valley, she saw a couple of farms amongst the trees. The Saxons liked to follow rivers. They would come up the valley with only the slightest of encouragement, following the stream and muddying it with their boots.

She shuddered. Saxons! They dirtied and muddied everything. Yet, they were loyal to...and she saw the trap she was falling into.

To save Britain, they had to defeat the Saxons. To defeat the Saxons, they had to placate the Christians.

Britain would become a Christian country, the old ways surviving in odd corners, for the Christians would not tolerate them. That was the price of victory and she wondered if it was too high.

Too high, too harsh. She brushed back her hair...it had grown out again. She would ask Galahad to cut it. He cut hair well.

Blazer picked his way up the ridge, towards Badon. The fort was small, but well appointed. From this distance, she saw enough to make her most definitely not want to be on the attacking side. They would have to come up the hill, into the waiting cavalry.

All they had to do was get there quickly enough, and Arthur picked up the pace to a steady canter. It was close enough that doing so would not overly tire their mounts.

It was a shame, she thought, that the hill was likely too steep for chariots. Three or four coming down that slope would be enough to put the fear of every god there was into those barbarians.

She felt anticipation begin to flow through her, that odd mixture of fear and desire and hope and trepidation that always preceded a battle.

It was almost time.

The fort drew closer and closer. It was occupied, for she could see men on the walls. Arthur unfurled his banner, the one that showed the head of a dragon in red.

Some were calling him 'Pendragon' for it. The dragon's head. Or the chief dragon. It worked either way.

Persy would rather have seen an eagle fly at their head. The banner was not enough. Call and response, an establishment of identity. A runner had gone ahead, but these people were paranoid. No, they were wise. Arthur was as tall and fair as any Saxon and Kay...Persy would have had second thoughts about allowing Kay within her walls if she did not know the man. She would certainly never want to take him on in a fight, for he was fast as well as tall and strong.

Fortunately, it would not come about aside from the trials, and if he wanted to put her on the ground there, he could. A shiver went through her, the idea for a moment of their band splitting, of them fighting for real. Focus! The gates opened, and they rode within.

Arthur immediately dismounted and began to bark orders. The wagons were tucked in behind the wall, as close to it as possible. Fire arrows tended to arc into the center of the fort, and the Saxons were certainly not above their use...if they thought of it. They didn't, always.

The horses were fed and watered, and she tugged a brush out of her saddle bag, running it over Blazer. She was not going to neglect the horse, even as pre-battle nerves flowed through her.

The gelding did not shy away, but he did try to get his neck around her, as if in reassurance.

"It's okay," she told him. "I'm fine."

"They do pick up on the nerves, don't they," Galahad said from nearby, examining one of the forehooves of his own grey.

"Definitely." She turned towards him. "And sometimes on other things, too." She noticed that except for that spavined mule, none of the horses liked Cadan.

"They pick up on whether somebody's a good rider or not in five seconds flat," he pointed out.

"Can you blame them? You've seen...do you remember that lad at the trials?"

"The one who got dumped in the mud?"

"Yeah. He needs to be barred from ever *seeing* another horse." She tugged off Blazer's saddle, checking for burrs underneath it.

"Or at least have all of his bits confiscated. What was that thing he was using?"

"Something some of the Roman cavalry swear by. A crutch for a bad rider." She studied Galahad again. A good rider didn't need any kind of special bit, or ropes tying the nose down.

"You mean something the Roman cavalry officers who bought their commissions swear by, right?"

"That's about the face of it. Maybe we're better off without some aspects of Rome."

"Maybe we need our own Rome." Galahad ran his hand under the grey's bridle, frowning a bit. "Our own path."

That echoed within her mind. "Rome is dead," Persy said, softly. "The legions will not return."

"I accepted that a long time ago, Percival." He frowned again. "I need to walk her."

He was gone in a moment, leading his sweaty grey. Not an excuse, she could see clearly...Blazer was fine. Tougher, or perhaps it was a factor of carrying less weight.

She put the saddle close to him, he munched on his fodder, quietly. She ran her hand through his mane before she left.

Needless to say, there was not enough housing for all of them. A bedroll under the stars would be her lot.

Something in her cringed. Something in her was abruptly uncertain. She did not trust that place.

She did not trust the Saxons. As the darkness faded, she did not even try to sleep.

13

"Ho!" She heard that sound from the walls. Wakeful, her hand moved to the hilt of her sword, then her spear.

"What ho?" she heard an answer.

"I saw a torch. In the river valley."

The Saxons, attempting to move into position under cover of darkness. The warning she sensed. As long as that was all they were doing it was fine, but her scalp still prickled.

The Saxons might have magic too. That thought had not earlier occurred to her. Yet, they had gods of their own. Gods that would be on their side as those of the Celts and Romans were on hers. Would their victory be a sign of Christian supremacy?

She feared so. She feared it being remembered as such. In truth, battles were decided by men, not gods. Yet, her scalp still prickled.

Slowly, she moved towards the walls. If she admitted to the Sight, here, now...and then she almost bumped into Brother Cadan.

"Do they attack now?"

She shook her head. "It seems they're just looking for a good position, but if you have any weapon..."

It felt strange to be talking to him in such a civil manner, but for the night, they were allies.

He patted the stout cudgel he carried. "I think this will serve me, as I'm not trained in the sword."

She remembered the sacrifice and the dagger and tried not to shudder. A truce with Cadan was a deal not with the Christian god, but with their devil. Their personification of evil.

The Saxons might be better. She could do nothing about Cadan for the moment. Instead, she moved to the horse lines. If there was a night attack they could still sortie. Riders might be blind in the moonless dark but horses could see clearly enough.

She had ridden night raids herself. Blazer whickered to her, as if to let her know where he was. She slipped his saddle onto him in the dark, and was gratified to see Galahad nearby, his grey standing out in the shadows where Blazer's dun coat blended in. Arthur's spotted horse also had a shadow near it. She hoped for a false alarm.

She did not wish to ride in the darkness. She could sense a foreign power from the valley, but also one that was wholly inimical nearby.

Cadan.

She frowned, and then in the depths of her mind and heart invoked one far older, and one purely Celtic. Not Athena or Ares, no. The name on her lips was a darker one, "Morrigan" she whispered. The stormcrow, the goddess of slaughter. Yet it felt right, or perhaps she already felt the goddess' presence, descending upon the valley on dark wings.

At least nobody had seen her, or if they had, they kept mum, for anyone who saw her, who saw the Washer in the Stream, would die that day.

Simply being aware of her, though, was only natural. There would be deaths soon enough. Many deaths, perhaps.

The air suddenly felt clearer in her lungs. Blazer snorted in the darkness as she fumbled with his bridle. Fortunately, she had practiced. She could have harnessed him blindfolded, could have and had.

Then there was only the waiting. Would the Saxons dare attempt to break the fort at night, or would they wait until first light? Or were they searching the valley bottom for them?

That last seemed unlikely. Saxons were not overly bright, but nor were they stupid. They would have seen the fort, and they would know.

The sun began to peek over the eastern horizon, over the sea she could not see but knew was there. Somewhere along that shore the Saxons had left their ships. She hoped some fishermen found them and either stole them or burned them.

It was in that moment that the Saxons began to pour up the hill towards Badon.

"So many!" came a voice from the wall.

"Archers," Arthur said, evenly, moving his spotted horse to position inside the gate. "Kill as many as you can. My warriors, to me."

A sound plan, and they had the advantage of height. The Saxons had the advantage of numbers.

Numbers meant nothing in the face of superior tactics. Unless they were truly overwhelming.

She felt her heart try to rise into her throat, and then the gates were open and they were riding out into the dawn.

There was a sea of them, a horde. It seemed as if all of the Saxons currently on English shores came for the chance to slay the British war leader.

Her heart tried to leap out of her mouth. For a moment, her left hand tightened hard enough on Blazer's reins that he snorted and spun his quarters. "Sorry," she whispered, releasing her death grip. He snorted again as she shifted her grip on her spear. Her sword remained sheathed for the moment. She hoped not to need it.

The Saxons had archers as well. Most seemed to be aiming at the men on the walls, but a couple of arrows spun past her in, one closer than she would have liked. Arthur lifted Caliburn to the sky and dawn sunlight caught the blade.

That moment expanded into a short eternity. All Persy could do was stare.

Then she pulled herself together, more rapidly, it seemed, than the Saxons did.

They were a mass of men, the light glinting off of their raised steel. She lifted her spear and felt Blazer gather under her. Then Arthur's spotted mare leapt forward and down the hill.

Lean back, she reminded herself, shifting her weight so that Blazer could more easily carry her. He did not even slow down. The world became a blur. Arrows from the fort darkened the sky, falling amongst the Saxons. She saw men go down. Not just men, either. There were some women in the approaching horde, armed and armored. Would the Christians consider them easy marks? They would be fools if so!

Between the height and the horses part of the Saxon line broke beneath the hooves of the spotted mare. The hounds flanked Arthur. She thought she saw Cafall leap, tear out a man's throat.

Then she had no more thought to spare for anything other than her own small part of the battle.

And yes, the one facing her was a woman. Her breastplate did not reveal her sex, but her face did.

Did she guess? It did not matter, for the spear found her throat.

Thrust through it, blood falling to the ground, her head jerking back. Her helmet must have been loose, for it fell to the ground.

Then one of them got canny. A blade slashed...through Blazer's reins. A good horseman needs no bit. She sat back into the saddle, then shifted her weight again. The gelding reared, striking at the man, hooves crushing his chest, destroying his heart.

He was dead before he hit the ground. By seat and knee alone, she whirled her mount towards the third, the spear shifting into her left hand. Thrusting into the man's belly, he screamed, clutching at his entrails.

Three, and no injuries except to her bridle and, perhaps, her pride for not forseeing that particular move. She swore in a mix of tongues, but they had fallen back from her.

Perhaps they were afraid. After all, she should not be able to command Blazer without the reins. He leapt forward with no cue from her, selecting his target as a good warmount would. He barreled into a Saxon, the man's axe blade tearing across his shoulder.

That would scar, but a good warmount carried many scars. She dismissed it from concern, instead knocking the blade aside with her spear tip before it could also bite into her flesh.

Blazer did squeal, but he did not run or panic. Nor, as she thrust the butt of the spear into the man's chin, leaving him unconscious or dead, did he feel lame.

Good horse. Damn good horse. If he was lame afterwards, he would get the best care, she promised mentally. Then there was another Saxon.

Blazer tried to shoulder him aside, but he found something more productive than her reins to slash. Her saddle girth parted, and she fell towards the enemy.

She twisted in the air, barely avoiding being impaled by the knife, and struck him across the shoulders.

He had apparently not anticipated that and went down under her weight. She lost the spear. Instead, she punched him in the throat. He went slack, and she rolled back to her feet, grabbing for the nearest weapon. The Saxon's axe.

Not particularly helpful! She threw it at the closest enemy, hoping it would strike blade first as she scrambled for her spear. Found it. The axe handle bounced off the man's shoulder. Blazer reared. With the reins broken, they could not get their hands on his bridle. His hooves struck out, missing the man grabbing for it, causing him to leap backwards.

She spun the spear, using it for defense as much as anything else. Mounting Blazer bareback would only have made her vulnerable.

She stayed on foot, but close to the gelding. As close as she could, anyway. If the worst thing she lost was reins and a girth, then she would call it victory.

They were falling back. They were falling back! She heard two war horns sound, one after the other. The second one was Arthur's, calling to regroup. She followed the sound, no more of the men assaulting her.

They were dead or fled. The injured dun followed her. He was limping a little, now that the battle fever had gone from him. She left her saddle where it fell. If things were as good as they looked, she could get it later.

She saw no Saxons standing on the field of battle.

14

Persy sat within the fort, tearing the last piece of meat off of a chicken leg with her teeth.

Blazer would be fine...but he would also need rest. Arthur had offered to lend her a bay mare, which she knew she would have to accept. Her pony would be fine with the baggage string.

Yet, she felt uncomfortable, almost disloyal, even thinking of riding another horse.

"You look weary."

She looked up. Of all people, it was Kay.

"Is anyone not weary after a fight like that?"

His booming laugh echoed through the crowd. "The coward who tries to remain at the back, avoiding engagement."

"I don't think we have any of those." She regarded him for a moment. He looked tired, despite the incredible stamina he so often demonstrated. Everyone had limits, and he had reached his.

"No, all of those were on the other side."

"Easier to be a coward in a large army than a small one."

"Funny, we're still on the field and they aren't."

"That would be because they were cowards." Not stupid. "And disorganized. Very disorganized." She shook her head, glancing over at Blazer for a moment.

"They're good in a fight. One on one."

"Not even." How many had she killed? They blurred into one another. She could not envision each one as a person, except for that woman. Except for the fact that there was another flow of doubt within her.

The Saxons were pagan too. The Saxons also wanted to take their land. That was more important, yet...

"I guess you got some easy ones then."

"I'd bet their best people took one look at you and went 'Target'." She flickered a grin up at the big man.

"No, that was their archers. Fortunately, even I am not that big a target."

She laughed, suddenly feeling a lot better. Kay was not a man she knew well, but he did know how to put somebody at ease. Maybe that was why Arthur kept him so close.

They were as brothers, he and Arthur. Persy almost wished, in that moment, that Kay had been the one she loved, even though he would never be a king.

"You are a larger one than I," she pointed out, wryly. It was a bit of an irony to her that she had somehow managed not to be the smallest 'man' there.

"Size is not everything. Did you see Pellinore?"

She looked meaningfully at the axe he preferred to fight with, much like the Saxons. "I suppose that depends."

"Size...and its lack...is one of those things we need to adapt to. We should spar some time. But I have to go." He stood, heading back towards Arthur's tent.

When would the Saxons come back, Persy wondered? They had dead to bury...not many and nobody she knew well, but even one was too many. One made it all the more important that the battle had achieved something, even if it was only to buy them a month.

She heard a commotion near the gates, and her hand went to the hilt of her sword. Looking up, she saw Arthur and Kay striding out of them, a small knot following them. Despite her weariness, she struggled to her feet to follow.

Outside, on the ridge, stood three Saxons bearing a flag of truce.

It was a tangled web that might never be fully straightened out. It boiled down to the fact that the Saxons had become convinced Arthur...based off of his name, his prowess and something about that sword...was a direct descendant of one of their gods. Thus, he was not to be messed with.

Persy supposed his appearance helped. Yet, she knew they had won by superior tactics and by using the terrain, not some supernatural means. Except whatever spells Vivian had woven into the sword Arthur called Caliburn.

She knew there were some, for all that Vivian had downplayed their existence. She could almost see them, out of the corner of her eye. All that really mattered was that the Saxons had not just been defeated, they had been routed. And terrified.

The treaty was simple. Persy watched from a distance. The Saxons who had already settled and established farms would remain under British rule. There would be no more war, no more expansion, while Arthur's line sat the throne.

Gwydion, she thought, as she turned to walk away. They would have to wed him at the first possible moment, to somebody suitable. And it would not even be her decision, as it should be, She would not even be able to stick up for him if Guinevere decided to get subtle revenge by binding him to a woman he disliked. No doubt in the Roman fashion.

She feared that would be the way of the future, that no man or woman would again be free to leave a spouse they disliked. Cadan even spoke out against handfasting, and that was a great folly. Arthur and Guinevere were proof of its necessity, right there in front of him.

Another vision flickered into her mind, a vision of a powerful red-haired man who reminded her of Arthur, arguing with a much smaller man. She knew instinctively that his problem was women and heirs. A King, most definitely. Then she saw a dark, lithe woman. She stood at the edge, watching the argument, one hand across her belly. His mistress, perhaps?

Then she was looking at the fort again. The message was clear. Or was it? Had that been a vision, or her imagination, reinforcing her opinion that such inescapable marriages were bad.

She idly wondered who Guinevere was sleeping with while Arthur was away. There was bound to be somebody. She did not love him enough to endure the pain of celibacy.

Then, Persy thought, what was her excuse? Not being able to tell the one man who she was and not wanting to risk the other man's reputation or her own.

Gwydion's wedding. She hoped for some vision of it, but she saw nothing. Perhaps it was too close. Everything she had seen had been future generations. Sometimes the far future, where wagons rumbled with no horses. Human knowledge, it seemed, would increase.

What, then, might they some day be able to do? And that was when it hit her.

They had won. They had actually won. Now they could turn their attention to their own future.

    For some reason, a shiver of fear ran through her.

15

She remembered the ride north as taking a lifetime. The ride back to Camelot seemed to be measured in hours that happened to have nights between them. Persy supposed it was relief. By the third day, Blazer was sound enough to ride, although the fur on his shoulder had grown in white. It looked like he was marked with a lightning bolt.

There would be questions. But Persy knew it would not be her job to answer them. The question on her mind: did she leave court and then return as herself? Leave altogether? Or did she keep up the masquerade indefinitely?

A large part of her wanted to. She had felt so alive of late, and he would not allow her to ride with him as herself.

Yet, if there was peace? There would be no need for the warband if the Saxons kept to the treaty. Perhaps there would be a need for them to be on standby, available in case the barbarians did not.

Persy certainly did not trust them, but she had made no decision. Galahad kept to himself since the battle. On the last day, he finally pulled up next to her.

"I'm sorry."

"You saw a bad one, didn't you?"

"Yes..." His voice tailed off.

"It's not easy. If we are lucky, they will abide by the treaty and we will not have to fight them again."

"Then we will end up fighting somebody else."

His words were so likely to be prophetic that Persy frowned. "I will never fight you, Galahad." It had the tone of a promise. Perhaps even of a vow. "No matter what happens, no matter who tries to get us to take sides against each other..."

He turned towards her. Then, he simply nodded, before changing the subject. "What do you reckon Arthur will do about the inheritance?"

"What he has to do. I just hope his experience with Guinevere will encourage him to allow Gwydion to have a handfasting."

"Why? Gwydion can always take a mistress then legitimize that child. That...is what these Roman style marriages caused in Rome, is it not?"

"It is." Persy frowned. But the system could be made to work, that way. "Brother Cadan should think of that."

"Brother Cadan should think, period."

And then they were at the gates. The slender form of Guinevere awaited her husband. She had not been expecting him quite yet, and had donned no special garb to greet him. He dismounted, but he did not swing her into his arms. A peck on the cheek was all she received.

Persy could feel the coldness between them from where she was. Behind them stood Gwydion. He had grown, he was carrying a bow and arrow. Maybe one of the women had been teaching him, or one of the old men.

What would happen in three generations when women no longer fought at all? She shook her head. She knew what would eventually happen. Too many people, if women focused entirely on breeding. That was inevitable, and then there would be plagues and death.

She saw a stream of people moving along a street. Some of them were even Nubians. So many people that they did not greet one another, could not, for if they did they would never reach their destination.

Was that what they had earned? Crowds and, no doubt, stench. Even Camelot smelled. She longed for the baths.

Of course, she would have to sneak, at a time few others used, hide her clothes so she could use the women's pool. Yet, a bath was suddenly what she most craved in all the world.

Even more than Arthur's arms around her...except that was the vision that had most faded. Her words to Galahad held more truth as time went on.

She no longer loved him.

By the next day, she felt far more human. Bathed, clean clothes, no armor. Blazer was in the stables, and for once, she trusted him to the hands. They were competent enough. Guinevere's coolness towards

Arthur seemed to have faded. As Persy came outside after breakfast, she saw the two talking and laughing.

Her envy had faded as well. It no longer gnawed at her stomach, but rather rested there, grumbling faintly but not causing the harsh pain it had once been. She had not fallen out of love, but... She had perspective now. She was not going to win him back, not unless Guinevere died.

But she still wondered if Guinevere had, indeed, been unfaithful. Stalking behind a pillar, she saw Brother Cadan.

He had not fought at Badon. But then, he was no warrior. When would he have had the time to learn to be a good one? Never, was the simple answer in her mind.

It occurred to her that Merlin or Morgan would have fought in their own way. Even Vivian, too old to take the field...

Vivian was dying. Persy remembered that.

As if the thought had summoned her, Morgan strode into the room. She ignored Arthur and Guinevere and walked towards Brother Cadan. Persy held her breath. There was tension in the air, and Arthur gently took Guinevere by the arm and led her away.

Persy wished Merlin was there. Where had he been? Why had he not been...no, his help had not been needed. Or had been present, unsolicited and unknown.

But there was no fight between Morgan and Cadan. She stopped, facing him, regarding him as if she just found him on the bottom of her shoe.

He hissed at her, "Arthur is mine."

"I think not," was all she said, then dismissed him utterly, turning on her heel to vanish into the crowd.

Persy slipped out of the hall. Where was Merlin? The king needed him, even if Arthur did not know it. Even if he thought Brother Cadan was what he needed.

The fort gates stood open, a sign that everyone believed in the treaty. Or believed that even if the Saxons broke it, they would likely attack Ebor or somewhere further north and east first.

She stepped out through them, on foot, pulling her cloak around her. Fall was starting to settle in, and she knew it would be a harsh winter. The coats of the horses and the dogs told her, if nothing else. It might even snow there, in the south, where such was almost never seen.

Persy scowled at that. Yet, if the gods wanted to inflict cold winters on them, then the gods had their reason. It might be what the land needed. Or what they needed, to learn the lessons...

She frowned. Was what they needed the Saxons? It was this cold that had driven them from their own lands, rendered the north less fertile, if she was right. Was this the gods' way of trying to unite Britain?

A heretical thought entered her mind. Perhaps the gods had nothing to do with it. Perhaps it was the way of things. The world changed, by its very nature. Except, the gods decided the nature of the world.

It was still their fault. The Saxons coming was their fault. And she finally understood why so many had abandoned old gods for new.

Yet, how could they be sure it was not the new god? Or no god at all? The sky was very clear. Persy looked up at the stars. The hearthlights of souls in the Summerland? The lanterns of the gods? Something else altogether? Something she could not understand, perhaps.

She watched them, suddenly unable and unwilling to go any further. She felt so small, as if she was nothing.

They were the eyes of the gods, and they rested on that place, that moment.

Abruptly, she turned and ran back into the fort.

If anything more had happened between Morgan and Cadan it remained unknown. The two were both at breakfast, sitting as far away from one another as possible. Guinevere sat with the king, and their makeup seemed to have continued.

Persy remembered something about absence and hearts. She still was not sure what to do. She sat at a lower table, not quite next to anyone, trying to watch both monk and witch at once. She was not sure which of the two she feared more. A conflict between them was what she feared the most.

It was inevitable. Had they really won? Did they need the Saxons after all?

She shook her head and went outside. Outside, awaited another problem. Gwydion. He had hit a growth spurt, she was sure he had put on several inches in the bare weeks they had been gone. Would he...he had not recognized her before, why now?

"Uncle," he said, with some uncertainty, as if not sure he should be greeting her.

"You should eat breakfast," she told him. A mistake, for those were a mother's words. He did not seem to notice.

"I already did."

He was lying, she thought, but she could not act like a mother. She could not push the matter. She had to pretend he was telling the truth. "So, what are you going to do?"

"I'm learning to hunt," he informed her. "Do you hunt?"

"Sometimes." She smiled at him, a little. "Why?"

"Do you want to come hunting?"

She contemplated. "It would be good practice, I suppose. But only if it is okay with your father."

"He's never around," Gwydion complained.

"He has to do what he has to do. You'll have to do a lot of things too." She frowned a bit. "Gwydion..."

"What?"

"Whatever is asked of you for Britain, you have to do it. You understand that, right?" She was thinking of marriage. Of putting up with whatever girl they bound him to...unfairly, unreasonably, for the rest of his life. It was not right, but there was probably no choice.

"Does that include going to church?"

"It includes whatever you have to do. There are good Christians and bad, good pagans and bad." She did not want Gwydion to become a Christian, but the Saxons coming back was worse. Far worse.

"I don't know whether I like church or not."

"Let me tell you a secret, Gwydion...it's what's in your heart that matters."

And she wondered how many would try to make that compromise, paying lip service to the new god and heart service to the old.

"I don't know what's in my heart, either."

Then Galahad was striding across the courtyard towards them. She turned to face him.

"Percival. We must talk. Now."

16

They stepped out onto the hillside. She glanced at her friend as the wind caught her hair. "What is it?"

Was her cover blown? What did it say about her that that was her first thought and her first fear?

"I think Morgan is invoking demons. But I am not sure."

"Tell me. I probably know enough to recognize what she is actually doing." The wind suddenly seemed several degrees colder. Most likely, he had witnessed some ritual to the Morrigan. But it could have been something worse.

"I've seen plenty of pagan rituals. This one wasn't like any of them. She was dancing with fire."

"Fire is one of the aspects of her patron. But...I don't trust her. Not at all. Although..." If Morgan had intended to harm Guinevere to win Arthur, she would have done it while the king and Cadan...

...unless she wanted to somehow make it Cadan's fault. Frame him. Persy frowned.

"I really don't trust her. I'm wary of most pagans...no offense."

"Afraid we might seduce you?"

"Don't use that word!" He looked away from her, abruptly, as if it was a quite different and far more mundane seduction he feared.

"Galahad..."

He turned back towards her. "I know. It would never work. But I love you, despite everything."

Hopefully nobody was close enough to hear the words torn away by the wind. "Admitting that would be your disgrace."

"What if she came to court?"

"To sit around in Guinevere's solar?" It came out sharper than she intended.

"I don't agree with women not fighting. Not anymore."

"Arthur does. He is fully Christian on that matter. And he is forcing Gwydion to go to church. Or Guinevere is."

"It might be her way of trying to win the boy's heart."

"It probably is. Either way, her presence at court would not be welcome. You know that, Galahad."

He looked away. "And we cannot..."

"I will not."

His face snapped back towards her, searching her eyes for the truth of why she said that. "Persy."

"For now, this is the way things are. I cannot come between them now. And I would, even if I didn't intend to."

"He still loves her."

"Of course he does."

"And I love..." He tailed off, saying no more.

"Find somebody your own age," she told him, wryly. "Somebody whose heart is totally, entirely yours, who does not long for somebody else the way she does." She was careful to use the third person pronoun. "Or, worse, not even know if she longs any more, sure she no longer loves him, but not quite able to put things in the past."

"You're right," he said softly.

"But I will always be your friend." A promise, but also a request. She did not want to never see or speak to him again, either.

"Always," he agreed, before he turned to walk back to the fort.

She stayed where she was for a long time yet, watching a hawk soar ahead, and wondering if she had done the right thing.

There was something about winter at court that dragged. A lot of those who had fought at Badon had gone home, either for the season or for good. Those who remained seemed to spend most of their time dicing.

Persy had never been much of a gambler. Yet, it was too cold to go far, especially for those who were not of northern blood. The winter had shut down hard on them. While there was little snow, there were many days when the rain came cold as ice, slicing through the air at any angle, it seemed, other than down.

Definitely northern weather, she thought, miserably, trying to stay warm by the fire. She had even sneaked into the kitchens a couple of times, to get close to the stove. The second time, the amused cooks put her to work, and she had not tried it since.

She did not want anyone noticing how well Percival knew his way around a kitchen. What she needed was soup. Soup and a distraction. The skies were such a pale grey that she wondered if it would snow after all.

Maybe snow would be preferable to the rain and the hail and the sleet. The outdoor areas within the fort had turned into mud.

She should have gone home for the winter, yet she did not want to leave Gwydion. Guinevere was doing her best to turn him into a good Christian boy. In fact, she was spending more time with him than Arthur was.

There was a shout. It disturbed her reverie. A shout from the gate, and she made her way to her feet. Who traveled in the depths of winter? Who was, to be frank, that crazy?

Kay was on the wall. "Ho!" he called.

The response was muffled, but Kay turned towards the courtyard. "Open the gates, before this man freezes."

Persy moved to help do just that, the heavy wood was hard to move. It took three of them.

There, standing in the miserable weather, no horse, a pack on his back, but his eyes bright, was Merlin.

"Where have you been?" she could not help but blurt.

"Helping make sure nobody stabbed you in the back while you were fighting the Saxons," he said, wryly. "I would have come sooner."

She wanted to tell him that in his absence, Cadan had wormed his way further into the king's heart. She wanted to yell at him, but his calm presence pushed aside those thoughts. Later, his eyes seemed to say to her.

She still followed, tagging along like one of Arthur's hounds, following the man into the great hall.

Arthur was not there. Only Guinevere, sitting by the dais, talking to Gwydion. It seemed to be a question and answer format. Persy was torn by it. On the one hand, Guinevere seemed to have finally accepted the boy. On the other, she was indoctrinating him.

Merlin glanced at the two for a moment. Was he frowning? No. He did not seem certain of whether to approach.

After a moment he opted for turning to Persy. "Do you know where the king is?"

"Somewhere warm," she could not resist responding, her tone as wry as it could be. "In case you didn't notice, it's a cold day."

"The winters will not remain cold forever," Merlin promised.

She wanted to ask him more, but at that moment, Arthur came in through a different door, the great form of Cafall at his side.

He turned towards his old friend, and their eyes met.

"We must talk," Merlin said. Arthur nodded, and vanished back through the same door through which he had entered, the old druid following him.

Rather than stay in the same room with Guinevere, Gwydion and the new god, Persy slipped out through a different door. Follow them, she dared not, but it put her right back where she started. She did think she saw somebody else follow, somebody in brown.

Cadan? It could be nobody else. She tensed, then relaxed. If anyone could handle the priest, it was Merlin. He would not get hurt, or even lose an argument to the other man.

Then she saw somebody else. Coming out of Arthur's quarters, a cloak pulled around her. Morgan. The witch hesitated, then she walked towards Persy.

Persy tensed. She did not want to deal with Morgan, with the woman who came towards her cloaked in death. Death that she could feel, could smell. As if she had been practicing some sacrifice. Had she cursed Guinevere?

Had she...cursed Guinevere...and cold ran through Persy's soul for a moment. No. Morgan would not.

"I know who you are," the witch said.

The rain seemed to return, if only in her head. Rain accompanied by a lazy wind, one that did not bother going all the way around her. She was doomed. It was all over.

Morgan's steel-hard eyes fixed on her. "Of course. I don't have to tell anyone. Just remember this. Arthur is no longer yours."

Then she brushed past Persy, close enough to send static arcing between the two.

In that moment, Persy knew exactly what Morgan had been doing in there. Or, more accurately, who.

She could think of only one course of action.

It was very cold, but dry, the kind of day those in the north called 'Too cold to snow'. Merlin sat on a log, a cloak pulled around him.

"So, you think Morgan is now Arthur's mistress?"

Persy nodded. She regretted not having come back to court as herself. It would have been better had Arthur turned to her. "Guinevere does not know."

"I fear what she might do when she finds out."

"Guinevere strikes me as the kind to seek revenge in kind. But I think Morgan planned this all along." Persy frowned. "I can never prove it..."

"You think that Morgan may be responsible for Guinevere's barrenness. I do not know. It may not be beyond her power, but...in personality, she is more an opportunist."

Persy shook her head. "She is very determined. And she is blackmailing me...but I set myself up for that."

"Who else knows?"

"Galahad," she admitted, softly.

"A curious choice of friend. Or perhaps not. The two of you may well be the bridge we need."

The image of Galahad and the cup flickered once more into her mind. She shook her head, cleared it. "And I get no visions around Morgan."

"Your visions seldom appear to be useful, in any case." He held up a hand. "Most of what you see is too far in the future."

She nodded. "And a lot of it makes no sense. The world is going to change a lot."

"It already has. I remember before the Romans came. They brought knowledge we did not have, although no new wisdom."

Persy leaned against a tree. "I fear that the people of the future have much of the former and not at all enough of the latter."

"People are more inclined to seek knowledge than wisdom. And most people would rather have a clean bath house than the secrets of the universe."

Knowing he was absolutely right, Persy shook her head. "The secrets of the universe have about as much practical use as my visions."

"You might be surprised there." He studied her. "I will keep an eye on Morgan. There is little more I can do. If the two of us actually got into it..."

"It would not be pretty. Or safe for anyone around. What about Cadan?"

Merlin frowned. "If the two of them actually get into it, I suspect she would win, but it would not be as easy a fight as she thinks."

That told her much of what she needed to know. "I thought the church frowned on magic."

"It frowns on any magic other than its own. Cadan, however, is not practicing their kind of magic, which from what I have seen seems to involve much use of numbers and symbols...it is very masculine."

"You were studying it?"

Merlin considered that. "Not studying, no. I felt it best to be sure that they were not inclined to do anything..." He tailed off, giving her an opening to speak.

"But I still think Cadan killed that girl."

"I do not."

Persy turned towards him.

"At that time, did Cadan not lack all of his wits?" Then Merlin stood up, leaving without another word.

She watched him go, frowning, but understanding only too well.

Cadan had not made that blood sacrifice. It had been made for him. Or, worse, that was not Brother Cadan at all.

17

Persy could think of one person she could tell about Morgan, however an opportunity to do so did not come. Said person would blow her cover, but she was willing to sacrifice her place in the warband for the sake of getting Arthur away from Morgan.

Oddly, it seemed of little importance whether she gained him for herself. Perhaps the final blow had been seeing Guinevere and Gwydion actually getting on.

Gwydion was happy, and she suspected he had worked out who she was. He knew he had no uncle named Percival and he knew she would not send some stranger to watch him. Even at his age he knew to keep his mouth shut.

There was always the small chance that Guinevere would not tell anyone. However, any action she took would alert Morgan.

Revenge in kind. She would probably try to seduce Kay, and Persy laughed inwardly. Kay struck her as eminently un-seduceable. However, to talk to Guinevere, she had to get her alone.

Guinevere was, like a lot of the Christian ladies, uncomfortable being with a man un-chaperoned.

There was an obvious solution and as spring began to melt the ground, Percival left for a brief visit home.

She wished she knew somebody similar enough to herself in coloring that they could be Percival for a while, but that was not possible.

Three weeks later, Lady Persephone showed up on a dapple grey palfrey. The horse, recently purchased, had rapidly become...the exact opposite of one of her favorites.

She was delicate, pretty, with the dished head of horses from the south of the Empire. The man she had bought her from claimed she came from Africa.

Whatever. Unlike other horses she had encountered of the type that were perfectly sensible, that one was a mess. She spooked at everything in sight, dancing sideways and avoiding the bit. Her favorite speed was 'as fast as possible'. And she was a mare. She was very determined not to let the mare near any of the stallions around.

Last thing she needed was another horse like her. Besides her, her servant rode on a pony...a much more sensible horse.

She was welcomed by Guinevere...and there was actual welcome in her eyes. Persy realized that the poor woman believed she had Arthur's heart secure.

Arthur? As usual, he wanted everything, wife and mistress both. He could rule Britain, but not his own affairs.

She followed Guinevere into the hall. Gwydion was there. He saw her, but did not rush to hug her. Rather he stood, absolutely dignified, walked over and reached to grasp her wrists.

"Mother."

He was trying to be a man, she knew. She sought his eyes for signs of his true feelings, saw nothing. Or at least, nothing he was willing to betray. Guinevere's eyes were on both of them. She too showed no sign of what she felt.

Persy schooled her own face into the best neutrality she could. It was not something she found easy, but the practice she had of late helped. "I came to see my son. Nothing more, nothing less."

She realized that her choice of words, if not her tone, was defensive, even uncertain. That had not been her intent, but it had come out anyway.

Guinevere shook her head. "Come. We must talk." She led Persy to her solar. Gwydion did not follow.

"I feel that I am not welcome here."

"I simply do not wish you...confusing Gwydion. He is at a difficult age, when the first stirrings of manhood come."

"Confusing him?" She knew, oh, she knew what Guinevere meant.

"There is only one God. You may not be willing to accept the truth, but he must."

"No. He must make his own choice." Things were not going well. "He is still my son."

"You gave him up."

"I followed the king's wishes. I suppose that it is not something you well understand, but..."

"Perhaps there is truth in the tradition that mothers of rank should not raise their own children."

She had a point. Gwydion would likely have been fostered anyway. "Mothers are also supposed to have some say in how their children are to be raised. I never agreed that he would be forced into Christianity."

"It is his choice."

Persy, who knew that not to be true, shook his head. "As you pointed out, he is at a difficult age."

"Difficult it may be, but I am informed it is the age at which Christ's own people considered a boy able to make his own spiritual decisions."

"And what about a girl?"

Guinevere shook her head. "Women follow the lead of their menfolk on such matters."

"Yet Gwydion follows yours."

"It is a moot point. There is only one truth. You wander in darkness, Persephone."

"Only until spring." A reference to her name-patron. And it was winter. Not the small winter, but the greater winter.

Maybe, though, there would not be another spring. Perhaps the change was a change, that would last until the end of the world. Perhaps it was even the beginning of the Norse Ragnarok.

"You are lost. I will not permit you to lead Gwydion astray. You are absolutely forbidden to discuss religion with him."

Persy nodded. "Fair enough. Catching him in the middle would be unfair, I agree with you on that."

But it told her much. Christianity was...or was becoming...a religion of coercion, even with Constantine gone. Especially on women...although she was sure that Guinevere had made her own decision. She had to win her confidence.

The one thing that obviously would, however, she was not willing to do. She would not lie to the gods, so pretending an interest in Christianity was beyond her. She could pretend curiosity, ask to understand it better, but that would unleash a hardcore conversion attempt. That was not how she wanted to spend her spring.

Of course, she could go to somebody else...but that would awaken all of those confused feelings. Feelings best, she thought, laid aside, even if she wanted his lips on hers again.

He was far too young.

"Precisely. This land will have a Christian king."

Her goal went beyond that, Persephone knew. Her goal was for it to be a Christian land. For every child to be raised knowing only the one God. Did Arthur share it? Women following the lead of their menfolk, pah!

"I care only that the land has a *strong* king," Persy said, standing. "I will speak to Gwydion now. We have much to catch up on." She made it a tone that would brook no argument.

Of course, she suspected the first words out of his mouth would be about religion.

Fortunately, Persephone escaped any hardcore conversion attempts, either from Guinevere or Brother Cadan.

The former appeared to have decided she was a hopeless case. The latter just scowled at her from a distance, as if not wanting to approach. Perhaps Merlin had warned him off somehow. Perhaps he was simply giving her some rope to hang herself. Most likely he felt her beneath his notice. She was probably nothing more than an insect to him.

If that was true, it gave her a certain amount of freedom. He would be paying all of his attention to Merlin and Morgan.

Morgan. Apparently, the other woman thought she was a threat to her status as Arthur's mistress. She walked through the court, then turned to face her. "Persephone."

"Morgan." In the past, her dislike for the woman had been jealousy. It had been twisted around. Now it was Morgan's envy of her that caused it.

"Stay away from him." She did not need to mention which him she meant.

"He is not yours either. He is the queen's." Persy kept her words even.

"Not any more." Morgan smiled. "Stay away from him, or I will tell him who Percival really is."

The threat was a real one, although not as strong as it had been before, when the war with the Saxons had been at its height. Persy studied her. Dark hair, the features of the western Celts, almost unadulterated. If Merlin spoke the truth, then fae blooded. Even if he didn't, she could see it in her. She would not speak the truth, for that would give Morgan more power. "You are welcome to him," she said, finally, gathering unfamiliar skirts as she turned away, going in search of Merlin.

She found him outside the fort, sitting under an oak tree.

"Morgan is still blackmailing me," she said, after a moment, making sure nobody was close enough to hear.

"What does she want you to do?"

"Stay away from Arthur."

Merlin actually rolled his eyes. "Some days I think Kay would have been the better choice."

Persy shook her head. "Men won't follow Kay. Maybe kings are supposed to be flawed." But Morgan? Well, she had hardly been there to tempt him.

"Or maybe Morgan is up to her usual tricks. It is not like she does not have plenty of those." Merlin frowned. "Perhaps we should tell Guinevere."

"I was hoping to get into her confidence, but all I got from her was a lecture about leaving Gwydion alone about religion."

"Don't worry about Gwydion. She is treating him in a way all but calculated to ensure he rebels against her. She seems to know little of how to handle boys. Especially ones approaching puberty. When he does, somebody will be there to catch him."

"Unless she's right." Persy held up a hand. "There are those who will settle for nothing less than every child in the land raised as a Christian."

"I know."

"And with the Saxons neutralized for now..." Persy tailed off. "How do we stop them?"

There was a tired expression in his eyes. He showed his age...something he had never done before. "What do your visions tell you?"

"We don't." She knew that with sure certainty. "We were doomed to lose to one or the other from the start." Probably from the moment Constantine converted.

"There are Christians and Christians, Persy. You know that."

"Do you worry that they might be right?" She did not want to consider it. She knew the gods, she loved them. If the Christians were right, then what she knew and loved were demons.

"Have you ever thought that there might be truths that we do not yet understand?" With that, he turned and left.

She watched him go. Truths that we do not yet understand. Typical druid cryptic comments, she thought, wryly. Yet, she did feel, oddly, strengthened by the entire encounter.

There are Christians and Christians. She thought of Galahad. Tolerance was possible, darnit. Just because you thought somebody was wrong, did not mean you could not live with them, deal with them. Possibly even marry them. Not that she had any intention of ever marrying anyone at this point. She would stay single, be content with the child she had and keep herself free from entanglements. Especially entanglements that were supposed to last the rest of her life.

She stepped out into the courtyard, then climbed up onto the fortress walls. Persephone would not stay much longer. All she had to do was talk to Guinevere.

Guinevere enjoyed sewing. Persephone had found that out very quickly. Specifically, she enjoyed complex embroidery, with no purpose other than to look good.

Fingers used to holding a sword found that hard. So, when she kept Guinevere company, she did simpler work.

"You need to improve your sewing," Guinevere said.

"I have other interests. I'd say good horse flesh, but..."

The queen made a face. "You got bilked on that mare. You should sell her."

"Who would be stupid enough to buy her? Other than me."

"I hope you didn't spend too much on her." Guinevere's expression was wry. "She is a nice color..."

"...and when that's the best thing you can say about a horse..." Persy tailed off. "So. I have to ask. How is Arthur?"

"Distracted," Guinevere admitted. "I am not sure what's going on with him."

"Could be another woman." Persephone feared Morgan just too much to tell the truth outright, but not enough not to drop hints.

"I hope not." Guinevere sighed. "He...well. You know more than any. I have days when I think I would be happier if he had married you."

"Do you love him?" Persy asked, forcing her needle through the cloth.

"Sometimes I think I do. At other times..."

Persy resisted the temptation to mention that there was an escape. "Does he love you?"

"I don't know. He has said he does, but a lot of the time, it appears to be a man's I love you, spoken for one purpose."

Far from a virgin herself, Persy did not blush, but nodded. "I know some women who use it that way too."

"Less commonly. A man is less likely to be reluctant to come to the bed."

Persy thought about the men she knew and nodded. "Or rather, less likely to admit to reluctance, as we are less likely to admit to passion."

Some, she recalled, seemed to think women had no such needs. That was a blatant falsehood that she wished they would learn to set aside.

"They do. And my need cannot be fulfilled."

Persy wanted to hug her. She realized in that moment that she had completely forgiven her. "I know. Sharing Gwydion...it is not enough."

"It is not enough. Nor does it make my father happy that his line will not sit the throne."

"Of course not." And, ironically, her father cared little for that. "If he is with another woman, then you should..." Persy flickered a grin. "Get Kay to sit on her."

"Kay would do it, too," Guinevere mused. "Of course, he would call it sparring. I'll keep an eye on him. After all..."

"It's not like his eye never wanders. But I think you can keep him tame." Against Morgan? Persy was not sure, but she had to make Guinevere more confident for her to have any chance.

"Talking of such things. I realize it is a little soon, but we do need to start thinking about Gwydion's marriage."

"I would prefer a handfasting. Just to make sure..." She tailed off.

"I doubt any of the lords would allow it. Handfastings give too much room for doubt." Guinevere's face started to form a shadow.

"And not doing one risks not just his happiness but the line." Persy frowns. "We cannot wed him to a woman known to be fertile, not with the way some of the lords are these days."

The queen sat as upright and straight as her needle. She said nothing, but the pain in her face was so obvious that Persy almost regretted saying it, but she knew it had to be said. And perhaps she was the one who could say it.

Some of them, it seemed, expected women to go to their marriage bed virgins. How often did that really happen? Possibly too often, but most certainly, it was a bad idea. One's first experience should be with somebody who, for one thing, knew what he was doing.

"It will be a difficult choice. I do not want him to be unhappy, but..."

"And whoever is chosen, somebody will be angry about it." Too much politics would go into this. Persy half hoped Gwydion would find a mistress.

But that would not be fair to his wife. Then again, would she be more than a broodmare? Some women were happy that way. Persy might have been, had Arthur married her.

No. She would not have been happy not to fight at his side, because of pregnancy or any other reason. Most certainly not because of politics. She was more Celt than Roman after all, she thought wryly.

"True. Which is part of why I wanted to talk to you about it."

"You want another opinion. I've given you mine." And it would avail nothing. Gwydion would be shackled to a woman he barely knew with no chance of ever escaping. Only luck would save him from misery.

"I want you to think about some names, nothing more. You may see something I have missed."

Persy sighed. "Christian names."

"This land must..."

"This land must have the right king. We have to move past Christian, pagan, whatever. Whoever the girl is, she must be strong enough to handle a boy who will grow up to have that much power. Not a non-entity." Persy felt herself warming to her topic. "And Gwydion would become readily bored with a woman who is nothing more than a quiet little mouse. Those are my thoughts."

"However, she must not overwhelm him."

Persy shook her head. "Gwydion will not be easily overwhelmed. I think you do not need to worry about that."

What Persy feared was that Guinevere would care more about finding him a nice Christian girl. A nice girl was not what Gwydion needed. Heck, he needed somebody who would fight with him. Some of the best relationships she knew were stormy. Guinevere...

Guinevere knew only that she could not control her man. Maybe that would be enough. And maybe her words, too, would be enough to cause the queen to set her house in order.

Except for one thought. What if she could not get a leash on Arthur?

18

Most of the girls Guinevere wanted to consider were not at court. Persy used that to stall. A decision did not need to be made just yet. Gwydion would not be old enough to wed for a few years. If she could push for a slight delay, she would. Enough to give him the chance to...well.

Somebody would have to introduce him to certain things. Kay might be a good choice. Galahad was too much of a prude.

As if her thought had summoned him, Galahad was suddenly next to her. She was on the grassy slope outside the fort, kept clear in case of attack.

"Galahad. I was thinking about you."

"Good things, I hope."

"Yes and no," she said, mischievously, not supplying any further details.

He laughed a bit. "You are a lot like your brother."

"I know." She glanced around. Nobody close, but they could be readily observed from the wall. The thought that if she kissed him, it would shock Brother Cadan came into her mind.

No. She would only kiss him if she meant it. She had broken it off, had insisted it could not happen. So, she could not mean it, could not let herself.

"Except a lot more attractive."

The tone was comfortable banter, not trying to push past the barriers she had set. She felt no qualms returning it. "I'm too old for you," she evaded. "Far too old. A man should seek a younger woman."

"I know that. I haven't met any I like," Galahad admitted. "Well, like, yes. Like enough to want to marry, no."

And he would seek a permanent marriage, no doubt. Persy smiled inwardly. Galahad had good enough blood to be a reasonable 'consolation prize' for one of Guinevere's girls. Perhaps she could kill two birds with one stone. It would hurt, when she wanted him herself, but...

...but it would be the best thing for him. He would not be happy with an older woman, and she would be too old, soon, to bear more children. In only a few more years. If she wed again, it should be to an older man who already had some...that way if she did not have more...

She did not intend to wed again. Even if Arthur were free, he too should wed a younger woman, now. That thought was cold and she wondered at its cause. She wondered, for a moment, why she thought like that. She glanced at the wall.

Morgan. Her eyes narrowed. "We're being watched. Let's go somewhere else."

Galahad nodded, moving around the fort. Once out of her view, he said, "That woman scares me."

"She should. She has her own agenda, I don't know all of it, but I do know it has to do with power. Power for herself and power for the old gods."

"I thought you would be all in favor of that." His tone was more amused than bitter.

"There are ways and ways. She is as bad as the Christians who wish their god the only one acknowledged. Except that she is a powerful witch. I worry one day that she and Cadan will collide and explode."

Galahad frowned at that. "Cadan is not...I don't know."

"I'm not sure Cadan is Cadan."

He came up short, turned towards her. "What do you mean?"

"The first time I saw Brother Cadan he was the half-wit gardener of a monastery. There was a murder. A desecration of the chapel to boot. He vanishes, then shows up as a brilliant advisor to kings. I don't think it's the same person."

"Meaning a ringer."

"Meaning I don't know. I don't know at all." Meaning, she thought, something else occupied Cadan's body. "Do you...believe in possession?"

"If he was possessed by a demon, would he be able to walk on holy ground?"

"I don't know. I don't know anything about your demons. And it could be something else. Or as you said, he could be a ringer. Whoever he is, he's dangerous." Persy frowned. "So is Morgan. Sooner or later, they are going to clash. My money's on Morgan, but I wouldn't want to be anywhere close to it when it happens."

"So, what do we do about it?"

"I don't know." She felt as if a cloud had lifted from her, and when she looked at Galahad she knewshe could kiss him and mean it. Morgan. Hexing her. No proof, though. Nothing she could go to anyone with, except maybe Merlin.

She would have to try and get herself a protection charm against that kind of thing. Influence hexes were hard to fight at any level, hard to deal with. Damn her anyway.

That, Persy suddenly thought wryly, was about the most Christian thought she had ever had.

The rider came the next morning. His horse was lathered and on the edge of being lame. It had clearly run flat out for some time.

Persy wanted to go to it, and she decided in that moment that it was time for Persephone to leave and Percival to return.

"Raiders..."

"Saxons?"

He shook his head. "No. Britons."

Well, it was hardly surprising. There were bad apples in every basket. But she felt painfully trapped, with no way to help.

She could not even leave. If there were raiders that close, then Arthur would lock the women in. Desperately, she looked around. Wait.

There was a back door. By the women's quarters. If she could get out that way...

...where would she go? Sitting locked up would be unproductive, but so would being out there in a gown with no weapons.

She resigned herself to being trapped for days, even weeks. Merlin had slipped away that morning. He might be back in a few hours, a few days or next year. Or never, the way things were going.

Guinevere beckoned to her. She supposed that at least, now, they were friends. To a point, anyway.

Not knowing what else to do, she followed, into Guinevere's solar.

"The raiders are not that close, but none of us should go outside the fort."

"I was planning on leaving tomorrow. But I suppose you are right."

"Arthur will deal with them quickly. It would help if your brother was here."

Let me go and I'll find him, she wanted to say. However, it would have led to suspicion.

"I could help," she said, softly. "It is not like I have children to worry about."

Gwydion was not there. She hoped he had not wandered out of the fort before it all started. Being a boy, he had a habit of doing exactly that, sometimes at the most inopportune times.

The women and the younger children gathered around Guinevere.

"You must not, Persephone. And you know why."

No. She did not know why. The attitude had never made sense, whether it came from Rome or Christ.

Or both, the two starting to overlap with one another. She finally understood. That was how they clung to Rome. It was how they tried to maintain themselves as Romans, not barbarians. She did not need it, or rather, she had found her own balance between Roman and Celt, Latin and foreign.

Yet, she finally understood why Christianity was necessary. Why the old ways had to fade into their odd little corners. If they did not, then there would be no preservation of the good parts of Rome either.

Except that it was wrong. Her eyes flickered with vision again. A different woman, sitting in a different solar. She was pregnant. Her eyes said it all, how trapped she was, how miserable.

A bad husband? Persy did not know, because the vision flickered away again. She saw a great church, half-built. The top was being formed into a dome. It was larger than any temple of Rome. Around it, there were the charred remains of houses, a city through which a fire had swept. Like as not, not a fire that the Christians had set, but they took advantage of it nonetheless, to build their temple.

She shook her head. Anyone would. And those houses had been built entirely of wood and too close together. Foolishness. Then she was back in Guinevere's solar.

Well, that had made even less sense than usual. Unless the woman had been Gwydion's future bride. No. That room was not at Camelot, or at any place Persy had ever been. It had been further in the future than that.

A great church with a great dome. The wealth of Christianity, its power. Power that might last centuries.

The door was not closed. The raiders were not that close. Quietly, Persy slipped from the room while Guinevere was talking to a child.

She did not look back.

The raiders were dealt with while she paced the fort, not wanting to leave and definitely not wanting to stay. No casualties, at least, and the second the warband returned she was taking her leave of Arthur.

She took the grey mare with her, determined to rid herself of it at the first opportunity. There was absolutely no way she was going to keep the animal, who tossed her head into Persy's nose and tried to run, dancing sideways across the road instead.

"Having problems there, your Ladyship?" came a voice.

A farmer, in his field, regarded her over the hedge.

"I'm half tempted to feed her to the hounds," Persy grumbled. She released the rein, hoping the mare would settle, but instead she leapt forward.

"Heh. I'd offer to trade her for a donkey, but the donkey's worth more. Where did you get her?"

"Back south of London." She'd found herself using the short form herself. "I'd give you the dealer's name if it was closer...so you'd know not to buy anything from him."

She felt oddly relaxed. The teasing, even from a stranger, made her feel as if she was back in the role of Percival. Where was Blazer? Too far away. And this mare was likely to dump her in the dust. "Where's the nearest market?"

"Hoping to fob her off on somebody unsuspecting?"

"Maybe. Maybe as dog meat." The mare tried to plunge forward again, as if she heard and understood. "I don't think I can ride her all the way back. I'd almost take that donkey."

"She's definitely not right, but you have good hands for a rich woman. You aren't on her mouth the way so..."

She didn't hear the rest of his sentence, because the mare took off completely, sparing her from any responsibility for answering, but also giving him the last word. It took a couple of hours for her poor maid to catch up.

19

When Percival returned to Camelot, there was a lot on her mind. More, in fact, than when she had left. The only good thing was that she had been able to get rid of the mare. The animal was nothing but trouble.

Blazer's reliable hooves took her back up the road, her disguise well in place. The only question on her mind was whether Morgan would leave her alone. If Guinevere had confronted Arthur, then...

Of course, confrontation was not exactly in the queen's style. Revenge in kind. That was not a pleasant thought, nor had it been Persy's intent to trigger such. With luck, she would have more sense than that.

Nothing seemed to have changed except that Cadan's chapel had grown bigger. She did frown at the thought of Gwydion being forced to pray to an alien, desert god...with such a priest.

No. Cadan was not a priest. But Galahad's words, too, echoed. If he was a demon, then how could he walk on holy ground? She realized she had never seen him do so. She had never seen him enter a church other than his own. The obvious answer was that that church was not, in fact, consecrated ground. Cadan was cheating.

Which meant, in Christian terms, that nothing done in there really counted. They were obsessed with their consecrated ground, valuing it beyond all reason. And if Cadan baptized anyone...

Well, he was still a monk. Whatever he had become, he was still that, and they were in good faith. The ritual had to respond to their intent as well as to his.

Yet, she shuddered. She resolved not to enter that chapel's walls, no matter what anyone...even the king...had to say about it. How did she protect Gwydion?

She could not. And the one person she could ask to do so was...no. Wait. There was another.

She stabled Blazer and sought out Galahad.

"I'm so glad you're here."

"More raiders?" she asked, quietly.

"That's part of it." He headed up onto the wall, she followed him, seeing some answer in his eyes.

"Cadan and Morgan?"

"Actually, no. Not exactly. I think Morgan and Arthur are sleeping together, and I think Guinevere knows about it."

"I pretty much knew that."

"You knew they were considering it."

Persy looked out towards the woods. "No. Morgan...has been planning on how to get Arthur for years."

"What is it about the guy that women throw themselves at him?"

Persy shrugged. "Maybe he's good in bed. I don't know." She tried to be nonchalant. She could not be entirely sure that they were not being overheard. "Maybe it's just because he's the king."

Women would always go for the king. Who else could provide better for one's children?

Galahad breathed in, then out, looking at the woods. "I suppose he's lucky it's mostly women."

Persy choked a bit on that. "Mostly. Is Bedivere still…"

"I think he still wants to, but he's actually with that nice young Welsh man, Cadogan."

Persy blinked. "The things I miss while away. Cadogan's Greek? That has to have broken the hearts of several village maids."

Galahad laughed. "You're assuming he isn't still chasing the village maids. He apparently likes them clean-shaven."

"You should be careful then."

Galahad lifted a hand to his chin. "If you saw what the beard looked like, you'd understand why I cut it off." His tone was rueful.

"Straggly, eh?" Persy was glad at least that some men still shaved. The trend was more and more towards full beards, and if it became the normal thing...

"Almost as bad as yours," Galahad teased. "Arthur, on the other hand...has a beard any man would envy."

"And hair any woman would." Persy flickered Galahad a smile. "Maybe it's the hair that does it."

"Maybe. But I think you were right about it being because he's the king. I've seen how the serving wenches all drool over him." Galahad's tone drifted wry.

"Serving wenches just hope somebody will knock them up so they can claim patronage." Not all of them, but Percy still laughed softly. "You sound like you have some experience with them."

"Every now and then."

So, he wasn't a virgin after all. Or he was saying that so people would think he was not one. She was amused at the thought. "You can do better than that, Galahad," she chided gently.

He frowned, then, "No, apparently I can't. I fall in love with the wrong girls constantly and the only way that's going to change is if I get myself married off."

"And like any sane man, you'd rather have the choice."

"Maybe. Maybe not. I am tempted to ask Guinevere to keep an eye out for me while she hunts brides for Gwydion."

Having had the same thought, Persy nodded. "Why not do it? It's not like you'd have to marry the girl. Just meet her."

He looked out at the woods. "Anyone Guinevere brings in right now is going to be like twelve."

"Then ask her to round up a few older sisters. You have royal blood. You're not at all a bad catch. And besides, it wouldn't just be you. Kay and Bedivere are still single." Not that Bedivere seemed likely to marry.

"Bedivere may do it for the inheritance. Maybe. Kay doesn't want to get married."

Was Kay that way too? "Why not?"

"You didn't know? Kay's terrified of small children."

Persy's laughter disturbed quite a few people in the fort itself.

It seemed as if life was determined to settle into a routine. Whatever was going on between Arthur and Morgan and Guinevere was kept between the principals. The raiders eventually gave up, enough of them having been killed or captured and humiliated to scare the rest back into normal lives.

As Persy watched, two boys sparred on the hill. Gwydion was one of them. The other was some cousin of Morgan's. She was proud to see that Gwydion was the better. He had managed to get the high ground on the other lad.

Gwydion was twelve. And already betrothed. The girl was a year younger...the wedding would take place in four years. Persy was not entirely happy, but she was not as unhappy as she might have been.

The girl, Elaine, was neither stupid nor a walkover. She knew what she wanted, and she would get it.

Gwydion needed that to counter his own stubbornness. They would do well enough, she decided, starting to turn to walk inside. She changed her mind in an instant.

Brother Cadan.

Gods, if Cadan officiated at the wedding, then as far as Persy was concerned her grandchildren would be bastards. He had no right to do so. His eyes rested on her, then he strode past her, apparently looking for a good place to watch the bout.

She shook her head, not wanting to leave with him there, but most certainly not wanting to stay, either.

In the end, her dislike of him won and she slipped back into the fort. The summer smell was in full force...mostly courtesy of the horses. They were turned out at night, but during the day corralled within the walls.

Blazer whickered to her as she passed, and she could not help but smile. She did wonder what happened to the awful mare. Not her worry. She had been absolutely honest when she had sold her, unlike that broker.

She rather suspected even so, that the animal would end up as food for hounds...a fate that was no less than the mare deserved for her behavior.

She walked over to the edge of the pen, and Blazer came over. That was where she was when the alarum took over.

Without bothering with bridle or saddle, or anything but her sword, she leapt onto Blazer's back, riding him towards the gates. If Gwydion had been harmed?

No, he and his playmate were running in through the gates, looking for weapons made of something fiercer than wood.

The men behind them were not Saxons, but rather looked like Goths. Which was to say, they could be working for anyone. Mercenaries.

The leader reined in his black horse. "We only want to talk!" he called.

Arthur, on his spotted mare, came trotting through the gate a moment later. He had bothered with a headstall, but the mare, too, wore no saddle. Perhaps the Goths were impressed by the horsemanship being shown.

Either way, their leader nudged his mount forward.

"Talk about what?"

"The Saxons have stopped raiding," the Goth said, quietly. "The Norsemen have not."

She might have known. And the Norse would be even more affected by the string of bad winters than the Germans. Persy rested a hand on Blazer's mane.

"And you need our help."

"No. We offer our help. Or rather, a brief alliance. We are too few and they are harrying the fens. We were hired to help, but we need more men."

Arthur scowled. Persy could tell he was thinking that the fensmen should have come to him.

She knew better herself. Clannish, secretive folk they were, never remotely tamed or even touched by Rome. They were more likely to trust foreign mercenaries than their neighbors. It was a common joke about the fen people that they would not give directions to the next village because, after all, who would want to go there.

But through an intermediary, they could keep their pride. The last thing she wanted to spend the rest of the summer doing was helping winkle Norsemen out of the fens...a good place to go a-viking if there ever was.

But that was like as not what she would be doing. She heard a sigh from behind her that, from its size, could only have come from Kay or maybe Bedivere.

"Fun summer."

Bedivere. She glanced over her shoulder at him. "Yeah."

"Trudging through mosquito-infested water up to our waist. We'll all get malaria."

It wasn't like him to make such dour predictions. "Sounds like you just have a reason not to want to leave Camelot."

Maybe something to do with his relationship with Cadogan. Or maybe it was just that he had become used to things as they were. Arthur, Kay, Bedivere. The three were so close, although it did sometimes seem like a duo with a third planet orbiting. That third being Bedivere.

"And what if I do?"

Persy grinned a bit. "Welshmen."

"Like you'd know. You're even chaster than Brother Cadan, and there's bets on you being one of those who has no interest."

"No, I've had my heart broken once too often."

"Don't let them have your heart, then," Bedivere suggested. "Isn't a warm place to put it enough?"

Persy laughed at that, turning Blazer back to the corral. A warm place to put it was enough for many. Or a warm thing to put in it. It had never been enough for her.

20

They rode out the next morning, Arthur with Kay on one side, the Goth mercenary on the other.

It had been two years since Badon, but the cameraderie of the road came back within what seemed like seconds. Galahad fell in next to her. He had a new horse, his bay having been retired. This one was black with a white face and a little larger.

Blazer snorted at it, then ignored it. Persy wondered how much more she would get out of the horse. She wished, not for the first time, he had been foaled a mare. That way she could...she knew exactly which stallion, too.

She would have to settle for buying one of that horse's foals. Now there was an idea. "I think I'm going to buy a yearling next year."

"Raise it up right?" Galahad asked, turning towards her. "I don't blame you. Look at what somebody sold your sister."

She was never going to live that down. She wrinkled her nose. "I think he had it on monkswort and probably other stuff too. It seemed fine at his place."

"Probably. And I'm sure it never set foot anywhere near Africa."

"He claimed its sire came from Africa. More likely it's great grandsire."

Galahad patted the black. "This one's a good 'un. He'll do, anyway. No mares for me."

"I've ridden some good mares," Persy argued. "And be careful what you say..."

He considered it, then he laughed out loud. "You're bad."

"I don't have much choice about being bad, do I? I hang out with you."

"Me? I'm pure as the driven snow." Galahad was already starting to laugh.

"After about three days and some rain." Persy grinned across at him.

A voice from nearby sounded clearly, "Anyone would think that the two of you were brothers."

Persy glanced over to see one of the mercenaries. "Just brothers-in-arms."

"I can see that."

The mercenary was not a Goth. His skin was dark brown, and his hair long, in tight braids secured with small glass beads. Nubian, and one of the darkest she had ever seen. A handsome man, too, handsome enough to make her hope she was not visibly blushing. She already had that reputation, or at some levels that fear associated with her. She did not need more gossip.

"You're a long way from home," Persy finally voiced.

"Not the only one to make this journey." He smiled at her, his teeth seeming very bright in contrast to his skin.

"I've seen others." She wondered, for a moment, why the gods made men that color. Or for that matter, the reverse, why they made men as pale as the snow. Some of the Norsemen she had seen made her look swarthy herself. Maybe it was so each race of men could tell each other apart. His tack was in the Roman manner and two short spears were secured to it. Throwing spears. Not a common weapon, although perhaps more so where he came from.

"Are you sure? From the way you are looking at me, I would think you had never seen the like of me."

Galahad glared at him. "There's no need to keep embarrassing him."

The Nubian's smile faded, but only for a moment. "Ah, I get it. Only friends are allowed to tease."

Persy looked up from the horse's mane, confident her blush was under control. "Friends know how to tease. Strangers can never quite find the path."

"Point, point."

Persy decided in that moment that she was not sure she liked this man. It was hard to tell whether he was just one naturally prone to banter, or whether he was being cruel. She gave him the benefit of the doubt...for now. "I'm Percival."

"I am Uluru," the stranger introduced himself.

The name sounded at once strange and not strange to her ears. Who was this man? Somebody she would have to trust to watch her back, but then, what was new? She had not known quite a few of her comrades well when they rode to Badon.

She was suddenly afraid...in a way she had not been on that previous ride. Was she growing old? Was it the presence of mercenaries?

No...she realized after a moment. Her subconscious was reminding her of a simple and, to her, unfortunate fact. Mounted combat could not happen in the fens.

The edge of the fens was a small line of so-called hills that would have been pimples anywhere else. Beyond them, it extended until it faded into the sea, past what her eye could reach. Blue and green and brown. The land sunk just beneath the surface of the sea, forming a mire the size of some kingdoms.

A stray mosquito buzzed past, reminding her of Bedivere's dire prediction about malaria. The place had to be infested with it. The fensmen, she supposed, were either immune or simply dealt with it.

They were a strange lot for a reason. The land had to breed a race as peculiar as came on Earth.

"Like the Nile delta. Just a lot colder." It was Uluru who had spoken.

"Oh?" she could not help but ask. She was starting to revise her opinion of the man.

"The river breaks up into little strands, flowing through the mud on the way to the sea. People go out onto those flats, even though it's dangerous."

"Why?"

"Because anything dropped into the river or lost in the floods is likely to get caught somewhere in the mud. You can make a good living by finding small, valuable items and selling them."

Which was not theft, for the owners had no doubt given up on them. Finders keepers. Salvage. "Is it true that they worship cats in Egypt?"

"They have a goddess who takes the form of a cat...a fertility goddess, I believe, although with some other aspects as well. She's considered to own every cat in Egypt, and there are dire penalties for harming one."

Persy nodded. "And I bet at least some of those cats are spoiled rotten."

"Definitely. And when they die, they're buried with the same rites as humans. If the owners can afford it, they're taken to the shrine of Bast and placed in a special cemetery there. It's strange, but...I suspect you worship some gods they would consider odd, too."

Persy could only think of the Christians for a moment. She set that aside. "We have a goddess who takes the form of a crow, but she's not very nice."

"I'd say not. Crows aren't very nice creatures. Useful, but not nice."

Persy nodded to that. "Do you have crows in Nubia?"

"I'm not from Nubia," Uluru explained. "I'm from the west side of Africa. I was caught as a slave, but earned my freedom."

Judging by his current profession...and size...she suspected he had earned his freedom in the arena, a not uncommon path. He was not a young man, either. "So, what gods do..."

She did not get to finish the sentence. The fensmen just...appeared, around them, as if they had grown out of the ground. Their clothing was in colors that blended in with the vegetation and they were all armed.

None of them bowed to Arthur. She sensed men who bowed to no one, perhaps not even to the gods.

"Good," Kay murmured from somewhere nearby. "We could not have gone further without a guide."

He was probably right. Even Blazer balked at the water, up above a man's knees at this point. Strange grasses poked through it. There were no trees. Arthur talked in a low voice with one of the men.

Persy was not even sure how they could help. The horses would be all but useless and these men, surely, could fight far better in that terrain than she. There was also a smell. A soft, sweet smell, almost like rotting flesh.

She supposed that would disappear as her nose became accustomed to it, but maybe that was why Blazer balked. Horses were far more sensitive to scents than their riders.

The fensmen moved off into the water again. Arthur followed, although the spotted mare hesitated then snorted and tossed her head. She trusted her rider, though.

The water never got above their stirrups. Even that was enough, though, to make horses and riders alike nervous. Mist floated in the air, clinging to them. Mosquitoes and, almost worse, midges, formed clouds at intervals. She felt as if she was being eaten alive. At least there were no horseflies, but the mosquitoes were bothering Blazer as well. He snorted and kicked, lifting his feet through the water. She could almost feel his misery.

There. A small island in the fens ahead...but no, perspective switched. A larger one, a long way ahead.

It would take all day to get there, and she slumped in the saddle. For a moment, the scene shimmered, and she saw a different landscape. She saw cattle grazing in fields that were bordered not by hedges but by straight ditches filled with water. And ahead, not an island, but a small hill.

It vanished a moment later. And late that day they came to the Isle of Ely.

21

The village had clearly been raided, and not that long ago. The remains of dead cattle lay in a heap by the corral, and the survivors still seemed nervous. There were no horses. Had any men been slain, the bodies had already been buried.

How, Persy wondered, did one bury bodies in this? Even on the island, where it was relatively dry, there was still the pervasive water. Almost as if they were moving across the bottom of the sea.

It took her until after nightfall to get Blazer's legs dry. She barely had the energy to eat the poor provender offered. The people had little before the Norse came and less now. Well, except that the mercenaries had been wrong.

The raiders had been dark haired. Danes, not Norsemen. A small difference, except if it came to negotiating...their languages were not quite the same. And Danes were often insulted by being mistaken for Norsemen.

She found her pallet and would have thought to fall right into sleep, as tired as she was.

Instead, she tossed and turned, her body absolutely refusing to cooperate. It was not pre-battle jitters, or even anxiety. It might have been the mosquitoes, but she did not think so.

She laid on her back, staring at the ceiling. They slept in a cattle barn, but she had slept in nothing at all and not had the same problem. What was wrong with her? It felt almost as if something warned her not to doze off. As if...

She shook her head a little. As if they were going to be raided again. As if her Sight had finally decided to give her something useful.

She shifted position, tugging her sword closer to her. Of course, if she had to fight in a nightshift there would be a problem. But if she got dressed, people would wonder what she knew.

The Christians in the camp would mutter 'wizard' and 'warlock'. Neither accurate, but...

Nonetheless, she pulled on her breeches and tunic, then decided she had an excuse after all. She stood, exhaustion flowing over her, and walked to the entrance of the building. Outside, there were no stars visible, the greyness of the land seeming to have encompassed the sky.

She heard a faint slapping sound in the distance that, after a moment, she realized was...no.

There were no trees there. It was not a beaver. It was an oar. She frowned. Arthur was in the main house, of course, with the local chief. And Kay stayed with him.

She contemplated for a moment, then simply moved and quietly woke the man nearest the door. It was Bedivere.

"There's somebody out there."

"Are you sure?" he grumbled, groggily. "You're dressed."

"I couldn't sleep. Gave up. Stepped outside to get some air and heard what I think was an oar in the water."

"Sure it wasn't a beaver?"

"Nothing for a beaver to eat around here. Place is probably full of otters and the like, but no beavers."

Bedivere stepped outside. Persy followed him. Another slap, and a muffled curse. Not in Danish. Or Norse.

The fensmen themselves were what was out there. And the vague suspicion that they walked into a trap came over her. The raid had been real.

Had it been the next village, not the Danes after all?

Then there was another shout and she actually relaxed. That one was in a viking tongue. The fensmen must have gone out to try and intercept them.

"Wake everyone. Quietly," Bedivere asked her.

She went back inside, quietly shaking each man awake. Or that was the intent. One of the mercenaries shrieked and grabbed her by the tunic. He'd been in some bad ones, she knew from that.

"Hush. Save it for the Danes."

Fortunately, he had enough presence of mind to release her, grumbling about his interrupted sleep.

She moved on. Galahad called her some interesting names, but by the time he had finished, they were both grinning.

As she came back outside, now with her spear...the sword might be a better weapon, but having both struck her as a good idea, she heard a scream somewhere out there. Then the thwang of a bow and another scream.

She hoped it was their side doing the shooting. Of course, in that darkness, she would not have tried it. She was worried enough that she might stab an ally. Dawn was not even beginning to stir, although it would come early here, with nothing east of them except fen and sea.

Not knowing what many of her allies looked like made little difference. She would have needed a Sidhe's eyes, or a cat's, to see well in the gloom. She closed her eyes, trying to orient herself by sound. Her nose seemed to go on strike. She could no longer smell the fen stench...or anything else.

Somebody came up behind her. She whirled, blade swinging towards him...to stop it at the last moment.

It was Uluru, the one person she could well distinguish in the darkness. He nodded, then moved up next to her.

"It's just too dark," Persy muttered. "Can't tell friend from foe in this."

"Which makes one wonder how the Danes manage it, does it not?"

"I have no clue." She kept her voice down, although part of her thought it might not be a bad thing if the Danes came to them. At least then she would know where they were.

An arrow spun past her. She frowned and ducked into the grasses. Whoever fired it, it had come far too close for her comfort. Far too close, and she glanced at Uluru.

He had a bow, but he was not pulling it out. An odd bow, made of black wood, darker even than his skin. Perhaps it had come all the way from Africa.

Perhaps he had made it himself and it was only stained that color. And then the Dane came out of the mist towards them. He wore grey clothing, almost as good camouflage as the fenmen's apparent rags.

Persy, in green and brown, felt like a target. She lifted her spear, but Uluru threw his in that moment. Skewered, the Dane fell into the water...and his two friends behind him charged.

She used her spear almost as a barrier, parrying their weapons to one side. They were both axemen. She hated fighting axemen.

At that , she hated fighting altogether. She was exhausted, hungry, she had not slept and she felt as if she had been pulled out of her home by those...stupid Norsemen.

If they even were Norsemen a-viking. Could they be Danes, also trying to take British land? Would anybody bother taking this land? But yes, that was the language. They were Danes A thrust, and a second Dane went down. The third danced with Uluru, whose style carried with it traces of the arena. She actually thought he might have been a net man at some point, from the way he used his off hand to distract, and then that one was down.

Later, they guessed there had been no more than a dozen of the Danes...and that none had escaped alive. That was hailed as a victory, but Persy did wonder.

She thought they should have let one get away, to tell of their utter defeat. That way, at least some would pack their longboats and go back to Denmark.

She wondered what Denmark was like. She wondered what Africa was like.

Persy stood at the edge of the Isle of Ely, looking out into the fens.

She would be glad to get out of there, but until they ensured that the Danes were gone, one way or the other, she was trapped. She did not belong in that landscape of mist and water. Two of the mercenaries had came down with malaria. It looked like they would live and recover, but it worried her. Once you contracted it, it had a tendency of coming back. Some people were never healthy again.

The image of the fens drained and turned into cattle land flowed through her head again. She wondered if that was a good thing or a bad thing. The people might be close-mouthed and clannish, but they had their own culture and way of life. If she valued hers, then she should let them value theirs.

Even the Saxon way of life should be valued. In Saxony. She made a face. If they really were struggling to survive in the new, cold winters, then she actually had some sympathy. Yet, she would...she was determined...protect her own people.

It had long since ceased to be about staying near Arthur.

"As for them?" asked Galahad, stepping up behind her.

"Just thinking that as crazy as the fen people are..."

"They're just used to living here. Bound to make a man strange."

She turned towards Galahad. "Uluru's the strange one."

"I noticed. I wonder why he doesn't go back to Africa."

"Maybe a woman. Maybe he likes it here. Who knows what Africa is like?"

"From what he says, depends on which part. It's a far larger place than Britain, and look at the difference between the Cymry and the fensmen."

"Heck, I swear some of the people here are more Angle than British."

"One way to deal with them, if you don't get too many. Bring them in, make them part of us."

"And what if we end up part of them?" She turned towards Galahad. "What if we end up being the ones who lose ourselves?"

"I don't know. But the occasional bit of intermarriage can't hurt anything." He paused. "I mean, people like Uluru marry Britons all the time."

"Look at Bruenor, or that girl in the kitchens." Persy smiled a little. "Maybe it's just color variance, like horses."

"Depends on what God decides, I suppose." A pause. "So, maybe some of our descendants will be part Saxon?"

For her, that was already true, given Arthur's own Saxon blood. Maybe that was it. Maybe the gods decided... "Except that there's always a pattern to these things, I've noticed. Part of the tapestry of the gods, I suppose. You can't get a bay horse from breeding two chestnuts."

"Maybe God does these things because He likes variety," Galahad suggested. "It would be boring if all horses, everywhere, were bay."

Persy laughed. "Yeah, it would. But most horses are bay or dun. That's the way of things."

"And most men are light colored."

"Are they? If Africa is as large as Uluru claims, more men might be darker. Maybe cold winters make people pale. He said that Africa has no winters."

Galahad shuddered. "How could the crops grow with no winter? Eh. I suppose the plants are used to it."

"And the people. It seems strange to us, but so do the fens." She saw how the fen children could handle boats almost before they could walk. Slender, lithe children, quite different from Gwydion. Of course, he had inherited a good part of his father's size.

She wondered about that, too. Eh. If people did not pass on traits to their children, then how would you know who's were who's?

"I'll be glad to get home."

"So will I. Although at least I seem to have gotten used to the smell."

The next few weeks were spent almost entirely on the water as they harried the raiders through swamp and lake alike.

22

"If I never see another boat, it will be too soon," Persy complained to Galahad, throwing a saddle on Blazer.

"And we may have to come back next year."

"Don't remind me." The idea of having to spend several summers in the fenlands did not appeal. But winter approached. The way things were going, the marshes would freeze, and nobody, Dane or Briton, would be able to move.

They were leaving before that could happen. The fensmen guides waited for them. She tightened the girth slowly and carefully. Blazer, who had been in a corral for weeks, snorted at her.

"Yeah, I know. You don't want to work." She glanced over at Galahad's black, just as the other man yelped. "Galahad?"

"He stepped on my toe."

"Ugh. I hate that." Persy usually managed to keep her feet out of the way, but it was always an occupational hazard.

"Makes me wish I'd bought a smaller horse."

Persy laughed. "I don't know. The little moor ponies hurt more. They have such small feet."

She finally had Blazer's saddlebags in place. Getting into the saddle felt odd. She hoped that she had not actually lost some of her riding fitness...although with all of the climbing around and wading she should have been in better shape.

"Ugh." Galahad adjusted his seat a couple of times, but still did not look comfortable.

"Forgotten how to ride, have we?" she teased.

"You look like a sack of grain in the saddle yourself," he quipped back. "But no. I remember how to ride. I'm just not sure my legs do."

Persy nudged Blazer with her knees and discovered she did, indeed, remember how to ride. He snorted again, grumbling, but subsided after a moment, moving forward.

Then there was a thud from behind them. She looked over her shoulder. Bedivere, of all people, had fallen off his horse. She decided to spare the man's blushes by remaining silent about it.

The edge of the fens looked like home to her, the ground rising back up into solidity. She never wanted to go back there, she never wanted to hear the call of the marsh birds again.

She did wonder about those people. Had they come to their own accommodation with the Saxons. Of course, would anyone even want their land? Maybe they could afford to welcome any who liked it.

Maybe anyone who wanted to live there, they assumed was one of them.

Camelot was the most welcome sight Persy had ever seen. Several children, younger than Gwydion, ran to greet them. Another winter here might be less than appealing, but the alternative was far worse. She did not see either Gwydion or Guinevere.

Uluru still rode with them, although the rest of the mercenaries had gone to their own wintering grounds. He had settled in with the group in a way the others had not.

Persy, though, was still not entirely sure about him. He had proved himself in a fight, but she did not know, beyond that, what kind of man he was. Was he one with whom she could share a game of dice? He had Egyptian dice, the ones that were almost spherical, and had promised to teach a game with them. They rolled as high as twenty.

She saw Guinevere. The queen seemed relieved, but Persy noticed something. Her eyes rested on Arthur for the most part, yes, but there was also the way she looked at Uluru. A look Persy recognized and understood. The dark-skinned man was handsome in much the same way Arthur himself was, despite the huge difference in coloring.

Brilliant. Maybe they should not have brought him back.

Blazer recovered most of his fitness on the ride. So had she. Her legs did not turn to jelly when she dismounted. She even had the energy to rub him down.

She felt eyes on her when she did so. Morgan's eyes, she knew, without even turning around. Was the witch about to betray her? No. There was something akin to understanding there.

She wondered what had happened. But for the moment she simply turned to face her, nodded, and then went back to what she was doing.

It was only then that she realized the only reason Morgan would have stopped hating her would be if she was sure and certain to have Arthur for herself. The witch did not wear one of her tighter gowns, either, but something looser.

A horrible suspicion flowed through Persy's mind. For Morgan not to show off her waistline likely meant she no longer had one, and there was only one reason for that.

She hoped and prayed the child was a girl. Morgan would not be at all above harming Gwydion, if it came to that. If it would allow her child to be king.

Of course, a girl from Arthur and Morgan would make a fine queen, but the Christian lords would never accept her. They would give the power to her husband. If she was anything like either of her parents, she would hate it.

Morgan would not let that happen to her child, if she was still alive. Her child would be the one person safe from her manipulations, and she would do all she could to protect her from others.

Safe at some levels, her worst victim at others. Blazer taken care of, Persy went in search of Gwydion.

She found him in the main hall. He had apparently just finished a game of something, looking up from the table. His opponent had already left.

"You're back."

"I've had time to take care of my horse. You should be faster to greet your father."

"Why?"

He was, as Guinevere had said, at a difficult age. "He's missed you." Not that she knew that for sure, but it was a reasonable extrapolation. Arthur did care about Gwydion. She would give him that.

"I don't know that I like him any more."

Persy moved to sit on the bench next to Gwydion. "He had to leave. You know that."

"It's not that." Gwydion looked at her for a long moment, then, "I don't know that I trust him any more."

"Morgan," Persy said, softly.

Gwydion nodded.

"That's completely separate from whether he is a good father. Which he has been. You know that."

The boy nodded again. "Brother Cadan says, though, that a man who breaks his marriage vows is weak."

"Yes, but only weak in one specific area."

"I won't break mine."

"You aren't married yet. You don't know what will happen. What if she can't have babies?"

"I don't know." He looked at her, his eyes hooded somewhat. "I guess..."

"You're not a man yet, Gwydion. You have a lot to learn. Just watch out for Morgan. She might try to get you set aside."

And Gwydion was no more legitimate than the bastard in Morgan's belly. The only angle of attack she would have would be doubt over the paternity, and Arthur stamped his stock. At least as far as Gwydion was concerned.

Maybe a witness account of Morgan with somebody else would do it. She had hardly been faithful to one man in the past. Maybe the child was not even Arthur's.

"What does Brother Cadan say about a woman who breaks her marriage vows?"

Gwydion frowned. "That she is evil and should be destroyed." A pause. "He's not very fair, is he?"

"Women can be weak as well as men. Men tend to find it harder to keep their feelings under control, but women can certainly lose control too."

"But then how could you be sure who the father of a child is?"

"Before the Romans came, it did not matter. Who your father was, that is. Everything was inherited from your mother. That is why we have to have these ties of marriage now, firm and unbreakable. So people can be sure." She studied Gwydion's face. "Of course, sometimes...sometimes it is unmistakable."

"I guess I do kinda look like him, don't I?"

She laughed. She would have ruffled his hair, but he was too old for that. He would object, as boys his age were prone to do. "You are his spitting image, with almost nothing of your mother in you. Most of what you get from her can't be seen. Like your curiosity."

Arthur was not curious. He did not wonder much about how the world worked and he knew his place within it. He had probably never looked at the stars and wondered what they were.

She recalled that some of the Greeks claimed the Earth went around the sun, not the other way around, and wondered.

Cadan confronted her the next day. He had not bathed recently, based on the smell. He was definitely one of those Christians who thought dirt was somehow holy.

"Percival."

"Brother Cadan," she said, with all of the respect she could muster. It was more than he deserved, less than she might have shown.

"Walk with me?"

She had no reason to say no, even if spending more than a few moments in his presence was almost frightening. She sent a quick prayer to Lugh for protection before falling in next to him. "What is wrong?"

"You are putting ideas into the head of the future king."

"I only said..."

"Women are the vessels. They have a strength men do not. There is no excuse for them to commit adultery, and if they do so, then they must be destroyed."

She thought of Guinevere and frowned inwardly, but kept her face neutral. "I don't know. I think it depends on the woman...and the man."

"You cannot seriously think that women and men are equal?" Cadan turned towards her, his thin face odd in the sunlight. He had lost weight.

"I think that male and female make less difference than some would think. Not saying there's no difference." She had, even, agreed with Cadan's point about women being more capable of resisting sexual temptation. To a point, anyway. But did that apply to, for example, Morgan? She did not think so. No. Morgan used her sexuality, used the men she slept with. Discarded them once she was done. That was evil, plain and simple. What Guinevere was doing was just...stupidity.

"If men and women were equal, then God would not be male."

She held her tongue for a moment, then snapped out with, "Why would God create half the population as inferior?"

"The first woman, Eve, was made as a helpmeet to the first man. Women exist to support men. But it was also Eve who was the first to be touched by darkness. She fell into the devil's trap and pulled Adam with her. That is why there is suffering and why much more of it falls on women. Women have Eve's taint within them, and must overcome it." Cadan's words sounded like he had taken them from one of his sermons.

Eve's taint, indeed. Persy decided, not for the first time, that Cadan's god was a cruel one. "At the same time, didn't your God sacrifice himself to remove taint?"

"Only if the sacrifice is accepted." His eyes pierced her. "You have not been baptized."

"Nor will I be." She was firm on that. If she was the last person at court not to go through the ceremony, then so be it. She had heard that some of the Christians had taken to baptizing infants. That felt very wrong to her. A child should not be bound to the service of a god before it could even walk and talk.

"You will suffer for it."

"So be it. I will at least suffer as myself, not as a liar."

"You will see the truth. I hope in time."

Christians believed in the strange concept of eternal damnation, she recalled. To her, that was beyond alien. People changed, people learned. Hopefully, they grew up. "I'm sorry," she said, finally. "I can't accept a god with the habit of giving up on people." She turned to walk away, her shoulders set.

"He only gives up on people who give up on him."

She let Cadan have the last word. Cadan's god was a woman hater and a vengeful fool. Why did she never get that impression from Galahad?

23

The murder happened the next day. Someone found one of the kitchen girls out on the hillside. She had been roughly bound and stabbed through the heart, then left lying there on the heather with her blonde hair spread around her.

The same way the chapel at Glastonbury had been desecrated. Except it had not happened in the chapel at Camelot. Of course, Persy still thought that land consecrated by Cadan had not actually been made holy. One could not desecrate that which was not sacred.

Her face showed fear, as if she had seen something horrible before she died. It was a message, Persy thought as she helped move the body, limp weight in her arms. But from whom and for whom? If it had been Cadan again...then that destroyed her theory that it had not been him in the first place. That the halfwit had just been a vessel.

He had called women vessels. And both times, a woman had been killed. No. Both times a maiden had been killed. The kitchen girl had not, likely, known a man...she had been all of thirteen. A maiden.

What did that signify? Eve's taint? She needed an expert, she needed somebody who really knew what he was talking about.

She needed Merlin. Even as she had that thought, he rode up the hillside on a dun horse. The animal was trying to get away, perhaps eager to greet the other horses, but then it smelled death and blood. It shied, and the druid barely kept his seat.

Persy set the body down. They were at the edge of the small graveyard - one side where the Christians buried their dead, the other where the pagans did their rites. She thought she remembered the girl was Christian. She was not sure.

Then, she escaped, moving over to greet Merlin. "We have trouble."

"I smell it." He could mean that literally or metaphorically. Most likely both.

"Can we talk? Before anyone is foolish enough to blame you for this." Persy feared it might happen. The coincidence was a little much. As if whoever had done it had known Merlin was coming and sought to kill two birds with one stone by raising power from the death and blaming him for it.

"I...you are, of course, right." He turned his horse around the edge of the fort, at a walk. Persy fell in next to him.

"Cadan did it, I suspect," she voiced.

"Or Morgan."

Persy shook her head. "No. It's exactly the same thing that happened at Glastonbury. The same method, just a different location."

Merlin nodded. "To the detail?"

"Except for not being on an altar, yes."

"So, instead of cursing a building..."

She turned towards him. "Could there be demons? I know..."

"There could be," Merlin mused. "They might or might not be what Christians claim them to be, but I have dealt with evil spirits before."

"Cadan..."

"Cadan is well shielded. Too well." Merlin slipped from his horse's back to walk next to her. "You believe he may be a demon himself?"

"Yes," she admitted. "I do. And Morgan...would not resort to human sacrifice."

"Not of that kind."

She glanced at Merlin. "She is pregnant. I suspect it is Arthur's."

"If necessary I will take Gwydion, hide him as I did his father."

One of her eyebrows arched. "You did?"

"His mother and father were not married. His mother's husband did not appreciate this."

"Cadan was implying that adulterous women should be killed." She shuddered.

"Some Romans believe that, as you know. It is not something Celts have ever tolerated."

She smiled. "Some Romans are fools. There are far more important things than who beds whom."

"Except when inheritance is involved."

Inheritance. Would Gwydion's children sit the throne...or Morgan's? They would have to wed him as soon as possible and pray Elaine was fertile. "Inheritance is a good reason not to push for permanent weddings."

"I know that, you know that. But this girl."

"A kitchen girl, all of thirteen. Probably a maiden." Persy frowned. "The other girl was supposedly a maiden too."

"That makes a difference. Potential, you see, not actual." Merlin frowned, rubbing the tips of his fingers across his palm.

"And if they..."

"Healed Cadan's wits? Or do you still think Cadan may be a demon?"

"I think he is one, yes." Persy frowned. "We should watch for anyone else acting odd."

"And Morgan would not kill somebody to sacrifice them. Her offering will be her child."

"That's wrong. But then, the Christians have taken to doing it."

"And you were named for a goddess. Don't tell me it's different, because it's not."

She frowned a little bit, then nodded. "I am hoping the child is a girl."

"Morgan probably is too, at least in her heart. A boy might be better politically, but I doubt she would prefer to raise one, if she was being honest with herself." Merlin studied Persy. "You know about boys."

She laughed. "I do indeed. But I fear for Gwydion's safety."

"I will make sure he is protected magically."

"Guinevere may not allow it. She is likely to insist the Christian god will protect him."

"Trust me," Merlin said, then turned to vanish within the fort.

Persy realized that her hands and arms ached. She could smell the faint stench of corpse.

She went to the bath house and locked herself in.

They buried the girl in the Christian graveyard. Cadan officiated, but Merlin stood quietly in the background, his eyes hooded.

Persy could feel him ensuring that the girl's spirit moved on safely. After the last incident, she was glad of that. She would not have wanted to try it herself, although she would had there been nobody else.

The words of the unfamiliar litany washed over her. The only thing she wanted to do was leave, but her honor would not allow it. She tolerated, thus, the ritual, her mind on her own gods the entire time.

Then she left, not fleeing but walking in a dignified manner.

Thankfully, nobody followed her.

She kept walking, to the edge of the woods. Merlin said he would try and investigate, try and get something done.

She watched for anyone who might have changed in behavior, but saw none. Whatever the intent that time, it had been different, and she had not sensed the horrible trapping of the girl's soul. It had not been necessary, and thus, she could only presume less energy had been needed.

It might well have been to renew whatever was keeping Cadan the way he was, rather than anything new. "I hate him," she muttered to the trees. There was no response. If there were any fae in the area, they were ignoring her. Like as not they were nowhere near. There were too many humans wandering around, and most of them of the kind that would not be popular with the fae. She shook her head.

A fox wandered through the trees. Seeing her, it froze, one paw lifted and its white-tipped brush straight out.

"I won't hurt you," she told it.

It shook its brush and trotted away, head held high as if to say it wasn't really fleeing her, just had business elsewhere. That was right. Business elsewhere.

She laughed a bit, feeling a lot better for the encounter. It was a good moment, and she needed one of those. She needed one to expunge the guilt and grief she felt.

She felt ineffectual. She could see Arthur and Morgan and Guinevere heading for disaster, a disaster that could well pull in Uluru, given how the queen looked at him. She could sense that everything was going to fall apart, sooner or later.

Maybe Merlin could keep everyone from ending up at each other's throats. Cadan, she knew, would only make things worse. Far worse.

She shook her head. There was nothing she could do...except perhaps gently remind all involved of the terms of the treaty with the Saxons. Arthur's line had to hold the throne of Britain.

It would not, a small voice told her. The red-haired king, though, if he was not of Arthur's line...he sure looked like him. Except, he also could have been pure Saxon. A Saxon king?

The idea made her shudder. But, as if her thoughts had conjured him, she saw the red-haired king. And his slender, dark haired queen. The two faced each other, and she saw in the background a man with a sword and a hood.

She knew what was about to happen. Except that for a moment the face of his queen was superimposed over that of Guinevere.

Whatever happened, she realized, Arthur must never know about Guinevere's affairs. The way she had looked at Uluru. The way they kept looking at each other..

She turned to walk back to the fort. She should speak with Uluru. She should tell him what Cadan had been saying. Especially as it might well be her fault, at least to a point.

Revenge in kind. Of course, Guinevere's adultery meant little beyond those involved. She could not bear a child that could be used to Arthur's shame. To Cadan and those like him, that would not matter.

Guinevere herself was Christian, but perhaps she thought that teaching could not apply to her. Not to the queen. Not to the woman Arthur had taken to secure the throne. The fact that if she were dead he could simply marry Morgan would like as not escape her.

Morgan needed rid of both Guinevere and Gwydion. Revealing Guinevere's adultery would be the easiest way to force the other. Perhaps even the Christians would allow Arthur to use that as grounds to set her aside and take another wife.

The dark-haired queen, lovely and lithe, walking to the headsman's block. Why? He so obviously loved her, so obviously cared. Had he been given no choice?

Or had she too been barren, and had he been given no other way to rid himself of her?

"Christians," she grumbled.

"What's wrong with us?" A clear voice.

Galahad. "Present company definitely excepted."

"Can't we all get along?" He regarded her with a thoughtful expression.

"Apparently not. The second we don't have anyone else to fight, we start on each other." Maybe they should have all gone home for the winter. There was so much snippy behavior already. Only the other day Uluru and one of the younger men had demonstrated that men could, indeed, fight like women. Of course, who knew what the men of Uluru's land did.

To make it worse, she had seen the girl Elaine watching Uluru. She was thirteen, prime age for a crush on an older man or an older woman. She hoped Uluru had the sense to grasp that and would cut her off cold if things started to go further than they should. Although he apparently did not have the sense to keep his eyes, and possibly his hands, off of the queen.

He was not, she thought, a stupid man. A strange man, though.

Or perhaps that was not so odd. The Christ avatar had supposedly lived closer to Africa than to Britain. More likely, he had learned the faith in the arena. It had for a long time been the faith of women and slaves.

Women. Yet the teachings of the church placed them second best. Or perhaps that was Constantine. Constantine and how he had, possibly, twisted those teachings.

"You're drifting off again."

"I know," Persy admitted. "I think I need to go get some rest or something." She still was not quite herself, and she knew it. Funerals did affect her.

"Funerals," Galahad complained, shooting her a sympathetic look.

"Do me a favor. If I die before you, make sure they don't stick me in the ground like that."

"Pagan," he accused, clearly trying to lighten the mood.

"Proud of it." She was, too. But...Galahad was walking proof that she did not have to hate Christians.

"One day we'll come to some accommodation."

She shook her head. "Too many people have been told that they are right." And she walked off before he could say anything else. Or before, perhaps, his sudden naiveté annoyed her.

Told that they are right. Those words echoed within her as she picked at her food. She did not feel much like eating, but forced herself to do so anyway. It did not help that the cooks, distracted and upset, had not done a particularly good job with the stew. The ratio of herbs did not seem to be quite what it was supposed to be.

She shook her head a little. She would be fine by tomorrow...no. She would not be entirely fine until the murderer was caught. She herself was safe from him, but...there was Elaine.

Then, Uluru sat down next to her, setting down his bowl. "I need a shield."

"Who from?"

"Elaine. She won't stop asking questions about where I'm from and I think she has something other than answers in mind."

Persy made a wry face. "I noticed. Just turn her down cold. She'll move on to somebody else. Girls that age..."

"Should not really already be promised. What of her choices...but, of course, you go by Roman ways here."

"You give your women more freedom?" She found herself interested.

"With my tribe, it is the woman who chooses the man, not the other way around, and if she no longer wants him, all she must do is set his belongings outside the hut. You would think after many years amongst the pale people, I would have learned your ways, but some things still..." He lifted his hand.

"You have learned some of them."

He considered that. "Not really. What does it matter what you happen to call God? He certainly doesn't care, as long as He is honored appropriately."

She digested that. Perhaps there was a way hidden there in which she could find a solution to all of their problems. No. There was no way the likes of Cadan or even Guinevere would accept that. "I wish the Christians felt that way."

"People like to be right."

"I like to be right myself. I suppose I'm just as stubborn as they are." And Gwydion was becoming more Christian with time. His children would be amongst those baptized at birth, she feared...but if Uluru was right, then perhaps it was not something to worry over-much about.

"Still, if I am right then so is everyone else," Uluru quipped. "Yes, I worship with the Christians. Their star is rising. One day it will also descend. That does not mean God is going anywhere."

The last vestiges of her dislike for him had faded. "But I agree on the promising. We have enough troubles of that nature without..."

"Without forcing them on the next generation. I'm not blind. I think the only person who doesn't know everything that's going on is maybe Brother Cadan."

"Who would preach hellfire against them all." Persy paused. "What's your opinion of him?"

"A small man, with nothing to recommend him. He only thinks he serves God."

Persy paused, then, "There was another murder. Almost identical to this most recent one. Cadan was in the area and then fled."

"He's not fleeing this time. It could just be coincidence." But Uluru's eyes had darkened. "On the other hand, I do not trust that man. Arthur should get rid of him."

"There are other priests. I'm not sure why he keeps him around."

"Because, as far as I can tell, the only people who don't trust him are you, me, the witch, and the druid."

"Add Galahad. He doesn't trust him either. But put like that..." Persy tailed off. "I don't trust Morgan either."

"That one dances with serpents. Sooner or later one of them will bite her. I suspect it's name will be Cadan."

She smiled at him as he stood to leave, suspecting that he was right, although unsure which of them would likely win the contest. She would have bet on Morgan, but the murders told her something deep and dark was going on.

Winter was closing in even faster than it had in previous years. Persy began to wonder if the kingdom was going to freeze shut. If spring would even come.

Now, though, she followed Morgan into the woods. Her pregnancy was no longer hidden. In fact, Persy wondered that she moved so freely so close to giving birth. When she had been that far along with Gwydion, she had waddled like a duck.

She was not sure why she followed her. Perhaps because she was still not entirely sure that there was not something going on with her and the murder. Or with her and...Guinevere.

Yeah. She was still wondering if Guinevere's barrenness was the result of a curse.

Then Persy lost her. One moment, the witch strode ahead. The next she was gone. Either she realized she had a tail and occluded herself or Persy was just too tired for this.

She searched briefly before giving up. Whatever Morgan was up to, she was not going to find out now. Maybe not ever. And if Morgan had seen her...

Who was she kidding? Morgan would not touch her, because that implied she was a danger to her. She knew well that she was not. There was simply no competition between the two women.

Morgan had won. For now. The battle, Persy thought, not the war. Where was her son?

She found him in the horse corral. He was brushing a dark brown animal she had not seen before. "Look what I got."

"Is he yours?" She stepped around Arthur's spotted mare to get a better look.

"I was getting too big for the little one."

"Getting?" He had hit a growth spurt and was heading for his father's size at a fast gallop.

"Yeah." He flickered a grin at her. "Elaine's going to ride her until she gets too big too."

Then, Persy supposed, they would find another child to ride the tiny pony. "Looks like a good one." She assessed the brown quickly. That reminded her of her plan to buy a yearling. She needed to make her selection soon.

"My dad picked him out, so of course he's good."

Persy grinned a bit. "Yeah. He's a good judge of horseflesh." Persy fancied herself a better one, grey mares aside, but she could not have done much better than the brown. Assuming his temperament was suitable.

She stepped to the brown's head, reaching her hand up around the side, to his neck. He promptly attempted to mug her for any treats she might happen to have.

Gwydion laughed. "He's silly."

"He's greedy, is what he is. I don't have anything." The gelding practically had his muzzle in her belt pouch.

Gwydion laughed again. "Neither do I."

"Would that be because he already scrounged anything suitable?"

The boy looked sheepish.

"Don't spoil him. It's as bad to spoil a horse as it is to spoil a child. The end result is pretty much the same." Except worse, because a spoiled horse would learn to bite and kick, but she didn't voice that yet.

"Okay."

"You want a partnership, but you are always the one in charge. He needs, to learn to trust you too. When you see a horse refuse to go through a stream, that's the one that doesn't trust its rider."

"I took him to the stream, he didn't want to go through."

"They don't. Especially if they can't see the bottom. It's natural. They don't want to get stuck in the mud. Besides, wolves hang around near stream crossings."

Gwydion shuddered. "I hate wolves. I wish they were all dead."

"Don't say that. The wolf has its place, just as we do." His words, though, had the echo of a prophecy. Would England one day have no wolves? Because people had killed them all?

"A long way away from me."

"Eh. I don't think any wolf is going to mess with Cafall." That thing had to be twice the size of a wolf.

"Good point. Dad says I can have one of his pups, too."

Persy would kill for a pup from Cafall, but held her tongue on that subject. "Don't spoil that, either."

He laughed. "I won't."

She slipped from the corral. It had been good to just talk to him, and about subjects other than religion. She only hoped he would listen to her and not spoil the horse, which was then likely to dump him. At least it seemed a sensible animal, if a bit too friendly. She probably should have pushed it away harder.

She stopped for a moment, and looked at the rest of the fort. There were hounds chewing on bones outside the kitchen, two very young children sparred with wooden swords. For a moment, though, she saw the future...or something. She saw the fort disused for generations, trees growing on the earthen ramparts.

No longer needed, perhaps? Or made obsolete by some better design that was easier to start on a new site? Two children ran along what had been the wall, laughing.

A fort turned into a children's playground. Maybe that was a good vision after all, a vision of peace. She did not see the adults before her vision snapped back to the present.

Peace. When would they have it?

24

The answer did not come that winter. Of course, peace did last through the cold months. No sane person would start a war during the winter.

Maybe that would change one day as well. She felt as if nothing was stable any more. Gwydion grew tall and strong. He also seemed to develop some fondness for Elaine. It was more brotherly than loverly, but it would have to do for now. Perhaps better, in the long run. If they could be friends, then maybe they could make it work. She did not, however, miss the fact that Elaine was still looking at Uluru.

Peace extended into the summer.

Life became a routine. Days blurred together, although Persephone did not again visit her son. Having to deal with being one of Guinevere's ladies was not something she could face. It was far better to ride out with Galahad into the summer air, away from the fort where they could talk...although never more than that.

Far better to spar with Gwydion outside the fort, with people yelling tips and encouragement to both of them. The first time he beat her, she grinned up at him. "You're learning."

The tension, remained. Morgan gave birth to a son in the depth of winter. She named him Mordred.

Persephone was sure he was Arthur's get, but with hair and eyes darkening to his mother's hues. His similarity to Gwydion as an infant was obvious and disturbing.

Gwydion hated him.

As summer faded to fall, she found herself spending more and more time with Uluru.

Elaine was still watching him. She was starting to take a woman's form at this point, but her eyes never drifted to her future husband.

Girls that age went for older men. Not uncommonly for older women; hence, perhaps, the songs of Sappho.

Of course, the Greeks once paired boys with older men. The same thing, perhaps.

Uluru regarded her. "I have wondered something."

"What is it?" They walked along the ridge, and she wondered...she had wondered quite a bit lately if he was not Greek.

"I still don't understand Celts," he said, finally. "You can't make up your mind what you are."

"Blame Rome. They tried to turn us into an extension of themselves, but instead we sort of..."

"Integrated. I wonder what would happen if you integrated with the Saxons." He lifted a hand. "I'm not saying you should."

"You're saying it would be interesting to see what ended up happening." Persy frowned. "It may happen. It may be the only way to have any kind of peace in the end. But..."

"You can't welcome people who come as thieves. Who could? Where I come from, they do worse than that. They take slaves."

"We've taken slaves. Not any more, but that's mostly because Rome isn't there to buy them."

"And what did they sell as the price of lives?"

Persy's mouth watered at the thought. "Olive oil." A pause. "Who wants to cook with lard?"

"Ugh. Well, maybe one day trade will resume."

"Yeah. But not in our lifetime, I don't think." And in the interim they would be stuck cooking with lard and drinking English wine. Such as it was. The vineyards were dying. Soon, it would be beer and mead. "I miss good wine, too."

"I don't. I never did care for wine," Uluru admitted. "A good beer, that touches the spot."

She laughed a bit at him. "People...you know what people think about you?"

"Yeah. I do. I need to find a serving maid willing to parade around on my arm for a bit." He chuckled at that.

Was he...she was sure he was sleeping with the queen, but he did not seem too bothered by the rumors...both those that said he was Guinevere's paramour and those which thought him more interested in Bedivere.

"I sometimes wonder if we make too much of a fuss about such things."

"Maybe so, but I also think it's human nature to fear that which is different. Where I come from, we make a fuss about it in a different way."

"Oh?"

"Yeah. We usually turn people like that into priests."

She glanced at him, arched an eyebrow, and then laughed. "Some of the Christians think priests should be celibate because Christ was celibate."

"Who says he was? Didn't he have a woman following him around?"

"I'm not that familiar with the actual stories." Persy brushed back her hair. "I don't know. The Christians seem to have so many different versions of their religion already." She remembered her vision of the great church in London. "And they do seem to be on the ascendant."

"It won't last. No view of God lasts forever, not yours, not mine, not theirs."

"What if people stop believing in God altogether?" The thought fell cold within her for a moment. If people did, then...

"They would stop believing in themselves if they did that."

"I know plenty of people who already don't." Persy frowned a little bit. "Believe in themselves, that is."

"God created the world. He created us to enjoy and appreciate the world. That is what I believe. If you do yourself down, you aren't appreciating yourself, and that's not what He wants."

Persy was unable to come up with a good response to that, leaving Uluru with the last word. How, she wondered, did he know so much philosophy?

She had gone from wishing he would disappear to being very glad he had chosen to stay.

Winter fell again, and it bid to be an unpleasant one. Not just by virtue of the weather, but by the fact that a lady named Linnet and her entourage had become trapped by early snowfall.

Linnet. Her voice was more like a crow's. It was raised often, and always in complaint about something.

Worse yet, she was relatively young, a widow, and pursuing any male whom she might be able to entrap into marriage. About the only one she did not go after was Uluru, who was, perhaps, too exotic for her tastes.

Her primary target, however, was Kay. Persy found him hiding in the kitchens, a ridiculous sight.

"Kay?"

"Somebody save me from that woman."

"We could accidentally lock her in the bath house?" Persy suggested, ruefully.

"Tempting, but Guinevere would let her out in five seconds. Honestly, I'm half tempted to find Merlin and ask if he can put a silence spell on her."

Persy laughed a bit. "He'd say no, and you know it. Morgan might say yes..."

Kay shuddered. "Let's lock her in the bath house too."

Persy was pretty sure that would not hold her. Morgan was quite possibly the most powerful person she knew, period. "Well, we do need to do something about Linnet. Like...convince her that this is not a fun place to spend the winter."

"Guinevere likes her."

"Guinevere pretends to like everyone." At least, it seemed, her affair with Uluru was over. Persy had seen the two of them avoiding each other. Even Cadan had noticed that, and the looks he kept giving the queen held curses within them. Fortunately, those curses did not seem to have landed.

"She's too polite to act otherwise." Kay shook his head. "What the heck do I do, Persy? I keep expecting one day to walk into my room and find her naked in my bed."

"I'd suggest visibly taking up with somebody else, but I don't know that that would stop her."

"Wish she'd go after Uluru. I think he'd know what to do with her."

"She's probably afraid her kids will come out some kind of weird muddy color." Galahad rolled his eyes. "I don't get why that would bother anyone."

Persy considered that for a moment. "Probably. Or she might be afraid they'll be mules or something."

"Uluru's not an ass."

"She is."

Kay burst out laughing at that. "Walked right into that one, didn't I?"

She grinned at him for a moment. "Kay, you have to just tell her to back down. In public, so that she'll be thoroughly embarrassed if she continues."

Kay nodded. "Maybe she doesn't care about that."

"Then get Arthur to toss her out as soon as the roads are clear eno...no, I have a better idea. Set Guinevere on her."

"What?"

"She enjoys finding spouses for people. Let her find somebody who actually wouldn't mind being married to Linnet. I've seen Guinevere on the matchmaking trail. More than a match for Linnet."

Kay laughed. "Okay. You're probably right. Would you do it? Guinevere keeps eyeing me and certain women speculatively. I haven't seen her do that with you."

Persy realized that she was about the only single person Guinevere had not tried to pair off. She knew. Guinevere, somehow, knew her secret.

Spring came, and trouble with it. It was not bandits. With the Saxons gone, the lords were starting to chafe at any bonds that kept them from fighting each other. It was barely March when word came that there was fighting in the west country.

At least not the fens this time. And at least spring had come early this year, bright and clear after the cold winter. It almost felt like she was a child again.

The real issue, she realized, was that she did not want to leave Gwydion at all. And this time, Merlin rode with them. Cadan and he placed themselves as far apart as they possibly could in the line, but they were both there. That struck Persy has a recipe for trouble.

Or at least a recipe for conflicting advice. She knew which of the two she would listen to. Did Arthur? And Merlin looked...

...not good. He had always struck her as ageless, fae blood in his veins. An immortal who would remain forever. Now he just looked old.

Perhaps there was a limit to how long he could remain alive after all, and if he died... If he died, that left Morgan as the most powerful. And she had no idea who would be Chief Druid. If anyone. Vivian had not been seen since she had given Arthur the sword.

The sword which had served him well. There was definitely something about that sword. Nothing complicated. It simply seemed that when he drew it the morale of his friends increased and that of his enemies...

It was hard to withstand that sword. He drew it only in honest battle, never in tourney.

Honest battle. She hoped they could avoid that. If the Saxons found out they were fighting amongst themselves, they would almost certainly come back. In greater numbers. That was the way of any predator...to watch for a weakness.

There was no weakness in Arthur. He was not getting any younger, but he sat his horse as lightly as any boy.

He had acknowledged Morgan's child, but insisted that Gwydion and Gwydion alone remain the heir.

Persy was not sure she liked that. Morgan might harm Gwydion, even kill him, and there was little protection for him. Except, of course, his own wits. She thought he was smarter than his father. He took after her in that regard.

But he could not face Morgan alone. Especially as Guinevere had bound him to Christianity, and any magic in his blood slept, for now.

It was their time. Did that mean that the old gifts would be cast aside and forgotten? For a moment, her mind flickered with another vision. A woman performing a ritual she had once witnessed Vivian offer to the gods.

Not forgotten, then. A reassurance from the gods. That no matter what, things would not be forgotten. Just hidden for a while, perhaps.

Cadan was two horses ahead of her, sitting his mount awkwardly. The horse he rode now was a gift from Arthur and the two were not yet used to one another. Persy half hoped he pissed it off. It was a sort of steel grey color, and too good a horse for a priest. In comparison with the mule Cadan had owned before, it was the best horse ever.

She shook her head. Unworthy thoughts. Yet, he looked over his shoulder at her. His eyes said everything. He didn't trust her or she him.

But had they not had that moment of cameraderie, that moment when they had been ready to fight together? Was that not, at least potentially, proof that he was human after all?

She did not know. And she booted Blazer forward, until she did not have to look at him.

It only later occurred to her that turning her back on him might not have been her smartest decision ever.

25

The real trouble started as they rode into the western hills. Small scruffy cattle grazed in fields interspersed with apple orchards. Most of that fruit would be turned into that odd substitute for beer, cider. Persy had never developed a taste for it. Kay had, and he stopped at the side of the road, negotiating with the farmer for a jug.

Of course, one of the things about cider was that one could never be entirely sure how strong any given tankard was. Beer, one could make a guess. Cider?

It was just too variable. By the end of the ride, Kay was so drunk that Bedivere and Uluru had to ride on either side of him, supporting him.

Arthur, of course, gained much amusement at his friend's expense. Persy rode tensely. With one of their best fighters so thoroughly out of action, it was the perfect moment for an ambush.

Or for treachery of another kind. They had taken on more fighters that spring, and one of them suddenly made a lunge for the king's unprotected back.

Persy saw Cadan make a quick gesture, nothing more, and the man fell from his horse. It was the first direct evidence that he did, indeed, work magic.

She gave no sign that she had seen, but rather rode forward. Merlin, ahead of the king, had only turned to look at the thud.

Score one for Cadan, she thought cynically, slipping off a horse next to the would be assassin. "What do you want done with him?" she asked Arthur.

"Bind him."

Persy nodded. She tied the man to his horse. The saddle girth had somehow come undone. A very simple curse.

Cadan was, at least, protecting Arthur. Why? Because Arthur would turn England into a Christian kingdom?

If he was a Christian demon, then the more people followed Christ, the more people would be open to such influence. Their Satan would want recruits as badly as their God.

It was so much simpler the other way. Even Hades, whom the Celts called Arawn, was not evil. Death was an essential part of life. Everything had its place. Evil was only what stepped out of the place it was intended to be.

She finished binding the man and then hopped back on Blazer. He stood like a rock with nobody holding him.

It would not be fun to train his replacement. She wondered what Arthur would do with the assassin?

Feed him to Morgan, maybe. Whatever else, she was more than capable of getting the truth out of him. Or what she wanted to hear. Persy shook her head. She would not trust Morgan with an interrogation, but who else was there? Cadan would be even worse.

She glanced over at Merlin's head. He still seemed old, bent as if under a great burden. Perhaps it was the changing of the age. Perhaps the gods themselves grew old, to be replaced by the dynamic, the new.

There was no more trouble until they reached the next town. It was almost a city, albeit not a very Roman one. No walls, only a staked palisade, but houses were packed within it. Some of them were even square. It was a classic example of the mixture of old and new that dominated those parts of the land never fully brought under Roman rule.

For a moment, she saw winding streets and houses packed even closer along them, touching. A strange wagon, with no horse, sat outside one of them. Okay. What use was that?

Sometimes she thought that it was all completely random, that what she was being shown had no connection to anything. They were east of Glastonbury at that point...that would be their next stop.

She wondered if Cadan would try to come up with some excuse to avoid the place. He had to have little or no reason to wish to return there.

Maybe he would develop a mysterious sickness. Of course, they were not to make it to Glastonbury.

The runner came from the east in the middle of the night, his horse half dead from the exertion.

Camelot had been attacked. The entire thing had been a set up. And the attackers had taken Gwydion, Elaine and the infant Mordred.

The language Persy used varied in origin, but all of it was bad. They did not wait until morning. The kidnappers had to be found, and quickly. Visions of Gwydion and Elaine murdered flowed through Persy's head.

If only her Sight could show her the present as well as the future. They did not hesitate. The horses could see in the dark even if their riders could not.

Cadan was left behind, unable to keep up. Merlin too seemed to have hung back. There was no marching order. People traveled as swiftly as they could, and Persy worried about Blazer. He was too good a horse to founder on a forced march. Yet, she could not hold back. The images in her head came from a mother's concern. What was happening to Gwydion?

Why could her blasted Sight not show her anything useful? She crouched low over Blazer's neck, letting him carry her easily.

If he foundered, she would never forgive herself. Yet, she also could not forgive herself if she fell back, if she was not there to rescue her son.

She wished she could rescue him as herself. The masquerade had become second nature; it felt once more like a burden. Like a veil that fell over her.

Four beats flowed under her, Blazer had gone into a gallop unasked. Perhaps he sensed her urgency. She reined him back a little. She would not let him run to his death.

Arthur was doing the same thing, concerned for the spotted mare. Neither horse was young any more. Neither could keep this pace up for long.

She glanced around. They had already covered what would normally have been half a day's ride. Yet, even at this pace, even if they killed every horse they had, they would not get back in time.

No. They had to think about this. Persy sat up, narrowing her eyes. She forced her thoughts into focus. Gwydion, Elaine and Mordred. If the two boys died, Arthur would be forced to choose another heir.

So, why steal them instead of killing them? If one wanted to control the next king. Or to bait a trap by taking those most valuable.

In that case, why take Elaine? She glanced around. Uluru seemed upset too.

She knew Elaine desired Uluru. She knew Uluru would never act on it, not with a girl so young. But he also seemed to like the kid.

And then Arthur was off again, having let his horse catch her breath.

It was Morgan who greeted them at the gate. She was doing nothing to hide her distress.

"We need fresh horses."

And they had, of course, taken their best. But Blazer was exhausted. He needed a warm bran mash and several hours of rest.

Persy needed several hours of rest and something similar. But men could be pushed further than horses and women, often, further than that.

"I ride with you," was Morgan's response to Arthur's comment. Her tone brooked no argument.

He looked like he might protest, but who was going to argue with her?

Besides, the fury in her eyes might switch to him if he said no. Persy resolved not to get between her and the kidnappers. As unnatural a woman as Morgan might appear at times, the fact that she loved her son was visible in her eyes and stance. In every line of her face. There was no hesitation within her on the matter.

Persy was glad her cover identity allowed her to show some worry, although she could not get away with a woman's open emotion. Which was stupid. Men had all the same feelings women did. Why were they afraid to let anyone know?

Because they saw it as a sign of weakness. There was nothing weak about worrying about a son. Or a nephew.

Arthur's face was set in stone. His eyes were completely implacable. Men would die, and soon, those eyes said.

Lacking a spare of her own, Persy found herself mounted on a black and white mare. She was too tired to argue, but still found the strength to swing herself into the saddle. The mare stirred a little under her, but did not object strongly.

However, when Persy picked up the reins, she threw her head up, trying to hit her face with her ears. She frowned and relaxed her grip. One of those, she thought, who needed a light hand.

Then they were out. And Morgan rode next to her. The witch traded court gowns for riding garb, and tucked her luxurious hair under a helmet.

Persy wondered if Morgan had any skill at arms. Likely not...both magic and war required a lot of time to study and it took a rare individual to be good at both. Morgan was a rare individual, but not, Persy suspected, in that way.

She felt the need to speak. "We'll get them back."

They were not riding at a headlong run, but at an easy, ground-covering pace, while Cafall and the hounds streamed ahead.

They had a scent. Hopefully it was the right scent.

"Whoever did this will suffer," Morgan promised.

Persy had never felt kinship with her before, but she did then. "Let's try not to kill anyone until we actually have the kids. We don't want to kill the people who know where they are."

Morgan's smile was unpleasant. "They'll tell me everything they know."

Persy decided she did not want to know what the woman planned. She was only glad that the witch's attention was pointed in a direction other than at her. She would not want to face that anger. For the mment, they were on the same side, or were they?

It would be the perfect opportunity for her to help rescue Mordred and...let something happen to Gwydion. Would even Morgan be that cynical?

Yes, Persy knew. "I'm not going back without both boys, alive. And Elaine, of course."

She worried almost more about what might happen to the girl. Rape? Sacrifice?

"Elaine will not be harmed." Morgan turned towards her. "They will find it very hard to physically harm any of the three."

Morgan had set wards, then, but on Gwydion? It came out before Persy could stop herself, "Why do you care about Gwydion?"

"Because I care about Arthur."

The truth? Persy could not be sure. "So do I. Even if he is...difficult."

"My plans do not encompass Gwydion's death. I promise you that."

But what about Mordred, as he grew? How would he view his half-brother, who would have everything? Gwydion was the heir, Mordred merely an acknowledged bastard. Guinevere had accepted Gwydion as her own. She would never tolerate Mordred.

"You have to understand why I don't trust you." Persy kept her voice down.

"You think I want nothing but power."

"You did threaten me."

"Only to get what I wanted." Morgan looked at her. "Arthur's bloodline must sit the throne, or we will become a Saxon land. You know that. I will not harm Gwydion, but I can't always protect him. There needed to be another line."

"Arthur should have married one of us."

Morgan surprised her in that moment. "He should have married you."

That was the one good chance she had to talk to Morgan. Galahad decided to play shield for her after they rested.

"Is Morgan giving you trouble?"

"Surprisingly, no. She's so worried about Mordred I think it's unfrozen her heart a little."

"You mean she has one?"

"She's still a woman, and I also think she's angry that she wasn't able to prevent the abduction."

"I'd like to know how they got past her. She's...formidable."

"But not skilled with a blade. Don't forget that. She's not even a very good rider."

"I noticed that." Galahad paused, then, "You've seen how Uluru is acting."

"He likes Elaine. Unfortunately, she takes that as him returning her crush. We'll have to deal with that."

"Yeah. We don't need Gwydion getting woman trouble before we've bought him his first woman."

"You mean you haven't yet?"

"He's your sister-son."

Persy's eyes widened at Galahad, then she realized he was teasing. That he didn't really expect her to find a camp follower to initiate Gwydion into the ways of men and women.

"Don't worry. I'll take care of it. What are friends for, after all?"

"Getting friends in trouble, from what I've seen." Not that she was too worried or upset. By this time she was mostly immune to Galahad's teasing, although occasionally he still managed to nail her a good one.

He was, after all, a man. And he had a man's sense of humor, except more refined. Looking at him, she shook her head. "When are we going to get you a woman?" she added.

"You know me. I'm finicky. She has to be just perfect. And the only one I've met who's perfect is too old."

She ducked away to hide the inevitable blush. "You'll find her,

Galahad. And when you do, you'll be the one with kids to worry about."

Except that even as she spoke the words, she knew they were untrue.

26

The hounds led them well, despite several attempts the kidnappers made to lose them. Running water stalled them for a while, and they bayed along the bank. It was a pitiful sound, not at all unlike the wailing of a bereaved woman.

Morgan sat her horse the entire time, murmuring what Persy suspected were incantations. For her part, Persy kept one hand on the piebald mare's mane. She had become accustomed to the horse's quirks, but she still missed Blazer.

When they finally reached the place, it was almost dark. A valley, cut by a stream, with a few houses tucked in the bottom of it.

"They're here," Morgan said, her voice soft but clear. No one had any reason to doubt her.

Persy shivered, as much at the tone of that voice as at anything else. Morgan scared her at the best of times, and right now...right now, she knew the witch was restraining herself from something stupid only with an effort.

It was Kay who spoke, the obvious: "It's a trap."

"Of course it's a trap," Arthur said. He turned to face both of them. "The question is how strong are the jaws?"

Badgers, Persy recalled, would roll on a trap and then eat the bait. That was what they needed to do here...roll on the trap. Not as easy as it sounded. The mare stirred under her, impatient despite the long journey.

"Perhaps," Kay added, "We should wait until dawn."

"They will expect us at dawn." Their voices were soft, only the occasional jingle from bridle buckles and bits might have betrayed their presence.

That was still more than Persy would have liked. As much as she wanted to swoop out of the night as an avenger of justice, Kay was right. The valley was the perfect site for an ambush.

Arthur hesitated, then, "We leave the horses here." He had had an idea, and Persy thought she saw the shape of it.

Almost. That was why he was the warleader. Because he thought of such things and took care of them for the rest.

They tethered the horses relatively loosely. If they did not return, the animals would break free and have a chance of survival. Or, more likely, be stolen, but Persy did not think about that. Blazer was safe, and she cared little for the mare. Only for her son.

Arthur moved along the ridge. Ah, yes. There was a trail leading down the side of the valley. Not much of one, perhaps made by fallow deer. It was enough, though, to transform the descent from foolhardy into reasonable.

Quiet, quiet, quiet. If they were heard then it was entirely possible all three children would be killed.

That thought kept Persy from even breathing, until she caught herself at it. No. Holding her breath would achieve less than nothing. Far less than, in fact. Yet, she could hardly resist the temptation to do just that. Any sound...

A twig snapped and she held her breath again. Below them, she heard voices. What if the children weren't there? What if they had been moved on, quickly, before the men could attack?

Had she been the kidnapper, she would likely have done just that. Trying not to think too much about it, she moved through the trees.

If they had been moved on, then they would still find them. Besides, Gwydion, if he could get to a weapon, might well be competent enough to rescue himself. The question was whether he was competent enough to rescue his betrothed and his brother. Elaine, Persy knew, was a good Christian girl. That meant she carried no weapon. And Mordred was a squalling infant.

Gwydion was the one she counted on to keep his head and do something, if he could do so without getting himself and the others killed. He might not be able to...and he was still a boy, lacking a man's judgment. That part did bother her.

And then they were in the valley. There was a house and several outbuildings, put together any way they fell. The house was square, Roman fashion, but the outbuildings were round. Stone mixed with wood and with the older wattle and daub. It was getting too cold to build that way.

How long would the winter last? Persy did not let her thoughts dwell on that, because a large, heavy dog launched itself at her.

Damn big dog, she thought. Damn big. She hated to do it, but she lifted her sword, slashed its throat. With an odd whimpering yelp it fell to the ground. She could not let herself feel bad for more than a second. She saw a second one leap past her. Somebody dispatched it, but from her current angle she could not determine who.

For a moment it seemed as if the dogs were alone, left there to protect on their own cognizance. Then came the men.

They were not Saxons, Persy noted almost clinically. They looked like Celts. Of course. This was about control and the fact that not everyone cared for Arthur. She let her thoughts flow away so that there was only the blade.

An opponent seemed to appear before her, as if transported by the gods. His blade slid through her sleeve, but she felt no pain. That did not mean she had not been hurt, and she slid her sword across his chest, opening a thin line that leaked red fluid sluggishly.

He did not react to the injury, but swung his own blade around, attempting to gut her. She parried, and then thrust into his stomach, slightly upwards. With a surprised yelp, he went down.

It took her a moment to free her sword. She heard Arthur's voice. "They're not here."

As she had feared, they moved on, leaving that small force behind to guard. She swore in Latin, wiping her blade on the grass.

The men were all dead. There had only been three or four of them. Enough to create the illusion that the place was occupied.

No. Not all dead. One lived, one little more than a boy. Perhaps not for much longer, as Arthur stood with a sword at the young man's throat and a grim expression on his face. "Why?"

"Ransom."

Good, Persy thought. If they were held as hostages for ransom or gain, they were far less likely to be slain. She had a chance of seeing her son again.

"Where?"

"They went towards the coast. They told me they would send a runner to you once they're secure."

"They won't have to bother. I will come to them." Arthur sounded as if he existed in that space beyond anger. "Bind him."

He intended, then, to make use of the boy to some purpose.

Obviously, the young man did not mean enough to any of them for an exchange, or he would not have been left behind. Perhaps a demonstration of mercy? Persy did not know. She looked at the dead dogs and sighed.

The south coast, facing Gaul, was marked by high cliffs of the purest white. Sailors spoke of them often. That was where they had taken Gwydion. Did they intend to take him to Gaul? Persy frowned.

The young man could have lied, even with his life at stake. Perhaps his words had been carefully prepared and planned. Had he said what he had been instructed to say?

From the top, of course, you could not see that the cliffs were white. You could only see how they fell off towards the oh so blue ocean. There was a legend that once you had been able to walk from there to Gaul.

Persy did not believe it. The land was the land, and it did not change that much. It remained while the generations of man passed. It was the one true constant. Of course, some also said that a giant had once walked from Wales to Ireland too. People told such stories, and they were true but not literal, their meaning at levels which she often could not understand. Or simply exaggerated.

She heard a "What ho!" in Kay's voice, and paid her attention to the road ahead. There was a shepherd, a young woman. She smiled coyly at the men, a smile that spoke of much invitation. She might not want the warriors, but she probably wanted their children. Morgan shot her a look. A look probably designed to warn her off any designs on the king himself.

Like that would stop Arthur...although he might well avoid wenching with his mistress standing nearby. Kay had no such limitations on him, and Persy thought he smiled back at her. Had she been closer, she would have elbowed him. They were on a mission, after all.

It was no time for men to fulfill their appetites. Still, the girl was pretty enough that it was hard to entirely blame them. Kay leaned down out of the saddle a little, talking to her. His horse was as big as he was. She wondered how he found anything large enough to ride. Even the Roman horses were not that big. She had a sudden image of a girl about the size of the shepherd leading a horse larger than any she had ever seen...no, it was an actual vision. The animal was black with white face and ankles. A true beauty, taller than the woman and with a proudly arched neck and rippling muscles.

She could only assume that such horses would be bred in the future, to lend their strength to man. Why, that horse could shift as much weight as a pair of oxen! And besides, she well recalled that once they had had only chariot ponies, before the Romans came. A man the size of Kay would not have been riding then.

Kay's conversation with the shepherd girl appeared to achieve something, for they turned to ride inland slightly. A valley formed a rift through the cliffs. It felt like another trap, but was that a hunch or just paranoia? The latter, she decided. Besides, if they truly wanted ransom....

But in what coin? Not, she feared, the coin of Rome. Mordred as hostage-fosterling? Morgan would never agree. Never in a million years, Persy thought. The witch rode stone-faced, although she did seem more relaxed with the talk of ransom. Not that she was likely to have any intention of paying it.

She was more likely to turn them all into toads, Persy thought wryly. She did not doubt that Morgan was capable of such an act. Unlike Merlin, she had no true higher nature to hold her back.

Persy reminded herself, she was human enough to love her son. Human enough to want to keep him safe, to want vengeance if he was harmed. Human enough to truly care for him.

Her one redeeming quality, perhaps. And she had said she intended no harm to Gwydion. Persy was not fool enough to believe her.

Nor was she fool enough to keep her blade sheathed as they rode into the valley. All of her instincts told her Gwydion was there. Elaine and Mordred she could not swear to.

Then fog rolled through the valley. She knew at once it was not natural, and her eyes sought Morgan. All the witch did was nod, however. If it was a spell, she was doing nothing obvious to counter it. Perhaps she did not want whoever it was to become aware of her presence.

There were but a few scraggly trees, yet Persy felt them reach for her, flow for her, their leaves rustling as if with the words of fairies. If there were fairies they were hiding. Like as not none among them were young enough or gifted enough to well perceive them.

Persy had not seen or felt the presence of so much as a pixie in months. Yet the valley felt almost like a fae place, but twisted. Perhaps the fair folk were angry? That would explain why none had been seen of late.

Of course, Cadan insisted fairies were demons. Naturally, they would avoid somebody who kept insulting them. Who wouldn't? She wondered what would happen if that belief spread. A lot of people's butter would be soured, that was for certain.

Well. She had no problems with fairies. Of course, they sometimes caused trouble, but no more than small children. Unless one was dealing with the Sidhe.

Morgan had Sidhe blood, as Merlin did, for the Sidhe would often take and then abandon human lovers. Was that what she sensed?

"They're down there," Morgan breathed, then she glanced at Persy. For a moment, it seemed as if the witch was going to ask her something, then she thought better of it.

"My nephew had better not have been hurt," Persy muttered. She did worry more about Elaine. She was too good a girl for this. Good by their standards.

"Don't go any further," Morgan warned. "Whoever is with them is quite competent."

For a moment, Persy almost wished Cadan had come along. Extra magical support. But he was not here, and in balance she preferred that. She would prefer it if the monk vanished permanently.

But for now, she waited, forcing her thoughts to stop wandering. Her mind tried to evade the reality of being here, with the cold fog licking up towards her. With her son somewhere in there. And none of the three had magical talent. Well, Mordred almost certainly did, but he was an infant. However...

Persy nudged her horse closer to Morgan. "I have an idea."

The witch frowned. Accepting advice from others was not her strong point. But she did not say nay.

"I know how strong the bond is between mother and child. For those magically talented, it must be stronger. Perhaps you could...connect with Mordred somehow. Maybe use a link to find out what's going on in there."

Morgan arched an eyebrow. "I tried to scry, but..."

"They can't block *that*." Persy kept her voice down, not wanting anyone to hear a man speaking of mothers' matters.

"I would ask you to help."

Persy frowned. How could she let her disguise get in the way of saving Gwydion? How would Arthur react?

Did he know anyway? Did she really think she had everyone

fooled? "We need to get those kids."

Galahad looked at them. At her, in that way of his. It made her feel odd. No, she did not love him. Or did she?

She had to think of Gwydion. "Let's do it."

Galahad watched them.

"Just think of Gwydion. I'll do the rest."

Persy focused in her mind. The image of the boy, with his hound puppy running at his side. An image of a happy day, such that if he felt it, if he sensed it or her, he would remember that day. He would remember it and feel some hope, feel less trapped.

The breeze seemed to be scented better as she closed her eyes. She had, at some point, dismounted...she did not quite remember doing so.

Morgan did have fae blood. The blood she had inherited from Merlin. And her own gift resonated, through the connection between them.

In that moment, she was able to forgive Morgan everything. Even if the moment did not last.

27

It was Morgan's voice that broke the spell. "They live and are unharmed. However, there are alarm wards ahead of us. Please, let me deal with them."

Arthur look right at Persy. Did he suspect? Of course, it was entirely possible he knew all along. Those who shared a bed often developed a bond of their own. Some claimed they could recognize a lover through any disguise.

Arthur, though, could barely tell his lovers from his enemies. She dismissed the idea. He was not a perceptive man where women were concerned and she had never given him a lovers' gaze. Not since he had chosen to marry Guinevere.

She still did not understand why. Perhaps Morgan had tried a love spell and had it backfire on her. Or perhaps it really was politics, ill-considered but making its own sense. The witch murmured under her breath.

"What were the two of you doing?" Galahad asked.

"A bit of...similarity magic."

"Wouldn't Arthur have been better?"

"Not in Morgan's terms. By the old law, before the Romans came, Gwydion would have been my heir, not Arthur's. He's my sister-son." Galahad, of course, knew the truth. Her words were for public consumption, an attempt to salvage the situation.

"Aha." That came from Morgan. "Got you, you..."

The fog abruptly vanished. It did not clear, but was simply gone. She saw the beach and the sea beyond. The perfect place for smugglers or raiders, she thought. Or for sneaking away by sea. Could they prevent that? Supposedly, Arthur had bought a couple of sea captains against just that contingency, but a small boat...especially under cover of fog...could often sneak past a ship.

But the valley took on a different aspect. It was no longer a frightening place, but rather a beautiful one. Definitely beautiful, Persy thought. There were even flowers in places. Bluebells.

"Okay, now it seems too nice."

"Indeed." Morgan nudged her horse forward, to glares from the various men. None of them wanted her riding next to Arthur. Well, perhaps not none. But very few. Too few, Persy thought with some sadness. The Christians were winning out.

Morgan seemed like a fragile figure. Unbelievably dangerous, possibly even evil, but also threatened. Perhaps everything she did could be excused. No, not everything.

She had seduced the king. She threatened Gwydion, whether she admitted it...or even intended to...or not. What did she intend? To survive, Persy realized. She had, perhaps, bound her soul so tightly to her patron that she stood or fell with the old religion.

Persy shook her head. The gods would wait. The gods were patient. Then they were walking through the valley itself. She saw the danger. The flowers were more and more numerous, better and better scented. A trap, and a subtle one. Morgan kept moving, though, and Arthur followed her.

She had his soul more ensorceled than any spell, but it would not last. He would tire of her as he had tired of Persy. As he had tired of Guinevere. And then, suddenly, Uluru was moving past them. He seemed hypernaturally alert, and moved with surprising silence. Arthur started to signal him to wait, but Kay murmured, "Let him go."

And then he was gone. He had vanished so thoroughly that Persy wondered at it. How did a man disappear in a forest? She supposed, the same way the fensmen vanished. Training and practice. What more was there? Magic...but she had never suspected him of that. Morgan frowned but kept moving.

Coils of bramble lay close to the trail, waiting to snare the unwary. They were the flowering kind and white blooms glinted between the thorns.

Persy thought she could live there, settle down when her fighting days were well and truly over. A little cottage, close to the beach, tucked in the base of the valley. Set just above the lines of tide and flood.

She shook her head. And learn to fish? Persy was no fisherman, and she knew it. She would be better off raising horses on the edge of the hill country.

The place had a magic about it. She wondered at the outlaws who had chosen it for their home.

Or were they outlaws? She had no clue what they wanted, beyond ransom. It could just be that they were desperate men. Desperate men might do anything, hurt anyone. Did they want money, or some other coin?

Some other coin, she decided. A place, perhaps, a place for themselves in the world. Why did she have that insight?

And then, the arrows started to fly.

The ambush was as inevitable as night following day. Those who sought to slay them would have a harder time of it than they likely suspected. Persy went down, quickly, neatly, pulling out her own bow as she rolled back to her feet. Her arm still hurt from the previous fight, but not enough to be serious. Not enough to bother her with her adrenalin up.

As she loosed the arrow, it did not even hurt. But she missed, the shaft burying itself in a tree. She was not the best archer, though, and other shafts flew past her. The yells indicated that several had found their way home.

She could not help but smile at that. She had not been hit, but she was sure others had been. There were shouts. Somebody nearby groaned with the pain of a bad wound. She hoped it was not one of her close friends. That sound was an audible prelude to inevitable death.

Well, they could not have expected to handle it without somebody dying.

Then she heard a shriek. Elaine's voice. She turned and ran towards it. So little disregard did she have for her own safety that the gods must have been with her, for she plunged through the trees and reached the small cabin set amongst them unscathed.

A guard had a knife to the girl's throat. Gwydion stood there with a sword, presumably taken from a second man. That man lay on the floor in a pool of blood.

Good work, Gwydion, Persy thought, but she stopped, ducking to one side of the doorway, hopefully before she could be seen. The thin, high wail of an infant also echoed within.

"You woke up the baby," Elaine said, her tone hysterical.

Maybe Persy could snatch Mordred...but no. Elaine was the one in danger, even as the battle expanded outside. She forced herself to breathe evenly, forced herself to remain quiet.

Gwydion lowered the blade a little. He could not risk the obvious threat being carried out. Apparently, he had not seen her, or if he had, was ensuring that even his gaze would not betray her.

What did she do? When they came charging in, Elaine would die. She had to prevent that. The girl was not blood family, but Persy cared for her nonetheless. Yet she had no magic to help her, nothing but a mother's love and her wits. The windows? Boarded and shuttered, the light came from the door and from a Roman style lamp on the table. There was no getting behind him.

Mordred was still crying. "Shut up," the guard said, turning a bit towards the crib...more like a box...they had placed him in.

Like a kid that age listened. All he knew was that he wanted his food or to be cleaned. Or, most likely, for everyone else to shut up.

Elaine did not scream again. She stood there, her eyes wide for a moment. Then she did the last thing Persy would have expected.

She stepped on her assailant's foot, grinding her heel into his instep. It was a surprisingly effective move. The man dropped the knife and she spun away towards Gwydion.

Persy stepped into the room. "I see we weren't really needed here."

"What kept you?" Gwydion asked, his tone amused as he advanced on the guard, placing himself between him and the crib.

"Hey, we got here as quickly as we could." That was about when everyone else came charging into the room.

28

It was a rather subdued party that rode back. Only one of the kidnappers survived other than the boy. He had died rather than talk and the boy had turned out to know nothing.

Morgan rode with one hand, Mordred in her arms. Gwydion and Elaine rode together. That relieved Persy. She saw a new chemistry between them. They might, after all, make something of this marriage. At the very least, they could be friends. A marriage between friends could work.

She herself hung back. They were calling her a hero, but she knew the real hero was Gwydion himself. And Elaine. Perhaps especially Elaine. How many good Christian girls would fight back?

They waited until they heard the battle before trying to break free, and they had come close to succeeding.

But they had also come close to getting themselves killed. Arthur had some choice words for his son.

Elaine seemed a lot less moonstruck by Uluru than she had been, although she did give him a look. If the kidnapping had gotten that crush out of her system, it would almost be worth it.

Almost.

Although it was summer, there was still the slightest of chills to the air, at least to her perception. Persy wondered if people would get used to the cold, to the wet. Perhaps their children would know nothing else, until the cycle changed again and the warmth came back.

By the time it did, she suspected people would have forgotten. People would not believe they had once grown grapes not far south of the Wall. The Wall itself might one day crumble, the Picts and Scotti emerging from their woods to mingle with the rest. She laughed inwardly. Supposedly there was a lot of graffiti scribbled on the Wall. That would probably survive until the end of time, including the crude comments left by soldiers. Soldiers on what was considered the worst...or at least the coldest...assignment in the Empire.

Maybe that was the real reason the eagles had flown. The Wall had gotten too cold for them. Persy shook her head, pulling her thoughts back to the fall of her horse's hooves on the road. Such as it was.

Her mind flickered with a vision of horseless carriages tearing at speed down a black surfaced road, and then back to the present. How were such things powered? With magic?

No, with knowledge they did not yet have. She knew that. Yet, she also knew magic and the fae would survive in odd corners.

Then Morgan called a halt. It was hard for her to ride while carrying her son and at first Persy thought she was tired or needed to feed the boy.

Then she felt it herself, like an electric current in the air. Somebody was using dark magic, and for once it was not Morgan. Persy breathed in, then out, and her eyes sought Gwydion and Elaine. She prayed briefly to Athena, a much more pleasant war goddess than the Morrigan.

Then she saw it. She was not the only one...this was no vision or hallucination. It was dark and wild...not evil, but uncontrolled, raw power.

It was a dragon, a red one, and it rose above them, the horses whickering, on the verge of panic.

Then it turned, a despairing cry, and flew into the west and was gone. It left behind it only a sense of great loss.

"The age truly is over," Morgan said, softly. "The last of the dragons has departed."

Persy felt it too. Would they ever return? She did not know. She only knew that the amount of magic had decreased again.

Yet, that dragon had made sure they saw her, made sure they knew she was leaving. Why? Was it a warning?

They would call Arthur Pendragon and forget that it was only a banner. Persy shook her head. Would she be remembered as a woman or as a man? What would they call her?

The horses settled, and Arthur turned back to the road. Persy was not close to him, but she fancied the man was weeping.

29

The winter did not go well. Tensions were high, and everyone was picking fights with everyone else. Morgan and Guinevere catfought then retreated to opposite ends of the high table, glaring at each other. Gwydion got into it with Uluru over Elaine, who was back to admiring the older man's view at every opportunity. The crush did not seem to be fading.

Uluru, for his part, spent more time in the queen's bedchamber than Arthur did, and Arthur spent his time alternately with Morgan and with various of the servants.

For her own part, Persy found herself snapping at Uluru, Galahad and even Gwydion.

She hid in the place she preferred at such times...the corrals. She brushed not just her own horse, but Gwydion's pony. Arthur had found him a good one. Yet, it was not enough. Merlin had vanished again, but mercifully so had Brother Cadan. At least they did not have to deal with those two sniping.

She decided to stick to the horses for now...but her peace was not to last. Galahad came slipping into the corrals.

"I see I'm not the only one looking for a mane to hide in."

Persy made a face. "I'm about to hit somebody myself. I swear there's something in the air or the water."

"I think it's the odd weather."

"I don't think the weather's going back to what it was," Persy admitted. "And it's going to get worse this winter, look at their coats."

"They always know, don't they." Galahad moved over closer to her. "Instinct, I suppose."

"I doubt they know. It just happens. They're only horses, and not

178

nearly as smart as we are. But they can't exactly choose to grow a long coat."

"Or we'd all have better hair," Galahad quipped. "Percy..."

"What?" She paused. "Who is she?"

"Nobody," he said. "It's something else. I'm not sure what, but I feel very restless."

"Probably whatever's making everyone else snippy. The snow, the cabin fever." Even by the standards of recent years, it was a bad winter.

"I don't get cabin fever," Galahad complained.

"You have it now. Let's go for a walk?"

"People will..."

"I don't care what people say. I'm tired of people talking about who is, or might be, bedding whom, anyway." She gave him a wry grin. "We know nothing's happening, who cares about anyone else."

They stepped out into the snow. Persy hoped the next winter would be milder. If this harsh weather carried on...was that why Camelot was eventually abandoned?

No. It would have to be more than that, a far more significant series of events. More likely it was no longer needed. A better fort elsewhere, perhaps? Or perhaps the Saxons won in the end.

Perhaps nobody won. "Galahad..."

"Yeah?"

"Do you think we can really keep things as they are?"

"Nobody can. What we can do is make sure something survives. The important stuff, like, say, the children."

She smiled at him. "Yeah, the children matter." Now that was one couple that was not sniping at each other.

In two years they would be wed. Two years. Five minutes, in any reasonable awareness of time. But they were not 'her' children, not any more. She wanted to see Elaine present Arthur with a grandchild, but... She shook her head.

"You wish you had your own?" Galahad spoke carefully. They were not that far from the fort.

"Some days," Persy admitted. She wished she had a second child, one she could have kept. A daughter, perhaps. Her son was no longer hers in any meaningful way, most certainly his betrothed would not be. Their children would probably think Guinevere was their grandmother.

"Me too, except..."

"Finding the right woman is the hard part, isn't it? What about that new cook?"

"She's..." Galahad frowned. "Almost too good looking. Know what I mean?"

"As in, you wonder how somebody that pretty isn't married yet and assume there must be a good reason."

"Right!" He flickered her a grin. "Like a tongue as sharp as that sword of Arthur's."

"No," Persy considered. "It's not her tongue. It's definitely something else. Maybe she's lousy in bed."

"Could try her out. Or maybe she's known to be barren."

"She's too young to be sure of that. I bet it's that she's burdened with a *mother*." Persy emphasized the last word.

"Oh God. Maybe that's it. What is it about some women that they turn into harridans in the presence of their sons-in-law?"

"They don't want another man around their daughter." Persy frowned.

Yes. And thus she placed a firm finger on her own uncertainty, her own concerns. It was nothing more than a mother's normal feelings when a son was married off, risen premature by the circumstances.

"I think I can see that. Why are women so untrusting of men?"

"Because men think about sex." She ducked from him, laughing a bit. She felt safe, now they were that bit further away.

"Like women don't think about sex. That's one thing that Cadan says that is emphatically not true."

"He thinks that way because he's never had a woman. Maybe a man."

Galahad snorted. "No. I don't think any man would want him. Any woman, either."

"I wonder where he is."

"Snowed in. Hopefully somewhere miserable."

As that was, indeed, the most likely explanation for the priest's absence, Persy fell silent. There was only the snow and the trees, and somewhere the wings of a pheasant clapping together as it took off.

Then another and another and a small flock of the birds aloft. Galahad made a shooting motion in their direction, and then gave her a regretful look.

"Yeah, I wish I had a bow too." Her mouth watered a little at the thought of fresh pheasant. "We should get back. It's cold."

"Too cold."

But she felt a lot better as she trudged back up the hill. The question was, did he?

That question was never answered. Spring returned, and Cadan with it. The grey horse had vanished. Instead, he had acquired a new mule, a white one that seemed even more of an obnoxious jerk than its rider.

At least it was primarily obnoxious towards Cadan himself, stepping on his feet and giving him a distinctly innocent mule look when he slapped it on the shoulder. Very clearly, it had done it accidentally on purpose.

Persy stifled a laugh, and then ducked into the barracks to avoid him. She was not in the mood for one of his transparent conversion attempts. From what she could hear, though, he went straight into the great hall.

She emerged and went over to the mule. It snorted at her. "Be nice," she told it. "A guy who spends as much time with books as he does is bound to be a lousy rider."

All she got for her pains was a forward flick of one large ear, and then it went back to its hay.

"Beastly beast," said Gwydion, from nearby, one hand on his pup's collar.

"It is a mule. The problem with mules is they're smarter than we are." For some reason, Cadan seemed to prefer them. Maybe it had something to do with his god apparently having a thing for donkeys? The priest was too big to realistically ride one of those, so he settled for a mule.

"Heh," said Gwydion, running a hand through the dog's fur. It was lanky and gangly, close on full grown, although not as huge as its sire.

"Pup's looking good. What did you end up naming him?"

"Snow," Gwydion said.

An appropriate name, the hound being pure white with black ears. She imagined the ears were roots sticking out of the snow and laughed silently to herself. Then she held out a hand for Snow. He sniffed it, and let her scratch him behind the ears. "Nice pup."

"Not really a pup any more. He's pretty much turned into a dog."

"He's as close to being a dog as you are to being a man, but he'll get there a little sooner."

Gwydion laughed. "Not that much sooner."

Like most boys, he saw his own adulthood as a wave he was cresting, not realizing it was really a hill, that grew larger each time you thought you got to the top. "Be patient. There is no sense being in a hurry on the matter."

The pup licked Persy's hand.

"I suppose not. He certainly doesn't seem to be."

She laughed. "Some dogs never quit being puppies. Some men never quit being boys." She definitely knew a few like that.

"I guess some women never quit being girls either."

"It's rarer. Women do not think or feel the same as men." Except that she had faked it so well for years she had begun to wonder. "Girls play at what they will do as women and reach for it. Boys tend to try and cling to their youth."

Gwydion considered that. "I wonder if women seek to regain their childhood through their children."

That was a remarkably insightful comment. Again, Persy reckoned Gwydion smarter than his sire. "Some do, I suspect. Or other people's children, depending." Some women surrounded themselves with any child that would hang out with them.

"Like old Mistress Lucia."

"Exactly like her." The old woman, her own children long since grown, would watch any child for anyone at any time. And did a good job of it, too. Persy might not be that kind of woman herself, but she understood. Sometimes, she even envied.

"Some men like children too, but I suppose it's different."

"You don't have the same feelings and instincts that a woman does. You'll see when Elaine has children. Even the husband had better not get between them and interfere."

He laughed. "I'll remember that. But you never married." He peered at her.

"I have a sister, remember."

"I wish I did," Gwydion said, rather abruptly. "I only have a brother, and he's not really my brother and too young to be any fun."

Persy laughed a bit. "He's your half-brother. But definitely too young to be any fun. Give him a few years."

Of course, by the time Mordred was old enough to be any fun, Gwydion would be a man with children of his own. He would be more like his nephew than his brother. She did not voice that for now.

"He'll take after his mother anyway," Gwydion predicted.

"You don't like Morgan?"

His face clouded. "I don't trust her. And she's spending far too much time with Elaine."

That, Persy did not like herself. But which was worse? Morgan or

Guinevere? She was no longer sure. "Could be worse. She could be hanging out with Brother Cadan, being told that she needs to be a meek, submissive vessel."

"She's already too much of one. Or was. I suppose..." Gwydion tailed off. "I don't know that I want to marry her, but I suppose I have no choice."

"You could do a lot worse. She's pretty, she's nice, she likes you."

"She's my friend."

"That's a good start. Just because you don't feel amazing passion for her...in fact, you're probably better off without it. Look at your dad."

"I...won't make his mistakes. But what do I do if she can't?"

"You very discreetly find somebody who can, but don't hop around and don't brag about it. Or, more importantly, let *her* brag about it. You're a catch." Women went for powerful men. Persy had felt that way herself more than once.

"Or have her find somebody."

"That might be the smartest of all. If she's level headed enough not to mind."

"I think she would be upset but understand the necessity. Maybe one day, we will come up with better ways to handle it."

"Maybe."

Then Persy heard a light voice calling, "Gwydion." Elaine.

"Your future wife is calling."

"I should go."

"Watch out. She'll get you trained up in no time." Persy quipped. She watched him go.

Yeah. Definitely well trained already.

30

It finally seemed that peace had settled on the land. Some of the men went home for good, but the most loyal, of course, remained. Persy was going nowhere. What else would she do? Putter around the family estate as an old maid? Their lands did not need her, and they would go to her cousin...who enjoyed being a farmer.

She supposed she should have felt some pride that her line would sit the throne, but it remained tempered. Especially by the battle for Elaine's loyalties. Morgan was clearly trying to convert her to the old religion. Guinevere was backing her adherence to the new.

The poor girl, Persy thought. She wasn't too surprised to see her seeking support from Uluru. As long as that was all she was getting from him. She was slowly filling out into a woman, but it would be another year before she could wed. If he touched her now, he risked putting her with child too soon, and then she might well die.

Not to mention the embarrassment if she pushed out offspring that was darker than it should have been. That was why Persy was cornering Uluru.

"I haven't touched her," he said, soft but defensive. "She's too young for me, not to mention promised to another man. No more than a child." A pause. "She is the daughter I never had, nothing more."

Persy nodded. "I know. But we can't have any talk, and people are talking." Another aspect of the tension that came when those bred for war tried to deal with peace. "And it takes so little to encourage a girl like that. She has got to accept that she is with Gwydion, nobody else. It's bad enough that Guinevere..."

Uluru flinched.

"Guinevere is barren. She can get away with her bed hopping, as

184

embarrassing as it is. Elaine can't even get away with looking." That flinch told her that he was, indeed, sleeping with Guinevere again.

Well, better Uluru than Bedivere or Kay. Kay had probably turned her down flat. He wouldn't do that to Arthur. Bedivere had no interest in women. Everyone else, though...was she the only one of the core group who hadn't shared Guinevere's bed? Galahad hadn't. He was far too much the gallant for that. Kay hadn't.

Pellinore? No, not with that harridan he was married to at court, sniping at the other ladies. He didn't love her, and she doubted he loved any woman, but... Realistically, it was probably only Uluru and maybe Gawain. Plus anyone outside that inner circle she had managed to seduce. There was no other word for her behavior.

Then Brother Cadan reappeared. He was accompanied by several other clerics. An entire entourage, in fact. Amusingly, they all rode better than he did. Persy stepped away from Uluru to watch.

They dismounted from their various mounts and walked towards the Great Hall. Giving the black man an 'I'll talk later' look, Persy followed them.

Arthur was in there talking with Kay. Both were very focused on each other, the easy chemistry between them yet more evidence that the latter had not touched Guinevere.

Of the queen, there was no sign.

"Your Majesty," Brother Cadan said, clearly.

He had the gall to disturb the king? But Arthur looked relieved to be disturbed, suggesting that the topic of conversation was distinctly less than entertaining.

If he was relieved by *this* crowd showing up, Persy reckoned it would have to be absolutely boring. She moved off to one side, positioning herself where she could hear.

"This," Brother Cadan introduced, "is Marcellus, the Bishop of London."

What was a bishop? The Christian equivalent of an Archdruid or High Priest, she supposed, from the reverence with which Cadan delivered the name and title. He was using the short form of Londinium, too, but the priest he introduced had a Roman name and manner.

Maybe things would always be that mix...and if Saxon customs ended up mixed in as well, who knew what British life would be like?

"Indeed?" Arthur's tone showed curiosity, but also, yes, faint boredom.

Persy decided he would rather be hunting, and the sleeping white shape on the floor not far away would also probably prefer that activity.

"He is here to properly consecrate the chapel. I cannot do it effectively."

So, Cadan was going to let the chapel be consecrated. What did that mean, if her suspicions about him were right? Persy felt some relief, though. Was that all? Well, Marcellus would no doubt try to convert her again, but like he was going to succeed where so many had failed? Not a chance.

He might sway a few. She studied him. No. He was overweight, for one thing, when they often had barely enough here. He looked like a man who never did anything physical...yet he was still a better rider than Cadan.

Maybe Cadan just hated riding. But that fat, well dressed, Roman man did not belong here. Not amongst the lean, hungry predators that dominated Arthur's court. Merlin could fit in. Cadan could fit in.

Not that guy. She dismissed him as anything of significance, and went to find her weapons.

The church was consecrated. Persy watched from outside, holding back deliberately. At least this Marcellus seemed to be genuinely a priest. She wondered that Cadan had brought him in, once more. Maybe he had no choice.

It might have to do with church hierarchy...but nobody would know that or care. There were also rumors that Cadan was not a proper priest, surprisingly not started by her. Which might mean he feared they would not see the chapel as consecrated. That would explain why he had not done this sooner.

Well, it was being properly done with him right there. So, perhaps, he was not a demon after all. Or perhaps he was a very canny one. Demons, most kinds, avoided any kind of holy ground, but somebody had murdered that girl right in that chapel.

Did that mean the Christian God was false? Or did it mean...something else? Perhaps it meant all of the gods had weakened. But if they had, so should the demons.

She thought of the dragon and shuddered. And then the fat form of Marcellus approached her. He was clearly aimed right at her like an arrow. She would have preferred the arrow.

She managed not to shudder. He needed to spend less time at the trencher. "Sir Percival," he greeted her. "You were not inside."

Did she lie or tell the truth? "I felt it better to leave the limited room to people more interested in the proceedings."

He huffed under his breath. "We should all be interested in the one, true God."

"Maybe, but I'd rather spend my time with a good sword." She watched for his reaction.

"Or a kitchen wench?"

She did not deny that, not wanting the man to think her a practitioner of the Greek vice. "I'm not very interested in the Church. Please forgive me."

"If I forgive you, I leave your soul to burn."

Her eyes desperately sought an escape. At least Cadan had given up on her. Of course, Marcellus did not know how stubborn she was. Finally, she came out with, "At least I'd be in better company."

He turned red from his collar to his receding hairline. "You do not talk to a Bishop like that!"

His alarm caught Arthur's attention. "What is going on here?" The king's voice, deep and rich, reminded her of when they had been lovers.

"Your man insulted me."

Persy's lips quirked. "You know I don't get on with clerics."

Arthur frowned. "You will be civil to the bishop, Percival."

"Then I think it is best if I avoid him," she said, clearly.

"He seems determined not to pay any attention to God," the bishop complained.

He sounded like a petulant child.

Arthur laughed a bit. "You can't win everyone over, Marcellus. Percival has not budged in several years of attempts. He won't budge for you. Let it be."

"And let him burn in hell."

Arthur's eyes narrowed. "Both of you. Let it be. Marcellus, come. We have some things we need to discuss."

Rescued by the king. Yet when their eyes met, she was utterly sure. Arthur did know who she was. Knew and was allowing the masquerade to continue.

Perhaps he had his reasons. Or perhaps she had actually proved herself, and he did not wish to lose a good warrior.

Either way, she made good her escape, heading back to the barracks. She was not the first to leave. Bedivere and another man were dicing in the corner. She ignored them, never having cared for games of chance. Most likely because she tended to lose.

Instead, she tugged out a pair of boots that needed to be fixed or thrown away, studying them. Finding them, in fact, very interesting indeed. Marcellus would be here all summer and he would not leave her alone. Should she leave?

No. She didn't wish to leave everyone else to deal with the...

"Asshole," somebody proclaimed as he entered.

She stared. It was Galahad, and such a word from him was the equivalent of a stream of invective from anyone else. "Who?"

"Bishop Marcellus. He's trying to talk Arthur into making baptism compulsory for everyone at court."

"Arthur won't go for that." Arthur might be Christian himself, but there was no way he would force his beliefs on others.

"What if the bishop forces him?"

"How could he do that?"

"There's this new concept being bandied around. Displease the church and the priests go somewhere else. Or...something. Marcellus is basically saying either everyone becomes Christian or he's going to order no priest to serve the people here who are."

"And Christianity is a religion where people are heavily reliant on their priests." It was a real threat.

Persy would not...she might have lived one lie for years, but she had no wish to add another. "Morgan."

"Good point." Galahad frowned. "We may lose the peace we have so carefully built."

"Arthur will send him packing. You watch."

For once, she got the last word.

Whatever Arthur said to Marcellus did indeed send him packing, for the moment. He took his entourage with him except for Cadan.

Perhaps Cadan was defying an edict, or perhaps one had not been given. Persy was just relieved that things had not come to too much of a head. She was even more relieved to not have seen Morgan muttering curses after the bishop...well, except for calling him a 'fat fool'. Persy agreed with the sentiment, but was a little less willing to voice it.

Morgan, no doubt, had influenced his departure, but like as not in purely mundane ways.

Persy stood on the wall, watching the last of their dust vanish on the road. "Good riddance to bad rubbish."

"Indeed." Morgan's voice, from nearby.

Persy turned. The other woman was clad in red. "I was worried he was going to split the court."

"Even Constantine was not so...forceful. As long as vague lip service was paid...but forcing people to swear oaths?"

"The only oath I'm willing to swear is allegiance to Arthur." Persy studied Morgan for a moment. "I follow the old gods, but oaths are a tricky thing.

Morgan nodded. "I trust that oath, and that is why I leave you be." She paused. "Especially as I suspect we now *know* we are on the same side and you are not..."

Competition, Persy filled in. "He will tire of you."

"Like as not. It is the kind of man he is. But I have what I want from him."

Mordred was growing into a sturdy lad. But Persy wondered if the witch might not have preferred a daughter. Then again, who had more aptitude for magic than Merlin? There were exceptions to the rule that women were generally stronger. "My nephew is still older." Stupid to remind her of that.

"You still think it is the throne I seek?" Morgan turned towards her.

"I honestly don't know. I know you seek power."

"I seek to ensure that if not the king then somebody close to him will always speak for the old ways. I know you neither like nor trust me, but Gwydion is coming to care for his brother. Like as not his oldest son will be even closer to Mordred. It is the only way."

Persy digested that. "They're winning."

"A battle here and there. Not the war."

"Does it have to be a war?" Persy turned her gaze back out over the parapet, back to the fields and woods.

"When they acknowledge none save their own, they give us no choice." Morgan's voice was dangerously soft. "I find it hard to believe their God truly demands that."

"Maybe somebody mistranslated something he said?" Persy suggested, still staring out at the trees.

"More likely mistranslated something a prophet said. Or, perhaps likeliest of all, thought somebody a prophet who was not."

"Or Constantine inserted that to consolidate his power. It's almost a shame it didn't work." Not in the end. Rome had fallen anyway, for reasons that clearly had little to do with religion. For reasons Persy could not see and understand beyond 'nothing lasts forever'.

"Given Constantine also stole his god's birth date from the Mithrans, that would not surprise me."

Persy had not known that. Her brow furrowed for a moment and then she laughed sharply. "Of course he did. Had to keep the loyalty of the soldiers."

"Indeed. I almost feel sorry for him. He knew his world was about to end, and he struggled to save it."

"Just as we are doing." We? With Morgan? But they were on the same side on the matter, if few others.

"The difference is that I know we cannot retain control. What I do is set the seeds that will some day bloom again. But you know that."

Persy frowned. "Yes, I do. I know it only too well." She saw no vision, though, even though she closed her eyes and sought one.

The gods clearly thought she needed none.

"Then, perhaps, we can be allies?"

"I still neither like nor trust you." The last word against Galahad, she had expected. Against Morgan? She wondered if the witch was sick.

31

Sometimes, it seemed as if five minutes had passed since she held Gwydion in her arms, a mere babe.

Suddenly, he was sixteen years old and a man, and taking one of those important steps toward adulthood. They had insisted on a Christian ceremony. Worse, Persephone had to be there. Percival was sick, confined to his quarters with something unpleasant and mildly contagious. She suspected even Arthur would back her up.

But a Christian ceremony made her profoundly uncomfortable. She wore a plain gown, not wishing to outshine the bride. Guinevere seemed to have no such compunction.

The vows would bind him and Elaine together for the rest of their lives. Except, of course, one or both would likely break them. It seemed few did not. As long as Elaine produced Gwydion an heir, though...

Things were so much more sensible when inheritance ran through women. A woman knows the child she has birthed, a man can never be sure. Yet, it was where they were. It was the world they lived in. It would change, the cycle would come back.

But it bothered her that Elaine, in her soft voice, swore to obey Gwydion in all things. The only thing he swore was to 'honor' her. As if those were...no, they were not meant to be equal.

Cadan and his words about adultery in a woman being worse than in a man. Everything else the Christians had said. She did not scowl. She knew that no matter what was sworn, Elaine would not be merely Gwydion's servant.

Oh no, there was too much quiet inner-strength in her for that. She would hold her own, vows or no vows. On the other hand, she had not hesitated to swear them.

She knew she had no choice. Persy was glad she had never wed. In fact, she was glad that Arthur had not wed her, had not forced her into those vows. It would have been the fight to end all fights had he tried. Possibly ending in one or both of them seriously hurt.

Elaine, though, had that knowing look on her face as she led Gwydion...clearly not the other way around...out of the chapel.

Galahad gave Persy a wry look. "And thus the son of the king goes to his doom."

"What do you know about it? You've never been married."

"Neither have you. But there has to be a reason every groom I've ever seen has looked terrified and every bride smug."

Persy flickered him a grin. "Because men only *think* they go after women. It's always the other way around."

Morgan, hearing them, just gave them both arch looks and then left the church. She made subtle dust shaking motions with her feet as she did so.

Persy was tempted to follow suit, but she did not quite dare. Besides, Galahad was scowling at Morgan's rear.

"At least you're nice about it."

She grinned at him. "I have no problem with anyone worshipping whatever god or gods they choose."

"Neither do I. Just don't ask me to pray to yours."

"Completely fair." She wondered if Gwydion and Elaine would avoid shivaree. Most likely not. She was certainly, though, not planning on participating. She planned on vanishing halfway through the party and then claiming drunkenness the next day.

He was too old for her to see him in a state of undress and besides she had never cared for the custom. Trying to draw no attention to herself, she finally slipped into the Great Hall.

Bedivere was already regaling people with a story about when Gwydion was about eight...that she had heard fifty times before. At least. Ignoring him, she moved over to a long table on which the kitchen servants had placed assorted food. They seemed to be serving in a less formal style than a high dinner, more suited to mingling. Grabbing a trencher, she filled it up, but she kept one eye on Gwydion. He seemed relaxed, although his eyes kept glancing to Elaine.

She still looked smug. Hopefully she had finally forgotten about Uluru and turned her attention towards the man she was supposed to be with.

Elaine could be happy with Gwydion. Would she?

Persy glanced around the room. She wondered if anyone was where they wanted to be, was even *who* they wanted to be. How many woven lies kept Camelot functioning?

And how many of their children and grandchildren would call it a golden age. Her mind swirled into a vision. A wedding, the bride in flowing white, her face veiled. The groom looking as terrified as they always did. They stood on an open field, not in a church or temple. The true temple of the gods, she thought, was all creation. Then she was back in the party.

A reminder, she supposed, that life would go on no matter what, and weddings would happen as long as there were people.

As long as there were women, too, they would get pregnant. Elaine's courses stopped coming immediately, and it was soon very clear that she was already carrying Gwydion's child.

It was autumn, and the men rode out hunting with spears. It was boar they pursued, a particularly large and fine specimen having been seen nearby.

Persy, having returned to male guise as soon as was reasonable, sat Blazer easily. The horse was old, but the youngster she had purchased was still a two-year-old, too young to be ridden. Gwydion rode with his father, laughing.

She would be a grandmother in a few short months. It would be Gwydion's last free hunt before he had a son of his own. Elaine, of course, did not leave the keep. She was with Guinevere. Probably the best place for her. The two got on very well indeed. Almost too well...they were like mother and daughter. Or two peas from the same pod. Persy was glad Guinevere, not Morgan, had won their brief battle for the girl's heart.

Uluru rode at the back, as far from Gwydion and Arthur as he might. Whatever he was doing now, it was not making him happy. It presumably had something to do with Guinevere. But he had never, as far as Persy could tell, been a truly happy man. Sometimes, he reached the edges of it. At such times, he was fun to be with.

Right now, he was nowhere close to that. Arthur and Guinevere were, most definitely, on the outs once more. Perhaps Gwydion's marriage reminded her she was not his true mother.

Or perhaps it was bedroom problems. Persy neither knew the reason nor cared. She only cared about how it affected the rest of the men.

Badly. Nobody was comfortable when the king and the queen

shared icy glares across the dinner table and slept in separate beds. She supposed it was an inevitable part of marriage.

But the king had Morgan and Guinevere, she was sure, had somebody, even if she did not know who. She suspected it was still Uluru, but she had no evidence to be sure.

"What ho!" Somebody had seen a stag.

"Not our prey," Arthur said, firmly. Even in these circumstances, he could induce discipline in the men with his voice and his eyes. The stag could be taken, maybe, if they had no luck with the boar.

Persy watched it run. It was a normal colored stag and young, not many tines yet on its antlers. For some reason, she shivered. Perhaps it was the obvious fear in his eyes.

Men would always hunt. Women, too, sometimes, although always fewer. Did the Christians have something of the right of it? That men and women were different, she seldom doubted. Seldom. There were times...

Then Arthur reined in. "This is the spot."

They would leave the horses there. A couple of boys had come along to watch them. Persy hoped they would do so and not wander off playing, abandoning the animals. One could never quite trust boys.

They should have brought girls, she thought, with amusement, as she slipped from Blazer's back. She unhitched her spear. She was lucky. Arthur had not forced her to be a beater, as he had with some.

Of course, she was sure he knew who she was. Which made it more of a surprise. For the first time, he allowed Gwydion to join the hunters in full as a man. Persy felt a twinge of nerves at that thought. Boar hunting was dangerous. Gwydion had been hunting deer since he was in single figures, but people almost never got killed hunting deer.

Boar fought back. That was the appeal, the challenge, but it was also the fear. She realized her knuckles were white on the spear and forced herself to release it a little. Not to relax, no, but at least not to grip so hard she risked spraining a wrist.

Arthur moved away from the horses, quietly. The trees arched overhead, and several pigeons flew between them. Some kind of small creature rustled through the bracken as it fled. Probably a fox.

Safe from the hunt. Who the heck would hunt a fox? Except, she supposed, for the sheer fun of it. Boar was good eating. Her mouth watered as they moved to form the line. But where would it or they break through?

She heard the beaters starting up. Kay led them, no doubt having volunteered to do so. Then again, at his size, stealth was not one of his better attributes. Giant blood, she thought, wryly. Probably not actually true.

It was a long wait. A still wait, during which her uncertainty slowly increased. For some reason, she felt that they should not be out there. She wanted to call out, to end the hunt.

Of course, all she would achieve by doing so was being sent back to wait with the horses, in disgrace. Arthur was determined to take that boar.

It was supposedly the largest that had been seen there in many years. Wild boar had become smaller and fewer. Persy supposed they needed to hunt them less often, but domestic pigs, kept in pens and fed on acorns, never tasted as good. Too fat. Which made her think of Bishop Marcellus.

He was a pig.

She knew Gwydion was to her left, and when she heard a crashing sound in that direction, she started to move. That was a boar alright, its tusks taking out brush and even small trees in its rush to escape the beaters.

She could move quickly enough to intercept it, and she was not letting Gwydion face the foe alone.

A mother's protective urge drove her as much as loyalty to her king. More. Then she saw it. The largest boar she had ever seen, and the fur on its back was tipped with white.

Gwydion was there, but she could not see him. The boar, however, could. With a faint roar, it charged.

So did she, from the side, spear first. She did not want to take the kill away from Gwydion, but it was not a beast any man should face alone.

Arthur was right. The largest seen in many years. It turned towards her, and her spear went into its shoulder.

Gwydion approached from the other side, trying to get close enough for a fatal blow.

Careful, she thought, trying to pull out her spear.

It was stuck. She swore in Latin, darting back to retrieve the second one that she had brought, but set down. Too heavy. What a fool she had been!

Gwydion thrust, but missed, the spear blade going under the boar's belly.

It turned, its tusks tearing into him. He screamed. They both did, and Persy charged again with the second spear.

She forgot her own safety. The spear plunged into the great boar's neck, and the creature went down easily, quickly.

Gwydion was down, bleeding. It was bad. She knew that instantly. She let out the loudest shout she could as she rushed to his side.

She might have betrayed herself to everyone, for she was in no state to disguise her voice. As she heard them come running, she collapsed at Gwydion's side.

He took three days to die. Three long, painful days in which the healers could do nothing for him. Elaine and Guinevere wept in each other's arms.

Persy...left the fort. She could not stay with him, she could not pretend nothing was happening. Something inside her had broken. Her misery was all she had, and she sat on the grass above the fort.

She should have stayed with him, but she could not bear it. There would be no other fruit of her womb. Elaine's child was the only thing that might carry on. Might. It was as yet a stirring in her womb, it might not survive passage into the world. She might not, especially not in the state she was in. Persy prayed to every god there was, but her prayer was a single word.

Why? Why? Why? It was a drumbeat, a litany. A word she could not escape. It should have been her. She had tried to put herself in the way, because she had known. For once, her Sight had told her something useful, and she ignored it. Set it to one side because she was afraid of not being believed.

She had let him die. As she sat there, a good mile away from the court, though, she heard a faint whimpering.

It was Snow. The hound padded up the slope towards her, his ears and tail drooping, and then flopped down next to her. He had somehow escaped and come here to find her. His head drifted into her lap.

He should go to...well, no, he would go to the kennels. Perhaps she could keep him, except he was not hers. She did not warrant or deserve one of Cafall's get.

She ran a hand through his short fur. He was grieving as well, but he, at least, would be spared the guilt. The dogs had been with the beaters, not the hunters.

Snow had not failed his master the way she had failed her son. With none but the dog to see, she wept. She wrapped her arms around him, buried her face in his ruff, and soaked her fur with his tears.

No visions guided her, and she felt that the gods had truly forsaken her. Had Cadan come to her, he might have had a chance of taking her soul. Except that Gwydion had been Christian, and that god had not helped him either. Barely a man, and already taken from her.

Her mind went over it over and over again. She could think of nothing she could have done better. She could think of no way she could have saved him. She could not live with having failed.

Would Elaine seek comfort from Uluru? It did not matter now, he could touch her without fear...she was a widow and pregnant. A widow having barely had a husband. She was, of course, still too young for him, but not everyone would care about that. Most likely, though, he was no more interested than he had ever been. Which could make things worse. She had to be redirected, but Persy had no idea how, and no strength to think.

The tears came again, freely. Then the horror, mingled in with them. Mordred. It was far more likely the lords would accept him over Elaine's child, with the slight difference in their ages.

Had Morgan? She had promised, but what did her word mean? Persy had never trusted the woman's words, why now?

No, Morgan would not have waited until Gwydion had fathered a child to kill him. She would have taken him out as soon as Mordred was proved healthy.

She had been there. It had been an accident. No foul play, no reason to suspect Morgan...or her family, who might also benefit.

An accident. The gods had taken him for a reason...that was what she tried to tell herself. It was not just cold comfort; it was none.

The gods had done it to her. Or she had done it to herself. Again, she went over it and over it in her mind, her arms wrapped around Snow.

It was many days before she returned, having run out of food for both herself and the hound.

Nobody asked her where she had been, but there was a quiet sympathy extended. If anyone determined her true identity, then they said nothing.

32

Three months later, Elaine gave birth, and Persy knew for sure her grandchild would not sit the throne.

The child was a girl. Elaine named her Bronwen. She seemed to have somewhat recovered from Gwydion's loss, but after the birth, she was plunged into deep despair.

"It is because," Guinevere ventured, "the child was a girl. Because it was not the heir she hoped for."

Persy, standing near by, shook her head a little, but it was Morgan who spoke.

"Sometimes, a woman who has given birth becomes like this, especially if she has other reasons for sorrow. You should stay with her, Guinevere, ensure she does not harm herself or the child."

Persy shuddered inwardly. She had heard stories about what women in such a mood could do. If necessary, she would take Bronwen away, although finding a wet nurse might be a challenge.

She would not allow Elaine to harm her. Physically, the girl was recovering well from the birth. Mentally, however?

Eventually, it was Guinevere who made the executive decision to give Bronwen to a wet nurse. It seemed to help Elaine, at least at some times. At others she would carry a doll in place of her child. At least that way she would not smother the babe, as young mothers in her condition had been known to do.

Persy spent as much time in the nursery as she dared. Again, that quiet sympathy seemed to remain. She was sure that her secret was, at court, an open one.

Of course, Guinevere also insisted that Bronwen be baptized. As much as the custom disgusted Persy, she could not resist it.

She contented herself with the thought that an oath could not be binding on one who did not understand it to swear it, but also refused to attend the ceremony.

She was not the only one. "She will be lost to us, I suspect," Morgan said, softly, in her ear.

"Perhaps, perhaps not. She will also have children." Persy hoped for that, anyway. Or did she know?

She had a vision, then. Bronwen, light haired, a woman, holding a child in her arms. "At least one."

"If they bind every child to their god at birth..."

"Such an oath is not binding, not in truth. Not on one who is, after all, far too young to understand its terms."

Morgan shook her head. "No, but if they are not even told other gods exist..." She tailed off, her voice almost dangerously soft.

"The gods will tell them." Persy had confidence in that. "Most will not listen, but some will."

Morgan considered that. She frowned. "The gods cannot talk to those not open to listening, and while the oath might not be binding, it may well shield the children."

Persy frowned to match for a moment, then she shook her head. "It will not last forever. It will not, Morgan. I know that for sure and certain."

"You know what you have Seen. You do not know what it means."

Persy shook her head again. She found it hard to be informal with Morgan. The woman's mode of speech was contagious. She tried it now. "No, I don't, but I know the gods are showing it to me for a reason. A good reason. It's too random to be anything else."

"Perhaps he whom the Greeks call Hermes has his eye on you."

"Maybe he does." Persy glanced up at the sky. "But I know part of it, and that is that it is a reminder that no matter what happens, the gods will not abandon us or our children's children."

She thought of Bronwen. Such a fragile vessel for her line...but she would live and bear, and from Persy's point of view, that was all that mattered. Even if her children would be raised as Christians.

Even if they had given her, the grandmother, no say in the path the child would be bound to.

"Not even if our children's children abandon them?"

Persy elected to give Morgan the last word, falling so silent that eventually the other woman swept away in a swirl of skirts.

She remained silent for a long time afterwards, staring out into space. If any of her friends saw her, they would tease her about woolgathering, but honestly, what else could she do but woolgather? She saw shattered pieces of images, like reflections in a broken mirror.

Nobody knew how to make mirrors any more. People were losing the knowledge the Romans had brought, slowly but surely. Ignorance was taking over, becoming the driving force, and it seemed the Christians were at the head of that force.

She saw women in clothes so complicated they needed a maid in order to help them dress. She saw people holding signs she could not read, in a language she did not know. She supposed it was so far in the future the language itself had changed. After all, people made up words all the time, and older ones fell out of use as commonly.

Then she saw a woman sitting on a black horse. Even the tack was different, and the way she rode was, too. She leaned forward a little, both hands on the reins, a clear look of concentration on her face as her mount tried to do whatever he wanted to do.

She laughed a bit in sympathy, remembering the crazy 'African' mare. And then she went to the corrals. Maybe taking Blazer out for a bit would help her overcome her mood.

Snow padded to join her. He was not, officially, hers. Unofficially, nobody wanted to interfere with their relationship. Sometimes, she wished they would, for every time she looked at him, her grief spiked like a wave on a Cornish beach. An undertow that threatened to drown her.

Maybe that was what truly ailed Elaine. Grief, and the fact that every time she looked at her daughter she remembered her husband. She was not supposed to be clad in mourning garb so young, and she had not yet set it aside.

Persy found Blazer's tack and rode out of the fort, finding some relaxation and some hope in the easy rhythm of his walk. A good horse. Such a good horse. Not like that black.

The next day, Elaine disappeared. The first indication Persy had was a frantic Uluru running up to her.

"Have you seen Elaine?"

Persy shook her head. "No, but I haven't been anywhere she would be. Where's Bronwen?"

"In the nursery. Elaine tried to snatch her, the wet nurse said no, she ran out and hasn't been seen since."

Persy's shoulders sank. "She probably went for a long walk. It's unfair that she's being kept from her child, but..."

"I have heard of women in such circumstances drowning their infants in wells or worse. But we have to find her before she hurts herself."

Persy nodded, moving towards the corrals. "She's likely to walk into a tree or something," she agreed.

The woman was in less and less of her right mind as time went on. "Uluru..."

"I finally just sat down with her and told her she would never...that I would never love her in the way she wanted. I think that may be what triggered this." He closed his eyes for a moment. "I thought I was doing the right thing."

"You did do the right thing. She wasn't in love with you now or ever, she was just after somebody to lean on, to depend on." What had happened to the strong-willed girl? Marriage and pregnancy, Persy supposed. Pregnancy could change a woman. Often for the better, but sometimes for the worse.

Blazer snorted and tried to avoid being saddled. "Stop that or I'll take Star." Not that she intended to take Star, who was still a young horse and prone to spook at whatever he saw. He had a lot of promise, but he also needed a lot of work.

The riders spread out. Nobody suspected foul play...it seemed most likely that she had wandered off, fallen down and broken something.

Hopefully not her head, Persy thought. She had always thought of Elaine has having a pretty tough head.

She had been wrong. The course she chose to ride was east from the camp, down into the valley. A small stream flowed there, one that met the river not more than a mile away. She let Blazer drink from it briefly before pushing onward, next to its course and sometimes splashing through it. Not the road. Elaine might have taken the road, but Persy somehow doubted it.

She heard hooves from that direction. Half the war band was out looking for the wayward princess. She would, at least, have that forever, even though she would never be queen.

Snow loped past her. She had not intended to bring the hound, but she wished she had thought of it. His nose had a far better chance of locating the girl than her own eyes.

"Not so fast, Snow."

He slowed to a trot, his tail sticking out directly behind him, splashing through the stream. In his dog mind, it was clearly a great game.

Of course, if she had gone through the stream, he would not catch her scent, not right away.

Yet, he cheered her, he made her feel that there was a good chance of finding Elaine. Arthur had probably taken Cafall too. She hoped so.

There was the river. It was not easy to cross here...there was a ford by the road, but even that short distance downstream, it became a tumbled mess of rocks and ravines. Not navigable by boat, either.

Snow gained on her by several horse lengths. He seemed to hesitate, then turned downstream.

She followed, not knowing which direction to choose. Might as well let the dog decide. He either knew something or he was being random, and random was the best she could offer herself.

Then, she lost sight of him. "Snow! Wait!"

As if in answer, the hound howled. She dug both heels into Blazer's sides, nudging him forward as fast as she dared in the tangled brush along the river bank.

Something upset Snow.

Elaine lay in the water, face down, her blonde hair and light blue gown both streaming with the current. Persy had never dismounted so quickly. She took no time to secure Blazer, but plunged into the water. With some difficulty, she lifted the slender woman out of the river.

It was clearly far too late, but she tried anyway...she tried to breathe for her, but there was nothing. By the time Uluru and Arthur found them, Persy held the drowned woman in her arms. They said she had slipped and fallen in the ford.

Everyone knew she had done it on purpose.

Morgan came up behind Persy as she stood on the palisade, staring out across the fields and woods with painfully dry eyes.

"Percival."

Persy did not turn around.

"Nobody here is close. So I can say it. I am sorry. I am sorry I failed to protect him."

Persy rounded on her. "*You* failed? You weren't the one who was..."

"...there. No. But not everyone can succeed in every endeavor, Persy. I had wards on him. They failed."

It felt like the truth, but could she trust it? After all, with Gwydion dead and only a female babe of that line, Mordred was the obvious heir. "I..."

"You don't believe me. Gwydion was the one who would have continued Arthur's line in unity, he would have brought us together. I can only drive us apart, and I am…far too old to change."

A very human admission there. "You are no older than I, if not younger." She was not sure exactly how many summers Morgan had seen.

"And how well do you change?" A wry tone. "It was always my intent to save Gwydion. I could not."

"But your son lives," Persy said, bitterly. "And my granddaughter."

"I will not harm her. I will not let harm come to her. She will be a queen, if I have any say in the matter."

Persy thought of Guinevere. Morgan would have far less say in the matter, but Guinevere might not object to a royal marriage for Bronwen.

Might even be all for it, as it would get a reminder of her barrenness away to another court. "Will that be what she wants?"

Morgan turned away, the wind catching her hair. "Do any of us ever get what we want, Persephone?"

The use of her birth name was a reminder. That Morgan was a danger to her. But in the moment, Persy also understood another truth.

Morgan was genuinely upset about Gwydion and Elaine.

"And Elaine?"

Morgan did not turn around. "I tried to save her. Her sickness was too deep and too wrapped up, too, in one who could not and should not sacrifice his own integrity."

She meant Uluru. "Somebody needs to talk to him." But he was absent.

"Somebody should. When he comes back."

A solid prediction. And perhaps a request. "Kay would probably be better. Or even Bedivere."

Bedivere knew how to be on the other side of such things. Kay, though?

"Kay fights them off, doesn't he." Morgan's lips quirked. "And before you ask, no."

Persy had not been about to ask. But she felt her mood lighten a little. Just a little, the clouds pushed back.

Morgan was no longer, at least for the moment, her enemy. Perhaps she never had been.

33

"Brother Cadan, you are a fool!"

Those words echoed through the dining hall, causing the heads of almost every man and woman present to turn. The accented voice was that of Uluru.

"I speak only the word of God. If the princess killed herself..."

Uluru was on his feet, stepping towards the priest. "If she did, then she did it because she was sick, not as some kind of crime against God."

By the gods, Persy thought. What kind of nonsense was the priest spouting now?

"It was a crime, and for it she is condemned. There is nothing we can do about it, and I will not...will not bury her."

He was refusing to conduct Elaine's funeral? Persy was on her feet, starting to cross the room. Out of the corner of her eye, she saw Guinevere do the same thing.

The queen was closer. "You will conduct my daughter-in-law's funeral." Her tone showed all of her pain, all of her anger at the situation, all of her grief.

"I will not. Suicides are not to be buried in consecrated ground. That is the law of the church."

Persy had never actually seen Guinevere angry. Even Arthur's various indiscretions had never caused this.

"So, you would condemn her to eternal punishment?"

"She condemned herself."

The rest of the room was entirely, completely, silent. Not even the hounds seemed willing to break it.

"We don't even know that she did kill herself." Guinevere's tone was absolutely cold. "But plain and simple. You will do the funeral or you will leave." This was the queen Guinevere should have been, and perhaps it took grief to bring it out of her.

Would Arthur back her up? Persy glanced around for him. He was watching with his face set. Unreadable. He had shown no emotion since Gwydion's death, none in public at least. Perhaps to Guinevere or Morgan. Bottling it up. Or letting it out only when it would not appear as weakness. She saw lines around his eyes, lines of pain.

He cared, she knew that. But he left this argument to his wife, seeming tired and drained. Or maybe he felt that Guinevere deserved to exert some of her own authority.

Cadan fixed his eyes on Guinevere. Then he stood up and walked out of the hall.

Eyes watched him go. Galahad glared at him. Even the most Christian of people there felt he had gone too far.

For a moment, it looked as if Uluru would follow him, the man's dark eyes hooded. Then he seemed to think better of it.

Persy frowned, then she left the hall herself. She wished Merlin was here, but he was off on his wanderings again. Perhaps he felt truly unwelcome. More likely he was just being Merlin.

But somebody had to find another Christian priest. Somebody who was not above lying to the man so he would do what was necessary. In the morning, Persy and Galahad rode out of the fort.

"I've heard his interpretation before," Galahad said, softly. "Suicide is a mortal sin, it condemns somebody to Hell. And because they are dead..."

"We don't have any proof one way or the other, and if she did kill herself...everyone knew she was sick." Uluru had spoken to nobody since, except for his outburst at Cadan. Persy thought he, too, was perhaps sick. Sick with guilt. It was obvious that the final trigger had been him refusing to marry her.

"Sick, yes, but..." Galahad frowned. "You're right. She could simply have slipped."

Nobody had discussed it until Cadan had said what he said. It was a taboo subject, as if leaving it unspoken had made it mere accident.

"Besides. No offense, but a loving god doesn't condemn people to eternal punishment. Sometimes I think your god has a split personality." Or was actually a bunch of gods kind of rolled into one. The Egyptians seemed to do that, from what she had heard. Their deities shapeshifting, flowing one into the other. Maybe that was where the idea of there being only one god had come from.

Maybe there was only one god, but if there was, it was not that god. That god who could not decide whether to love his people or to hate them. Persy desired nothing to do with that god.

If that was the only god there was, then she would sooner accept his eternal punishment than follow him. At least the company would be better.

Galahad spoke again. "See, I'm not so sure he does."

"Okay. To avoid it, you have to believe in his son. But what about all the people who have never heard of the guy, or who died before he was born?"

"I don't know. Of course, if we combine it...no, that doesn't work."

"Somebody like Cadan, or even Marcellus, wouldn't care. But I think the entire thing doesn't work. I'm sorry."

Galahad ran a hand through his mare's mane. "Persy..."

With nobody else around he apparently felt he could safely call her that. "If we could all agree to disagree, it wouldn't be a problem. But if you genuinely believe that somebody's going to suffer eternal agony if they don't convert, then how can you not try to convert them?"

That was why the Christians would not live and let live, Persy realized. Because no caring person could believe that and be tolerant. No caring god, therefore, would demand that of his followers. Would put them in that position. Yet, many of them did manage tolerance.

"I don't believe that he will condemn people for not believing in him, only for actually doing bad things." Galahad frowned. "It is a problem, though. It is..."

"It is what is leading people to bind children to him, Galahad. And that is wrong. I don't want to fight with you, but it is wrong."

Galahad shook his head. "You won't get any argument from me on that. We're supposed to have free will. Give the kid until they're at least eleven or twelve before asking them."

"Depends on the kid. Some kids at eleven can make their own decisions. Some will do what their parents say, and what if they then change their minds?" The oath did not seem to have any kind of get out clause that she was aware of. Only being too young was a possible escape. Unless one directly asked that jealous god to release you. "You're about the only reason I don't turn into Morgan."

Galahad shuddered. "No offense, but not all fanatics are Christian."

"She's afraid," Persy said, quietly. "Everything she does is born out of that fear. But it pushes her across the line, and there's no excuse for that."

"She's a complicated woman, but I will never trust her. Ahead."

A small village, a mixture of building styles. For a moment, Persy saw it as it would be in the future. How far in the future, she did not know, but there were square buildings with white walls, the wood of their frames visible and stained black, their roofs thatched with straw. A child ran down the street.

There was a child in reality, too. A different one, half naked as children were wont to be.

Persy was surprised they had been able to have the conversation they had without too much tension, but it ended. A few villagers came out to stare.

They were not wealthy people at all. Which meant that their mission might be easier. Their church would no doubt appreciate some gold. Assuming they had one.

Galahad did the talking. "We are looking for your church."

The specific word helped...separate from temple. One of the men frowned, then, "It's that way." He pointed.

Persy decided Christianity was not very welcome here. Neither, it seemed, were they. A woman grabbed the child and kept him close to her, away from the hooves of the ponies.

"These people aren't doing well," she commented as they turned in the indicated direction.

"A lot of people don't. Some people don't do well even when everything aligns in their favor, others are just unlucky."

The houses petered out, but there was one more building. Persy peered at it. "Not much of a church."

"Best they can afford, maybe." Galahad shrugged. "Or best they're willing to give."

He dismounted, walked to the church door and opened it. "Nobody here."

"We should have asked where the priest lived." Persy glanced around. Surely not far away. Maybe there wasn't one, and they would have to go to the next village...maybe he had stormed out like Cadan.

Not that Cadan wouldn't be back, with oiled apologies. Honestly, the man acted like eastern eunuchs were supposed to act. She did not enter the church, but rather started to approach the nearest house.

A tremendous barking stopped her in her tracks. She was not about to approach a dog she did not know.

Then it came bounding out, heavier through the shoulder than one of Arthur's hounds and leapt for her.

She had time to neither dodge nor grab a weapon, and the animal's weight bore her to the ground. She yelped.

"Brownie, get off him!"

Persy could not get the dog off her. He was...thoroughly licking her face. Including her ears. Galahad was too busy laughing to help, for which she would get him later.

Eventually, somebody grabbed the huge dog by the collar and pulled him off.

"I thought I was going to drown in dog slobber."

"I'm trying to break him of doing that to strangers," came the voice.

Persy brushed herself down. The voice came from a man almost as fat as Marcellus. He looked, in fact, a lot like his dog. "Better than using his teeth. I'm fine. Although if this lout doesn't stop laughing..." She glared at Galahad.

"What? I figured the great warrior could handle a dog."

She glared at him some more, before turning back to Brownie's master. "We're looking for the priest."

"And why would two warriors seek a priest. Confession?"

"No. Actually, we urgently need somebody to conduct a funeral."

"What happened to the priest you have?"

"He's away. He'll be back eventually, but probably not in time." Persy did not mention the payment. She did not want the guy claiming to be the priest when he wasn't.

"Well. I'm the priest. Call me Alban."

Not his real name, but that of a noted martyr. A religious name, then.

He looked after himself better than his church. Or his flock. Or maybe he was simply one of those men who was always fat, even when others around began to starve. She studied him again. His clothing was in good condition, but of poor quality. He could use the money alright.

"Can you ride?" Galahad asked. "And keep that hulking beast under control?"

"Ride, sure. Keep the beast under control, not so much." The dog sat next to him, panting and slobbering, its tail describing a slow semi-circle on the ground behind it. "Brownie, will you behave?"

"No knocking fine ladies into the mud," Persy told the animal. "Warriors, you can probably get away with."

Galahad laughed again. "Come on. Let's go."

They rode back towards Camelot in silence. The priest could ride and a stocky cob had been found for him. It needed a bit more weight on it, but that could be fixed easily enough.

"We've been having problems," the priest finally ventured.

"What kind of problems? You seem well fed enough."

"Eh, only because I needed to be less well fed. Local drought. Anything you can send us in terms of help will be useful. We lost most of last year's crop and that put us short of seed for this year."

Not uncommon. "And you don't have the money to buy it," Persy finished. "Talk to the King. I can't promise anything, but we can see what we can do."

Would Arthur help? Could he help? Did he even have the means? Silence took over again, only the sound of the horse's hooves and Brownie's paws.

Alban watched the road ahead. He did not seem at all nervous. Persy wondered at that. She would have been nervous. Perhaps he simply knew what he was going to do well enough that there was no need for fear. Perhaps he was one of those religious types who had precious little concern for earthly leaders.

That was most likely, she thought, then wondered in amusement if Brownie would bowl Arthur over. Actually, she rather hoped the dog would pick Kay to harass...he'd stand there, then wrestle the animal to the ground and teach it a quick lesson in manners.

The priest either could not or would not do so. Most likely could not...the animal was huge. Shorter than Cafall, but possibly heavier. At least Brownie was not a bitch...crossing those two really would make a horse. Of course, crossing him with one of Cafall's daughters might make something interesting.

"I hear that the king is Christian, but many at court are not," Alban ventured, breaking the silence again.

"That's right. There's a bit of a divide, but we manage. Just watch out for Morgan."

"She hates Christians?"

"With a passion. She probably won't do anything but annoy you, though."

"Don't worry. I won't provoke anyone. I'll just do the job and get out."

He hadn't asked more about Brother Cadan, and Persy was not about to supply any information that might lead him to react the same way. She almost wished they could keep him, but she knew Cadan would come back.

He would turn up the way a forged coin had a habit of returning to its creator. He was every bit as false and worthless.

She would have said her thoughts were uncharitable, but right now Cadan was perhaps her least favorite person. And she still wondered about his involvement in the murders.

Somebody was riding to meet them. She could not see who, only the horse, a dark bay. Flat out, they came, she could see that they were digging their heels into the beast.

It was Bedivere. "Ho!"

"Ho. We brought the priest."

"Good, but we have a larger problem. Come." He whirled his mount and took off up the slope.

Persy pushed Blazer after him. For Bedivere to act in this way, it had to be serious. Another kidnapping? Another murder?

"It must have been because Cadan was not here," Bedivere said, finally, riding towards the chapel.

Persy knew what she would find. She also knew that Cadan had waited until suspicion would not fall upon him. The worst part was that the girl was barely twelve.

34

"It's a good job I came here," Alban said softly, regarding the interior of the chapel. "You say this has happened before."

"Once here, outside the fort but the same thing. Once in the chapel at Avalon, the same exact thing." Persy felt the same result, too, as that time, the girl's spirit trapped. Screaming.

"I need to..."

"You need to do an exorcism. I know. Can I get you anything?"

"I got the impression you did not like Christians."

In, out. She focused on her breathing for a moment. "I don't like fanatics. I don't agree with some Christian practices, and I don't worship your god. But if you tolerate me, I'll tolerate you."

Alban cracked a grin. "What I really need is some people to help with physically cleaning the place up."

She rounded up a few servants to do so, then moved away. She felt cold inside. If it had happened...was she completely wrong about Brother Cadan? Had he been working against the perpetrators, not with them?

"I am tired of this."

A female voice. Persy turned slightly. Morgan. "Some people might blame you for it."

"Exactly."

Morgan would be prime suspect in the minds of quite a few of the men, Persy realized. There was no way she would not. "I know it's not your style."

"No, I would have killed that horrible priest if I was going to."

Persy's lips quirked. "I think at this point, you might have to get in line."

"I wouldn't be surprised if Uluru hadn't taken care of it for us."

"That might not be smart," Persy murmured. "I'm not sure, any more."

"Nothing's black and white, Persy," Morgan said, glancing towards the chapel. "You know that."

"I know my own loyalties. I don't know anyone else's." But she resolved to keep an eye on Uluru.

She did not have to go far to find him. He was sitting on the hillside, sharpening his sword. Like as not, his way of dealing with the grisly scene in the chapel. Not to mention everything else going on with him.

All she did was move to sit down nearby.

"I may leave," Uluru said, quietly.

"I would not blame you if you did." Persy considered that. "I almost did myself."

"When your nephew died."

"It's not supposed to be the kids who keep dying." She thought of Bronwen, who would not remember either of her parents. She would have everything she needed...and be married off to some lord Arthur wanted to favor. Well, such was the fate of princesses.

"No, it's not." He kept stropping the blade.

She sensed that he did not wish her company or anyone else's and turned to leave. She was not sure whose company she sought. With all the death, she felt something akin to the post-battle tingling within herself. A desire to reaffirm life.

Perhaps a desire to replace Gwydion, even if it was too late. Too risky, at her age. Was she old? No, but she was definitely not young. She would be old, sooner or later.

Then what? Keep up the masquerade, leave court, or become Lady Persephone again, at court, in Guinevere's bower?

She did not know. She only knew that she would put it off as long as possible, that she was still younger than the king...and a woman. Women aged differently than men, especially if they had not had too many children.

Perhaps it was the reserves they had for pregnancy and childbirth, and any left unused were kept.

Three days later, Brother Cadan came back to Camelot.

He said nothing about Elaine's grave, and when told of the desecration, merely frowned.

Persy avoided him. Uluru had indeed left 'for a while,' taking with him a spare horse. He would be back, she could sense that. His loyalties were there now, his friends. Everything that made him who he was.

They were all so dependent on each other, and hurting each other so much. Guinevere did not even try to hide her disappointment at Uluru's departure. And she and Morgan were catfighting over the education of the children.

Persy escaped it all by taking Star out over the hills. The young horse still tended to spook at anything in sight and occasionally at things he invented. Young horses did that.

Snow trotted at his heels. She wished she could take a lover. She wished she dared. But, apart from anything else, she might still become pregnant again. She probably would not survive if she did, but her body was still capable.

And who could she trust? Galahad needed a younger woman, and there was nobody else.

None of the men in the small remaining warband could possibly serve. The way they looked at her, if she put what came between a man and a woman in there, then something vital would be lost. True, Bedivere and Cadogan managed, but she was not sure what came between men who loved each other was quite the same thing.

She reminded herself that she had chosen her path, reminded herself that, no matter what, she had a good life. She had her friends.

It was only natural to feel regret about roads not taken.

She pulled the young gelding to a halt on top of a ridge. The land spread out before her, but so also did an odd sense of foreboding.

The peace lasted well. Almost too well. Well enough that one might suspect, or fear, that it would shatter dramatically when it did. She hoped not.

If Arthur fell, then that would leave Morgan regent for an infant king, except that the Christian lords would never accept her. They would demand Guinevere or Kay.

The country would split, and the war Morgan predicted would happen for sure.

She was probably protecting Arthur's life with every single spell she had, but that would stop once Mordred reached manhood. Or perhaps she would wait until he had fathered his own heirs. Two, preferably. It was always good to have a spare.

She realized she felt sorry for Mordred. With such a mother and such a destiny...and with Morgan and Guinevere quietly battling for his heart. He would be a pagan king over a Christian court...he would be even more caught between the two than his father.

She could do nothing to help, nothing except protect her king as best she could.

Her king, whom she no longer loved. That, though, she had well accepted. She might have stayed in love had they wed.

No, she would have; but parting had, in the end, led to indifference, not desire.

The land spread out before her. It would endure. She saw carts along the road beneath her, and it took her a moment to realize it was another vision. The road seemed to become a bit wider, then paved with something different, the same dark substance she had seen in other visions. Some kind of odd wheeled vehicle came down it, pulling a cart.

Why did they not use horses? Like as not, she would never have a good answer to that question. The future mystified her, and then she was back in the present.

Pointless. Why did the gods not show her something that would help? Something more concrete than the vague reassurance that Britain would survive in some form, that life would go on. She wished she could ask Merlin about it, but it seemed a lifetime since she had last seen him.

She dismounted, leaning against Star's shoulder. The horse searched her for treats.

She found a carrot in one pocket and fed it to the animal, who chomped it around his bit. He had no worries such as she did. All he cared about was his next meal and his next grooming. Snow padded along the ridge nearby, head held high. He had, apparently, forgotten Gwydion. Or, if he remembered somewhere deep in his dog consciousness, then it was not important the way it had been.

He had probably forgotten. Dogs did not live in time the way humans did, but rather in the moment. Horses, she suspected, even more so.

What was going through their minds? Some druids claimed to be able to tell. Persy simply re-mounted and rode back towards the fort.

What would happen next? She was not sure she wanted to know.

35

The young woman who walked into the great hall had a dignity to her Persy had seen in few men.

Could it possibly be Nimue? The age was right, the hair color was right, but the last time she had seen Vivian's apprentice she had not even been a maiden.

Besides her, Galahad drew in a breath. He was surprised too, but it was more than that.

Nimue was beautiful. She held a beauty that eclipsed Morgan's, that eclipsed Guinevere's. Persy had forgotten if she herself was ever beautiful, but knew that even if she had been, then Nimue would be as far above her as a sun above the stars.

Both men and women turned their heads, not all of the latter in jealousy.

Nimue's hair was the color of spun gold, and fell to below her waist. Her gown was deep blue, cut in the Celtic style, not the Roman. It revealed her breasts nicely, firm and tight.

Persy wondered, uncharitably, who she planned on seducing. She narrowed her eyes at the thought. It was unfair. Nimue was Vivian's apprentice and even if she did seduce somebody it would be harmless.

In one corner, she saw Brother Cadan watching her. His eyes burned. He probably wanted her to cover herself a little more. Or he wanted her, and he did not want to admit it. Him and his celibacy. Because he thought he was following in the footsteps of his God.

Like there was any proof or evidence, one way or the other, that their Son of God had remained chaste.

Nimue was enough, though, to challenge any man's vows...celibacy or marriage. Quite a few women's, too.

Persy pulled her eyes away from her, then elbowed Galahad in the ribs. "Psst. She's a witch."

"I think she just cast a spell on the entire room."

"That's just normal women's magic." Women had it...it was, in a way, what Persy had given up. That ability to control men that Morgan and Guinevere both used so freely.

Well, it was worth it. Freedom was worth the sacrifice of that magic. Nimue, though....

Guinevere had just poked Arthur in the ribs, the two, for once, sitting together. Persy stifled a laugh.

"See. Everyone."

"With him, it's not that difficult. Look at Brother Cadan. I think he wants to do something horrible to her."

Galahad glanced over. "I'll hurt him if he does. She's just after a husband, like as not."

Morgan was not after a husband. Persy did not think Nimue was either, although if she was, she would have no problems winning one. There would be a duel fought over her before it was over. Possibly more than one.

Persy, of course, did not fight duels, let alone over women.

Nimue's eyes scanned the room, however, then she stepped up to Arthur and whispered something to him.

He shook his head, ignoring Guinevere's baleful eyes. The young woman frowned, and then turned and strode out of the hall.

Persy wondered if she was looking for the absent Merlin. Or if she had asked him something far too deep and personal. She might never know. Her departure led the room to return to its normal volume; if anything, higher.

There could be no other topic of conversation but the woman herself. Even Galahad seemed smitten, and Persy had thought him mostly immune to such.

She finished her food quickly and headed, for some reason, to the nursery. Bronwen was asleep in her cot, watched from a distance by her nurse. The nurse gave her a bit of a look, but did not throw her out.

What would become of her? A decent life, if one more prescribed than her grandmother enjoyed.

Persy did not feel like a grandmother. She did not feel old. She still felt like the young warrior, but when she looked at her hands, she saw otherwise.

They were not as fair as they had once been.

Nimue did not stay at Camelot. The theory that she was looking for Merlin remained foremost in Persy's mind.

Or perhaps she had not wished to stay under Cadan's gaze. The man had already driven the much nicer priest out. He had reclaimed his place, but only to a point. Arthur was asking, softly, for Merlin.

Hopefully Nimue would find him and convince him to come back. Persy wanted his presence.

Arthur needed him. Cadan skulked around, he had lost weight. Almost, she felt sorry for the priest, yet...

She still could not be sure he was not a murderer. Why else had he fled Avalon? Or, perhaps, there was something even more complicated going on.

In any case, the way he had treated Elaine would have instilled a dislike for him in her had there been no other cause. Men, of course, did not understand the difficulties of women and vice versa. Even she, who straddled both, knew there were aspects of being a man she could never grasp.

Nimue's beauty caused her to reach the edges of one of them, and she no sapphist by any stretch. Maybe it would even work on Merlin.

She feared his disappearance meant he'd given up. Giving in to depression and to pain and to loss. Morgan fought in her own way.

Persy? She had also given up. She had accepted that the Christians had won; it was only a matter of preserving what really mattered. Some things would preserve themselves. She could not imagine that people would stop dancing the May. Or burning the Yule log, even if they thought it had something to do with Christ's birthday.

They would not completely give up on the fae, either. How could they, when brownies hid behind logs and the Sidhe rode on winter nights?

Or would the Sidhe still ride? No. She shook her head. Magic could not die. Could not, or the world itself would fade and become grey. It had not been that way in her visions. She ran the brush through Star's tail again.

It had not been that way. At the moment, the world was pretty grey. Mundane grey, caused by the threat of rain. The trees in the valley seemed to droop. Most of the people drooped as well.

Persy tried her best not to droop. The prevailing mood ranged sullen to darkly angry, grey clouds hovered over Camelot both mundane and metaphorically.

Part of it was that the men needed something to do. There were no bandits to hunt and nobody wanted to hunt boar.

Half of the court had been put off the taste of the stuff by what had happened. That would change, but...

There was only one outcome, and that was the dispersal of the war band. Back to their homes, and then what if the Saxons broke the treaty?

Yet, if they stayed together...

Bad stuff would happen. Very bad stuff. There could be years more of peace. She could hope so.

Years for Mordred to grow, to find and claim a bride. A Christian bride, perhaps, to unite the two divided halves of Britain. It was a shame Bronwen was his niece, not his cousin. It would make a perfect match were the consanguinity not so close.

They would find somebody. Bronwen would probably marry one of the Orkney royal house or similar. Now that would be a good thing. Her descendants would be away from most of the trouble. The Orkneys only had to deal with the occasional viking, and most did not stay. The islands were too harsh even for them.

The next day, a good number of the men left.

36

It was winter, a cold, chill day. Not as cold as some had been. The weather seemed to have finally settled into new patterns.

Or rather to patterns that would last for a few generations. If there was one thing Persy had learned it was that the world was mutable. That everything could change. It might even be true that lands off of Cornwall sank into the sea, to become a name and a memory, or that men had walked to Gaul.

She stood on the wall, a wool cloak pulled tightly around herself. Only the hardcore loyalists remained. And Merlin.

He and Nimue had shown up a few days before. It was obvious to all that the two were lovers. Their words, their gazes each to the other. Persy did not know who Nimue was, perhaps never would, for she had only seen her as a child. And the age gap would have bothered her, had it not been Merlin.

Except that he seemed old. Very old. All of his ageless quality had gone. Persy, of course, was not about to ask what had happened.

The fae were seen less and less. The Christians called them demons, so could they be blamed for hiding?

Perhaps Merlin would depart into fairy to avoid dying.

Or perhaps his liaison with Nimue had only one purpose...to produce a child, to secure a bloodline that could wait through the ages until magic came back. Until he could be reborn.

She watched Merlin and Nimue leave the fort, out into the snow. No doubt they went to do some ritual, but she felt an odd sense of foreboding. A sense of something wrong.

Last time she had ignored that sense, her son had died. She would not ignore it.

She took her sword and swiftly followed. The snow crunched under her feet. Their tracks led into the trees and then vanished.

No, appeared to vanish. She was no fool, she knew what a glamor was and knew for sure that they were using one to keep from being followed. Maybe if she had brought Snow...

No, dogs were as easily fooled by glamors. Snow would be no help. Only logic could allow her to find them.

Where, in the wood, would a couple of druids most likely go? It was far too cold for them to be go out there for sex. Or for anything but some ritual that had to be done in the heart of winter.

There. A disturbed branch, they had forgotten. As quietly as she could, Persy followed. She knew that she should not, yet all of her instincts screamed at her to hurry.

It was hard to hurry when she didn't know where she was going. The winter woods were entirely silent. Birds had flown south or remained in warm spots as balls of feathers. She saw the dreys of squirrels, but none of their inhabitants. The only thing that stirred was a red fox that crossed her path on business of his own.

No. She would never find them like that. She closed her eyes. If her own gifts were warning her, then perhaps they could guide her. Taking on two such powerful magicians was foolish...

...but for their own good. She did not know what evil would befall...a wolf would never be a threat to them. No, the threat had to be men. The threat was always men.

Snow began to fall again, blanketing sound and filling the air with white. It was colder than it had ever been, here, in the woods near Camelot. It was as cold as she imagined the Wall to be.

The bracken turned into frost, and she realized that more was going on than just the weather. That it was not just that the sun was hiding behind the clouds, but that some magic flowed outwards. She followed it, breaking into a run. Now she knew where they had gone, to what clearing in the forest.

Something had gone wrong with their spell. She was no witch, but she felt that, sensed it, deep in her bones, which themselves threatened to turn to ice and shatter. Her skin turned blue.

She had never been in the presence of this so power. As she approached the clearing, trees leaned away from it. One had fallen completely, crushing the bracken and dead brambles under it. How had she not heard?

In the center of the clearing, Merlin lay. He was curled into almost a fetal position.

She did not stop running until she reached his side. When she grasped his wrist to check for a pulse, his hand and arm shattered in her grasp.

She screamed.

When Persy came back to herself, she was kneeling in the clearing, and the only thing that remained was shattered pieces of crystal. Of Nimue, there was no sign.

Her own tears soaked her, and she did not care if she was revealed as a woman. Nothing mattered any more. Her son was dead, her granddaughter orphaned, and now the one being that had been the compass and rock, the reminder that she was not, in the end, wrong was gone.

She did not know what they had been trying to do. Something desperate. Something drastic. Power still glowed in the clearing.

Then she saw something else. It was a brooch, and one absolutely familiar to her, even though she had never seen it before.

She picked it up and slipped it into her pouch. One of them must have been wearing it. It buzzed with power.

She knew it was not hers, but to be passed on to another...she would, she supposed, realize who in time. No, she did know. It was for Bronwen, for some future time.

Then she stood, the tears streaking her face. Did she go back and report on what had happened?

Nimue would become a hunted animal. Or they might even blame her. Well, Morgan could vouch for the fact that Persy had nowhere near enough power to do such a thing.

Or, perhaps, it was best to leave it be. Slowly, she walked back towards the fort.

The snow fell heavier, and she realized she had lost everyone, one way or the other. She had lost Arthur to another woman, Gwydion to the boar, Merlin to this.

She only had Galahad, and the best thing she could do for him was, had always been, to give him up. To not pursue what might have been.

She said nothing about Merlin's death. Let them think he had simply vanished again, as was his wont. Let them not know what had happened. Instead, she would leave.

The decision had made itself, no conscious thought involved. But one thing she would not negotiate on.

Another decision had wormed its way into her mind. Without Merlin...but then, the court had managed without him often. Things had been smoother when he was there.

Yet... No. She had to tell Arthur, and Arthur alone, the truth.

She found him in the salle, although he had no partner currently. It seemed he had come there to be alone. Perhaps to avoid his women.

"Percival."

"My king." She approached, her shoulders set.

"What is wrong? Do you cry like a woman?"

"Merlin is gone. This time, he will not return." She did not say dead. He was dead, surely...but his spirit must still exist, somewhere. Perhaps in Faerie.

"You are certain?"

"I am certain." Persy frowned. "And I too wish to take my leave. There is..."

"There is peace, and you do not wish to be in a court where the only spiritual advisor is Brother Cadan." Arthur's tone was firm. "I understand. But you will return..."

"As I am needed. I promise." She was, perhaps, getting old. Yet, she was younger than the king.

"Then I ask something of you." He regarded her seriously. "Foster Bronwen."

Her eyebrow arched.

"She needs a woman who can be as a full time mother to her. Your sister...she has no man, no children. She could easily handle her." His eyes still rested on her.

The very favor she had intended to ask him, handed to her on a plate. "I will take her."

"Good." Then he paused. "She should stay away from court. Just in case."

Persy understood. He was protecting his bloodline. Bronwen could be queen. Or her husband king. Yet, she would not be seen as a threat by those who considered women unfit to rule.

He was protecting her from another destiny. From being surrounded by suitors before she was old enough to be wed. From, perhaps, Elaine's fate.

"Send for us when you wish," Persy said, finally, understanding the trust she had been given.

But then, by the old law, Bronwen, with Gwydion dead, was Percival's heir. She was sure and certain, though, that he knew. That

Jennifer R. Povey

Arthur knew there was no man named Percival.
  That man might never return to court.

37

"Bronwen. What have I told you about playing with swords in public?" Persy, dressed in a simple gown, stepped towards her granddaughter.

"Why shouldn't I?"

"Because some people frown on it." She had insisted her granddaughter learn to defend herself.

She had, of course, not realized that the person Bronwen would take after was not her pallid mother, nor even her father.

Oh no, Persy knew exactly who Bronwen resembled. She finally understood just what her own mother had gone through.

"But you don't."

Persy crossed the short space between them, reaching to rest a hand on Bronwen's sword wrist. "The times have changed, Bronwen. I hesitated to teach you to fight at all, but I would not have you reliant on men for your defense."

She had grown into an attractive young woman who much favored her father, but had her mother's slightly dreamy eyes.

Persy wondered how Uluru would react to her. He had stayed at court, having no other place to go. Likely he once more shared Guinevere's bed. Guinevere was not a woman who would have lost her looks.

Persy...had, in some ways, sacrificed hers. She was well aware that she bore the visage, now, of an old woman. Yet, a few minutes would turn it into an old man.

She kept in practice. And she was not weak, she was only grey, her hair having faded. She had lost her looks, but none of her strength.

"Does this have to do with my other grandparents?"

"In part. And in part because your grandfather might ask you to go to court at any time."

"To marry some stranger." Bronwen's eyes fixed on her, full of fire. "Why can't I do what you did?"

"Because if anything happens to your uncle before he has children..."

"I don't even get to be queen." The girl just sullenly turned away, shoulders set.

By rights, Persy thought, Bronwen should be queen. But she had been so careful not to put that idea into the girl's head.

She had either come up with it herself or somebody had been talking out of line. The worst part was, Bronwen would make a good queen. It was, she thought, for the hundredth time, a shame she and Mordred could not wed, bringing the two lines together.

Persy watched her granddaughter go, then headed for the horse corrals.

She had another young horse now, a black mare with a star. She would have named her Star had she not already used that name. Horses did not live long enough.

Hounds...a hound she no longer had. She had never successfully bred Snow. No, nothing lived long enough. Especially not sons. Had she treated Bronwen too much like a son? Too much like a replacement for Gwydion?

Guinevere might be able to fix it, except that Persy did not really, in the depth of her heart, want to. Whoever wed Bronwen would just have to deal with her wildness.

Then she heard hoofbeats on the road. The rider was a man no longer young, but still handsome. "Galahad!"

"Persephone." He used her full name, perhaps to emphasize that he was there on some business, not one of his rare social calls. He slid down from his horse, one she did not recognize.

"Come. Please. Accept our hospitality."

"Where is your brother?"

"Hunting," Persy lied. A lie they both knew was one, for Galahad full well knew who 'Percival' was.

A charade, then, for the benefit of whoever might be listening. A stable hand came forward to take the horse.

"It is time for the princess to come to court. We would all very much like it if her uncle would come with her."

All except Brother Cadan. Was the man even still alive? "What's the catch?" She could tell from Galahad's manner that he did not truly wish Percival to come back.

"It's..." Galahad sighed. "Come on. Let's talk in private."

She led the way to the small fruit orchard. "What's wrong?"

"Arthur is not aging well. Guinevere is the true power in the court now. She and Cadan are at odds on some things, but..." He frowned, the mask of formality fading away. "There are expectations there were not before."

"Everyone is expected to be Christian." She had predicted this. "Bronwen will chafe."

"Bronwen will not have to tolerate it for long, trust me. But I hesitate to ask you to come back...even in your other identity. They will try to haul you into church." Galahad sighed. "Most especially you. You're fairly notorious."

"I don't wish to send Bronwen with no support, though."

"Is she Christian?"

"In a sense. She seems to have found her own balance. I fear to damage it. But she has to wed."

"She does. And her uncle would have a good influence on the choice of groom. But her uncle would likely be miserable to see what has become of Camelot."

"Her uncle will come." She could be uncomfortable and give lip service to ensure Bronwen was not shackled to a man she could not abide. Yet, there was something in Galahad's manner that disturbed her.

Whatever was wrong at Camelot was clearly affecting him, and it had clearly developed since they had last met. The imbalance. Whatever was happening to Arthur.

She grieved, once more, for Merlin.

Persy's seat and legs reminded her she had not ridden all day in some time. From the look on Bronwen's face, she felt much the same way.

The girl wore riding gear, the fine garb prepared for court in the packs. Persy...was back in the role of Percival.

It was amazing that even after well over a decade away, she still found it easy to slip into it. Galahad seemed more comfortable with her too, his coldness perhaps only discomfort at seeing his friend in female garb and the reminder of what had not passed between them. Yes, it seemed to be that, for as they rode, they began to fall back into their old ways.

The sky was clear. It was early summer and as of late the weather had been milder. Not returning to what it had been in her youth, but definitely easier to handle.

The horses' hooves echoed on the old road. The cobbles parted in many places, grass growing through them. Nobody remembered how to build roads any more.

They would, of course, relearn it. She had seen that in her visions...visions which had faded away and departed once she had left Arthur's side.

She glanced at Bronwen. The girl rode without looking where she was going, but rather staring out into the trees. She was, perhaps, enjoying what they passed.

A fox trotted across the path in front of them, ignoring the riders. It was fat and sassy, no doubt from raiding somebody's henhouse. Somewhere in the trees, she heard the alarm of a pheasant as it took off. It had probably noticed the fox. The black mare started a little bit at the sound, but settled quickly. She was almost as good as Blazer...the one horse Persy regretted having had cut.

And missed...he had died two years before, of old age. She had never been tempted to feed him to the hounds.

The black, though, was still a little rough around the edges. She had never been tested in battle.

Neither had Bronwen, Persy thought, but if the court had its way, she never would be.

It was right as she had that thought that Bronwen, staring into the trees, tensed and then yelled "Uncle!"

At least she knew better than to betray the secret, but as Persy turned, the black mare whirled with her, facing what was off in the trees.

Bandits! Bronwen's sharp eyes had spotted them before they had intended to be seen. Seeing only three riders, though, and one a woman, they chose to attack rather than run.

A full dozen of them, screaming from either side...a couple of them actually doing so, war cries startling the horses.

They were Norsemen! Persy had her blade out before they hit, as did Galahad. She saw Bronwen draw her own sword and was very glad she had said nothing about her riding with it.

The black shied, then settled again. Persy turned her towards the nearest of the men. Norsemen? There? But they undoubtedly were...their armor and manner revealed it.

The mare reared, bringing her hooves down on the nearest assailant. She missed his head, but struck him in the shoulder, sending him flying with a yelp. As she came down, Persy's blade slid through the neck of a second bandit. It had been so long, and yet her body remembered.

Everything came back to her. She could pay no attention to Galahad or Bronwen, but only to those attacking her. Her blade slashed again and again. The black mare squealed as an axe hit her shoulder.

A flesh wound. It would scar, it would make a line of white fur, but Persy knew the horse would be fine. Blooded now. As was Bronwen...as the last two bandits fled, she could see that was literal as well as metaphorical. She was covered in the stuff.

"It's not mine," the girl said, quickly.

"Dismount," Persy ordered. She did so herself, stiffly. "Sometimes one can be hurt and not feel it, perhaps even for hours later."

She was indeed hurt, a shallow cut along her upper arm. Persy tended to it while Galahad, unscathed, handled the horses.

Norsemen, so far inland? She wondered if the princess had been deliberately targeted or if they were just opportunists.

Most likely the latter, she thought. Or perhaps whoever was behind it had assumed that Percival had forgotten how to fight and Bronwen never knew.

Like two of Arthur's war band could not handle a dozen Norsemen.

Galahad casually looted the bodies. Bronwen trembled. Persy slipped an arm around her. "It's okay."

"I..."

"It's a normal reaction, the first time. Just don't tell anyone at court." If they all thought the girl was a good Christian woman...except she was. Sort of.

She had found her own balance, and court would wreck it. Marriage would wreck it further. She would just have to pick up the pieces. Pick them up and carry on. Just as they needed to now.

38

Persy almost did not recognize Camelot. The fort still stood on its hilltop, but there was a village in the valley beneath it. An inevitable development, she supposed. Children stopped playing as the riders approached.

She insisted Bronwen dress up for the final arrival. The girl argued so little that Persy suspected she was up to something. She watched her like a hawk.

The chapel was gone, she noticed, replaced by a larger church in the town. No doubt it served both court and townsmen alike. In front of it was an active market, with farmers presenting their wares.

It all seemed much less stark than when she had been there, much more civilized.

There was even a proper bath house...of course, that would make sneaking around to bathe somewhat harder. Merlin had been wrong about the older bath house being the last, although given some Christians...

The road up the hill had been roughly cobbled, and she gave the mare her head for the climb. The fort itself did not seem to have changed much.

"Ho!" Galahad called at the gate.

She let him take care of it. Who knew if anyone would recognize her? The gate was opened from within, and she rode inside.

The gatekeeper was a stranger, to her eyes little more than a boy. Had she ever been that young?

No. Gwydion had been, what, seven when she had first come here. She could not have been *that* young. But young, yes. Too young. Now she was too old.

At least he did not call her grandpa as they rode into the courtyard. Here too, the signs of peace and prosperity were visible. No more corrals, but rather proper stables, a second gate nearby no doubt leading to the pasture. Where the barracks for the war band had once stood was a two storey building, the lower floor built of stone.

Yes. The court had prospered. Persy had prospered herself. Peace did that. It was a wonder men sought war so much.

Guinevere stepped out of the great hall. She had aged well, her beauty still remained. Her blonde hair did show grey, but it was more a silvering of the gold. She wore a slender coronet and a green gown.

She took charge of Bronwen in seconds. The girl gave Persy a somewhat despairing look over her shoulder then followed her.

"Some things never change."

"For a moment," came a soft voice from nearby, "I mistook her for Elaine."

The pain in that voice, undimmed by years, identified its owner before Persy even turned around. "Uluru."

He stepped towards her. "Percival." A pause. "I have missed you."

"There was nothing for me here any more. I have been enjoying the peace."

"You should change from the journey."

She did not argue. He showed her to a private room...no more barracks, to her delight.

Once changed, she made her way into the great hall alone. It was empty and ill lit...of course, it was too early in the day.

Where was the king? A servant came into the room and she turned. "Where is Arthur?"

"His chambers, I believe."

She would not disturb him. She walked towards the dais and realized a large, circular table had been placed there. The seats were engraved with letters. No, not letters. Names. Galahad. Gawain. Uluru Lancelot. Percival. She stopped at that name. A seat saved for her, over all of the years, but still...what had she missed?

She did not know. She felt lost and confused, and then the door at the back opened and Kay stepped in.

"Percival!" The huge man crossed the intervening space and pulled her into a bear hug fierce enough to threaten her secret.

"I have ribs!" she reminded him.

"I am so glad you're here." He took her, gently, by the arm. "How much did Galahad tell you?"

"That the court was far more Christian now." He had tried to warn her off, so what sense did Kay's enthusiasm make? Persy found herself tensing up. Kay had never been so close to her.

"Which would be a problem for you, yes." Kay tailed off. "But he did not tell you the rest?"

"No."

"Perhaps he is right. It might well be better for you to see for yourself. Come." He turned back towards the door.

At one point, it had led to the King's private bedchamber. Now, that had apparently been demolished. There was a short corridor, and then a large room, circular as the table had been.

Arthur sat on the far side, and Persy felt something curl up within her. His hair was almost white, and he not that many years older than her. A staff lay against the wall nearby, and from the wear on it, it saw regular use. His heavy frame had shrunk in on itself.

Arthur was old. Nay, Arthur was ancient. He had aged beyond his years, for he was not so much older than her. Care, perhaps, had worn on him, or some sickness during her absence.

"Percival," the king greeted her. He did not rise.

She bowed to him. "My King. I have returned."

"My granddaughter?"

"Guinevere has her.

The king chuckled. "Ah. Yes. I think it best to leave her to it, then. Kay, have you prepared a place for Percival?"

"Yes." Kay glanced at Percival, then turned his gaze back to the monarch.

"Good. Although I fear there will be little for him to do."

Peace... Well, she would find something to do. Perhaps help train the young colts. Then again. "I am less sure of that. We were attacked on the way here. By Norsemen."

Arthur's form suddenly seemed to fill out. He leaned forward a little. "Indeed."

"They were a good bit inland. They grow bold."

"We will have to keep an eye on that and perhaps prepare a party then. For now...I am afraid I will have to say I will see you at dinner."

Persy knew a dismissal. She moved to leave and Kay followed her. As soon as they were out of the room, "What happened to him?"

"He fell from his horse and injured his hip. He has not been able to walk properly since, or fight."

Persy cringed, feeling a bit of her heart break. Arthur was a war leader, a warrior. That was who he was, and without that? "How is he holding up?"

"Frankly not well. Guinevere is running things..."

"She always was the better administrator," Persy pointed out. "I don't see any harm in that."

"And he'll still send some of us out to scour for Norsemen, although I am older than he."

Persy studied Kay. "You don't look it. Arthur is letting himself grow old."

"I doubt he will live that much longer. Which leaves us with Mordred." Kay's tone tightened.

"What?"

"I don't believe it's Morgan's fault, what has become of him. But he is not fit to be king."

The mood of the court was lively. Persy found herself greeted as an old friend by men she had never considered herself that close to. She realized that she and Bronwen were being used as an excuse for a party.

Bronwen had been transformed. Guinevere had apparently been practicing, because her deft hand in hair and makeup had, Persy swore, doubled her granddaughter's beauty.

"Your niece is going to be knocking them out," Galahad murmured from nearby. He seemed more relaxed now.

"She is definitely prettier than her mother." Persy could think of Elaine without pain now. All she cared, though, was to spare Bronwen her fate. She would not have her granddaughter die like that, but could it be prevented? Such things often ran in families, haunting daughter after daughter.

Well. Bridge, cross, come to. For the moment, Bronwen sat at the high table, next to Guinevere. She was every inch the princess in a blue and silver gown Persy had not seen...no, she had seen it before.

It had been Elaine's. Of course. Well, only right that she should have it. It and jewelry that also had belonged to the dead princess.

"Yes." Galahad frowned. "Half the court will have their eyes on her."

Persy shuddered. "Including the ones that need more mature women and don't know it. Speaking of ones who do know it, is Uluru here?"

"Uluru's here. He never did marry, you know."

He was probably sleeping with Guinevere again, Persy thought.

Why get married? "I think we all know why."

Galahad sighed. "All along, and Arthur past caring."

He glanced at Bronwen again. "There are two possibilities for her. One is my cousin, named Arthur for the king. They are much of an age, if she would not mind living in Orkney."

"I'd almost rather she did. Away from the court, away from the intrigue, away from any war."

"The other is a kinsman of Arthur's through his mother....the current King of Cornwall. He is a little older, but a good man. She would be a queen, of course."

"I would have to meet both of them to offer any opinion," Persy admitted. An older man was not necessarily bad. More women ended up widows than did not anyway, and being wed to a man the same age did not protect one from that fate.

"Wise."

"What would you do?" She trusted Galahad's judgment. She remembered when they had been strong together. Now? It would be younger men who rode out after those Norsemen.

"I honestly am not sure."

"An honest answer. A less ethical man would tout his cousin."

"I think, though, that Cornwall is ahead in the running."

She wished that her Sight would return to guide her. She wanted Bronwen to be happy. Or at least to be content. Happy was a constant struggle. "You have seen Bronwen fight. Which would be more tolerant of that?"

"My cousin," Galahad said, without hesitation. "They are old fashioned up there."

Now she knew for what she would push, yet, she also knew that Arthur had politics to consider. Cornwall was a powerful force. If he wanted Bronwen, he might well get her.

Right then, any man would want her.

The church was empty. Persy forced herself to step within. As Galahad warned, attendance was all but mandatory.

Just as Constantine had forced Christianity on the Empire. Yet, Arthur had never done so before.

He had always welcomed anyone who wished to follow him. Had he become bitter through age and injury? Most likely, yes. Or perhaps it was his way of mending the rift.

She turned away from the church...and Mordred stood there. She had not seen him since he was a babe in arms, but she recognized him...his father's cast to the face, but his mother's raven hair.

The next king. She wondered if they had a bride for him yet.

"The wayward one."

"I did leave for a reason."

"To be a nursemaid." His face twisted into a sneer. "I won't have nursemaids in my court."

Persy did not respond right away. It was worth the risk of giving him the last word to fully assess him. Young men were sometimes bitter like that. No, she sensed there was more to it.

Mordred was not fit to be king? Well. No, he was not ready to be king. And with the state Arthur was in, who knew how long before he had to be ready.

"I was fighting Saxons and Norsemen before you were even thought of. Don't forget that. Obviously, you're too old for a nursemaid, but you should think about listening to, say...Kay."

"Kay's old."

"Youth needs age. And vice versa." She studied Mordred. All she saw was a particularly frustrated and bitter teenager.

"Things will change around here when I am king." He glanced at the church.

The look in his eyes was that of a boy who wanted to tear it down. Persy shivered a bit. Forcing Morgan's son into a church, perhaps, had done that. "They always do. But I hope it will not be for some time now."

"Why? The old man's just that. An old man. He can't lead his men into battle any more."

"Fortunately, we have less need for that than we did." Which was a good thing. Could Arthur stand to remain at home while others did the fighting? Likely not. It might even kill him, quite literally.

Mordred had no answer for that. He just turned and stalked away. She could not determine whether it was true that he was unfit. He was at a difficult age for a boy, hard to judge.

Gwydion had never been like that, but Gwydion had not had Morgan for a mother.

It seemed as if that thought had summoned the woman. She moved to Persy's side, glancing after her son. "What am I to do with him?"

"You should have fostered him on the Orkneys."

"I should have." Morgan breathed in, then out. "But I wanted to keep an eye on him. He is not what I hoped for."

"He is a boy. He may well turn into a better man."

"I hope so. I raised him to preserve the old, not destroy the new."

"Perhaps he feels the only way to preserve the old is to do exactly that." Persy let out a breath. "Cadan."

"Cadan is a fanatic, although he has mellowed a little with age."

That might indicate Persy had been wrong about him. "Whatever happened with those murders?"

Morgan tensed. "Cadan did not commit them." A pause. "Neither did I, before that thought enters your mind."

"Not your style," Persy said, quietly. Which she knew was not true. Morgan would do whatever it took, she could not forget that.

Morgan's laugh was sharp and bitter. "Then the thought did enter your mind."

"Only briefly. Do you know who did it?" It was worth the question.

"No." Morgan frowned. "Believe me, I wish I did. That kind of thing can only lead to trouble."

Persy frowned a little more. "Who was at all of those places." Not Merlin. Merlin was incapable of such an act.

"Other than Merlin, who would have died rather than harm an innocent, I do not know. You might be a suspect."

Persy drew in her breath, then nodded. "I didn't do it, but I could see that." What about Nimue? Too young...

And that first murder had taken place before she had even come to Camelot. "Of course, I could also be the target."

"Unlikely, but not impossible."

"How do you know it's not Cadan?"

"He has a solid alibi for the third of them."

"And if he is...or is associated with...a demon?"

Morgan fell silent. "He is bound to dark power. I do not believe he truly serves the god he claims to follow. However, he was not there."

"Physically." Persy shuddered. She a suspect? It was logical, though. She had found one of them, been fairly close by for the other two. Nobody had thought of it. Perhaps that said something about the person she was. Something good.

"Of course, he could also have convinced somebody else to do it just to give him an alibi. But..." Morgan tailed off. "It all seems very strange."

Bronwen. Persy abruptly turned and walked away. Perhaps it was a flash of her sight, returning after all of those years. Perhaps it was simply a mother's concern. She had been far more mother to Bronwen than she had to Gwydion.

She found Bronwen leaning on the fence of one of the horse pastures. Relief flowed through her. "Hey."

"She won't let me do anything fun," Bronwen complained, immediately.

"We'll work on that." Persy turned to face her. "Guinevere is a lady. She will teach you much you need to know. If that means not doing anything fun for a while..."

"She's even hesitant about letting me ride."

"I'll talk to her on that. She's not the best rider herself, but if I can vouch for the fact that you're competent enough not to be taking random tumbles, she should back down." A good compromise.

A hound puppy padded over towards the two of them. Persy glanced at it.

"Dogs everywhere."

"That one reminds me of Snow."

"I remember Snow," Bronwen mused. "He died."

"Dogs don't live very long. But they might be related." Persy did miss Snow. She reached down and rubbed the puppy behind the ears. It licked her hand, its tail wagging slowly.

She missed having a hound. Maybe she could buy one. For Bronwen to have one, though...Guinevere would consider that improper.

How much did she care? She wasn't sure. And there were more important concerns. Was Arthur dying?

"I just...I don't mind being a lady, but why does it have to involve sitting around and embroidering?" Bronwen paused, then answered her own question. "Because that's what she's good at."

Persy laughed. "Guinevere has skills other than that. Skills you need."

"I don't need to be able to embroider."

"No, but you do need to be able to manage your husband's household." Persy studied her. "I wish times were different. I wish you had been born when a woman could get away with more. They will be different again, but we have to..."

"Why? Why not show them they're wrong?"

"Because we're outnumbered." Persy was blunt. "Because anyone who tried to change things now would be ostracized." And when Mordred tried to change things there would be civil war. Arthur's line would fall. She could see no alternative.

They had to keep Arthur alive for long enough to sort the boy out.

"So were they, once," Bronwen said, mulishly.

"It's their time. We just have to make the best of it. I'm sorry." She meant it. "Be careful, Bronwen. Don't go anywhere with strangers. Don't forget your parents were abducted when not much younger than you."

Bronwen was less of a target for that kind of thing, not being the heir. She was still a target for other things, for things her grandmother did not wish to think of.

39

The harvest was approaching. Persy should have been celebrating First Harvest, but the Christians apparently did not care for that festival. The best she had managed was to sneak away and pray on her own.

She asked for forgiveness for her hypocrisy. Not that she was pretending to be Christian per se. She lied and said she had been baptized. She had no intention of being forced to go through that ceremony. A lie was better than swearing an oath she would not keep.

The gods would forgive her. Bronwen was enjoying the way her two primary suitors vied for her attention. Persy, though, already knew how it would fall out. The Orkneys were going to lose.

Bronwen would be Queen of Cornwall. Not yet, they were talking of waiting about a year so Guinevere could finish her education. So she could develop a bit more physically.

Persy did not like Cornwall. He struck her as a man who would all but lock Bronwen in a solar and keep her pregnant. He was not cruel, simply one who bought into the new attitude about women.

Bronwen would teach him, eventually. She would not simply bow, but she also knew when to bend and when not to.

Persy still did not like it. She made her way back up the hill toward the fort, hoping not to bump into Cadan. He would know enough to know what she had been doing. There would be a sharp lecture.

Now there was somebody she wished would grow old. It was not right that he should be alive and Merlin, whom she had always seen as immortal, dead. Like as not, the old druid had already been reborn, but that did not help them.

Nothing would help them, except to plant the seeds of remembrance where they could. The fort loomed over her, and she hesitated for a moment. Did she stay after Bronwen's wedding or did she leave again?

Nobody wanted her to leave, of that she was certain. She was living a lie, however, and would be until she walked away from the situation. For Bronwen, it was worth it. For her friends...were they even her friends any more? As if the thought had summoned him, Galahad came striding from the fort, towards her. He, no doubt, knew what she was doing.

Now that was a true friend. In fact, he had been the only friend to visit her during her self-chosen exile, albeit rarely.

She wondered how different her life would have been had they ever acted on their other feelings for one another. There was still a faint tension between them. He had never wed.

He stopped, hesitated, then approached her fully. "Percival."

"Is something wrong?"

"Nimue showed up at Glastonbury, apparently, harassed the monks and showed off, then vanished again."

Persy frowned. "You know she didn't kill Merlin." Deliberately. Or had she? Had she done it to steal a measure of his power?

"Can we be sure of that? And she is causing trouble. She tried to attack their precious tree."

"Oh, not a good idea. Besides, the tree can't help who it's dedicated to." No druid would ever harm a tree.

"Which does make me wonder. You did not see what happened."

"She loved him." Persy's voice was almost dangerously soft. "I saw that."

"Then perhaps she lost control. Or perhaps what happened sent her mad."

"Quite probable." Nimue. Persy would have to talk to Morgan, whether she liked it or not. Vivian was undoubtedly dead. She would not have allowed this to happen had she lived.

It was ironic that Persy thought Morgan would make a better Lady, a better high priestess, than Nimue. Nimue had been groomed for it, trained for it, raised to it. No doubt she was of common birth. A princess would not be chosen for such service.

Which brought her thoughts all the way back to Morgan. "I have to find Morgan."

"Rather you than me." Galahad shuddered. "No offense."

"I don't trust her either, but would you rather ask Cadan to deal with it?" Not that the thought of doing so was not vaguely tempting. They might take each other out.

"I wouldn't know who to cheer for in that case. You might notice I'm only in the church here a minimal amount."

"You're going somewhere else. I don't blame you." Persy wished she had the same option.

"Somewhere where the priest is sane." He studied her. "I'd invite you, but I know I lost that battle many years ago."

"No. You won it. You don't let it come between us." That made him so much better than everyone else. "But I really must go."

She found Morgan on one of the gate towers. She was as high as she could get, and she was staring at the sky.

"Nimue's out of control."

"I heard," Morgan said, softly. "And thus you come to me."

"Who else might be able to stop her?" Persy studied the other woman. Her eyes did not show disbelief, they showed curiosity.

"Other than maybe Cadan..."

"The temptation to set them on each other is fairly high."

"If I leave, somebody needs to keep a leash on Mordred." Morgan turned towards her former rival.

Persy frowned. "He needs some good, honest battle. He should go with those hunting raiders."

"An interesting thought. It might work. I suppose you know men better than I."

"Maybe. I think it depends on what aspect of men we mean." She actually smiled at the witch.

It was funny how she had gone from enemy to something almost like an ally. Sometimes, Persy felt as if she was in an armed camp. At other times, she remembered these people were friends. Comrades in arms. That the difference should not be that important.

Then, why did they keep making it that important? It seemed as if nothing she did, nothing she achieved, made them stop caring.

They all wanted to save her soul. Morgan didn't. Morgan cared about nobody except herself, and that was refreshing.

"It does. Of course, it also depends on the man. Mordred, though...he is not a man. Not yet."

She had the right of that. "He is a boy who thinks he is a man. Those are often the hardest to deal with."

But there was more to it than that. Mordred was heading down a dark path. "And he will do anything to restore the old ways."

"As would I. I am simply more...aware...of my limitations."

That was maturity. Persy looked out towards the village and its church. One day, she knew, they would build churches in stone. Churches large enough to hold hundreds of people, that almost dwarfed Stonehenge in grandeur.

But people would still, she also knew, dance the May. Couples would still slip off into the Beltane fields. People would, too, bar their doors against ghosts on Samhain night. "They will not win in the end."

"They are taking all of our children."

"They cannot win," Persy said, softly. "They cannot win until they acknowledge that only those who choose to follow a god should. That might take generations. And once they have, then we have all won."

Morgan looked up at the sky. "And what will happen in the interim. Women forced to be nothing but baby factories? Too many children, too many people."

"War," Persy murmured. "There will be so much war." She might, at some levels, hate peace, but peace would be an anomaly. From that moment until...she did not know when.

"So, do you blame Mordred?"

"He is simply not mature enough to know his plan will not work. But I'll try and work with him." Persy sighed.

"Thank you. Galahad might also be able to help." With that said, Morgan turned away, though, effectively dismissing Persy.

She turned to descend back into the fort. What would any of them try next?

Her attempt to slip away was stymied by Arthur himself, beckoning her to the table.

She knew the story he was telling as the boys and young warriors gathered around.

"So, the lady uncovered her head and Gawain could not take his eyes off of her."

Gawain gave the king an arch look. "What? She was a redhead. I like redheads."

"He was so distracted that he fell off his horse."

Persy remembered the incident herself. "No," she cut in. "What actually happened was that her hair was so bright that it spooked his horse."

"See, I have a defender," Gawain said.

"And you can't tell me." Arthur leaned back in his seat, "That you should not have sat that spook."

"And then she turned out to be worse than Linnet," Gawain mused. "If she hadn't been, I'd have married her."

Persy shuddered. "Didn't Linnet marry a Welshman in the end?"

"Owen, from north Wales, and I assume he had joy of her." Gawain made a face. "But Lile was almost as bad."

"And then she turned out," Arthur said, "To be married!"

Persy laughed. "Married to a guy who was so far in his dotage he wouldn't have noticed her taking a second husband."

"True, true. Join us, Percival."

Percival took his seat. This was all Arthur had left. Old stories, stories of battles and court shenanigans.

As long as nobody brought up Guinevere and Uluru, it would be alright. But there was a sorrow to it. Once he would have been on his horse, riding. Taking them on a hunt or simply a joyous romp through the countryside.

"So, time to embarrass your sister. That grey mare."

Percival laughed. "Oh gods, that mare. She would have made good hound food."

As if hearing the word, a hound flopped across Persy's feet. Absently, she reached down to pet it.

"But not much else," Arthur said with a grin. "You sure wouldn't have caught me riding her."

Kay cut in. "You'd have squashed her almost as badly as I would have."

Persy grinned at the huge man. It felt for a moment like the old days. A feast, in which they could all partake. A time of joy.

But it was all faded glory now. As soon as she could do so, she quietly slipped away.

She could not stand to see Arthur, who should still have been a strong warrior, like this.

40

She could not have anticipated what happened next for all the world.

Everyone was in the Great Hall. Those who had fought for Arthur in his glory days gathered around the table. Servants and others sat in long rows. Guinevere sat next to her husband, but seemed to have eyes only for Uluru.

In short, everything was normal. The food was decent, although not good enough for a feast. It would do, Persy thought. Morgan's absence was conspicuous. From one of the lower tables, Mordred occasionally glared at his father.

It was obvious he thought himself old enough to sit with the warriors. Perhaps he was. Perhaps he was not.

Most likely, Arthur was waiting until he comported himself like one, instead of like a spoiled brat.

The doors had been closed...the main doors, that is, not the one direct to the kitchen, to one side, or the ones behind the dais.

Abruptly, they flew open. A moment later every torch and taper in the place was extinguished. Persy felt a sense of foreboding as deep as when Nimue and Merlin had left together.

Nimue.

Who here would remember what she had looked like as a maiden? She would be a matron now, a mature woman.

Yet, the three women who walked into the room were all young. Very young. The first one carried a wooden spear, stained with old blood. The second, a piece of wood. The third a cup covered in a white cloth.

She knew the symbology, but she also knew how the Christians would read it. It represented the divine to both. To them...spear, cross, grail. To her, it was about fertility and rebirth.

To them...the very symbols of their redemption. Every man, woman and child in the room stood. Persy got to her own feet, even though the sense of warning throbbed through her.

Her eyes sought Galahad, but he was staring at the maidens, and not as a man looked at women.

They walked up to the round table, regarding the men sitting at it. Then, they vanished, a wind seeming to relight the tapers.

Glamor, Persy thought. The entire thing had been a glamor. A trick. An awe-filled murmur started through the room.

Grumbling to herself, although not even under her breath...no, it was entirely in her own mind...Persy quietly stood and left the room.

Nimue. What could she possibly be planning? That was assuming Persy was remotely right in her concerns. What if it was her imagination? Or even a prior bias against the woman?

Except she had none. She had not believed Nimue to be evil until she heard those rumors from Glastonbury, and even then she had not been sure.

Maidens dangling what appeared to be relics of the Christian God in front of the men. Of course, they could just as easily have been the Fisher King's spear, a piece of wood from a grove and a chalice used by the priestesses. Or they could have been entirely fake, intended to represent those things.

Fakes intended to make people think they were the relics of Christ seemed most likely...except, why?

She would not have chosen that combination if her intent had been to remind the pagans. Or would she? Just as it was possible that Merlin's death had been an accident, it was quite possible that the girl had not thought things through.

No, not a girl any more. She quite likely had children. In fact, at least one of those maidens could well have been modeled from her daughter. The third one, with the chalice, had borne a certain resemblance.

So, it might have been something ill-thought. Yet, no. She remembered the looks between Nimue and Merlin, none of that had spoke of a woman who would deliberately slay her lover. A woman who had not been seen since, who might not even be alive. Persy walked to the wall, climbed up onto it. She looked out into the growing darkness. No, it slowly dawned on her. She knew all three of those girls, where all three illusions came from. Would Arthur? Yes, because she had told him, had ensured he knew.

Hopefully, it would be put down as some kind of sign that they were on the right track and otherwise ignored. She felt the cold air flow into and out of her lungs. It was the very edge of night.

Whoever had done it could not be that far away, but they would still be long gone by the time anyone found where they had been. Reluctantly, Persy decided any search was a waste of time.

She slipped away and nobody followed her.

The next day, Galahad cornered her at breakfast. "So, explain last night."

"I can't," Persy said. "But if you think it's going to convert me…"

He laughed. "I don't think it's going to. I was just wondering if it could have meant anything not obvious to me."

"It could have meant quite a few things pagan, as well as things Christian. Or been some kind of trick."

"It's going to stir up the hornets' nest." Galahad closed his eyes, opened them. "What if they really do have those relics?"

"What if they do?" Persy turned to face him. "It's possible. If somebody really did come here from the Holy Land, who witnessed the events, he could have brought them with him. It's not as if said relics are in danger, correct?"

"Not that we know of." Galahad ran a hand through his hair. "But why show them to us?"

"To let you know they're there? To improve morale, which you have to admit is screwed up lately. Or, it could all be some kind of trick designed to have the very opposite effect."

Galahad scowled. "Cynic."

His tone, though, was that of the old Galahad. "Idealist," she quipped right back.

"I suppose I want to believe that they're real and here. To touch…" He tailed off.

She could see it in his eyes. "I get it, Galahad. I do get it. I might not share your beliefs, but I respect them."

She could accept that a god's son had sacrificed himself to gain followers. She simply could not accept the entire monotheism thing.

"You do better than so many on that." Galahad's chest rose, then fell. "But I need to know. You understand that."

"I do." She reached for another piece of bread, using it as an excuse not to say any more immediately.

If Galahad was reacting like this, then how would those who were more fanatical act? Would they insist on finding the relics and bringing them to Camelot? Or maybe to Glastonbury? Would Bishop Marcellus demand them for his cathedral in London?

She saw war and division. And she saw Galahad dead on the floor. "Galahad. Whatever you do, don't go looking for them."

He regarded her. "I don't think they're dangerous, Persy. Seriously."

If he did not listen to her, then she would have to make him. Coming up with a way to do that would take time. "I don't mean the relics, Galahad. I mean those women."

Glamor it might have been, but there was somebody behind it. Somebody who had been around long enough for this. Which meant Morgan or a player she did not know. Vivian was presumably dead. Nimue was too young.

"Persy, do you know something?"

She took a deep breath. "The three maidens are the three girls who were ritually murdered, one at Avalon and two here."

Galahad frowned. "So…either their souls, which should be rights be in heaven, or somebody using their images. But that doesn't mean…"

"It probably means this is a trick put together by a murderer." And there was, in the end, only one suspect. She did not want to think it, not after how their relationship had improved. Morgan had not been at Avalon for Persy to see, but that did not mean she had not been there. A small detail swum up in her mind, an old woman watching. A woman who had looked like Morgan's grandmother. It all fell together. She had come to like Morgan, even to respect her. Perhaps she still respected her, but Nimue could not have done it, and she only had word that it had been Nimue at Avalon.

"It might."

But he did not, she noted as he finished up one last bite of food and walked away, promise not to go looking for the relics.

Nothing less than that would have made her happy. Without that satisfaction, she left.

She tended to the black mare herself, as she always did when upset. The rhythm of brushing the raven coat helped. So did the soft nuzzle as the horse tried to check her for treats. "I forgot to bring anything," she apologized. Maybe there were some carrots around here somewhere. Right now, she did not feel like looking.

The mare snorted, affronted, and pretended to ignore her. She laughed a bit. Sometimes, dealing with horses and dogs was so much easier than trying to handle humans. Especially men.

The situation with the maidens was not going to end well, and she knew it, but she also had no clue what she could do about it. Nothing except hope that, like Guinevere's indiscretions, it sorted itself out in the end.

It sometimes seemed almost as if Arthur did not care what his wife did or did not do. Most likely, he did not love her any more. He had. Persy knew that.

She was, once more, glad she had never married. She fortified herself with the knowledge that this group of people had weathered so many storms.

Persy's strongest ally in the quest to keep people from looking for relics was, oddly enough, Brother Cadan.

She wondered if he was really against them or playing mind games. He was no longer young, except for his eyes. Those pierced as strongly as ever. She still wondered how he had been cured. By black magic.

But had it been his black magic? Had he even sought it? Was his craziness a desperate attempt to cleanse taint from his soul?

She had never thought of that before. But if not him, then who? They stood at the entrance to the church.

"I won't ask you to come in."

"Thank you." She studied him. "I think that's the most respect you've ever shown me."

"Right now...I would not quite ally with the devil himself, but close, if it would cause those here to realize this is trickery."

"It was Morgan." She was certain of that. Morgan had still not returned. "She left, claiming she was looking for Nimue, blaming her…" Persy tailed off.

Cadan frowned. "If it ws Morgan, who's side is she on?"

"Morgan is on her own side, nobody else's. This serves her agenda, somehow." The idea that Morgan had a side to be on was almost humorous. "It may be as simple as trying to get all the devout warriors to go relic hunting so she can work on Arthur."

"Okay. Now, those three women."

"They look like the three girls who were…"

"Ritually sacrificed." Clearly he had the thought in mind too.

For Cadan to bring that up. Softly, "You realize you've been my prime suspect for years."

He sank against the church wall. "I know who did it. But from me, it would have been taken as bias.

"You know? Why would I believe you?"

He cut her off, but there was no real sharpness in his tone. Scissors cutting a strand, not a sword a limb. "I did not do it. I would swear, but that is forbidden to Christians."

"Tell that to most of the warriors."

"A minor transgression. Whilst I..." A pause, then, quietly. "I did not do it. It was done for me. By Morgan." There was pain in that voice, the pain of long-delayed realization.

"By Morgan? Why?"

"I don't know." He looked at her. "I don't know, but she condemned me as well as herself." He paused. "I always thought it was a displaced druid who did it. But now I understand. She set me up to be her foil, to be somebody she could point at to say how bad Christianity was."

No truly good god would condemn him for this. The insight that struck her was as sharp as any knife. Cadan was condemning himself.

"But it might have given me the power to stop her," he added, quietly.

"Do you think those relics might be real?"

"I did not see what was under the silk. I have no clue whether it might be the real thing. If it looked like the real thing, then she must have seen it or heard it well described, as I did."

"Except that if somebody described it to you, then..."

Cadan nodded. "It is nothing special. It is a plain stone cup, inscribed in a language none in this land speak. If she shows a cup of silver or gold..."

"But the men expect silver or gold. Not stone." Stone? Perhaps that was a custom of the land their god's son had walked...to make ceremonial vessels from stone. Or perhaps he had been too poor to afford silver or gold.

"True." Cadan frowned.

Persy shook her head. "Morgan. This is so twisted, and I thought. I thought she was better than this, I thought she was a fanatic, yes, but not a murderess." But she had known, in truth. Morgan was capable of murder, she had always known that.

"I have tried not to be what she made me, and it got easier with time, but for a while. And then there are other sins. Bedivere's...sin."

Ah, so Cadan was Greek himself? It would explain why he felt driven to be celibate. That which the Greeks celebrated, the Christians abhorred. Bedivere's tendencies were known and tolerated because he was too important and too close to Arthur to drive out.

Yet another reason to regret their ascendancy. She studied Cadan's face.

"It's not a sin. So, what do we do about the grail?"

"I don't know. I'll come up with something, though."

"Perhaps a sermon about being presumptuous before the gods might help?"

His eyes brightened. "Perhaps."

Was he doomed? Only if he let himself be. But if she told him that, he would not believe her. It would only, she decided reluctantly, make the situation worse. "It's worth a try. I have a dark feeling about what might happen if anyone goes after that stuff."

She could hope it was a mere distraction, but she feared it was a trap of a deeper nature.

"So do I," Cadan admitted, and stepped back into the church.

Had he really...could he be innocent? Persy had entertained the possibility, but then flipped back into refusing to accept it. Him acting like a human being was almost alien to her.

Almost. It was still Brother Cadan. Still the man who interpreted the teachings of his God so strictly that he was often cruel.

But it was a lot more complicated...was anyone truly good or truly evil? No, she decided. Everyone, including her, was a mix of both.

It was only a matter of which one allowed to rule one.

41

The hunt rode out with laughter. Arthur was with them...he could not fight, but he could still ride. Thus, they hunted stag with bows. No boar hunts.

Persy would not have gone on a boar hunt. She had not hunted boar since Gwydion's death. In any case, there seemed to be fewer and fewer boar. Maybe it was the cold winters killing them off, or too much hunting.

Very few wolves, too, except, she had heard, north of the wall. Wolves would be no loss. Boar, though, were a loss as much as part of her wanted them to disappear.

There were still plenty of deer. Always would be, Persy thought. Often too many, for they would invade the kitchen gardens of the goodwives and eat the prized vegetables.

Her mouth watered at the thought of venison. For a time they had had no luck.

She rode with one hand on the black's mane, the other on her bow, her eyes scanning the trees. It would be a better hunt if they could dismount, but Arthur needed the chance to lead again as some men needed air.

What had happened to him was not right. Not right at all. But then, life dished out such unfair situations regularly. There was nothing to be done about it. Merlin might have been able to heal him.

No. Persy doubted even Merlin could have fixed the problem. A specialist healer might have had a chance. But having driven magic out, there had been none. Except for Morgan, and she had no talent in that area. No question but that she would have tried.

No deer, still. No wildlife at all, it seemed, as if something had scared off all of the creatures. The silence that seemed to descend through the air was absolute. Persy's scalp prickled. "We should turn back," she said to Galahad.

"You going to tell Arthur that?"

"I mean it. There's danger here." No visions, though. No clarity, only that vague hint of foreboding.

The trees seemed to close in, forcing the riders down one particular path. It seemed that the sun dimmed, and then she saw the candles amongst the trees.

Had she not had that feeling of foreboding, she would have suspected the fae. Sending a message, perhaps.

The fae, though, had never made her feel the way she did. It took everything she had not to turn and ride back the way she had come. Only the fact that Arthur might need her stayed her.

The horses seemed not to notice. Glamor again, she supposed, and canted only for human eyes. The light ahead flickered, definitely candle-like. She shivered.

It was not cold. If anything it was warmer. Galahad's eyes widened.

The trees formed the shape of a church, their trunks columns, their branches the vault. She knew no clearing like that existed in those woods.

An altar of wood was ahead of them. On it was the cup, covered in silk. Slowly, Arthur dismounted, limping towards it. He reached to remove the silk.

As he touched it, the entire thing vanished, the trees returning to their normal shape and configuration.

There was only a female voice. "Come to us."

Persy knew it was a trap, which immunized her against the allure in that voice. The men clamored forward, towards where they thought it had come from. It pained her to see Galahad among them.

There was nothing to be found, though. Empty-handed, the hunters rode back to the fort. They had no grail and, worse, they had no venison. It would be pork stew again tonight, no doubt.

Or perhaps only vegetables. Persy regretted that. There was animated talk, in which she did not join.

It was all about finding the woman and the chalice. Those less entangled by Christianity even used the word 'goddess'.

Galahad pulled up next to Persy. "You still think it's a trap, don't you?"

"I know it's a trap."

"Why can't I go?" Bronwen asked Persy.

Persy frowned. "Because..." A pause. "I am absolutely sure the entire thing is a trap."

"You're going."

"Only because Galahad will likely get himself killed without me." Going with him was the only way she could think to prevent the persistent vision...Galahad dead on a stone floor, a silver chalice on the ground nearby. Red liquid, like blood or wine, spilled from it.

That image was in her dreams and caught her at moments in her waking life. Clearly, she was supposed to protect him, or try to. He was not listening to her. He did not believe Morgan was behind this. He truly believed his god spoke to him.

She had failed to protect Gwydion. She had failed to help Elaine. She was not losing Galahad as well.

"You think he can't look after himself?" Bronwen teased.

"I think he is not thinking straight right now. None of them are. It's not the grail they're after, not really. It's the woman. And I know who she is. She's a dangerous witch."

Persy wished Nimue would show up. She had her doubts about the young woman, but she was the only one with the training to possibly stop this. Perhaps, though, she and Morgan had already dueled and she had lost. Whatever power Morgan worked with now, and Persy was sure it was not the Morrigan she was named for, was placing her at a higher level.

"I still want to..."

"Bronwen. You are needed here. With so many of the warriors gone, the fort will be ripe for some kind of attack. And somebody needs to keep an eye on your uncle."

She made a twisted face. "He should have been drowned at birth like a mutt puppy."

"He's salvageable, trust me. But it won't be easy." And if he would not listen to Persy, he would not listen to Bronwen, that was for sure. "For now, he just needs to be kept from doing something dumb."

"Even the hounds don't like him."

Persy had noticed that. It was sometimes a sign that a person was involved in dark magic. It was far more often a sign that a person was afraid of dogs. Mordred might well simply not like them. "That doesn't necessarily mean anything sinister. Hounds like people who like them."

"I asked Arthur for a hound, but he said no." Bronwen made a face.

"He probably doesn't want to encourage your tendency to sneak out and go hunting."

"I don't see any reason why I shouldn't hunt stag. I can see him not wanting me to hunt boar, that's dangerous."

Persy regarded her. "I would kick your butt if you hunted boar. I don't trust those things."

She knew it was something akin to a grudge or a phobia, but the very idea of anyone kin to her ever going after a boar again was utter anathema to her.

"Maybe..." Bronwen chewed on her braid for a moment.

Persy reached and pulled it out of her mouth. "You grew out of that when you were five."

Bronwen laughed. "Sorry. I know, I know. It's not good for my hair."

"And you will need to look...I do promise one thing. I will be back for your wedding." To Cornwall. It had been, in the end, inevitable.

Still, they would work things out. She knew what would happen if the man sat on Bronwen too hard. She'd poke him with something. Which he'd deserve at times.

"Good, because I'm going to need some support." Bronwen regarded her. "Although, it could be worse. He's not in his dotage."

"I wouldn't have let Arthur do that to you." Could she have stopped him? If he had gone that far, then she would have taken Bronwen home. Any sane mother would. An older man was a good thing. An old one made the wife a nursemaid. Only widows who already had children should be put in that situation.

"He's still a sour grape."

"Well, we can work on that. For now...stay safe. And keep your blade sharp." Persy knew that there might not be enough men to defend Camelot from a major raid.

Nobody was thinking straight. They were all too enthralled by that female voice. Some were saying it was Mary, their god's mother.

Persy knew better. Cadan was trying to tell them. He was, in the end, trying to stop this, but it was his own past voice he thought against.

Nobody, including Arthur, seemed to want to accept the truth. Perhaps especially Arthur, who had loved her.

"Don't go," came a voice from nearby as Persy prepared her horse.

Its tone implied that its owner wanted the opposite. She turned.

"Greetings, Mordred."

"You really shouldn't go hunting wild geese. Something might happen while you're gone." His tone was wry, but there was a hint of a threat to it.

Had he been a few years older, she would have taken that threat more seriously. As it was, it was the noise of a boy. "You make a lot of noise, boy. Give it a few years."

"What difference will a few years make?"

"Wisdom. Just ask your mother."

He scowled. "A man should not listen to women."

"A man should *always* listen to his mother." Not that Morgan was the best role model, but Persy rather thought she was all that was keeping the boy in line.

"Besides. She's not here."

Persy frowned. He was right, Morgan was absent. "Then listen to wise men. Listen to Kay and Bedivere, if not to your father."

"And to you?"

"I never claimed to be wise." She turned, leaning against the black mare's shoulder to remind him. The mare snaked her head around and gently breathed on her.

"But you dispense plenty of wisdom now. Go, then. Enjoy your search for relics that don't exist."

"I never claimed they *do* exist." She studied him. "What do you want, Mordred?"

"You claim loyalty to the old ways then leave on a Christian quest. How can I trust you?"

"I am loyal to the king and to my friends." She couldn't help but add. "You have a lot to learn about loyalty, Mordred."

"You need to learn to be loyal to me. Like I said, go ahead. Leave."

See if I care was the last echo. Persy shook her head. "By the time you are king I will be too old to be anything but a voice by the fire."

"Then be a voice by the fire somewhere else." It was a threat. It was a hint that she would not be welcome in his court.

So be it. She had no intention of staying in or near Camelot a second after Arthur's death. If she had not already retired, she would then.

Arthur's line had to sit the throne. "You are a young fool, Mordred. For the sake of Britain, try not to become an old one."

It wasn't pleasant words, but they had the echo of things Merlin had said. Perhaps she was more wise than she knew.

He snorted and stalked away. As he did so, she saw him hesitate.

Bronwen was standing in the gateway. His eyes lingered on her.

42

Persy and Galahad rode north in silence, which he had broken only with.

"I would more believe it was Cadan than her. Morgan wanted Camelot intact and at peace."

"Morgan also wanted it pagan," she had pointed out before dropping the matter. She was here, and she could try to protect him.

Well, she could stop him from drinking from any silver chalices. If it was the real grail, then she believed Cadan when he said it was likely to be stone. The very fact that a stone cup seemed strange made it more likely. The customs of people who lived in a desert were bound to seem odd to her.

Uluru had made it clear that there were many different ways in which humans could do things. Legend had it that even further east than the place of Christ's birth there were men who lived on endless plains, who could ride like they were one with their horses.

Some versions of the legend had them as centaurs. Persy was not entirely sure she believed in centaurs, oddly enough. Perhaps they were a kind of fae. More likely, they came from envy. The envy of men who wished theyhad such skill themselves.

She certainly did not feel particularly one with the black mare as she rode. The horse was in a mood and kept pretending to spook at things she had seen a hundred times before. Mares could be so difficult.

On the other hand, when they cooperated, they were better than geldings. It was a toss-up. She glanced at Galahad, then past him at the bright salmon of a jay.

It seemed, in fact, a day for birds. As they crossed a river, the azure blur of a kingfisher darted along it. The songs of other birds followed them, flowing after them with joy. It was early enough in the year for that.

They had all summer, and there was no need to return for the winter, simply find somewhere to hole up.

Finally, Galahad spoke, "Any thought on where?"

"I would have said Glastonbury, but if it was there once, it is not there any more. I doubt it ever was, or they would have been showing it off to all comers." Attracting pilgrims was a business of shrines, after all. Even stolen ones.

"Then you won't mind if I follow a rumor?"

"Rumor?"

"There is supposed to be a monastery on an island in the sea, off the north east coast, north of the wall, even."

Persy nodded. "You think..."

"It would be a good place to tuck such an item away and keep it safe, and those three women we saw could easily be nuns."

Persy nodded a bit. "And it would, even if we fail, be a good story to confirm the existence of a legend." She hated playing along, but she had no choice. If she pushed further, he would ride off without her.

"Exactly." He turned onto the north road. "I vote we make Ebor our first destination."

Persy wondered what Ebor was like now. Did they have peace and prosperity, or was the Norseman always at the gate?

The former, she suspected, for the latter they would have heard of entirely too quickly. Where else would the townsfolk come for help, after all?

Still, she wondered. Yet, the land through which they rode seemed quietly prosperous. Woods interspersed with small villages and the occasional farm. Squirrels scolded them from what seemed like every tree. Deer peered from the clearings and a swineherd guided his charges through the woods, rooting for acorns.

She felt a sort of doze come over her. It was as if it was the way things had always been and would always be. She could not imagine that it would ever change.

Perhaps she did doze off in the saddle, because for a moment she soared with the birds, watching the landscape change and alter. She saw the forests retreat to be replaced by fields of wheat and cattle. She saw a village grow into a town.

Too many people, she thought. When one encouraged women to have as many children as possible, they ended up with too many people. Then she was on her horse again, riding through the woods.

Except, was it really too many, or just more? She shook her head. It was not her place to judge. All she hoped was that Bronwen's children survived.

"You seem deep in thought."

Galahad's voice broke into her reverie. "Sorry. Woolgathering," she responded, turning slightly to look at him.

"Nothing wrong with that. I assume that your horse won't let you ride into a tree."

She laughed. "No trees in my direct path." The Roman road remained more or less clear. It would probably be used for all eternity.

It might even be that people would forget the name of Rome, but still use her roads.

Ebor had changed little, as it turned out. The walls still encircled it, although it seemed as if the townsmen had piled earth around the base to strengthen the foundations. That made them effectively lower, for a good man could climb the embankment easily.

Of course, he would be open to any archers on the walls. It like as not remained a sensible course of action.

The gate was guarded, but half-heartedly. They were barely challenged as they rode into the city. Within was a hotchpotch of crumbling Roman town houses and more recent wood and mud construction. Had the stone buildings not been in such obvious disrepair, one might have assumed the wood ones to be the older. As it was, it was a visible reference point.

Would the Romans be remembered as giants? The smell of manure and cooking fires mingled unpleasantly in Persy's nose. It was not quite as bad at Camelot. But cities always smelled. Always had and always would. The tang of urine betrayed, most likely, a tanner's work. A deeper, richer scent was that of a stable, and Galahad reined in his horse.

"I see an inn." He peered ahead, along the road.

"So do I. But is it a good one?" She dismounted, leading the black mare. A child chased a small dog across the road in front of her. From the look on the child's face, she decided to root for the dog. Its tail was in definite danger.

A cat yowled from somewhere not that far away. It sounded like its tail had already been yanked. Children did such things.

The inn was stone and had seen better days. At one point, it had even had glazed windows, but only fragments of the glass remained. Would people forget how to make glass?

A narrow courtyard next to the inn could have used somebody to spend a bit more time sweeping it, but at least it did not stink too much.

Persy decided to try and discourage Galahad from spending more than maybe a day in Ebor. Yet, it might be worth exploring the city. She was mometarily torn. If she could keep him there...but could she stand it? It would be better to stall somewhere else.

A boy took their horses and they walked into the common room of the inn.

Heads turned. Persy very much doubted the people were used to seeing warriors, even older ones. The few people in the main room, most of them nursing ale, seemed to be of the trader classes. There were few women other than a fairly pretty maiden who was probably the innkeeper's daughter and probably not really a maiden.

Galahad ignored her. He went instead to the bar, which was stained from many spills of ale and wine and mead. The faint smell of alcohol dominated.

Was it really a good place to stay? It would serve, Persy decided. It was reasonably clean, and she could only smell booze, not vomit and urine. She would, oddly, have been happier if the serving maid had been comelier.

She might have distracted Galahad from the memory of the lovely voice.

Persy claimed a corner table that currently stood empty. Galahad came over a moment later, and slid a tankard to her.

"We have rooms, and there is stew coming."

She sniffed at the ale, then took a sip. It was decent ale, but she would have preferred wine. It would have to do. "As little as I want to stay in this city, I think we should explore some."

"I agree. There might be things to learn here, and I suspect the king would appreciate a report."

"People seem reasonably prosperous." Then the vision flowed over her with such completeness that she gasped.

She saw Ebor in flames. Dark haired Danes rushed through the streets, pursuing the fleeing townsmen. The fire destroyed wooden houses and charred stone ones beyond recognition. When? It gave her no idea, no clue.

"What?"

Very, very quietly, "Ebor is going to be destroyed. But I don't know when. It could be a hundred, two hundred years in the future."

Galahad let out a breath. "Is there anything we can do?"

"Keep Britain united." Even as she said the words, she knew it was already too late.

The stew was tolerable, if bland, the room clean if small. The next day, Persy slipped out without Galahad. She needed to clear her head and get some air.

She headed towards where she suspected the old forum was. She was not surprised by what she found...it was a market now, farmers touting vegetables and milk. Goodwives and apprentices moved amongst the stalls. She almost envied each and every one of them.

Almost. No, she would not, truly, trade her life for theirs. However, they at least had to worry only about themselves and their families.

Beyond, the old administrative buildings were being used as a stone quarry, the land cleared. Not unexpected.

She did wonder what they were building. Perhaps the first of those great Christian temples? She saw a fairly sizable wooden building. If that was the church, it would be destroyed when the Danes came.

Why would the Danes sack Ebor? It seemed too destructive, almost, for mere viking or for settlers.

Unless they had demanded the city surrender and the townsmen refused. Or, perhaps, there would be the reasonable assumption that taking Ebor would give them control over much of the north.

It likely would. There was nothing Persy could do, except feel the pricking of tears behind her eyes.

In the end, they were going to lose. She knew that now. And Nimue was going to be in no small part responsible. Persy blamed Nimue. She blamed Mordred for being a brat.

She blamed Merlin for showing that even a wise man could be a fool where women were concerned. Arthur was walking proof of that. How many men were sensible where women were concerned?

Not many. Not that women were much better. Morgan was walking proof of *that*.

Maybe the idea of celibacy was not such a bad thing. It would at least keep a few people sane.

Of course, she had been celibate herself for so many years that she sometimes felt that she would not know what to do with a man if one showed up in her bed. It would be safe...she was far too old to get pregnant. But...she was also so used to being alone. At this point, she definitely would not know what to do with a relationship.

She might have been happier if she had had a relationship with Galahad after all. Was it even too late? He had never married.

She turned away from the construction and walked down a different street, essentially at random. Ebor was not built on flat ground but dipped down towards the river. That was the way she went, seeing the dark water flow through the city, under the old Roman bridge.

There were few buildings close to the water. Like as not they were afraid of floods.

She was not afraid of one right now. The river was, in fact, likely close to peak, given how early in summer it was. She walked down to its edge and regarded it.

Nobody approached or spoke to her. Typical townsfolk, evading any contact with a stranger. Unless, of course, they thought they could get money out of her. Of course, village people closed up too, but it was different, somehow. Less...she almost detected malice from the people. It might be because she was armed.

The river, she thought, would be there forever, and her mind flickered with another vision. The ground under her feet was stone. As she turned slightly she could see an inn that had been set dangerously close to the river's edge. The old Roman bridge had been replaced by a splendid edifice of stone. The faint roar of horseless carriages sounded from it, but it towered over her and she could not see the top. A large boat with glass sides glided along the river. Its top deck was full of people in fine clothing. A party barge, as it was rumored the Egyptians sailed down the Nile during their festivals.

It was an Ebor prosperous and joyful. A future that was not so bad, after all, but the flames had to come first.

Was the true message of her visions that she was wrong to fight for the old ways? She regarded the inn. It was not busy; it was too early in the day for day customers and anyone spending the night would be out on business. She took a step towards it and was back on the grassy riverbank, the ground slightly damp under her feet.

She would have cursed, but she knew she could not truly explore that future. It was beyond her reach and outside of her reality.

She only had here and now, and the wind from the river dampening her hair, cooling her. Strengthening her.

The thought that flowed through her next, though, was whether Galahad's death was also needed to create that future.

She also wondered, once more, whether, as prosperous as it seemed, it was a good future. Would it be better for people to keep living quietly? Their farms tucked in the eaves of woods that would some day be destroyed to make room.

Persy decided she did not know and could not, should not, judge. Perhaps nothing she did could change that future. Perhaps nothing she did could make any kind of a difference in the world.

The thought was enough to make her want to start drinking, as early as it was. Instead, she made her way back up to the road, and headed up a nearby street. It arced up a hill, and she wondered if the street would stay where it was, or whether it would move with time and change.

Only a few buildings were set along it...the houses of reasonably wealthy individuals. Kitchen gardens surrounded them, full of green shoots. Again, Persy felt that strange mixture of envy and satisfaction. She would not want to be one of those people...or would she?

She shook her head. If she was one, then all she would know was that life, dull and plodding and yet with its own rewards. There was no sense to wondering about it.

She stopped at the crest of the hill, turned and looked back. The old walls covered a wider area than the current population needed. One day, like as not, they would be full to bursting again, but that day was not yet.

The street flickered, and she saw it cobbled, with carriages parked outside of elegant stone houses. Nobody she knew knew how to build like that. Nobody outside Rome. A woman in flowing garb was being helped out of one of the carriages by a servant. Wealthy indeed, Persy thought, admiring the horses for a moment. Then the vision faded.

Had her Sight returned because she was on the right path, or the wrong one? Should she have stayed at court?

She would have been called a weakling and a nursemaid if so. She wished she did not care about such insults, but in truth she did. She did when they came from people she had considered her friends. Still did, even with this madness that seemed to have swept over them.

There was, though, nothing, she could learn there.

Persy and Galahad spent the next three days gathering rumors. Persy asked about the women, Galahad about the monastery to the north.

The division of labor was tacitly agreed on. Persy was not enough up on Christian theology to adequately fake being a pilgrim to some shrine of theirs.

That, she left to Galahad. Meanwhile, she gained her impressions of Ebor.

She stood at the construction site. There were men working, stripped to the waist. The sweat poured off them. She thought of labors she herself had performed.

"Do you need something, sir?" came a voice from nearby.

She turned. "Just curious. What are you building?"

"It will be a monastery," the man said, simply. "And a church for the Christian citizens."

She nodded a little. "I suspected as much." Perhaps one day there would be one of those great temples here after all.

"Are you Christian?"

"No, but my traveling companion is. He might be interested." She definitely intended to mention all of this to Galahad.

"I...see." The man seemed uncomfortable all of a sudden.

"Don't worry. I'm pretty tolerant." Of course, it was sadly likely that the man was not tolerant and would immediately start in on the conversion.

"I'm sorry. But the last pagan I talked to, I honestly thought she was going to..."

Persy tensed. "Dark hair and eyes, fair skin, maybe a little older than I am, but still quite the looker?"

"You know her?"

"Yeah."

"She seemed…" He paused. "I would say unstable, but she was too controlled for that. Trying to expertly sow doubts in any souls she could encounter. I suspect she served the Devil, not any pagan god."

Persy nodded. "That's her, alright. I'd just...stay out of her way."

"You can't tell me what's going on?"

"Given I don't want to know about it, I'm sure you don't."

He laughed, although it was a somewhat sharp laugh, unpleasant in its tone. "Got it. But she's gone anyway. She rode north. Nice horse, I'll give her that, but crazy to travel without a man."

So, Morgan was ahead of them. Good. Maybe she would... "How long ago was this?"

"Maybe a week." The man glanced at the monastery. "I suppose it could be worse. She could have cast a spell on me."

"You do realize that the vast majority of pagans know no more spells than you do, right?"

"Yes, but..."

Persy shook her head. "Thank you." She turned to walk away, but did spare him a glance over her shoulder. He seemed frightened. Or at the very least, concerned. Well, there was nothing she could do about it. He'd get over it.

Morgan. Barely a week ahead of them. Persy had that. She felt an odd mixture of tension and relief within her. Part of her was oddly glad the witch was still alive.

They could catch up with her. Then what could they do? Force of arms might or might not stand against her, even if she could convince Galahad.

He was not always easy to convince, about anything. A good man, but even more stubborn than she was. Besides, she did not, in truth, want to catch up with Morgan.

A strong gust of wind caught her as she turned. It carried with it an odd scent. It smelled like battle. Surely not? No, she realized. It was a charnel house, the wind shifting to blow the stench of butchery towards her. Needless to say, she did not linger, quickening her pace back to the inn.

Galahad came to her room later. "Percival?" he whispered.

She let him in. "We're a week behind Morgan."

"Seriously?" He seemed less surprised than she might have thought and more vaguely concerned.

"Seriously." Persy breathed in, then out. "I don't know whether we want to catch up with her or not."

"Depends on which of us is right."

Persy stepped over to the room's small window, looked out at the narrow courtyard. "I'm not wrong about her, Galahad. I wish I was. I don't want to be anywhere near her, not anymore."

She would, in fact, rather like to be in the next province. Was Gaul far enough? Of course, they were going north of the wall.

43

Riding out the next day was true misery, enough to make Persy seriously consider suggesting that they wait another day.

The rain fell in thin streams, soaking through cloaks and manes. The black mare kept tossing her head, as if annoyed by the falling water. The road they took was the road to the wall, west of Badon.

She remembered that as if it was yesterday. Her hands tucked under the black's mane for warmth, she glared at the mist and rain.

"Okay, this is miserable."

"We should have stayed in Ebor," Persy grumbled.

"I don't think we could afford any more time, especially you're right Morgan's on the rampage."

"Morgan's not on the rampage. She has far too much control for that." Persy could not help but snort a little.

"Whatever you want to call it." Galahad snorted back, amused. "Maybe she's trying to…"

"To spring the trap for us."

"It's not a trap. The grail is real." He sounded a little sad.

Even the animals sheltered from the rain. Not bird nor beast stirred. Persy frowned again. She felt as if the world was closing in around her.

It was the perfect setting for trouble, and surprisingly, that thought caused her to relax. If it looked like there should be trouble, then there would be none. The trouble would wait for the bright, clear day.

The sun struggled through the clouds all day, and by its end Persy was further north than she had ever been.

Roman messengers, switching horses, had gone from the wall to London in a day. They were slower, taking great care of their mounts. At nightfall, they reached a small village. It seemed to sleep already.

There was no inn. Galahad talked a farmer out of a meal and space in his barn.

Yet, there was also no sleep for her that night. She stepped out into the darkness.

The rain and clouds had cleared. The full panoply of the sky extended above her, stars upon stars and no darkness of space. She began to doubt the traditional explanation of stars as pin pricks in heaven's canopy. No, there were far too many for any fabric to maintain its integrity.

There was nothing but stars, as if stars were the stuff of which the world was made. Perhaps they really were the hearth fires of the dead.

Most likely, they were something else altogether. Something beyond her understanding, something only the gods could grasp. Her mind's eye shimmered, and she saw something like a great arrow fired towards the sky, burning as it went, reaching for the stars.

Reaching for the gods. Had they abandoned her, flown with the last of the dragons? The visions had come back, but she still wondered.

Perhaps the stars were the gods. Or at least some manifestation of them.

An owl hooted, its querulous 'Towhit' answered by a 'Towhoo' after a moment. Husband owl, calling to his wife.

She knew she should go back to bed, yet something held her out there.

Something. Then there were lights in the trees, dancing ones. "Fae," she breathed, softly.

She could not see their forms, not clearly. Had they come to remind her they were still here, or, in her worst fears, to say goodbye?

The most beautiful of all creatures and beings, they danced around her, pulling her into their dance. She knew the dangers of giving in, she knew that they might steal hours, even days from her.

She also knew that if she refused them, she would earn their anger, something she could not afford. She stepped into the dance, let them take her, let them claim her.

Let the night become only their dance.

She woke up on the ground. Her memory fuzzy, she did not remember half of the night. Only the stars and the fairies. There was, though, no more rain or darkness.

She felt a strength within her, something she had needed more than she realized. She no longer felt abandoned.

Far from it. They had gone out of their way to remind her that she was loved.

"Percival!" Galahad, frantic.

She picked herself up, moving towards the barn. "I'm sorry!"

"What happened?" He approached her, worried and angry.

"I couldn't sleep, went for a walk, sat down on the grass and..."

Galahad stared at her, then just burst out laughing. "So, when you could have slept in a reasonably warm barn..."

She hated lying to him, but the truth would only have caused them both pain. "Pretty much."

"I hate insomnia. Are you fit to ride?"

"Definitely. Although if we can bribe breakfast out of that farmer's wife...given how good supper was."

Bribing breakfast proved easy. They hit the road filled with bacon, eggs and black pudding. Nothing beat the latter for giving one strength.

The clear weather, too, continued. Ahead of them was the wall.

The Emperor Hadrian had given up on the Picts. He had declared them such barbarians that they would never be civilized and built a wall to keep them out.

That was history. The reality was still incredibly solid. No legions manned it, but the wall and gate still stood firm. There was nobody to open the gate for them, but nor was it locked. It took both of them pushing to move it, the mechanism creaking. Galahad's mount decided it contained a horse-eating monster, broke free and fled south.

Persy was on the mare in a second, pursuing the errant animal. It did not seem to want to stop, plunging down a dip. If it lamed itself, they were in deep trouble.

She followed, finally getting ahead of the gelding. It was slipping out of panic mode now, the ears no longer quite as flat, the eyes not rolling, but there was foam around the bit. "Easy...Whoah. Easy."

Horses. For such large creatures they could be inveterate cowards.

Then she saw the men. Two of them, and ragged enough that she hoped they would not see through her disguise. One of them tried to grab Galahad's horse, but the animal was having none of it, closing its teeth onto his arm.

"Ow!"

Persy took the opportunity to claim the reins, but with two sets in her hands, she was not going to be able to fight if these men chose to attack her.

"A wealthy warrior. You don't need two horses, do you?" one of them asked, almost wryly.

Bandits. But there was something in their eyes that told her they were desperate, not malicious. "I'm afraid I do, but I might have other help for you." She could hear something moving in the brush behind her. She hoped it was Galahad.

One of the men turned, to cover the entering stranger. "Ah, yes, there are two of you. And ten of us."

Persy laughed. She could not help it. "I have faced worse odds with better opponents."

Their swords came out. So did Galahad's. Persy released Galahad's horse. The animal had settled now, it could be trusted not to run off unless it needed to.

One who had not been bitten lunged for the bridle, tripped over a root, and fell flat on his face. Persy laughed again.

"Where did you find these fools?" Galahad inquired.

"They seem to fancy themselves as both warriors and horse thieves."

Galahad did not bother with the horse, he simply drew his sword. "Shall we teach them what a true warrior is?"

Persy's blood was not even coming up. Against men such as this, she could probably win with one hand tied behind her back.

One of them struck at her. She disarmed him with a neat move. "They are not worth the effort of killing."

At that point, they rushed her. Two of them collided. A third practically impaled himself on Galahad's sword.

"Oops," the other warrior said, tugging his weapon free from the body.

That was enough to cause no less than three of the bandits to run and the rest to hesitate. "Come on," Persy said. "Honestly, we don't actually want to kill you, but we will if you persist."

She did not want to, she felt a certain sorrow within her. That there was so much prosperity, but still those desperate men. It might be inevitable. That did not mean she had to like it.

The men stepped back. "We surrender," said one of them.

"Good. Now. How did you reach such straits?"

"You were too nice," Galahad said as they rode north from the wall.

"No. There is a difference between evil men and desperate. What would killing them have gained us?"

He hesitated, then he nodded a little. "Nothing," he admitted.

"Nothing at all."

"Whilst leaving them alive and showing them a few tricks to stay that way will give the people around here some protection." Persy glanced north. A road led to a second wall that had been built further north but supposedly overrun. Supposedly.

How would they...

"We need to turn east," Galahad mused. "The only way we're going to find this monastery is to follow the coast."

He was right. "Leaving what road there is will slow us down, but..."

He started to turn his horse from the road. The gelding balked.

Persy hesitated. The horse might merely be being difficult again, or it might have noticed something they had not. They were in wild country now. North of the wall were only the Picts and Scotti. Barbarians. That did not make them bad, necessarily, but they were dangerous. They might not appreciate southerners in their territory.

"Come on," Galahad said softly, and the gelding elected to cooperate. He snorted and stepped into the brush.

They found some kind of trail quickly. It might have been made by deer or by Picts. Or perhaps started by deer and enlarged by Picts. That was, often enough, how trails started in the south.

The Picts could not be that much different from her own people. They were rumored to have somewhat strange customs and to be very fond of body paint. Beyond that, she knew little of them.

The terrain was no different from that immediately south of the wall to start with, but the altitude began to increase, slowly but surely. Then they crossed a ridge and started to descend again. That was all she was aware of.

The trees were smaller and stunted, but remained a tangle, hard to navigate. "This is a wilderness."

"Yes. I wonder where all the people are."

"Maybe nobody lives this close to the wall. Maybe the legions used to ride north and hunt Picts for fun." She wished that was less plausible than it was. She knew what restless soldiers could be like.

"Maybe they did. Or to hunt other things and the Picts just thought they might be hunting them."

Even more plausible. "Whoa!"

The ground suddenly dipped away from them. Galahad's horse stopped not far from the edge. Was it the coast? No...it was a steeply cut river valley.

They turned north along it. "I hope this monastery of ours is actually real." Galahad expressed doubt for the first time.

"We'll have to see. It's a long wild goose chase if not, but..." She hoped it was real, but that the grail was not there. That, above all, Morgan was not there. The few days she might have would be more than enough.

She did not want to be on the right track. Not, when the right track led to Galahad's death. She knew that, so why wasn't she trying harder to stop him? Because it would only make him more determined. She knew that just as thoroughly. They found a place they could cross the river, continuing vaguely northeast.

The worst part was, with no settlements, they would have no place to spend the night.

No place other than miserable bedrolls under the stars. It rained, of course, and the trees here were not enough to give shelter. She wondered, if you went far enough north, if there would cease to be any trees. Then what would there be? What kind of land? Grass and bare rock?

She shivered a bit, from imagined cold. How much worse, too, would the colder winters have been to those who dwelled here?

A shout in a language she did not know disturbed her reverie. She sat up, reaching for her sword.

The Picts had them surrounded.

44

They were a short, dark people not so very different from the Cymry. In the darkness, she could only vaguely tell that they were wearing some kind of paint, but struggled to see pattern, let alone color.

Persy stood up. "I don't speak your language."

She heard Galahad turning.

The Picts turned to one another, exchanged words in their own tongue. Finally, a slender woman stepped forward and spoke in accented Latin. "Southerners. What doing here?"

"We are pilgrims," Galahad said, "seeking the monastery that supposedly lies off the coast."

The woman's reaction was distinctly odd. She licked her lips.

Galahad stared at her.

"Monastery. Yes. How do we know you go there, not try to take our cattle?"

"We don't have any need for your cattle, don't worry." Persy studied the small woman. Their cattle were clearly important to them.

"Well, we will make sure you go there, then. Or rather I will." The woman tapped her weapons. "Besides, southerners get lost, without guide."

Persy glanced at Galahad for a moment. She nodded to him.

"Alright. Frankly, I think we're already a little lost."

His Latin was not quite as good as hers, but it was serviceable. She wondered where the Pictish woman had learned it.

In the morning, they moved out, leading the horses. The Pictish woman, who gave no name, stayed ahead of them, as quick on her feet as some were in the saddle.

Persy kept one hand on the reins, the other on her sword hilt. She did not trust the Picts. It could be a trap, and the lip licking still disturbed her. Why would the mention of the monastery trigger such a reaction?

Then...the land suddenly opened up. "Wow," Persy could not help but say.

"You like the sea, yes?" came the Pict's voice.

"I like open spaces." The land fell away in a cliff, and fell away more to the north. She saw along the coast, the blue water, and ahead some kind of fishing village. Beyond that, the land seemed to extend out into the sea. If it was an island, it was very close in.

"Danger comes from the sea."

"You have Norsemen problems?"

"Yes," the woman said, shortly. "We send them running." She glanced up at Persy for a moment.

"Good." Even though Persy was sure the Norsemen had reasons come here, that did not give them the right to take other people's land. Or destroy Ebor, if, they truly intended to do so.

Yet, what would she do if it was her land that was suddenly cold and barren?

"You like them not."

"They've tried to kill me before." Persy glanced at Galahad, who was having a minor argument with his horse. Then back to the woman.

"But you would still take our cattle."

"I wouldn't. I won't deny there are some who might, though." She thought of the ragged bandits. They would not be above cattle rustling.

"Ah, good. You have enough wisdom to know you do not command all of your fellows. Even your king cannot."

"He commands those close to him, but he admittedly can't be everywhere at once." Nobody could. And that was part of the wisdom this barbarian spoke.

Well, there was no law saying that a Pict could not be smart. She might even be a witch, Persy thought. She might...well. She might be anything.

They walked on in silence. Neither Persy nor Galahad was willing to ride when their guide remained on foot. The grass crunched under her boots, seeming oddly springy. It appeared to be a different kind of grass from what she was used to.

The village was fairly primitive. No Roman building techniques here, only roundhouses with thatched roofs. A couple of boats had been pulled up on the beach. As they approached, she saw light glint from bronze weapons.

It seemed everyone down to the children was armed. Norsemen troubles indeed. Those weapons might well have been turned on them. And....there were islands. Or an island, anyway, although she saw no monastery.

"We cannot go to the monastery now."

"Why not?" Galahad asked.

The woman smiled. "The tide is in."

She led them down into the village. A quick exchange of words between her and one of the men, and the weapons went back into belts and sheaths.

"So, it is not a true island," Persy commented to Galahad. A young woman brought them food, accepting coin in payment.

They were not entirely uncivilized...cattle might matter most, but they were not above the use of money. She did see some cattle...small, shaggy creatures well suited to the north. They were brown or black.

Fine beasts, Persy thought, in their own way...they had good reason to worry about them being rustled.

"Tide?" she asked their guide, accepting a bowl of stew...it seemed to contain mostly mollusks.

"In a few hours."

Persy nodded, and moved over towards the water with her stew, settling down comfortably. A few hours. There was so much tension here, though. They were not poor, no, but they lacked security. This place was not safe. She wanted to curse out the Norsemen.

Then, she often did. In between pitying them. What a world, she thought.

Still, the Picts did not seem horrible and aggressive and violent, not like she had envisioned them. True, they did wear body paint, but they also wore clothes. They were warriors, but also fishermen. And very proud of their cattle.

Fierce, they might be, but they were not what she had envisioned...men and women huddling in the cold, against the night, barely human.

She looked out at the island. All she saw was grass. If there was a monastery, then it was out of sight.

How did she kill a few hours in a Pictish village? Galahad tended to the horses. Smart, she realized, to take on that task when there was little else to do.

She did not dare wander far, either, in case she was mistaken for an enemy. About all she could do was sit and watch the waves lap against the beach.

Something cried, a lonely sound. She looked up, and the largest seagull she had ever seen glided above the water. Grey and white wings carried it on the wind. She watched it fly.

For the birds, she thought, nothing ever changed. They had the wind, as they had always had. They ruled far more of the earth than could men, and they cared nothing for politics.

The seagull cried again. It did sound as if it was searching for something or someone, but that was applying human emotions to a bird. She knew better, having spent enough time with horses.

Dogs came close. Dogs and horses had emotions. Just not human ones. She missed Snow.

She needed to get another dog, once this was over. It would not have to be a hunting hound, but she did need a dog. Having somebody who would worship you the way a dog did was good for the soul.

The seagull drifted away. A couple of half-naked children ran along the beach, playing some kind of tag. Kids...the same everywhere, she thought wryly. Some things were universals. The games of children. The very different game played between men and women. The ultimate game, too, that of power. Of politics.

For a moment, it seemed as if she was on the verge of some insight, of some answer to all of her questions.

"Percival!"

In that moment, she could have killed Galahad.

They rode out, eventually. A trail led through muddy flats that had been exposed by the tide. The horses liked it little.

Persy wondered what would happen if the tide came in? Well, perhaps the monks had a couple of spare cells. Actually, they undoubtedly would have some provision for stranded pilgrims.

This would not, she thought, stop the Norsemen, who came from the sea. But it would certainly slow down any attack on the monastery from the land. That and those armed villagers. She wondered if they were Christians...or if they protected the monks for some reason connected to their guide's odd reaction. About which Persy had not found the courage to ask.

Then the full extent of it hit her. She had sort of expected the monastery to be on the far side of the island, behind it.

No. This was only the first island, and now the road stretched out across what was, at some times, the sea bed. She saw the monastery now...low buildings. A few sheep that would give them meat and wool...the latter had to be vital so far north, especially now.

It took a couple of hours to cross. Persy wondered if anyone had been caught by the tide in the middle and swept away. More likely, she thought, people got trapped on that first small island. That would be a miserable, but not particularly dangerous, fate.

The black shivered some, not liking it at all. A good horse, she carried on. Galahad's gelding threatened to run right back to land more than once. Seagulls were the only other living things they saw.

Finally they were on solid ground again. Persy thought that if anyone remembered Roman road building techniques, building some kind of road through the water might be a good idea.

The sheep made various sounds as they rode through them, moving away. Maybe they were worried Persy had a set of shears hidden away somewhere.

A monk moved to greet them.

"Brother. I brought you a couple of lost pilgrims."

"Welcome."

Persy watched the man's body language. Why did he seem so tense? Perhaps because the pilgrims were armed warriors.

"I suppose," the monk continued, "you'll want some to take with you."

The woman licked her lips. "Of course! Usual payment?"

Lamb? No, the Picts seemed to prefer cattle to sheep...unless that was why.

Persy slid down from the mare, leaning against her shoulder as the monk vanished into one of the buildings and came out with some bottles filled with something yellow.

Mead. The monks were paying the villagers for their protection in mead. She wanted to laugh for a moment. Then she wanted to try some. As much as she preferred wine, the Pict's face spoke clearly of the quality of the mead.

Her scalp prickled and her body started to tense. The monk was acting perfectly normally. Smiling, even.

She glanced at their guide, but the woman's attention was entirely on the mead. She took the bottles, and rapidly headed back for the water road.

"So...pilgrims?"

Galahad nodded. "We heard of this place and thought it a legend."

The monk glanced over his shoulder. "That would be a good defense...if we could convince the Norsemen of it. Or..." He tailed off. "Come. What has happened here needs to be witnessed."

"Happened?" Persy was abruptly very tense.

She did not want to think about the likelihood of what it was, especially as the hair on the back of her neck was trying to escape its sockets.

"Yes. A great miracle. We thought you knew."

"I suspect word has not spread that far, or you would be overwhelmed."

The monk nodded. "Come. It is in the church. But..." He paused, she saw his chest rise with a deeper breath. "Please. Be respectful."

Galahad's eyes brightened. "It is here. The chalice!"

"Yes..." The monk paused. "So, you knew of it, but did not know..."

"We did not know. It was...a hunch." Galahad was almost out of breath.

Persy frowned. Whatever he was caught up in, it did not affect her. "Is it stone?"

The monk looked affronted. "Of course not. It is pure silver."

"Galahad. Do not enter that church." She moved into his path, murmuring, "It's a fake."

Galahad brushed her aside, quickening his pace. "Percival. Don't be ridiculous."

She glared at him. "Galahad. You're the one being ridiculous."

"I have to see it."

The monk was sort of staring between the two. He could, perhaps, see his advantage slipping. "Come. I will show you."

Galahad followed. Persy realized the only way she was going to prevent him was to physically grab him.

She had no illusions as to who would win in an actual fight. All she could do was follow.

If she could keep him from touching it, perhaps she could save him. "Has anyone touched this chalice?"

"Of course not. It is far too holy. The virgin who placed it in the chapel is the only one, and she has vanished."

Of course. Probably not even a virgin, Persy thought. Not uncharitably...she did not place any great value on virginity. Over-rated. Yet, the dishonesty bothered her.

The church was a small wooden building with a stone floor. It was the place.

"Galahad..."

"Leave me alone."

The monk took that literally. Persy was not moving. Galahad strode into the chapel. He saw it, there.

It was silver, and ornately decorated. Its surface was marked with symbols Persy did not recognize.

"Galahad. Do not."

He was reaching to touch it.

"It's poisoned!"

"Persy...it's...it's the..."

"Trust me, Galahad. If you touch that cup, if you drink from it, you'll die."

It was clear he did not believe her. "If I die, it is because God wanted me at his side."

"You have never spouted this nonsense before. All gods...even yours...guard best those who guard themselves."

He stepped towards the grail.

"If you do this, Galahad, you are no longer my friend." It was a low blow. It was all of the ammunition she had left.

He looked at her, stricken. For a long moment, he remained there, frozen. Then he made his choice. Or it was made for him. She knew in that moment that her friend had lost his mind, that he was a victim of the maidens and their manipulations. Turning, he reached to lift the grail in both hands.

She leapt towards him, but it was too late. He fell to the ground, boneless, without making so much as a sound.

She knew he was dead without even checking. She too fell to the ground. The darkness that claimed her was absolute.

45

Persy awakened slowly, her eyes struggling open. She lay on a thin, narrow bed in a strange room.

She was at a monastery, and they had put her in one of the cells. Had they uncovered her secret? Had they cared if so?

She was still fully clad, so she could hope that they remained clueless. Galahad.

Dammit. Damn him. The tears came, freely. She did not care if anyone thought she looked like less of a man. She did not care if they thought she was worthless, even.

She was worthless. She had failed to save her best friend, and all she could do was regret that they had never been lovers. Regret, also, her last words to him.

"Why do you weep?"

She looked up. One of the brothers stood in the doorway.

"Why do you think?" Her anger snapped outwards, for a moment the monk's form was veiled in red. She pulled it back.

"God has taken him."

"Don't let anyone else touch that cup."

"That is not possible. It has vanished."

The cup might have been entirely glamour. Yet, it had been intended to snare Arthur, not Galahad. Why had it vanished?

The next thing that had to be made to disappear was her. The witness. She resolved to eat and drink nothing until she had left the island. "I'm leaving."

"Is that wise?"

"I am leaving now. I am taking my friend's body with me."

"I'm...afraid that will not be possible."

"What?"

"He too has vanished. He was taken into heaven."

Nice. A very nice, tidy little legend. And the prospect, the possibility that Galahad was still alive. She needed an answer to that.

"I have to see the church, then."

"Drink something."

"No." She got up, feeling a little weak. "Please. I'll be fine."

The church was empty. No blood, no wine, nothing...no sign any of it had happened. And within those walls, she did not dare ask her gods for a sign.

So, she did something she would never have done any other time. She asked his.

She felt the presence for a moment...sorrowful, most definitely real. The sense that the chapel needed to be cleansed.

They would not do it. They thought they had a miracle, and she knew the consequences of that. The church would be destroyed. It would burn, and it would be rebuilt. The legend would survive. The pagans would tell it as what it was, as hubris. To the Christians it would be proof of faith, and it would make them even more likely to seek death in the service of their god. It would make them want to be taken directly to heaven, as Galahad had been. Morgan and her spiritual descendants would laugh at each of those foolish deaths, as she no doubt did at this one. Persy could not even cry. Could not even seek vengeance, for she knew who would win...

The monastery would burn and be rebuilt, and that was sorrow too. But the answer to her one question was simply...pain.

Galahad was dead. She knew it for certain, but as she stepped out of the church, she knew one other thing; the mead recipe would survive.

She had not even had the chance to try any.

Only pain followed her across the causeway. Galahad's horse was unhappy about leaving without his master. He kept shying at nothing and anything. She could not even be angry with the beast.

She was hungry and thirsty, but the need to put as much distance between herself and that place as possible overwhelmed everything else. She did not so much as pause in the village. The mist that covered her eyes at intervals was, she knew, tears.

Tears that wanted to come even more freely. She had nothing left. She could not even say, for sure, that she remained loyal to Arthur.

Was Arthur even still alive? Had the trap caught any more of her friends? She had been protected, perhaps by her own faith, but Galahad had not been.

That was not fair. She had lost the last person she truly loved, and it had been his own fault, and he was not here to yell at any more.

She wanted to hurt somebody. She wanted to hurt that god that seemed unable or unwilling to protect his true and loyal followers most of all. Was he weaker than Morgan?

She wanted Morgan dead.

No, she wanted Morgan destroyed. Dead beyond all hope of reincarnation or resurrection. She wanted to never have heard the word 'grail'.

She wanted to find the real thing so she could smash it into a thousand pieces. Her horse, picking up on her mood, skittered sideways.

She tried to calm the mare, but how could she when she could not calm herself? Galahad was dead, his body taken and no doubt desecrated.

He would not be buried in hallowed ground, either Christian or pagan. And he would be falsely remembered as a martyr.

Persy vowed to remember the truth, to speak the truth. She vowed that if his soul was trapped she would find it and free it...that being all she could do for him.

That and wish she had acted on those long-repressed feelings, wish she had taken him within herself.

There is no regret keener than not having loved and then lost, for had she loved...

Where did she go? Back to Camelot? Or did she continue the quest, not for the grail but for her revenge?

Revenge burned the soul, she remembered. She knew that. Yet her soul felt already charred and cindered. She saw no escape for her from that. Time would heal, but she did not want to wait.

She barely cared, in that moment, if Morgan killed her. She also cared nothing for where she traveled.

West and north, then, without any thought, where mountains towered.

She could not face Arthur with the news. She could not return to Camelot, not yet.

Not until her own soul was quiet.

It was not quiet. Nothing was quiet. She walked alongside the horses up a rocky path. The sky threatened rain, but did not yet offer it. She was glad of that, for if the path became slick...

What was she doing? Her reason had returned to a point, but her fear of returning to Camelot was so intense she wondered if she had been geased. Arthur's face floated in her mind.

Everywhere she went, there was death. The trees were not stunted, but many of them seemed to be dead, their needles turned grey and brown, their bark peeling. Some blight or sickness, perhaps.

Or Morgan. Had she become so dark, so tainted that her touch did it? Persy thought not, but she could not be sure.

She was sure of nothing. No visions had come to her, and she sensed the presence of neither gods nor fae. Like as not, it was grief that kept her from them. Grief and guilt.

Yet, perhaps, she had always been doomed to failure. Was what she saw fated to be? She did not know.

And thus, she wandered, lost in the lands north of the Wall. Halfheartedly, she sought the grail and Morgan, but neither was her true goal. It was her own soul that she had lost. She lived. She survived off the land...rabbits and hares were plentiful, as were berries and nuts, although she saw no fruit. It had never been a highly fertile land, and it was less so now things were colder. The most common form of life she saw were deep red squirrels, scurrying from branch to branch in search of nuts and seeds.

Her depression had reached its deepest as she rode out of the forest and onto a heath. Purple flowers decorated the ground, bushes touched with brilliant gold surrounded her.

The sun came out from behind a cloud, transforming the scene into bright color, but she barely saw it.

Then, the bird sailed overhead. Broad wings carried it, its body dark, its head almost as gold as the gorse. It was not that high. She could have shot it easily, except there was no way she would.

She knew exactly what it was. Circling above her was the eagle of the Legions. The eagle of Rome. It cried out, as mournfully as the dragon once had, yet it did not leave.

It was calling to its mate, she realized. It was not the eagle of the Legions, it was simply a bird. Yet it was a bird touched with brass and gold. It was a golden eagle, and she had thought they, like the Legions, had gone.

Nay, simply flown north of the wall where there were fewer people to bother them. She could not blame the eagle. Was she not hiding north of the wall herself?

The Legions had flown. They had long flown, and they had taken with them something intangible. Something known by its absence more than by its presence. Not hope, no.

A sort of faith. People had believed in Rome, had turned to her to solve their problems, but then Rome had failed to solve her own.

There had to be a lesson in there somewhere. And a lesson in the eagle, showing up right now and reminding her of Rome.

Was it time to go home? No. Yet some vague sense of purpose flowed through her and she quickened her pace, turning slightly south.

West. What was west of there...no southwest? How would she know? She tried to put the map of Britain together in her mind, but she had wandered lost for so long that she did not know where she was.

She rode Galahad's gelding and ponying the mare. The mare was the quieter horse and she felt she needed the extra control on the animal likely to cause the problems. It had dropped her twice already, putting in a nasty little buck with a twist when it got fed up.

When she got home, suddenly a when, not an if. Yet, she also wanted to keep the horse. What else did she have? Galahad's sword had vanished with him. She had nothing of his except the horse and tack. And memories. So many painful memories.

She had thought she was leaving him free for another, younger woman, but the truth was he had wanted nobody else. She knew that now.

Where was she going? She did not know. The only place that might lie ahead was the Roman fort of Carlisle, at the end of the Wall. There was Carlisle at one end, Wall's End at the other.

That had to be her destination, but she was not the one who had chosen it. Perhaps it was the gods.

Yes, it was the gods who were guiding her. There was no other choice except some geas from Morgan. If it was the latter, then Persy would gladly sacrifice her very existence to stop the woman.

If she had Galahad's soul, then she could... That thought cut off. If she did, then she had to be stopped, she had to be destroyed. Not just killed, but taken out of the equation altogether.

Could Nimue do that? Persy knew she could not. Merlin was dead, and no replacement had ever been named.

The horses shied, both of them, away from the small glen ahead of them. Her own senses flared, a moment later. The stench of death and dark magic.

She had found Morgan after all, guided by those feelings. She had found her.

And she was dead. An odd, disturbing mix of grief and relief went through her. The witch lay where she had fallen, pale skin and dark hair, a Pictish arrow protruding from her.

After all that, with all her power, a skilled hunter had brought her down. Persy dismounted, stepped over to the body. "After all that. The mighty always fall." A pause, then, maliciously, to whatever spirit yet remained. "Your son will be no more king than mine."

In truth, she would miss the woman; yet, she would also have no reason to fear her. She would also eternally regret that the arrow had not been hers.

Persy herself was alive, and while she did not relish that right now, a small voice of reason told her she would.

Reminded her that grief was part of life. Yet who, now, had she not outlived? Arthur himself...and she would outlive him, she had little doubt of that.

She had outlived parents, her only child, her best friend and several of her enemies. That could only mean the gods still had work for her to do.

That was the only thing it could mean.

46

Persy came on the fort of Carlisle from the north. Unlike the gates they had first entered, these were manned. Armed mercenaries took aim on her as she approached.

"Whoah! I'm not Scotti!" She was aware that she was as filthy as one, however. When had she last bathed? She had missed her chance at the monastery.

She hoped people would at least keep that habit from Rome. There was nothing worse than a man who did not bathe. Well, except maybe, a woman who neglected to do so at certain times.

"You speak Latin?"

"Yes. I was on a mission for the king that took me north of the Wall."

That magic word got the gate open, but they still watched her warily.

"Did you lose a companion, warrior?"

She nodded, hoping that in her current state she would not be outed as a woman. "I did. To foul deeds and magic."

"That is not the story we have heard."

She shook her head. "It is the truth. As all men know, the truth can change in the telling...and sometimes two witnesses see different things."

She would make herself unpopular, she realized. So she did not press the issue further. "Is there a bath house here?"

Getting a bathing chamber to herself was not difficult. She would have, she decided, to seriously contemplate burning what was left of her clothes. Still, the water washed a good part of her remaining grief away.

It would remain with her, but she was no longer a madman, a wild woman who survived on berries and uncooked meat.

Yet, she was sure she would not be believed about Galahad's fate. Was it even wise to perpetuate the truth, or would his memory be better served by letting people believe the lie the monks were telling?

People would believe it anyway, and she knew what Morgan had truly succeeded in doing...ensuring the ascendancy of Christianity.

Why? What would she have gained by that? Or perhaps the faster the climb, the faster the fall.

As she left, she was approached by a boy. "You must ride to Camelot now."

"Why?"

"I don't know...it might be a rumor, but the rumor is that the king and the prince stand opposed."

"Mordred?" Without his mother to rein him in, with much of the warband gone, had the boy decided he did not want to wait for Arthur's death? "Where are my horses?"

With two, she could probably get to Camelot in a few days. It was almost certainly too late. Yet, she had to try.

With food in her saddlebags, she rode out from Carlisle at the fastest pace she felt she could sustain. There was an old Roman road beneath her hooves and the day was bright and clear, albeit with the promise of fall.

Had she really rode out with Galahad only that spring? Galahad. Dammit, but she needed him. The king needed all the loyal men he could get, for the young would likely side with Mordred.

What if it turned into battle? Then Cornwall's son would eventually become king. Cornwall and Bronwen's. What if Mordred did something to either of them?

The thought was almost enough to make her push the horses to founder, but she could not afford to do that. Nor could she afford to be like the messenger who had run to Marathon and then dropped dead.

He had run twenty-six miles in one day. She wondered if somebody could do that and live? Probably, if they prepared for it properly, if they built up to it, but who would put that much time into achieving such a goal?

Somebody who had nothing better to do, and she knew nobody with nothing better to do.

She rode. She crouched low over the horse's neck, the rhythm of its hooves becoming the litany of her life.

She reckoned three days. Three days, and she would be at Camelot.

What if it was a false rumor? What if, heck, somebody had sent the boy to bring her home by whatever means it took?

That could be it. She had been gone only a summer, though, and before for years. Why would she be missed unless, of course, it was...

...the story, that must have been passed from hand to hand as if it was heated in a stove. Of course they wanted her back. They wanted answers. She would have wanted answers herself.

They would not like and possibly not believe the ones she would give them. Not want to believe, rather.

On the third day, she reached Camelot.

The village beneath the fort was deserted, the church locked and barred. She saw all this as she rode, the black mare beneath her, Galahad's horse walking alongside. He was finally too tired to cause her any trouble. Instead, he only snorted and pretended to shy at a piece of cloth blowing in the wind.

The fort gates too were closed and barred. "Ho!" she called.

"Who?" It was Kay's voice, but she had never heard such suspicion and uncertainty within it.

"Percival."

Slowly, the gate opened, barely wide enough for one horse. "More, I need more."

It almost seemed to yawn reluctantly the rest of the way, and to practically close on Galahad's gelding's tail hairs.

"What is going on?"

"You don't know?"

"I know nothing except some rumor about Arthur and Mordred arguing," she admitted.

Kay just looked at her for a long moment. Then he turned to the two boys who had helpd him with the gate. "Take his horses."

Persy slid down. Her legs trembled from the long ride. "They need bran mashes, both of them."

She could barely walk. Kay moved to support her, guiding her towards the warrior quarters.

They were half empty. Most of the older warriors and many of the younger ones had gone off in search of the grail.

"Percival," Kay started gently.

"Don't be gentle. I've lost my best friend, nothing you can tell me..." She tailed off, catching the look in his eyes.

"It started when Arthur caught Guinevere and Uluru together. He told Uluru to leave court. So he did. He and I were pretty much the only old guard who hadn't gone off after the grail."

"Which was a trap." Percival looked right at him. "No matter what you have heard, it was a trap."

"You were there. But rumor has it Bedivere saw it in Cornwall, and Uluru, after he left, found it in Wales. But only Galahad, supposedly, touched it and God took him straight to heaven."

"But that is not the news. If it was only Arthur and Uluru fighting..." Persy tailed off.

"Mordred took advantage of the situation. A group of the younger warriors followed him. They took the queen and...and they took Bronwen."

Her eyes widened. "He wouldn't. She's his niece!" She knew suddenly what Mordred had planned.

"He has made no offer of ransom. I rather suspect the two women are bait. Why would you think he would..."

"I have no idea, beyond...beyond my extremely negative impression of him. Which might be bias. But..." She let out a breath.

"He demands Arthur face him, but you see what we have here. The villagers have gotten out of the way, and most here are old men, boys and women."

"Some of the women could probably fight, but most...would not know how."

"We have been trying to recall everyone."

Mordred. Now it all made sense. The lure of the grail to get the Christian warriors and nobles out of the way. They had assumed the pagans would ally with Mordred. They might even have assumed correctly.

"You have me. But we may have to deal with this by another means than open battle." May? It was a certainty.

"I'm trying to tell him that." Kay ran a hand through his hair. "Arthur..."

"Remind him this happened before, and how we dealt with it then." When Gwydion and Elaine had been taken. Was there a connection? First Elaine, now Bronwen. Bronwen, though, would...would what? She had no clue what Bronwen would do.

Escape on her own, if she could. But likely not leave Guinevere. Both the queen and the granddaughter...and why take Bronwen if not to remove her from the line of succession? Nay, to strengthen his own claim by the very means she feared.

"I tried that. The problem is...Mordred has called him out, and he has his pride. And his desperation to regain his own lost youth."

Persy frowned. "If we face him in open battle, we lose, and what happens to the women then? I'm not doing it, Kay. I will leave again first...perhaps that will convince him he is on the wrong path."

Uluru loved Guinevere. "Somebody needs to find Uluru."

"He went to Wales. We know that much. The last heard from him was that he saw the grail, but it was snatched from his reach." A pause. "Cadogan is searching for him.

Bedivere's long-time lover. Persy nodded. Why Galahad? She did not know.

"Where is Morgan?" Kay asked now.

"Dead. I still believe she was behind the grail, and her son moving in..." Could have been Morgan's intent, could have not.

Kay frowned. "Are you sure?

"I found her body, north of the Wall. I was guided to it by the gods. It was not a glamor. She is gone."

"If her beliefs are true she will be back."

"Not straight away." Somebody would have to keep an eye out for her and whack her back down every time she showed up. There would have to be watchers. If the world really did lose track of magic, there would have to be those who kept it.

Bloodlines. It would have to be bloodlines. Bronwen's would be...key. And now she understood.

Cornwall would not wed Bronwen if there was any hint she had been dishonored. She knew that man well enough...inflexible on that point. Any child she had with Mordred would be tainted.

Or would it? Percival frowned.

"You really believe that...I have never been sure, myself."

Percival studied Kay. "There are so many different ideas about what happens. Any of them could be right."

There had to be something, though.

"What about the Christian idea?"

"I have real problems with the concept of Hell. It doesn't fit with any of the other stuff they say...their god seems to have a split personality." Of course, if there really was only one god...he would have to encompass everything and, by definition, have a split personality.

"I know what you mean. Or maybe just mood swings. On the other hand..." Kay considered that. "I think he just has a temper."

Persy laughed. "I always thought you were Christian."

"Nah. I reserve judgment. I figure their god is nicer than they are and won't be mad with me if I'm wrong."

He almost had to be nicer than his followers, Persy thought. Or some of them, anyway. "Some of them are...nice."

Grief hit her like a wave. She knew she would never get over her loss, that the pain would last for the rest of her life. It would end up in its own little place next to her grief and sorrow for Gwydion. For Elaine.

Anyone who lived grieved, it was inevitable.

"I'm..."

She looked at Kay, then set her shoulders. "We need to find Bronwen and Guinevere, and we need to do it fast, before Arthur does something stupid."

"If I leave, he'll know something is up."

"He'll know if I leave too." Who would not be noticed? There were so few here that there was nobody who would not be seen. "Is Brother Cadan around, by the way?"

"Of course. He's even more useless than usual, though."

Persy wondered at that. Or perhaps Morgan's death. "Is he losing his mind?" Kay nodded. "I'd ask how you knew, but...it was all Morgan, all along. All of it."

Persy set her face. "Yes. I'm tired," she admitted. "I'm going to sleep on everything. Please."

All of it her, all along, and how had she ever thought they could have been friends?

Things did seem saner the next morning. She sat outside, in the courtyard, eating porridge. The sun had touched the top of the higher buildings, but she was still in partial shade. It was cool, the breeze teasing at her, but she did not wish to go inside.

The few people around ignored her. She wondered what they really thought. An old warrior who had left and then returned. A nursemaid. Mordred was far from the only person to say it. Had Bronwen been a boy, it would have been different.

Had Bronwen been a boy, either he or Mordred would be dead now. Of course, in the old world, the old days before Rome, Bronwen would have been the heir, period. Perhaps she should have been, except that the Christian lords would not have accepted her.

Now she might be dead, might have been raped, or beaten, or scarred so Cornwall would not accept her.

Or even the rumor of rape might be enough, with that man. Mordred had to die...but then?

Then Arthur's line would cease to sit the throne and the treaty with the Saxons would be shattered. The British would not accept a disgraced woman, not in that day and age.

Mordred was a fool. She had known that. Morgan was evil, but out of the picture. Nimue was missing and the one person who could have solved this was long dead.

What she needed was guidance, but she no longer even knew where to seek it. She no longer felt that the gods were with her, as she had north of the Wall.

Maybe, she thought, the gods were also fighting, and those on Earth merely caught up in their dispute. The Greeks had legends of similar times. Maybe the Christian god was as unpleasant as the worst stories about him after all.

Or just greedy. Or... She tailed off. She had no clue any more. It was entirely possible the old gods were just fighting back against the Christian god's followers, not the entity himself. That all they were thinking about was protecting their own territory.

And they were losing. Of that she was sure, but whose fault was it? The fault of those on both sides who kept going too far. And then there were the Saxons, with their own set of gods.

"I almost wish the Christians were right. We have too many gods."

"Do you truly think so?"

She looked up. Arthur had aged even more, it seemed. Rapidly. He bent over a cane, but his eyes were still bright.

"Yes. Or perhaps too many people."

A bitter laugh came from him. "Tell me, Percival. What would you do?"

"Send a small, carefully chosen party to retrieve the women. Disinherit Mordred."

"I already have expressed my desire to do the latter, but Cornwall is now refusing to marry Bronwen."

"Somebody will take her, if only for the power. It is entirely possible Mordred has not harmed her." Percival set her empty bowl down, stood to face her king.

"I doubt that very much. From what he said before he left, he coveted her." Not a surprise, perhaps, for Bronwen was an attractive young woman, as well as the key to the throne.

"I had regretted that they were too close myself; it would have secured the succession. Had he not..."

"Had he not taken after his mother, except for her redeeming qualities." Arthur looked away. "I have been a fool, Percival."

"Only in one area of your life."

"I should have wed Persephone. I would have had several children, I would not have had to..."

"You had no way of knowing Guinevere was barren. None of us did. Including, like as not, the lady herself."

"But I knew Persephone was not."

It was the nearest thing she was going to get to an apology from the proud king. "We must retrieve Bronwen."

"And what? They will never accept her as queen. They would not have before."

"They must. We both know what will happen if the Saxons find out we don't." How did the Saxons view women rulers? They had some women warriors, but they were relatively rare. The Norsemen, too, but the two peoples were not so far apart from what she had seen.

No doubt they thought the British to be the barbarians. Heathens, too, most likely.

That was where the one god thing had come from. The genius of the Romans had been to say all gods were real. Most people did not feel that way. Most people felt their gods were real and everyone else's were myths.

Arthur shook his head. "Some of these men are so stubborn they would feed us all to the Saxons rather than accept the possibility that they are wrong about anything."

"We still need to send a party."

"Send who?"

"Me, for one." Was she still capable? She might have doubted that a few months ago. No more.

"I'll consider it."

She knew from his tone... "Mordred will wipe us out if we dance to his tune." She kept her voice as soft as possible.

"And if we do not...what will he do to Bronwen?"

Persy watched Arthur limp away. He could still ride. He could still fight...barely. He would die if he did this. Like as not so would she.

Unless they could recall the scattered warriors.

47

They had no witch to cast any spells to find them. Persy might have approached Cadan, but she still did not trust the man. There were two spirits within him; the priest who regretted all that had occurred, and the creature of darkness. Only the latter would have known how to scry. That was if the creature of darkness was still there. By Kay's report, it seemed likely Cadan was returning to his former status as a half-wit.

Nor was she willing to try it herself. Instead, she stood on the ridge, not far from the fort. Everything had fallen apart. All the years of peace and prosperity. What if she had stayed and not gone with Galahad? She had failed to prevent his death and succeeded only in not being here when her king needed her.

Kay had been able to do nothing. Kay, though, was not a subtle man. A fine warrior and a truly good person, but not subtle. It would have been more surprising had he stopped them. Uluru would have been the best.

Wales. Yet, when he heard of this, if he heard of it, he would come flying home, exile or not. Or possibly go straight in search of the women. If he could save them, then Arthur would take him back. Persy smiled a bit. Yes, that would be exactly what Uluru did. The man was not a fool.

Except in that one area of his life. Women. From her point of view it was men who caused all of the problems. It would be easier if they lived in a society where males and females were essentially the same.

Humans were not like that, however. The gods had laid down that men and women would walk parallel paths, but not the same path. A woman warrior did not fight like a man...and again, she wondered how many knew. A woman leader did not lead like a man. Persy wondered for a moment if the best system would not be to have a king and a queen who ruled equally, with no subservience of one to the other. A true partnership.

Pheh. That was sensible, and thus never likely to happen.

She knew what would happen. Mordred dead, Bronwen disgraced and exiled to the Orkneys. No child of hers would sit the throne.

The Saxons would then come back, and those who had known only peace and prosperity would never be able to fight them.

They had lost. They had lost not on the field of battle but in the realm of politics.

Then she saw them. A small, ragged group of men, yet she recognized the way they moved.

Pellinore. Bedivere. Gawain. Others whom she knew. The warband had been called, and they returned. Seeing them, Persy felt a little bit of hope for the first time. Even if there was no sign of Uluru.

She did not ride to join them. They came up through the valley, and she still desired solitude. Some bird flew overhead...a buzzard, she realized after a moment, smaller than the eagle that had led her out of her grief in the north, but built in a similar way.

The eagles had flown. They had done their best to preserve what they had and failed. The bird would not care. The horses and hounds would not care. The beasts in the field lived on no matter what. Only humans felt pain of that kind, only humans were cursed with the memory that made them long for what had been.

She was cursed with the memory of the future, with knowledge that she did not want. She wished for a moment to be some peasant in Wales, where the Saxons might not walk for generations.

She wished she was a horse, who only had to worry about the vagaries of its rider. She wished she had had more children and none at all.

She sat on the ridge, her mare grazing nearby, trusted not to stray, and let her head sink into her hands. She might have asked of the world what she was supposed to do, but she knew the world would not answer. The gods had, in the end, given her no guidance but only warned her of what would happen.

The inevitable, regardless of what she did. Softly, with noone to observe her, she wept.

By the time she got back to the fort she felt better. She knew she had done everything she could, even if it had not been enough. If she could find the right team, she could leave against orders. Find the women, kill Mordred.

Kill. She saw no other solution to the problem of him. He had to die. She had hoped he was only a foolish child, but she knew now that he had ingested poison with his mother's milk.

"Percival!" Bedivere's voice disturbed her reverie.

She hugged the man. "You did not find it."

"I hear Galahad..."

"It was a trick," Percival said, softly.

"Can you be sure of that?"

"Look at what happened in our various absences, Bedivere. A trick. It worked, too."

Bedivere sighed. He ran a hand through his hair. "I wish I could be sure you were wrong."

"We can't change the past. Let's focus on how we're going to get them back."

"Mordred wasn't beaten enough as a child."

Persy shook her head. "I don't think that was the problem." She did wonder about Mordred. A pawn of angry gods? Some mistake his mother made? Too much magic of the wrong kind worked when he was in the womb? Or had he been intentionally raised to be this?

"You think..."

"I think he was born that way. I think he inherited his father's pride and his mother's manipulative nature." They should never have got together.

"But that does not change what has to be done."

"Except that then, Arthur's line will not sit the throne."

"It will have to be Bronwen..." Bedivere tailed off. "Assuming she is still alive."

"Which we can't assume. It seems likely, though. She would be little use to Mordred dead. More likely," Persy added, her tone blunt and her eyes grim. "More likely he has raped her."

Bedivere shuddered. "His own niece. Then again, was he ever tied to her in such a way?"

"Not really, and Arthur believes he desired her from the start."

"She was fostered on your family pretty early, right?"

"Right. I think Arthur did not want her influenced by some of those..." Persy frowned, her brow furrowing, "...women."

"Morgan chief amongst them. She always took what she wanted. Is it any surprise her son is the same?"

"Morgan always had an agenda. However, she also had the wisdom not to..." Persy tailed off. "He is like her, only without the restraint needed to control his desire for power and work within the system."

"Perhaps we are all lucky *she* was not born a man," Bedivere commented, then glanced at the sky. "Do we know..."

Persy cut him off, "She's dead. She died a foolish death, focused I suspect so much on dangers spiritual and magical that she forgot the merely mundane. Her body lies north of the wall."

"I'm not believing that one's dead *with* a body." Bedivere glanced at the sky again.

Persy's lips curled wryly. "Nobody can cheat death to that degree."

"No, but...did you trust her?"

"No further than I could have thrown her. Which isn't that far, I don't think."

"I don't know. She was fairly light." Bedivere finally looked back at her. "What does Arthur have in mind?"

Persy sighed. "He's letting Mordred call him out. He's not up to single combat, we're not up to fighting Mordred's armies. And then there's the treaty."

"We can't let Mordred be king, even for the treaty."

They were doomed whatever they chose, Persy knew that. She felt as if they always had been. "Can't we?" She paused. "At least he won't sack every town in his path."

"You really think he won't...well, maybe not if Arthur surrenders. But come on...what would he do to Bronwen?"

"Wed her," Persy said, a little grimly. "And probably cite the Egyptian royal family as a precedent."

They had wed brother to sister. One way to secure the succession, she supposed.

"And break her. I saw what he did to one of the kitchen wenches."

"Bronwen knows how to use a blade if she must. If she can get a knife in her hand, Mordred will be dead before we get there." Persy was absolutely confident of that. Unfortunately, she was also certain Mordred knew it.

"That would be an ideal solution, wouldn't it?"

"Sadly, Mordred is far too smart to let that happen." He would try and break Bronwen. Was she smart enough to pretend to be defeated?

Then, there was Guinevere. Guinevere was every bit as capable of slitting Mordred's throat, given the opportunity. Or poisoning him.

That might be more her style.

What would Persy do? She knew exactly what she would do. Guinevere would not wait passively for rescue. What woman would? Even Elaine had done her best to fight.

"Let's hope the women rescue themselves." Bedivere's words echoed her thoughts perfectly.

"We can't count on it. Nor can we let Arthur get himself killed."

"We can't ride out against orders either. Besides, he has a small chance with us, he has none without."

Persy knew in that moment that if she rode to the rescue, it was likely to be alone.

48

It was a poor excuse for a warband that rode out from Camelot. Even poorer was what was left in its defense, women and the crippled. Any woman who could fight had gone with Mordred.

Well, except for one. Persy rode towards the tail of the group, looking them over. A handful of grizzled veterans...and she was pretty grizzled herself. Some boys. Some half-trained farmers. She was pretty sure at least one of the boys was actually a girl.

Not that she would ever be the one to say anything. The hounds fanned out around Arthur, Cafall's descendants, most of them. They were like as not the most valuable fighters here.

It was a doomed mission, and everyone knew it. Yet nobody could either talk Arthur down or refuse him. His old charisma was intact, flowing over and through them. Persy would have been called yellow for refusing to go.

Yellow was not supposed to equate to intelligent, nor brave to stupid.

She rode with them nonetheless, trying to work out how she was going to salvage the disaster. What happened was beyond fathoming.

They enjoyed years of peace and prosperity. She fought for those years, risked for those years, earned scars for those years.

They were over, cast aside like old clothes and red war took the land. Merlin. Gwydion. Elaine. Galahad.

Not the only deaths, but the ones which most mattered. Even the weather shared her mood, grey clouds descending to dull the countryside. Drizzle followed as sure as night after day, soaking through her clothes almost immediately. She growled a little under her breath.

By the gods. Did she have to be miserable as well? Apparently, yes. The gods were determined of that.

The worst part was that they were even letting Mordred dictate the field. A wide, open valley, good for maneuvering.

A place where numbers counted. She could hear Kay arguing with Arthur. Yet, the King would not bend.

He would break if he did not. Break beneath the force of the young king's strength. In some ways, that was the way of things.

Arthur was the Oak King and Mordred the Holly. Yet, it was no Yuletide play, where a young man would lightly tap an old on the shoulder, to signal the passing of the old year and the birth of the new.

It was no Saturnalia, where masters would, for one night, serve their slaves. That too was play acting. This was real and serious and people were going to die.

Perhaps she was going to die. Perhaps she would finally escape the curse of always being the survivor. It would be worth it to save Bronwen. Cornwall did not ride with them.

He refused to have any part of it. He retired to the west and told Arthur he could keep his shamed granddaughter.

Assumptions. They all assumed Mordred had raped her. Persy was guilty of that assumption herself.

She did not think it was shame if the woman was not willing. She did not think it was shame at the best of times. There was nothing wrong with not going to one's marriage bed a virgin, as long as one was certain one was not carrying another man's child. It was unfortunate that there was no way to be sure of that.

The drizzle soaked through her. She embraced the very real possibility of death and made it part of her. She rode to the end, anyway. The best chance she had was to get Bronwen and run.

The Saxons would likely be the only winners here. If Mordred won, he would be able to fend them off for a while yet. If he lost, then it was likely the Orkneys, who were more flexible, would still have a husband for Bronwen. If the child was born a month or so early, then that could be kept quiet.

She knew in her heart that was why Mordred had taken both women. Guinevere to anger Arthur. Bronwen to give him an heir. He only needed Guinevere for the 'angering Arthur' part of things.

Bronwen was lovely and forbidden. For a man like that, that was more than enough.

The black mare lowered her head and snorted. Startled from her thoughts, Persy glanced around. She saw nothing to cause such a reaction from the animal.

There was a village ahead. It remained, from what she could see, prosperous. Perhaps the horse had scented strange dogs or, more likely, pigs in the woods. She thought of roast pork for a moment, then shook her head. 'Pork' led inevitably to 'wild boar' and thus to 'Gwydion'. She did not want to go there.

She did not want to go anywhere except back to Camelot, back in time, back to the life they had made.

Or, perhaps even better, back to the villa on the coast and Bronwen in braids, laughing.

One could not go backwards. Her Sight never showed her own future, and it did not come now, as much as she would have wished it to.

Just a bone, she thought. Some hint that there was something more than death and destruction.

The villagers barred their doors against them.

Arthur's anger was terrible to see. For a moment, Persy thought he would order the place razed. Instead, he stormed away, remounting and taking off at a gallop.

Even Kay did not follow, instead moving off at a sedate trot. Of course, Arthur would come back.

Barred against them. Mordred's men had been here before, she could almost feel it. All of the trust in the king, gone.

Had it been words or deeds? She stopped and looked at their storehouse.

Not barred. Empty. Mordred had taken everything they had. Small wonder they would not offer hospitality.

With him as king...why had Bronwen not been born a boy?

Why could the fools not see that a woman could rule as well as a man? Or as badly, for that matter, but... Nothing could be worse than Mordred. Perhaps not even a Saxon invasion.

The Saxons would have left them something. Perhaps. She did not know any more, she was honestly uncertain of where she stood. Mordred would have tried to recruit her had she not gone with Galahad.

She had chosen her side. She had chosen the Christian king because the pagan one was cruel, yet her heart belonged to the old gods.

She was in between. She looked over her shoulder at the sullen villagers before she rode on. She had seen prosperity, but it had been a shell, an illusion. As she rode out she saw another building was a burned out shell.

She knew instantly it had been their church. Anger rose within her. One did not desecrate any temple.

Morgan had done that. She had done it in the worst possible way, showing no respect to other people's gods. Yet the Christians had started it, for was not reconsecrating a shrine to another god also a form of desecration?

Did the gods fight? She stopped trying to chase down her thoughts and pulled them from the unpleasant past to the even more unpleasant future.

Arthur had finally stopped at a clearing. They made camp, silently, none daring to approach him. Nothing at all could reach him when he got like this. With the possible exception of Guinevere.

That, Persy understood, was why he had married her, in the end. Because she could calm him down. When, of course, she was not herself the cause of his anger.

She leaned against her sweaty horse, feeling much the same way herself. They had been vaunted saviors. They had been everything the land had needed.

They had been eagles, laughing as they piled up the enemy dead at Badon. She had walked amongst those dead, giving them the honor owed to worthy foes.

Not that they had been that tough, but the honor was as much for herself as for them.

She felt the night close in around her, and it closed more tightly than it ever had. Mordred. How would his name be remembered? Not well. Nor would Morgan's, nor Nimue's.

Arthur's? Time would blend everything together, and the shining star of his rise would...and she saw it for a moment. Not a vision, simply a knowing. She rode with a legend. She was quite possibly a legend herself. The stories would live down the ages, and all of the foolishness would be forgotten.

Most likely, the foolishness would be remembered as bravery. The stormy marriage would becomes a great romance. She knew how things turned into the tales of bards.

Names would be changed, and personalities would grow. Yet, for the moment, all she wanted was to live. For Arthur to live. For the entire thing to be resolved.

The Saxons would take the land. She was as sure of that as she was of her own name...of course, some days, she was not sure of that. No. They would take the land, and they would no doubt blend with her own people, in the end, into something new.

Something strong? She did not know. She did not care. She did not want them, she wanted things as they were.

Everyone did. Whatever happened would happen without her, and again, the cold of death flowed through her.

She had to save Bronwen.

49

Mordred had taken a fort for his own. It was not as large or as grand as Camelot, but it looked over the valley. He had the same advantage they had at Badon. Perhaps somebody had gone over that battle with him.

He had picked up at least some of his father's ability. Persy feared that. With even half of Arthur's old skill...

Arthur had experience, or did he? It had been so long... She heard Kay urgently addressing Arthur.

They turned, remaining within the trees. Persy could envision it in her mind. If they went all the way around, they could come towards the fort from less of a dip. They could not gain the advantage of height, but they could lessen their disadvantage.

There had been a village in the valley. Persy looked out at it, and saw only emptiness. The Saxons could, she thought wryly, move right in.

What had happened to the barbarians being the true enemy? She knew what had. They had become barbarians themselves.

They had become that a long time ago, when Constantine set aside the doctrine of tolerance with loyalty, and ordered all subjects to serve the same god.

That was why Rome had fallen. Because it had become...that. Or perhaps it had started even sooner, when the Christians had been executed in large numbers for denying the divinity of the Emperor.

Pheh. Arthur was the closest to a divine king she had ever met, and he had more than enough flaws to prove his humanity. Along the ridge, behind the trees. She became, suddenly, highly aware of the moment.

All of her thoughts drained away. She knew they were about to be attacked. She could feel it, sense it, she was sure of it even before the arrow struck the tree.

Arthur ducked, low along his horse's neck.

They were in the trees. Of course. They had known no sane commander would brave the valley. So they had placed skirmishers along the likely routes, hoping to pick a few of them off.

The black mare screamed, but in defiance more than pain, whirling without any cue to lunge towards one of the men. She was probably injured, but Persy let her charge anyway, her sword drawn. It plunged through the warrior's chest, and it had started.

These were her own people she was fighting, but the only thing that mattered was the fight. Time slowed, and she whirled the mare again. There was blood under the animal's mane. Was she badly hurt?

Persy could not check on it. They had to get out of the ambush. She drove the mare forward. Not running, but retreating out of the trees to a space where she could at least see an attacker coming.

She was not the only one with that idea. She knew that they were being herded out into the open ground. What could she do, though? Had she stayed where she was, she would have ended up a pincushion.

She was going to die, and utter calm flowed over her, through her. There was something about knowing one had lost that made for a moment of peace.

Mordred rode onto the field of battle. His standard was not Arthur's dragon head. He had chosen for himself a black eagle, a conscious echo of Rome and all it stood for. It rested on a blue field.

You have no right to that, Persy thought.

"Arthur!" The young man's voice was clear. "Come out, old man."

Old man. That was his own father he spoke of, yet the only thing in the boy's voice was contempt.

"I am here." Arthur nudged his horse out from the trees, the animal side stepping nervously.

"Let us settle this."

"You propose single combat."

"Between you and I." Mordred was confident, and perhaps he should be. He lacked Arthur's experience, but not, most certainly, skill.

Arthur had lost much of his edge. "Terms?"

"Simple enough. Whoever wins, is king. No men, either yours or mine will be harmed, and they will swear fealty to the victor."

"Where are the women?"

"In the fort. I would not expose either to a stray arrow."

He sounded far too reasonable. Persy narrowed her eyes. It was clear that Mordred simply believed he could defeat Arthur easily, and once the old king was dead, he would immediately renege on any terms. On the other hand, not bringing the women out...

"If I promise that my men will not attack, will you bring them out? I would verify their safety before agreeing to any combat."

Mordred's eyes narrowed, then he turned to a young man, nodded sharply.

The man turned, cantering his horse to the fort.

Persy waited. She had no chance to sneak away, and at least if Mordred tried to have them slaughtered, she could fight.

He might decide to be honorable. Could she swear allegiance to him? In a way. She would acknowledge him as king and then leave. Perhaps to the Orkneys. Yet, there was Bronwen. Could she leave her granddaughter in his clutches? He seemed highly unlikely to give her up. He would, rather, keep her.

That would weaken any children he had, but she wondered if he knew that. Or if he believed it. The arrogance washed over her, radiating out from him.

The two women walked out from the fort. He might at least give them horses. Guinevere seemed unharmed, but Bronwen sported a shiner she had no doubt earned honorably. Neither showed any more significant damage. They wore clean clothes, although not as fine as would have normally befitted their station.

"As you can see...I would say unharmed, but your granddaughter, Arthur, is a feisty one."

Bronwen scowled as the two approached. "Let me go." She did not try to run...she knew better.

Mordred turned towards her for a moment. "Stay back, Bronwen. Or return to the fort. You may not want to watch this."

His tone had shifted to an odd mix of gentle and possessive. Was that how a man talked to a woman he had made his property?

It was how a man talked to a woman he had made his wife. However, there was nothing wifely in the way she looked at him. Nothing at all. Indeed, her eyes smoldered with something far closer to hatred.

She would stab him in bed some day, Persy decided. Guinevere, however, simply stood there. She did not seem upset.

She was, Persy thought, not letting him win in the only way she could, by betraying no emotion. She did not even smile at her husband, but rather reached for Bronwen's arm, pulling the girl back.

As if that was a signal, Mordred circled his horse towards Arthur. Arthur had his weapon out, and Persy thought the younger man held back just enough to ensure his opponent would be properly armed.

They met with a clash, swords striking off each other. Arthur's horse reared to bring his hooves into play against Mordred's slightly taller mount, which shied out of the way.

Despite Arthur's age, the combat was swift, the moving blades scarcely visible to those who watched. Sparks flew from them.

Then Arthur fell from his horse. Mordred leaped down a moment later, waiting, letting the man get up.

He was acting honorably. Well, except for deliberate patricide. Persy found her breath, let it out. She wanted Arthur to win, but the reality was he was too old. Too tired. Too burdened by old injury. The young lion was taking the old as the pride looked on. Bronwen did not look away. Guinevere was frowning.

Oh, she was hurting alright, even if she did not love Arthur now and possibly never had. Familiarity was enough to make her wish that he could live.

Persy willed with everything that was in her for Arthur to rally, but he did not. His breathing could be heard to be labored, Mordred's was fast but clear. The blades struck one another again, a small fire almost starting in the grass from the sparks from the metal.

It seemed to last forever, and then Arthur went down, the sword falling from his limp fingers. Blood streamed to the ground.

He was not dead, but he was dying. Mordred glanced down at him for a moment. Then, "Kill them all. Except Bronwen."

Had he thought they could be that stupid, as to not grasp that he was going to pull exactly this?

Persy's sword was out before the first word was spoken, and she did the last thing anyone would expect.

She rode straight for Mordred.

He leapt aside, striking at her with his sword. She felt the black quiver, but keep running. She heard hoofbeats, blade striking blade, but she was tunnel-visioned on one thing: Bronwen.

The choice was not a conscious one. Guinevere was not her own blood. As she slowed, Bronwen grabbed the saddle and her and pulled herself up.

She spun the mare to face the fight, feeling her granddaughter's hands wrap around her waist. The black shuddered again.

Kay, streaking towards them, clearly about to pull the same stunt with Guinevere. She did not look to see if it was successful.

Then she heard other hooves. A black mare and a black rider, riding straight towards Mordred.

The young king had time to turn, had time to look. Then a spear pierced him, a thrown spear.

Only one warrior threw spears from horseback. Uluru.

"No patricide will be king here!" the warrior exclaimed.

Mordred looked down stupidly at the shaft protruding from his chest and then fell.

Bronwen's grip tightened on Persy.

"We must go," she whispered. "Before they recover."

Bedivere dismounted to assist the wounded Arthur onto his horse then leapt up behind him.

Persy simply turned her mount and fled the field as fast as the mare could go.

50

They set Arthur down on the shore of a lake. Hopefully, they had come far enough to avoid Mordred's remaining supporters.

Persy assisted Bronwen to the ground.

"He..."

She slipped her arms around the girl. "It will be alright."

It would not. Bronwen was queen, but a queen nobody could accept. What man would take her, even with the kingship of England? A good pagan one, Persy thought, but for Arthur's line to sit the throne?

Bronwen had to be queen, not her husband king.

"I'm not stupid. It's not alright. None of it's alright, and I'm glad he's dead."

Persy did not argue with her. "I don't mean it's alright right now."

The weakest of smiles crossed Bronwen's face.

Arthur was still breathing, but some of the blood coming from the wound was a sluggish black. Persy knew enough to know what that meant.

Bedivere knelt next to him. The sword. It was supposed to go to the Lady of the Lake.

Nimue.

Who had not been seen in so long. Was it a good idea for her to have the blade?

Slowly, the circle contracted around the fallen king.

"Guinevere," Arthur whispered.

"I am here."

"I never was....a good husband."

"I never was...a good wife."

No talk of love, no sentiment. Only an acknowledgment of many years of fault on both sides.

"Bedivere...Bedivere, Kay...my friends...Percival. The sword...the lake." And then his eyes widened. "Morgan?"

And he fell back, and said no more.

Bedivere was the closest. He reached up and picked up Excalibur, carefully. He looked at Persy for a long moment.

Morgan? Had he died with her name on her lips because he knew or because she was in truth the one he had most loved.

Then Bedivere turned, stepped towards the lake...and flung Caliburn as far out into the water as he could.

The old way. The sacrifice of a warrior's sword upon his death. It was fitting for a king so bound between the old ways and the new.

Kay, meanwhile, knelt next to Arthur's body, and then closed his eyes. "The king is dead. Long live the...queen." A hesitation there, his eyes flitting towards Bronwen's slender form.

If they accepted her, it could yet be salvaged.

"No." It was not Bishop Marcellus, who had died some years back, but his successor, a Cymry named Llewellyn. "The church will not support a woman on the throne. Especially given the circumstances."

Kay rose. "The treaty with the Saxons."

"We can deal with the Saxons."

"Arthur's father and the last Romans said that. Look what happened. The Saxons cannot be trusted."

"And when she pops out the illegitimate and incestuous brat?" The bishop paused. "If she is married, and her husband rules in her name, and the child is removed, I may consider it."

He turned and waddled out of the Camelot great hall.

"Nobody is going to accept me." Bronwen glanced at Persy for a moment. She had one hand on her swelling belly.

"The child can be fostered, well out of sight and mind." That was Persy's suggestion.

Bronwen frowned.

"Your grandmother had to give up your father. Fostering is normal. You will have others." Persy knew her words were harsh. "That's hard right now, but it's the reality."

"Maybe it would be...best..."

Bronwen had chosen to keep the child, not risk an abortion. A wise choice at many levels, for trying to induce a miscarriage was well known to end, often, in the death of the mother. The fact that she had chosen to love it made Persy admire her.

A child of rape and incest. It would be tainted, and it might be best if it died at birth. Such things could readily be arranged.

Kay walked to the door. "I don't think that we are going to be able to do this."

Had Gwydion lived...that boar, that beast had changed the destiny of Britain. It had all hinged on that...and on Persy's inability to save him.

"I will take the child," Persy said, finally. "And I will make sure he or she disappears."

She doubted she could bring herself to kill the babe, but she could ensure that he or she was fostered, quietly, somewhere where he would have no power. Somewhere where he could do no harm.

"Bronwen, it's the only way."

"And who will wed me?"

"The youngest of the Orkneys is willing. He is not ill-favored and does not judge you." Persy breathed in, then out.

What was the point? Kay, Bedivere and Percival were the only ones loyal to the young queen. Guinevere had gone to Avalon.

Permanently. She had taken vows as a nun. Uluru had not been seen since that last battle. Having killed one monarch, he probably feared no other would trust him.

"Very well," the queen said, finally.

Then a boy rushed into the room. "The lords ride on us!"

"And what do they demand?"

Kay had fallen into the role of regent quite naturally.

"That Bronwen give up all right to the throne. Well, that's the nice ones." The boy was out of breath.

"Which lords?"

He rattled off the names, a quite impressive feat of memory.

"The Saxons will fall on us." Bronwen stood. "The treaty must be upheld. Tell them I offer this compromise. I will wed the man they choose, and the child I carry will be fostered at birth, if it lives."

Persy stepped over to Bronwen. Softly, "If they reject it, we must flee."

"You don't think they would?"

"They may. And we do not have enough men to fight them all, not any more." Most of Mordred's had sworn allegiance, sure, and then faded away.

Vanished. None had shown up as bandits, yet, so she suspected they were simply lying low, returning to their normal lives.

They forgot so quickly.

"The Saxons..."

"If that happens, they will have brought it on themselves."

The messenger returned. "They demand nothing less than the queen's surrender. It seems the man they have in mind as king is already wed."

Meaning they would eliminate Bronwen, one way or another. "My surrender and?"

"Your consignment to the monastery at Avalon."

"I am not Christian."

"Your conversion is apparently part of their demands. Or they will torch this place and leave none alive."

None asked about the child. "Then everyone must leave," Persy said. "Bronwen, come with me."

Her surrender or her flight and exile...both would violate the treaty. Flight gave some chance of return later.

Bronwen looked at her, then with infinite dignity stood and took her hand.

"I'm sorry," Persy whispered.

There were several rear exits to Camelot. To Persy's relief, at least one was not known to the men outside, and they had chosen to approach en masse, rather than surround the fort. Fools. The handful of men who had been within scattered except for Kay. He was opening the stable door, releasing the horses.

Persy dared not stop for her mare, but at least they would not be in the fort when it was burned. On foot, then, she guided her granddaughter into the woods. Perhaps the lords made only a half-hearted effort to stop them. They did not fear Bronwen, that was for sure. She was only a woman.

Persy was only glad she was not more pregnant than she was.

"What now?"

"We wait until they torch the fort, as they promised, then leave. There's less chance of being seen at that point."

"Where do we go?"

"I don't know quite yet." Persy was running options through her mind. Cornwall was completely out. The Orkneys were a distinct possibility...a long trip, but doable, and they would still get there before Bronwen's belly swelled past the point at which travel was reasonable. The other prospect in mind was Erin, across the sea, where the Romans had never come. "We'll discuss it later."

"I...think I have an idea." Bronwen's voice was quiet.

They waited. The lords were as good as they promised...some fired fire arrows into the fort. Others were rounding up the horses. Persy wondered if Kay had escaped.

She might never know, she could not go back and look. As they waited in the trees, night fell.

She prayed to the gods. At that juncture, would they answer her?

She sometimes felt they had deserted their people with the dragon. Or lost. Or planned the entire thing. Yet, the one hope was that young woman. She was the queen, and would be regardless of what happened.

Did she carry a savior or a monster in her belly?

Two dark shapes abruptly plunged through the brush nearby, far too big to be men. Her prayers might well have been answered.

The black mare and a spotted horse, the latter a dead match for Arthur's mount at Badon.

Wordlessly, Bronwen grabbed the mane of the latter and pulled herself up. Without benefit of bridle or saddle, they rode into the night.

51

The boat rocked beneath Persy's feet. Behind her the shores of Britain faded away for good. She would not return, and she knew it. Exile for the rest of her life, however long it might be. The fishermen adjusted the sails as they streaked out across the sea.

"What do you truly know?"

"It is an island," Bronwen said, softly. She wore simple garb, but Merlin's brooch was pinned to her cloak. "They have some problems with the Norsemen, but appear to be coming to an accommodation with them. An understanding."

Her descendants might be part Norse, then. Persy felt oddly resigned to that. "And not a place they would expect us to go."

"No. The Orkneys have been threatened with war for sheltering me. These people..." Bronwen placed a hand on her belly. "Will it be a monster, grandmother?"

"I don't know. There is a reason why such close breedings are avoided...sometimes the children that result can be deformed. And its father was a monster."

"I will just have to try and teach it not to be like him."

Unspoken between them was that it might be anyway. That there was no telling what inheritance of blood had been passed down from a man who would rape his own niece.

A man who had killed his own father for power, for politics. For the gods. If the gods had abandoned them, it was because they were tired of their own followers.

The shore that came up ahead was forbidding, rocky, a village tucked at the base of the cliffs.

Persy, no longer in the garb of a man, no longer being anything but herself, looked towards what they called Mannanan's isle, and suddenly knew.

The child would be neither hero nor monster, but the line would continue. Continue until it was once more needed.

Author's Note

I suppose it was inevitable that some day I would write an Arthuriana novel. At least from the time when I realized that "Jennifer" and "Guinevere" were forms of the same name.

The kernel of my approach came from a casual comment while talking about the Knights: What if Percival was a woman?

I have no idea why we picked Percival, but it stayed with me. What if one of Arthur's "knights" was, in fact, a woman disguised as a man.

This led me to combine Percival with an obscure figure from Arthuriana: The lady Lionors.

Lionors was Arthur's childhood sweetheart. By conflating Lionors into Percival (The name Persephone was chosen as a name a Romanized Celt might reasonably have named their daughter that shortened to "Persy") I was able to do two things at once.

I was able to include Arthur's son from the Mabinogion, Gwydion, whilst keeping the tragedy of Guinevere's barrenness intact. Gwydion's fate in the story became his fate in the novel.

Then, of course, I made a few other changes.

I'm following the tradition of setting Arthur in the actual historical time rather than the invented world of the later romances. I replaced the Medieval tournament with a trial at arms intended to help the King choose the best men to be his "officers" and the core of his warband.

For ease of reading I have used the anglicized form of names - Guinevere instead of Gwenhyfar, Bedivere instead of Bedwyr, etc.

And there are three other things I did that I feel warrant explanation:

1. The replacement of Sir Lancelot with Uluru. First of all, Lancelot is a later *French* addition to the stories. He was never in the original.

However, I needed him to show up at the end and finish off the tragedy. I know some readers will question the existence of an African man in Roman Europe. The fact is that there was extensive trade with Africa, including sub-Saharan Africa, during the Roman period. There was trade in spices and, yes, in slaves. Some black men may well have chosen to join the Roman army as part of immigrating. These men would then have been, likely, sent to stations in the north and west in accordance with Rome's policy of not having enlisted men serve in the province in which they were recruited. Uluru was a slave, but this was by no means the only way a black man might have ended up working as a mercenary in northern Europe. If you read carefully, he's not the only person of African descent at court. Black men and women were all over the Empire.

2. Elaine. Ah, my poor darling Elaine. In the original stories, Elaine is a rather pathetic figure who attempts to seduce Lancelot (who has eyes only for Guinevere) and then kills herself when he turns her down. There was no way I was going to do that to a female character in my book. I changed Elaine to Gwydion's fiancee (thus allowing the existence of the entirely-invented princess Bronwen), and the cause of her death to something which no doubt would have been understood but poorly at the time: Post partum depression. Post partum depression is often caused by stressful life events during pregnancy, which the poor girl certainly had. Another risk factor would be the fact that she was only seventeen at the time. Suicide remains the leading cause of death for new mothers. She was not weak. She was very, very sick.

3. Climate change. Historical fact: Europe got colder in the late Roman and early Medieval periods. This was a major driving factor behind Saxon migration and probably was the motivation for the viking expeditions that got as far as northern parts of the United States. So, no, I'm not making the climate stuff up or going for some kind of metaphor. It was the real background at the time. As the climate shifted, crop failures and hunger became more common, and it took a while for people to adapt. But during the Roman period, yes, England was a wine region, if not a fantastic one.

Oh and, of course, the monastery where Galahad finds the grail is Lindisfarne, and the mead recipe did, indeed survive...

Acknowledgments

Acknowledgements

As usual, full acknowledgements to my husband, Gregory. To my editor, Jennifer Melzer (everything that is good is her responsibility, all remaining mistakes are mine) and my cover artist Starla Huchton.

Also to my father, for introducing me to Arthuriana and instilling the love which remains to this day.

Other Books by Jennifer R. Povey

Other Books by Jennifer R. Povey

Transpecial
The Silent Years (Mother, Crone, Maiden)

The Lost Guardians Series:
Falling Dusk
Fallen Dark
Rising Dawn
Risen Day

Daughter of Fire